·RECKONING·

·RECKONING·

MICHAEL PYE

GRAFTON BOOKS

A Division of the Collins Publishing Group

LONDON GLASGOW
TORONTO SYDNEY AUCKLAND

Grafton Books
A Division of the Collins Publishing Group
8 Grafton Street, London W1X 3LA

Published by Grafton Books 1987

British Library Cataloguing in Publication Data
Pye, Michael
Reckoning.
I. Title
823'.914[F]   PR6066.Y/

ISBN 0-246-13118-7

Typeset by Columns of Reading
Printed and bound in Great Britain by
Robert Hartnoll (1985) Ltd., Bodmin, Cornwall

·RECKONING·

PROLOGUE

Sometimes he was sure there had only ever been one woman. They'd lived through a revolution, seen murder and stolen a billion dollars, all in a just cause, and he had been in the service of one woman. He could no longer distinguish the decorous Latin matron who took tea like a vocation from the brilliant Manhattan model. He puzzled over the woman's true name: whether she was Aurelia or Mercedes.

It was the circumstances, and the horror which made him know so much about her: so many poses, and so many fears. He knew about her appetites, and how she masked herself. He saw her like a diamond: an infinity of facets, giving dazzling light.

But then he would shake himself, and think again. He tried to pull together what had happened: the murderous course of a fantastical treasure hunt, the way the cold machines of banks and vaults had suddenly turned into traps and disaster. The slow, tearing fall of a dictator, and the final triumph of a supreme financial terrorist. The face, the shared dark face of Mercedes and Aurelia Zenon, that he had come to love.

He remembered the airport at Leon, which is the capital of Providencia in Central America. He remembered a little plane heating like a glasshouse on the runway, taxiing gently to make a breeze. Inside, Aurelia was waiting for him.

The papers took time and money, like everything in Providencia, and the guards came running at the sound of the plane's engines.

'Come on,' Aurelia said. She kept her voice low, like a lady and so the Guardsmen wouldn't hear. In a way, both reasons were the same instinct to survive.

He, Ian Carpenter, came sprinting out of the airport offices, a plume of permits in his fist. He swung himself across the wing and into his seat and shouted back to Aurelia: 'Everyone got paid.'

The doors slammed.

'You shouldn't say that,' Aurelia said.

The little plane crept up into the sky. There was a lake like black mirror and a volcanic cone under a sheath of steam and a few neat farms that were hemmed in by a weave of scrub and bush. The roads were like scrawls of white chalk against black rock, and then the roads disappeared under forest.

'I didn't think you'd bring me,' she said.

'I asked your husband's permission.'

She laughed, and her ceremonial mask of make-up came to life. She seemed very lovely, and very young.

'Besides,' Carpenter teased, 'you don't usually run off with your dinner guests. Do you?' He paused a beat too long.

'Just for the day,' Aurelia said, and settled into her seat like a cat. The plane filled with an assault of static from control towers and cheap music from the ground.

She lowered her voice. 'I come from Bluefields,' she said.

Great grey battlements of cloud smeared softly against the windscreen. Carpenter could see the Hidden River below, slipping out of the green forest in valves of brown water and then vanishing under great trees.

'I always thought you must be Pacific Coast,' he said. 'Some patrician family. You think the Atlantic Coast is devils and savages.'

'And Protestants,' Aurelia said. 'Don't forget the Protestants.'

He didn't laugh; it was not his country.

He'd expected to be her guide to Bluefields, showing her a smile of a town. But she must know it all already – how the river opens suddenly into a wide lagoon that is speckled with islands. He could see it through the window now, and as the plane went lower, the grey wood houses and their shadows separated into streets. Pretty black pigs went primping on the jetty.

Aurelia had pressed her spine against her seat, on guard.

'We'll be on the ground in a minute,' he said.

She said nothing.

The plane bumped down on rough crabgrass and fetched up

against the wall of forest. The door opened on tangible, harsh heat.

Carpenter negotiated for a moment with the pilot. 'At six,' the pilot said. And Carpenter jumped down, expecting to give Aurelia his arm, but she sat still in the plane, touching her face. Yet he knew already that she wasn't vain.

There was an ancient Ford by the field, its windows gone, an ominous scrape on the roof, smelling of new sweat and mangoes. Carpenter hailed the driver, who'd followed the sound of the plane in the hope of a fare. He waited for Aurelia.

She took a deep breath. Sometimes she could seem painfully young. She wondered what she was doing – coming home with a man from a dinner party. She'd been hostess for her husband's fellow academics – one crocodile, one donnish Dutchman, one chancer of a gypsy, one woman of fifty in a backless dress, all assembled for some anthropological cultural conference. She could have made a dissertation out of them and their rituals. And Mario had invited a banker called Ian Carpenter, the odd man out, to talk to Aurelia: a curly, big-shouldered man who talked about big ideas in simple words, because he'd learned Spanish without all the Latin rhetoric. He talked to her about doing when everyone else talked about things – glittering, women's things.

It was a risk, she thought. She came to the plane's door and jumped down. She fell against Carpenter.

The old Ford crashed its gears and began to roll down into Bluefields. It was the last dry days before the rains, when water trucks haul themselves along the back streets, taking down the dust. A parrot, powdery red and blue and green, went crabwise on the wires of a garden fence.

'You'll want to see friends, then?' Carpenter said. He hid his disappointment very well.

'I thought,' she said, 'I could come with you.'

'But your family –'

He saw her hands were forced together, a nail cutting her palm.

'Of course you can come on the river,' he said.

A pair of old ladies walked the road in starched white, black umbrellas above their heads to keep off the sun, fastidiously

3

rounding the cooking braziers that showered sparks. There were black and white goats, facing down the dogs. There were smells of sea, peppers, smoke, ripe fruit.

'It's like a Western town,' Carpenter said. 'The wooden houses, the saloons –'

'Do you have to work at once?'

'They know I'm coming. They probably heard the plane.'

She said to the driver: 'Stop at the park.'

The old car flopped when it stopped, as though only movement guaranteed its shape, and there was a square of green – a wide banyan tree, a food stand, and up concrete steps a slim pagoda of a bandstand. There were three plinths with ceremonial heads: one poet and two members of the Diaz family – the President for Life and his father, President for Life.

'Have a fresco,' Aurelia said.

He didn't argue. She went to the food hut and asked for two tamarind frescos and two pine tarts.

'We could have breakfast under the tree,' she said.

Three men in the olive drab of National Guardsmen watched the pair. They weren't sure what to do. Strangers meant trouble, but these were city-sharp strangers who might be important. But then why were they sitting under the tree with the little plastic bags of drink?

'You bite the corner,' Aurelia said. 'Then you suck.'

Carpenter tried. The sweet tamarind drink went trickling down his chin.

'Look,' Aurelia said, 'you sort of push the drink into your mouth –'

The Guardsmen went to report the strangers. They didn't want to be caught being wrong.

'Why are you here?' Aurelia asked. She had a shrewd look that startled him.

'To be shown the site of a dam.'

'But you won't lend money because you like the landscape?'

'Of course not,' Carpenter said. 'This is just politeness. They feel they have to show me the plan is real. I feel I have to let them show me. We're not very clever about things like that.'

She smiled, and tugged his sleeve. Two children had a spider monkey on a leash; and they followed as it went on feathery legs

4

from top to bottom of a lattice wall, and danced its delicate way.

'You have family here?' Carpenter asked, while their eyes weren't meeting.

'I suppose so.' But she wasn't indifferent to the question; he could see that. She made herself explain. 'I come from Leon now,' she said. 'Daughter of an old family. That's been my job for eleven years.'

'Job,' he noted as something he would have to understand.

'And your parents –' He couldn't bring himself to stay ignorant.

'My father died –'

The Guardsmen were back, a wall of olive and a busy man in a broad moustache.

'My dear Mr Carpenter,' the busy man said. 'Welcome to Bluefields. If only we'd known –' He looked at Aurelia with bleak dislike. 'And your charming companion –'

She dusted the stickiness of the tarts from her hand.

'Colleague,' Carpenter said flatly. Better not to explain.

They were walked to the government building, a shell of bright concrete with broken, gappy windows like bad teeth.

'We shall be pleased to show you whatever you wish to see,' the official said. He re-ran the day in his mind, taking out the women and the long lunch that he'd thought it might be wise to provide. A busy day, perhaps. A day on the river to see serious sights. The official wondered if he would really have to go along.

The wake of their speedboat broke against bright fishing boats, tied in bunches, and they tacked northwards over silver shallows to where the mangrove began walking the shoreline on high, fastidious fingers of grey root.

'This place would change, with the dam,' Carpenter said to Aurelia. He was ready to hear anything she had to say.

'It worked once,' Aurelia said. 'There were gold mines and logger camps. People didn't always ship out.'

'Traditionally,' the official began, 'the Caribbean Coast has not been part of the mainstream –'

There were shade umbrellas, and Aurelia had the air of a young matron inspecting the world. He was fascinated by the changes in her, hour by hour; he watched the long line of her legs

5

against the rough wood of the boat. She had cocktail manners, an almost mechanical helpfulness; but he thought he sensed heat.

'Of course,' said the official, 'I am not an engineer –'

He had no idea what she wanted.

'– but I think they call it anisokinetic –'

They scrambled back to shore with a sense of relief and took an official car – old but whole – to the airstrip. In the back of the car, the official moved a little too close and said: 'Madam, you'll forgive me – have we met? I was so sure, and I could never forget –'

Carpenter saw Aurelia hesitate, minimally. She said: 'I don't think so. Really.'

The official reckoned Aurelia had got above herself.

At the top of the hill they stopped in a cloud of dust and stared at an empty field. There was no sign of the plane.

'There seems to be a problem,' the official said, shifting from foot to foot.

At one side of the field there was a ramshackle tower. A man in braces stood there, pushing wadding through the barrel of a rifle, and looking carefully past the official party to a screech of a green parakeet in a tree.

'You,' the official shouted. 'Where's the plane?'

The man shrugged.

'Why is the plane not here?'

The man shouted back: 'Orders.'

'Whose orders?'

The man said, with an elaborate and mocking attempt at proper Spanish: 'El Maximo. El Jefe.'

'The President,' the official said, embarrassed now. 'Himself?'

'A secretary to his Excellency Anastasio Diaz Sacasa, President for Life –'

'I know the titles,' the official said. He shrugged as though gravity had doubled.

'We'll have to wait,' Aurelia said. Carpenter felt her move against his side. 'It's not too bad.'

'But we have to tell your husband –'

'There is,' the official said, dubiously, 'a hotel –'

Down at the Hotel Cueto a baby lay bare on the cool tiles and the steps had a guard of Indians and bottles.

The hotel boy said there was only one room. The official began to shout, unsure what he must do. Aurelia only smiled. Carpenter demanded a phone, but the boy said the phone had been out for two days. There was a plane tomorrow, and a room for tonight.

'The power's probably gone, too,' Aurelia said. 'Those generators were fifty years old when they dragged them out of the old Bonanza mine.'

The official wanted only to be away, not responsible for what went wrong. He had a cold feeling about married women on field-trips like this.

'We'll sort things out,' Carpenter said.

'But you are our guest,' the official said, desperately. 'We must arrange –'

'Thank you,' Carpenter said, and the official took it as dismissal. He was too grateful to be offended.

'I'll sleep somewhere else,' Carpenter said.

'Don't be stupid,' Aurelia said.

He wondered what she wanted afterwards.

Their room was a square of concrete, smelling of cooked beans and new insecticide. There was a shower walled off in one corner but no water, only two tall buckets.

'I'll find the well,' Carpenter said. He saw the threadbare sheets that just covered the mattress and was oddly embarrassed.

He walked out with the buckets, through a dining room with beans cooking on open fires to a covered well. He moved aside the planks and dropped the bucket down on rope, flicking it so it fell on its side. It was a skill he remembered from his grandparents' farm.

He opened the room door, and Aurelia was sitting on the bed with a pharmacy that spilled out of her bag. She was dissolving away the mask that had served her all day, and he was startled: her face was a private matter, alive and lovely, almost more intimate than seeing her body. He knew her skin must be hot like fever.

Kids in the hallway watched some ancient TV Western, laughing with excitement whenever the hero was in peril.

'We have to eat,' Aurelia said.

She led the way. Someone had parked a horse at the hotel steps

7

without tying it. Along Main Street, doors and windows opened like an Advent card on an evening's business. They passed GG's Club and a great cathedral of red and white wood, up a hill by five tall palms and out along hibiscus hedges. A boardwalk went off to the right over a spit of land.

He had to walk behind her because the boardwalk was so narrow. She could pretend not to hear him if she wanted, and so he could ask.

'What happened here?'

He thought she wouldn't answer.

'My father didn't die,' she said, flatly. 'He was killed. That's all.'

And she was gone. For a moment he thought she'd quit, but then he heard feet scuffling over a chute of oyster shells that led down from the boardwalk. He followed the sound. Down by the water there was a jetty roofed with thatch, with oil lamps burning and a few chairs and tables.

Aurelia ordered oyster soup, and said it with the proper Jamaican vowels – 'ais-ta soup'. It was hot and sweet at once, full of coconut water, specks of pork and peppers that stung. They drank beer.

'You really want to know?' she said.

At that moment, watching the shadows in her cat's face, he wanted to know everything.

She said the dawns were like white paper that's suddenly stained with blue. She'd never got used to living with sunsets instead of sunrises. And she had a sister, called Mercedes. Her twin sister.

Carpenter tried to put that face, with its dark, drowning eyes, into some other place. He thought of New York clubs, a life suspended like a high wire between rock music and the castled rich, a model's face that was very famous but not familiar. Nobody got that close.

Aurelia was talking about a morning when the streets were full of old flags, and carpenters were sweating over a new reviewing stand by the park. In a few hours, the President was coming.

There was a different Captain of the National Guard in those days: a flaccid man, soft with his own resentments. He hated being so far from Leon and all the prizes of the capital – a cut of the customs dues, a Porsche concession, a few girls to run. He hated wheat tortillas. But he smiled to see the twins, Aurelia and Mercedes. They had been pretty things a few years back, mirrors of each other, and now they went out walking in brilliant colours and high skirts, their bodies filled out freshly. The Captain loved to watch.

'Get that fucking stand in place,' he shouted. 'Just make it so it doesn't fall. So it can't fall.'

The girls went down to the jetty where they tethered their dory, a little dug-out with floursack sails. They climbed aboard and the boat sank down until the brackish water almost filled it; they struggled with a pole and a mess of rope and sacking. And quite suddenly, the dory darted out from shore like a dragonfly, and the girls were busy with the crude tiller and the ropes – absorbed in the wind.

It was good to be away from shore. They had to dress that morning in drum majorettes' costumes brought back by an uncle from Miami, and dance in a parade for the President. They loved dancing, but their father seemed nervous about the day. He kept saying it was an honour, nothing to concern them.

The Captain left the carpenters alone. He didn't worry too much about the look of the things; El Presidente did not expect much in the outlands. The Captain couldn't impress him.

He walked out behind the barracks. He didn't tell himself he wanted to see the girls in the water, but they were there – the dory stopped in the lagoon, one girl standing to pull her T-shirt over her new breasts and dive into the water. He felt jealous of the water that could tease the new hairs between her legs.

There were shouts behind him; he turned back to the day's rituals. He knew a man upstream who changed the traffic signs every other day to make money from the fines; he might try that. Soldiering was a business.

The girls came in reluctantly from the water. They dressed themselves in red and white and settled each other's hair. Their mother looked proud. But one of the skirts seemed to ride too high and she tugged it down; best not to take chances.

Down below the green and white houses, the crowd nudged itself into rough order. Kids like black polished stones lined up in their white shirts. There was percussion like a storm, bells and drums and cans filled with beans, and a streetside crowd that picked up the music and went strutting and cheering, but not for Diaz; this was a celebration of celebration itself. Banners opened across the street – church banners, praising a doe-eyed Lord – and the parade formed up. At its head marched Aurelia and Mercedes Zenon. They twirled the batons, flashed their long, brown legs, and turned back and forth to play the crowd.

On the stand, El Presidente beamed. He was the owner, complacent like a duke in his estates. He wore khaki like a soldier but tailored to control a spreading gut; he was a parcel, stained with sweat. And he accepted what he liked to think was homage. It didn't worry him whether he was liked in reality; he had fear to keep control. But he liked the games.

He pointed to the Zenon girls. The Captain, crossly, left the platform.

The procession went by, and out of sight of the reviewing stand it broke up in an old wood baseball stadium, and the dancing went on.

The Captain went down to the Zenon shop on Main Street. It was cool and high, stacked with plastic cups, popstar posters, dresses for kids and batteries and herbal cures from wise women in the bush. The girls' father was behind the counter, in a white guyabera.

'I can help you?' he asked the Captain.

'You should be at the parade,' the Captain said.

'I have the store to mind.'

'This is a holiday,' the Captain said, as though that was an order. He picked up and fingered some cheap linen. 'Your daughters did well. The President wants to see them at three.'

'He can talk to them now, in the parade.'

'He wants them alone,' the Captain said. 'In the uniforms. He particularly liked the uniforms.'

Zenon stared. And then, as though to settle his mind, he reviewed the high wood shelves of his shop: boxes, dresses, shoes, socks, jeans, cups, pots, towels, bolts of tropical cloth the colour of cut papaya. There was so much order in his little world, so far.

He went to see his wife in the back. She had her black hair pulled back sharply from an olive face, like an Indian.

10

'Diaz wants the girls,' he said.

She crossed herself. She was a good Protestant in her way, but she wanted all the protection she could have.

At three, El Presidente was settled in the barracks. He was ready for company. Around him the National Guardsmen were nervous, although one asked a favour, which was granted – money so his mother could go to hospital in Miami. Diaz knew how to keep the men happy. For the price of an air ticket, he'd be loved by the soldiers for another year.

The Captain fretted that the girls were late. He wasn't comforted by a stump of a man called Chamorro, a box-headed dwarf who sat high so nobody should patronise him, as if they would have dared. Chamorro always came with the President, the security man; but really a kind of priest who made ostentatious sacrifices for the sake of peace.

'You got the girls,' the dwarf said. He had a cop's voice: always cold and judging.

'It's arranged,' the Captain said.

'Better be,' Chamorro said. 'Better be.'

The Captain couldn't stop sweating.

An ancient Volkswagen, cut away to make a truck, began toiling up the hill to the barracks. It scoured up a biting dust that made people look away. A pair of Guardsmen fidgeted with their rifles as it came to a boiling stop.

El Presidente watched lazily. He thought about two girls tangled around him; possibly, probably, two virgins.

Erasmo Zenon stepped out of his rough truck and let down the tailboard. He dragged down two bodies, dressed like drum majorettes, their cheap gilt a sullen yellow in the sun.

El Presidente only watched.

Erasmo Zenon walked up to the barracks; the President nodded to let him through.

Zenon came to the President's chair. He threw down the bodies, which were things of straw and dirt, with stuffed stockings sewn to them to make parodies of legs and breadfruit heads.

'You said you liked the uniforms,' Zenon said. He was trembling with self-righteous terror.

El Presidente said: 'Where are the girls?'

11

Zenon was shaking now, an angry man who'd gone past the limit of his courage.

'I said, where are the girls?'

Zenon pushed the dummies forward.

'Scum,' said Diaz complaisantly. He picked up a dummy and buried his face in it; he could smell sweat. He said: 'They smell good. Now bring the girls.'

Zenon could not have moved even if he had known a move to make.

The Guards grabbed him. And El Presidente took out a cigarette lighter and lifted first one dummy and then the other, putting a flame to the sex of each one until they crackled, melted and burned up briskly, a mess of nylon and straw.

Zenon was staring. He wondered why he couldn't cry.

The dwarf Chamorro had a workroom under the barracks, and he left Zenon to spend time there: a vigil, watching the drummer roaches on patrol. Zenon thought of his wife and his daughters, all curled lovingly together in a great circle in a great white bed.

When El Presidente's plane had gone, the Captain sat out to watch the streets. He'd been given cigars; he smoked a serious one and he watched the stars. He knew there'd be trouble.

It must have been early evening when Chamorro went down to see Zenon.

'I've heard your name,' the dwarf said.

Zenon stood to a civilian kind of attention, the stubble on his chin like a rash. The dwarf perched on his stool like a hooded bird.

'You don't refuse things to the President,' Chamorro said. 'But you know that.' He lowered his box of a body to the floor. 'Now you can make up for it. Tell us about your Communist friends.'

'I don't know –'

'You need a wash,' the dwarf said, comfortingly. 'You'll feel better for a wash.'

The guards brought a bucket of water. They sat Zenon down and forced his head between his legs, deep in the water until he thought his brain would burst.

'That's better,' the dwarf said. 'And again –'

The rumours worked bar to bar round the town; Señora

Zenon had only to wait on the porch of her green and white house. The story would come to her.

She rocked back and forth, a motion so perfectly controlled it was alarming. She was terrified to know nothing, and more afraid to find out. Zenon didn't have other women, or drink; if he was gone, it was something terrible.

She got up from the chair and stilled it with great care, as though to hide where she'd been. She walked into the dark house and found a deep closet that smelt of cedar. There were two stiff white muslin dresses that the girls had worn to First Communion; she took them down, and stroked them, and laid them on the bed. They were like talismans.

Aurelia and Mercedes didn't doubt what they had to do. They dressed in the white; they kissed their mother. On the porch, the streetlight and the torches made the stiff white dresses glint. The people had crowded round the house out of a sympathy they didn't dare express; the girls shone in their eyes.

'We were going to save our father,' Aurelia said. 'We had to look so innocent –' She didn't finish the idea, but it was clear to Carpenter; when you use innocence, you lose it.

The girls walked down into the street, hand in hand through the smoke of the town evening. The pool hall cleared. The bootblack boys sat back against the wall, quiet. The girls went by like a Holy Week procession, their mother behind and a crowd following at a decent distance.

The Guards saw the white of the dresses first, and then a great firework of gold sparks from an unattended brazier.

Aurelia stepped forward. 'Please,' she said, 'where is our father?'

The Guards raised their guns.

The Captain told himself he didn't have to answer some girl. The barrack lights threw cold, blue shadows; he stayed in their shelter.

The frontline Guard asked Señora Zenon: 'What do you want?'

'We want our father,' Aurelia said.

The guard talked only to the Señora. It seemed safer.

The town was hot and close, and people began to seem busy, milling in the street.

The Captain came forward. 'Señora,' he said. 'At your disposal.'

But the girls were between him and the Señora. They wouldn't be moved.

'Your husband is in custody,' he said, over the girls' heads. 'Please explain that to your daughters.'

'I want to see my father,' Mercedes said.

The Captain was afraid they'd hear Chamorro working below, even through the shutters of concrete and steel. 'There is nothing I can do,' he said, which was the truth.

He told the men to put down their rifles, and the butts clattered on stone. The girls moved forward, eyes dark and steady and the white of the dresses dazzling.

'You will be informed.'

That was the moment, they found out later, the dwarf Chamorro took away the wet towel that he'd bound around the eyes of Erasmo Zenon and soaked it in acid from a car battery. He bound the towel back in place.

'Get out of here!' the Captain bellowed. He felt he was suffocating with the heat and the people. 'Get the hell out of here!'

The girls did not move.

'Get out or we'll shoot.'

The girls were still as angels in a church.

'Aim!' the Captain said.

The Guards brought up their rifles. They saw children in their sights, but they were still scared.

In the basement, the dwarf washed his hands elaborately in a metal bowl. 'Make a report,' he said. 'Put him down as an Amadista. Active guerrilla.'

The Captain clattered on steel heels down to the workroom. He saw Zenon's big clean hands crossed across his chest in a holy mockery; they were pulp around the fingernails. A guardsman dusted flies from where the eyes had been.

'You know what to do,' Chamorro said.

The next morning, the body was delivered to the undertakers' shack. Four women tended it; they were wattled and jowled like the birds that wait on death. And then, before the body went to the family, the coffin was sealed shut. Even the old women, who

14

had seen everything, would not touch the sacking bound round the eyes.

'It was just a box,' Aurelia said. 'It wasn't my father.'

They walked together to the burial ground – the widow Zenon, her eyes wide with astonishment, and the girls trying to be her strength and her sight. Their dresses were stained now by the clouds of rising dust.

The lane narrowed, and turned abruptly; there were Guardsmen blocking their way.

'No Amadistas here,' the sergeant said.

'This woman came to bury her husband,' the pastor said.

'No Reds. No Commies. No Amadistas.'

The procession had its own momentum; it could not stop. People crowded against one another, and the Guardsmen felt rushed. One fired into the air.

A woman screamed. The coffin slipped from the pall-bearers' arms and crashed to the road. The children and the widow watched the thin wood splinter.

'Where do we bury him?' the pastor said.

'I don't have orders on that,' the sergeant said. 'Just get him out of here.'

The widow Zenon turned from girl to girl, as though tied by their loving hands.

'Señora,' the pastor said, with a sense of horror.

'We'll take him out to sea,' one of the fishermen said. 'We'll bury him with honours.'

'Get out,' the sergeant said, and spat.

The procession was a warm, angry jumble of bodies that changed direction only with difficulty. The split coffin went back into the town.

The Guardsmen were left shrugging in the dust.

That night there was a crowd outside the house but Aurelia remembered her mother sitting very still, watching the people through slits in the wood shutters.

'Did you see him?' Mercedes had asked.

'We still have to live here,' her mother said.

Aurelia watched and guessed. Her mother wanted to be alone, so kind people would not stop her showing grief. She wanted to run out into bush until the vines had cut her and she knew she

15

had something left to feel. She went to the door and raised a finger to her lips, but she didn't want silence, only peace; sometimes she smiled at the sound of the women singing which came into the house as gently as a smell of baking. And she was awake all the night. Towards morning, she turned in her house like a dog does before a storm.

At eight the next morning, Aurelia and Mercedes dressed in their morning colours and walked down past the barracks to the lagoon. Breezes tugged at the wax yellow trumpets in the vines and made the palms shimmer. The sky was black and the town was lit like a stage.

They waited by the jetty for a moment or two, a tangle of warm, brown limbs. The Captain came out in time and saw them.

He was startled, they could see that.

They let the dory skim out a little way, and then they lay there. The water lapped round them.

The Captain was staring out, as they knew he would. Aurelia stood and watched him back.

The Captain was confused. The girls should be in mourning; daughters of his would be in mourning. But these creatures were amoral. They'd forgiven him; they were teasing him.

He began to undress. He waded into the water and struck out for the boat. He felt like a great fish in the water, ready to play between the girls' legs. He came close to the dory and basked there. He could see their breasts, firm and little, the nipples pink in a circle of brown. He smiled like a fool.

He did see one girl standing. He saw the blue-black hair between her legs. He was still smiling when the paddle cracked down on his head and a rope coiled round his neck.

The mast went up and the dory moved out from shore, sluggish at first because of its hidden cargo; the Captain's lungs filled up and his life blotted away. His neck snapped.

'And then,' Aurelia said, 'we went back to shore. Everyone agreed it had to be a swimming accident. They found him in the shallows.'

Carpenter sat very still. He knew she would watch his reaction with great care; he wondered if the story was finished.

'The night they found the body,' she said, 'the minister came to the house, and the bishop. I remember the lamplight on their faces. They looked like conspirators.' She sipped her beer. 'We listened outside the door, of course. They just said it might be time for us to go to school, somewhere else. They asked if we should go together. Mother just said: "They're very strong together."

' "You won't be lonely?" the Bishop said.

'My mother said: "I'll be lonely." '

They were on the boat three days later, girls standing under the open awning to catch the breeze. They watched the Indians pole the dories to mid-river, to miss the wake of the boat as it passed.

It took five hours to Rama. They ran to the buses for Leon; Mercedes bought peeled oranges and pressed one into Aurelia's hand. On the road to Leon, they saw smoke everywhere – curling up the sides of the mountains, blocking the road, and distant walls of soft, orange flame. The land was being cleared and fed for planting.

'I hate the smell of smoke,' Aurelia said.

He leaned forward and held her hands.

'You don't say anything,' she said.

He moved to hold her, so brusquely the table almost turned.

'Thank you,' she said.

They walked silently along the boardwalk. His mind was racing. He'd been in such a place before – a woman you half know, a hotel friend, someone you have dinner with, perhaps laugh with, and sleep with for the warmth you both need.

Aurelia was ahead of him. 'I suppose you do this all the time,' she said. She sounded defiant, but he could feel that the breeze off the lagoon had raised goose-bumps on her arm.

Carpenter said: 'I have a wife.'

But he couldn't make a living picture of Jill in his mind, only a kind of snapshot: a handsome woman tugged across the marshes by a large dog, smelling of bread, deconstructing Spenser in Wellington boots and smiling kindly, warmly as though every person and every thing gave her delight. He used to be jealous of her warmth until he realised it meant nothing in particular; and then he came to think her warmth to him was meaningless. 'My wife,' he said, inadequately, 'teaches.'

17

They didn't touch on the way back, because touch was going to matter.

The boy at the hotel yawned and grinned.

He handed them the key. 'God go with you,' he said.

In the bedroom, the airconditioner was thunderous. Aurelia went to wash in a basin of stale water; Carpenter undressed very quickly and sat on the bed. It was a moment awkward as a first seduction, complicated by what he now knew about her. He was tempted to find another room, even sleep in the corridor out by the Indians and their bottles; but he knew that was not what she wanted. He knew; that scared him.

She came into the bedroom, bare in the dim light; he knew more about her history than her body, he realised. But when she stood there, simply looking at him, he stopped thinking. He held her, the slick wetness of her body marking his. He felt his blood roar.

In the morning he could hear kids playing, cooking utensils crashing; the airconditioner wasn't such a good curtain of sound. He felt across the damp, thin bed and he missed Aurelia.

She was splashing, improvising a shower, soaped and naked; and he joined her, bodies slipping against each other as though they were oiled, and hands busy with each other's bodies. They muddled their arms and legs like one person, and they were joined together almost before they'd realised it. The act was furious and breathless.

When they turned off the airconditioner, Carpenter pulled aside the plastic curtain. There was no window behind it. He began to laugh.

Someone had pushed a note under the door. Their plane would return at nine, sharp.

Aurelia sat at a long wood table in the dining room with a quiet group of Indians, gobbling the red beans and eggs; and when she'd finished with the thin, woody coffee, she went to the room. Carpenter waited, content and impatient all at once.

She came back as someone else's wife, the make-up precise. He had to talk to her from a distance; suddenly she didn't allow any closeness. He had a moment of anger when he wanted to throw her story, their last night, in her face; but it passed quickly.

18

They were in the air before the pilot announced a diversion. He looked very young in his starch and cologne, and very unsure.

Aurelia spoke like a matron to a servant: 'Why?'

The pilot was fooled for a moment, but he grinned. 'Finca Esmerelda,' he said. 'We're collecting a Diaz. It can't be the old man because he's got a Boeing.'

Carpenter saw Aurelia showed no fleck of emotion, except annoyance at the inconvenience.

'They've had a meeting of the board,' the pilot said, 'comings and goings for days – the whole family. You can't get a limo and you can't get a plane out in Leon.'

Aurelia said: 'The whole family?'

The plane dropped to a bright white landing strip in the smoky hills. After a minute, a cloud came out of the smoke – dust round a jeep's wheels. It came to a nose-diving stop by the plane. The driver was a man with a moustache like a black label on his upper lip; he jumped down, neatly, an athlete who'd given up grace to be a soldier. And he handed down a woman in scarlet, who limped under the weight of her dignity.

'We are,' the matron said, stonily, 'sharing this plane?'

'I have to share the plane too,' her companion said, most reasonably. 'And I am Tomás Diaz.'

But the matron would not budge.

Carpenter wanted to know how Aurelia felt, so close to the family who'd ordered her father dead. The pilot had climbed down and was talking to the young Diaz; the matron stayed by the jeep.

'When we got to Leon,' Aurelia began, very softly, 'the nuns met us. They had a new compound – they had these ficus trees with big, rubber leaves, and there was a frangipani. It smelled like my mother.' She cleared her throat. 'One day, a man came – one of the sisters had been in the InterContinental, asking for money. She had a lovely smile. She used to make people feel lucky to stay in the hotel, and generous. She brought back a man called Vico.'

Ian Carpenter spluttered. Vico was one of those names that mean only one man: and not a philosopher any more. Now it could only mean that last surviving great financial criminal of the

1960s and 1970s, a man who stole the business of mutual funds, put it through a post box in Amsterdam and a third floor walk-up bank in Luxembourg and settled for exile.

But for some reason, Aurelia wanted to tell her story fast and quietly. She talked over his reaction.

'There was a room with shutters – I remember the walls were stripy, like tigers. It was very cool. It smelt of frangipani – blowsy. And the sister brought us out, both of us. We had our hair tied back. We wore shifts. And this man Vico, he hunkered down and he said he was glad to meet us.'

Aurelia looked at the figures by the jeep. It was as though she'd calculated this was the last opportunity to tell her story. But the scarlet woman was still obdurate, Tomás Diaz reasoning with her; and the pilot was standing to attention, and to the side.

'We knew it mattered, we didn't know why. Vico said we were lovely. The Sister said we'd lost our father. Then she brought Vico a drink. I don't know what. She said it was water, but when he drank it, it was like it bit him. Maybe it was *guarro*. I remember he looked up, at a crucifix with a great, pink bloody Christ and he hiccupped. Then he said he wanted to adopt one of us, and the Sister said that was complicated, and Vico said he was very rich. He said he'd help the convent.

'I think it's like that in a brothel, isn't it? They bring the girls, you make your choice, you make your deal. So Vico chose, and he chose me. The Sister kept saying he mustn't choose there and then, it wasn't good for us, but Mercedes stepped forward and she said – "Choose me." The Sister told her to be quiet.'

Tomás Diaz and the scarlet woman had come to a stand-off.

'I think the Sister thought Mercedes was being forward,' Aurelia said, 'but she was being brave. She didn't see the man like we did – like a big sea creature hauling his blubber with him and smelling of drink. We knew about men like that; we knew about the Captain. And then Vico began to wonder which one of us he'd take, and the Sister kept watching as though she'd finally realised what the risks might be, and Vico flipped a coin.

'The Sister said I had to pray for Mercedes, and I did. I cried for her, I lit candles for her. I remember the Sister's hand on my shoulder, how it smelled of strong soap.

'Then Mercedes wasn't there any more.'

Tomás Diaz and his cousin were grudgingly turned towards the little plane, which was hot and stifling.

'A family adopted me. The father couldn't have children, which was his shame, and he'd had three annulments so he couldn't bluff any more. They took me in and I became –' She spread her hands to take in her painted face, her neat skirt, her manners: herself.

Tomás Diaz said from the plane door: 'I'm sorry we have kept you waiting.'

'I'm Ian Carpenter,' he said as though this was an ordinary introduction, and Tomás interrupted, with an interested look: 'The banker?'

Carpenter nodded.

Aurelia said: 'Aurelia Dometz. My husband –'

'Husband,' Diaz said, and winked at Carpenter.

They put the scarlet matron, redder now with crossness and heat, in the very back of the tiny plane in a single seat; Aurelia and Carpenter, in the middle, served as a *cordon sanitaire*.

Tomás Diaz didn't take the controls, and the pilot was made to feel the concession. The matron squawked on.

'Nobody,' she said, 'tells you anything. In this family, we say nothing. Nothing.'

'Yes, cousin.' Tomás was impatient for the sound of the engines to shut the lady out.

'Your father said nothing. Nothing. He could die tomorrow and you none of you know where his credit cards are. Let alone –'

'They speak Spanish, cousin,' Tomás said.

But she was in full flood now. 'He calls himself El Jefe, El Maximo, El Presidente, and he's a Diaz just like us. He's so afraid of his clever little Yanqui bitch, he can't enjoy his money. He's scared of your mother. That's it.'

'Yes, cousin.'

'He has hidden one billion dollars,' the cousin screamed as the plane roared up into the sky. Until the very outskirts of Leon, there were still sharp, aggrieved barks from behind; Aurelia was half afraid of a sudden attack, a flailing handbag.

But Tomás was grateful for the noise, and he made quiet, unimportant talk. He was interested in Carpenter; Carpenter

21

knew about money, and perhaps about the old man's money.

'But you know the rules?' Diaz said.

Carpenter looked blank.

'Other people's wives,' Diaz said, conspiratorially. 'A wife can't be a mistress.'

'It's not my country,' Carpenter said, again.

'Nobody minds what you can't see,' Diaz said. He was checking his pilot's reflex to take control as they came into land. 'We do have nightclubs here. Dark. You see the feet, you see the candles, you never see the faces.'

'The plane was delayed,' Carpenter said.

'You'd be better off with the girls,' Tomás Diaz said as the plane came down in Leon.

On the ground, the cousin demanded a car. Tomás Diaz was talking about a party. And Aurelia was gone, abruptly. Carpenter wondered if she'd been offended by Diaz, or the male talk that seemed to cut her out, or whether she was bothered about what to say to Mario.

'I always wanted a Purdy,' Diaz said. 'A shotgun. Purdy of London.'

'They're fine things,' Carpenter said. He was startled at how the man expected bribes, even when he needed favours.

'Think of it like a tax,' Tomás said. 'And don't forget the party. Your lady is coming, with her husband.'

Carpenter took a taxi to the house that he'd borrowed from the local manager of an American bank. He sat out on the screened porch and looked at bougainvillaea in chains of purple and russet, the waxed and blowsy frangipani, the dead, gold boats of leaves from the rubber tree floating in a still blue pool. For the moment, it was better than looking up and seeing the broken plain of the city of Leon.

He poured himself a drink. It was good to hear the Diaz family squabbling; it suggested there really was a billion, and that only the old man controlled it. That was the point of being in Providencia, after all.

The phone rang and he padded over the cold tiled floor.

'I have to see you,' Aurelia said.

'You know where I am.'

She was there within minutes. The housekeeper, a sour sort,

still waited in the driveway when Aurelia drove up.

'My husband is giving a paper,' she said.

He wondered if she'd be more discreet when he went away. 'He didn't mind you were away?'

'The maid said he didn't understand.'

'We should be careful,' he said. He didn't know how to make another alibi as safe as Bluefields.

She wore fiery silk that caught at her body as she moved and seemed to tease it. She slipped the dress over her head and she wore only high heeled shoes.

'I have to go to Mexico City,' Carpenter said. 'Tomorrow.'

'I know,' Aurelia said, mockingly.

'And –'

She matched every inch of him.

·ONE·

There was a moment Mercedes loved on the way up: when the cable car comes out of its dock, pulls slowly over the rock and snow and then clears a ridge, and the rock falls away fast. She was flying again, risking in the cold, brilliant air. She saw a chapel on the spur of the mountain and wondered how people got there; she saw the *in memoriam* crosses stationed like soldiers. And ahead, at the summit, she thought she saw lenses glinting. The cable car began to tug up the last face of rock.

Two days in the Alpine sun, and the final shots for the magazine spreads: then she would have done everything. She could wander back to New York; she could wallow in the city for a few days; she could think about going to the Diaz party. It would be curious to be in Providencia again.

The car came into its dock and she walked the steep concrete jetty to the hotel. There was a receiving line in place – the photographer, a bearded Scot with a thin, bothered face; a pair of stylists, their spiky hair toned down for Switzerland; a make-up person, an art director, a publicist, a camera operator, two porters of sorts and the hotel manager. She would know all their names in a moment, and forget them all when she had to.

'Darling,' she said.

'It's perfect,' the publicist said.

'It's going to be tricky,' the photographer said.

Mercedes smiled. She was smothered in fur to the waist, and below that the legs took over – long and silky beneath a leather skirt. It was her job to be watched. And now she had to animate them all, persuade them to love her enough to make the pictures right: the autumn pictures to sell a new perfume, soft and floral so the makers said, to be signed Mercedes Zenon. She'd manufactured a name that was up there now with Paloma Picasso or Krystle of *Dynasty* or Estée Lauder's husband or some designer much loved by his business manager – a name that could sell. She tended her assets.

'The light,' said the photographer, 'is extraordinary. Quite difficult. You'll see.'

'You'll do it,' Mercedes said. She was glad they'd brought the Scotsman; for the first pictures, the cosmetics men had imposed a Germanic figure who liked his ladies with great white bottoms, or in leather. She'd been angry at being a fetish, but professional.

And they walked into the hotel, to a suite with a view of the blue-white powdery snow all around, and the wide wooded cross of the lake down below. She settled and let her mind go blank while the stylists and the make-up and the hair people fussed.

'– we need –'

She hadn't realised that coming back to Pilatus would upset her so; it mustn't show in the pictures. There, she was meant to be young, metropolitan, brilliant, successful: that to which people aspire. And playful, they'd said at the briefing, and sexy, of course. She'd nodded. But what she really remembered was five birthdays spent on this mountain, with George Vico.

They'd left Leon on a yacht, a great white dazzler that was more splendid than anything she'd imagined: it was the reality of some small encyclopaedia picture, some gossip-column snap. Vico had told her to carry suitcases that were heavy. When they got to Switzerland, the cases didn't hold the clothes he'd promised, only one-hundred-dollar bills. She hadn't been puzzled or surprised; she assumed someone was paying Vico, as he paid the nuns for her. She'd grown up abruptly.

But once a year, Vico bothered with something gentle and almost romantic – their trip together to Pilatus. They drove from Geneva, took the ski-run up over the trees, smelt the smoke from the woodfires burning under the path of the lift. And Mercedes, because it was her birthday, let herself remember the fires on the road to Leon, and all the other smells that she missed in this clean, breath-taking air: the smell of things changing, the smell of pigs, rind, smoke, river water. And Vico, blubbery as he was, seemed a hero.

As a father, he'd been tidal – sometimes close and overwhelming, more usually out. He always brought presents. When he was home, she heard things: phone calls, arguments, meetings in other rooms that suddenly fell silent if she walked in. There was always talk about money, and it was always urgent; Mercedes was alert like a scared animal, and Vico trained her to use her alertness, without meaning to. She shivered, and she learned.

The last birthday, they'd come to Pilatus as usual. She knew there was something wrong, but Vico had no idea how fine her instincts had become. He thought of her as his lovely, perfectible daughter – the glamorous one, not the pudgy child who'd gone off with her mother after an acrimonious divorce. He'd traded up.

The stylists had almost finished, and the photographer said: 'We'll start on the terrace.'

The retinue trooped to the narrow ledge that overhung snow and the line of a rack and pinion railway, and the dizzying view down valleys into the rocky plain below. They took positions.

Mercedes sat beneath an umbrella, and a black bird came up to her shoulder, a glossy creature with a brilliant yellow beak and quick eyes. They faced each other.

'Yes, yes,' the photographer said. 'Fine.'

There had been birds on the terrace that year, scavenging for all they could find, tumbling over one another in the snow after crumbs. When they went down the mountain, there was a hawk overflying the tall firs: she remembered that.

And she remembered the car park. As they came down over the meadows, and the apartments each with its screen of evergreen, Mercedes could make out blue-grey sticks of men in the car park. The lower the gondolas came, the clearer the faces and the fuller the bodies. She tried to tell Vico, but he wouldn't listen, and he was too vain to wear glasses in front of her and see for himself.

'Cops,' she said.

'You never see cops in Switzerland,' Vico said.

But when the gondola docked, the cops came towards them like filings to a magnet. They told Vico he had twenty-four hours to organise his affairs and get out of Switzerland.

'That's not how you treat a guest,' Vico had said.

'You're not a guest any more.'

They had driven back to Geneva too fast. Vico was pre-occupied, and Mercedes thought the whole thing unfair: she'd learned so hard to be Vico's daughter, to remould herself into a good Swiss schoolgirl, and now that was over. She had a very cold sense that it was completely over.

In the big Geneva house, Vico told her to pack.

'Where are we going?' Mercedes asked.

But he'd lost everything, and now he lost his temper as well.

She climbed a circle of stairs and went into her room. She would take clothes. She had her expensive education, her few fine years of graces at la Rosée. Vico would give her money, perhaps. The wardrobe held a few lives – teenage kid in jeans and T-shirts; girl-child playing the role to the gingham hilt for Vico; woman.

She could go anywhere. Anywhere was as good or bad as anywhere else. She felt sick, and terrified, but she managed to look self-possessed, more like a wife thinking out a long-expected settlement than a child thrown out.

When Vico came into her room, she said: 'Will you give me money?'

Vico looked red and bullish. 'You're my daughter,' he said.

She smiled.

'You can rely on me,' Vico said, but she knew he didn't mean it. He felt her lack of trust in the air, tangible as a chill.

'I know all about it,' Mercedes said.

He stared at her. She was a girl of eighteen, for Christ's sake, some peasant innocent taken out of the jungle and put down in Switzerland. What could she know?

'About Offshore Capital,' Mercedes said. 'I heard you talking. All the assets have gone, haven't they? They said you took them all.' She looked at him matter-of-factly. 'But I didn't know if that was true.'

He walked to the window and looked out onto the gardens. A little fountain kept a circular pond alive; abruptly, it was switched off. The hired staff in the hired house were taking no chances.

'They said you had this enormous – mutual fund. They said you moved all the assets – all the money, all the shares, when you were supposed to rescue it. They said you sent them to a post office box in Amsterdam and then to a walk-up bank in Luxembourg.'

'You understand all that?'

'I knew you had a big company with lots of investments.'

'And you think I stole that money?'

'They said it was a quarter of a billion. Maybe more.' He was too startled by his own predicament to catch the stone in her performance, the perfect, fake stillness that signalled her inexperience.

'I thought it was interesting,' she said.

Vico began to roar. He never found the words to match his anger. He only shouted about women on his territory, a daughter who didn't trust him, how she didn't know nothing, fucking nothing.

Mercedes was scared, but Vico hardly noticed.

'I give you a home,' he was bellowing. 'I give you a home and this is how you repay me.' He spilled out all his fury at being caught. 'A woman doesn't know about things like that. A woman knows what she's meant to know.'

She had the strength to run, but that wasn't enough. She tried to put a dress neatly into a suitcase and she spoiled the folds.

'Shit,' Vico said, and his menace collapsed into terraces of bellies, all shivering and close to tears. 'I am shouting at my baby. My baby.'

He had a glassed smile, and his arms were out. Mercedes was more frightened now.

'You like the mountain, don't you? You like Pilatus? We'll go back some day.'

'I have to pack,' Mercedes said.

He hit her sharply across the face. 'Where the hell does baby think baby's going? You think I'll take you with me?'

'I don't know,' Mercedes said, honestly.

'Tell me why I should. I don't need another daughter.'

And Vico threw himself at her, an awkward lunge that fell a little short of knocking her down but tore the white cotton of her dress. She stood there, a cloud of white enfolding her legs, her brown skin filmed with a nervous sweat that made her look oiled. She was firm and sweet as pears.

'We have to leave,' she said.

'You could stay. We could –'

'I'll need some money.'

He fell towards her, and she stepped aside. He lay, broad and awkward on the ground, looking hurt.

'Jesus,' he said.

And then it was as though he had sobered from a drink. He raised his great head and she saw only another performance, just something more she had not quite learned. She threw the cases shut and struggled out of the room with them.

She felt overwhelmed. All the things she still had to master and arrange – the rest of her life – swarmed around her like biting insects. She thought of being out on the lagoon when a sail falls and a wind is rising, and times when you can think about nothing except survival: she decided thinking was a luxury.

She stormed down the stairs, cases crashing against the light metal balustrades, and stood in the marble hall. The flowers were a little too old, the pictures a little too anonymous: the life had gone out of the house.

'George Vico,' she shouted through the house, so the servants and secretaries could hear if they hadn't already gone. She felt very ignorant and very young, and she wanted more than anything some person who would nurture and support her, take away this endless job of surviving. The hall was clean and cold; she was isolated in it like some specimen.

Out of a side room ambled a thin, neat man, Vico's secretary.

'You could go to New York,' the secretary said. 'I expect I'll go back to New York. You have your American passport.'

'I need tickets,' Mercedes said. She could feel how she'd planted her feet like a matron waiting for a bus at Rama, elbows out.

'You want everything, don't you, dear?' the secretary said.

She felt anger that seemed to bubble in her veins and skin. 'I want tickets and some money,' she said.

'I don't know if Mr Vico has money,' the secretary said. 'To be truthful, that's why I'm off. The police seemed to think he'd have a hard time getting his hands on his money.'

Mercedes put back her head and screamed: 'George Vico.'

He came to the head of the stairs. Somewhere, he'd fallen; his left eye was a glory of green and purple. He looked down on people he used to own, and he said, in a tired voice: 'You don't have to shout.'

She'd never seen him look shabby before. But still she stood four square at the foot of the stairs, like a market woman challenging a deal.

'I know the address,' she said. 'In Luxembourg.'

'I don't know what you mean.'

The secretary draped himself against a square pilaster; he was watching them as he would watch a soap opera.

'I know the address the Swiss want to know.' She looked triumphant now, her face completely without malice but animated by the knowledge that she had the key that guaranteed survival.

'Nobody wants to know,' Vico said with an air of sweet reasonableness. 'They know the money's gone. They know where. They know it's vanished. What else could they want to know?'

'They asked a lot of questions this morning,' the secretary said. 'Of course I couldn't answer all of them –' He supposed the kid deserved a break.

Vico said: 'You're a faggot and a fool.'

And Mercedes couldn't wait any longer. She stalked to the door, hoping that car and driver would be waiting there; evidently one servant still remained. She ordered the car to the railway station, and she checked her bags at left luggage. She went to the telephone booths.

Vico answered. 'Don't be so damn silly,' he said.

She watched the shoes of men who walked by. Brown brogues, military blacks. Sneakers.

'I can't come back,' she said quietly. 'The police would have to question me. I'd have to answer.'

She wondered how to play her hand. She wondered if she even knew what precisely was in her hand. She was in a small, closed booth with unfriendly faces passing the door, with nowhere to go and nowhere to be. Should she threaten Vico, just that, or should she play on his old affection for her? Did he want to lose her for ever? Should she offer him that?

'If they had the Luxembourg address today,' she said, 'they could get the money back.' It was a pure guess.

30

Vico didn't answer. She almost tapped the phone to test it. He was thinking that she couldn't possibly know how the money had been shifted from the world's largest offshore investment fund into the private accounts of George Vico; he'd stripped the organisation brutally, but neatly. But as it happened, she was right on one thing. The money was still in Luxembourg, because it takes time to hide cash, and he was too closely observed to give the final orders that would take it to safety.

'Where do you want to go?' he asked.

Mercedes thought for a moment. She had the American passport. She had nobody in Europe. She couldn't think of Providencia.

'New York,' she said.

'You can collect money there,' Vico said. 'I'll arrange it. You have your passport?'

'Of course.' She felt very wise at remembering her passport. She'd never travelled before without servants or Vico.

'And where will you go in New York?'

'Friends,' she said.

'What name is that?'

She had seen the right movies, read the right thrillers. 'If I told you,' she said, 'you'd follow me.'

'I don't think I can come to America for a long time,' Vico said. 'I wish I could.'

He added, like the tired and thoughtful father he still was in his own mind: 'You call them first. From wherever you are now. And you won't be able to get in touch with me.'

'I'll see the papers,' Mercedes said.

She was just a stray in the station, but she could not let it show. Confidence carried her. On the plane, when she asked for a drink, they gave her only one, and when she went to the Manhattan bank, they were suspicious and puzzled. But Vico had sent the money, and they opened an account. The bank proposed she should put herself into the Essex House for a day, and she did, playing room service; but the waiters wouldn't stay to talk. She didn't know how to tackle the people in the lobbies; she was afraid of the people on the street. She saw only towers and rushing people, and sad old horses pulling cabs around the park, and kids of her age in packs.

She needed friends.

She was out on the cable car now, suspended mid-way while the dour Scotsman Polaroided her with machine-gun speed. He said to his assistant: 'I never saw that look on her before.'

The assistant shrugged, not able to guess what the photographer wanted.

'It'll be wonderful,' the Scotsman said.

Back on the solid rock of the summit, she made herself walk out of her memories and back into the social business of a shoot. The hotel had been booked for two nights, and the sunbathing Americans had been cleared out; Pilatus could be visited but at night it belonged to the crew and to Mercedes.

She lay in bed, listening to the silence, which was like the smothered silence of a studio, without echo or resonance. There were sudden sounds, a little like barking in the mountains, a little like ice cracking over a sea. She slept fitfully.

The next morning, the publicist had brought some reporters up the mountain – the big-shouldered woman from the *New York Times*, a brace of Swiss, one cross and one indulgent, and half a dozen others.

Mercedes saw the publicist for the first time: a little, lardy man with busy white hands. He was nervous about reporters too close to reality, even the special reality of a shoot on the summit of an Alp. Mercedes would have to calm them down.

'Is it true –' she heard.

She said she might indeed appear on *Mainline*, for the glossy night-time soap opera was just beginning to sag a little in the ratings and importing names to lift its fortunes; she would play a character like herself. And what was she like?

'Dark, of course,' Mercedes said.

A little laugh.

'It's wonderful that blondes are the heroines nowadays,' she said. 'It's so much more fun for the rest of us.'

And were those shows fair to the rich, to her friends?

'My friends don't think so,' she said. 'It makes them too interesting. They always have Rolls-Royces on the show, and in real life it's Volvos. Volvo station-wagons. It's gowns on the show, and clothes in real life. Eighty hours a week working when on TV it looks like we spend eighty hours a week on our nails.'

The publicist frowned. The subject was perfume; Mercedes knew that.

'– and how do you feel about what's happening in Providencia?'

The publicist heard alarms in his skull; he washed hand over hand. It was out of control. The wrong person had arrived. He only knew the questioner was from some Central American paper, and who knew from the Guatemalan market – except they bought perfume in Miami.

'I haven't been there,' Mercedes said, 'for a long time.'

'You only left ten years ago,' the reporter said. He was a very tall, spare man, broad-shouldered but insubstantial from the side, wearing a scrub of beard; he looked young, and inflexible.

'I'm sure,' Mercedes said, gracefully, 'they will all be wearing Mercedes Zenon. It is a wonderful perfume. Perhaps we could have the samples, and you can be the first to – as it were – taste it for yourselves –'

'Perhaps we could talk later,' the reporter said.

Mercedes nodded. The publicist groaned. There'd be no holding them now, not if one had an exclusive. He'd said, particularly, no exclusives.

But girls from the kitchen came in with trays – crystal glasses, and champagne; crystal bottles, cut and inlaid like hibiscus flowers, and the perfume. Some syndicated bitch asked an awkward question, but it was lost in the greedy sniffings and posings and drinkings. The perfume had arrived and it had conquered.

But the reporter didn't go down the mountain with the others.

'I'm José Mantica,' he said.

'What paper?'

'*La Prensa* in Leon. Among others.'

Mercedes said: 'I know.'

He had suggested they talk on the terrace. The last light was vanishing, leaving only ghosts of red and gold on the mountains.

'You're from Bluefields?' Mantica said.

'A long time ago,' Mercedes said. 'It's not something I usually talk about.' She was puzzling over the man. She expected some pitch, some offer to write the great life story, some deal; there were always people who wanted to turn you into a TV movie. But Mantica seemed more driven than that.

'There's trouble there,' he said. He was mean with words.

'I guess the guerrillas are there.'

'The Amadistas,' Mantica corrected her. She knew what the correction meant. She could feel him trying to sense her attitudes, to slip under all the warmth and glamour she could so easily project and find what she was thinking. But the barriers were impressive.

'*La Prensa* isn't an Amadista paper,' she said. 'You support Diaz, don't you?'

'We support law and order,' Mantica said. 'Which isn't always Diaz, as you know. You do know?'

Mercedes was edgy. She never talked of Providencia, never went back; and now the moment she was considering one party, one insignificant party, suddenly the world wanted to talk about her earliest past. She was neither proud nor ashamed of those years, but they were childhood years, and they had nothing to do with the name she'd built.

'The Diaz family seem to have been there for ever,' she said.

'Maybe not for ever more.'

Mercedes shrugged. 'Look, I'm not political. I'm not even Providencian any more.'

'But you're a serious person.'

'You know my secret. You and a dozen others.'

'You're serious and you lost your father.'

The light on the mountain died out, and the ridges that had been faintly bronze were now a pale blue-white.

'Please go to that Diaz party,' Mantica said. 'That's all we ask.'

Mercedes Zenon shivered.

'I didn't mean to take up your time –'

'That's fine,' she said. 'Fine.'

But even until the plane was over Manhattan she could smell woodsmoke, and see her sister: the mirror of herself, her other half. Her lost Aurelia.

There were pencils of white light on the skyline, and golden domes, silver candles in concrete. Mercedes lay back in the limo, adrift in a sea of saffron light from headlamps and tail lamps and street lamps. She waited for the city.

'I suppose,' the consul said, 'you've been up to something profitable?'

The consul was a reliable irritation in Carpenter's life – one of those blond Englishmen who looks boyish into his forties and in his fifties makes Americans talk knowingly of public schools and the fall of the Empire. He always added: 'I don't envy you.'

'I've been in Mexico City, if you want to know. Dealing with forty thousand Volkswagens.'

The consul looked blank. 'That's what you were doing there last time.'

'Yes,' Carpenter said.

'But you're a banker.'

Carpenter said: 'We own the company – foreclosed on it. The company has some dollar futures contracts, to buy dollars at what the peso was worth five years ago, which is maybe twenty times what it is today. Only we can't get the cash unless the business is still trading, so we're selling Volkswagens.'

'Until you can pocket your profits and run.'

'Until,' Carpenter said, 'we can collect what we're owed and get out.'

The consul poured himself a beer, which was an affectation.

'And you're going back to Providencia?' he said.

'The Diaz clan is giving a party. Junior division but El Maximo is coming. Probably I ought to be there.'

'Do you mind telling me what you find so interesting in Providencia?'

Carpenter said: 'Yes. Just as you would mind telling me why you always grill me about Providencia. Why should Her Britannic Majesty's Government suddenly be interested in a little chunk of jungle in Central America?'

'I am consul to Providencia.'

'A job that's so important you live in Costa Rica,' Carpenter said.

The consul got up to fetch ice for Carpenter's drink. His steel heels clicked on the tile floor, a cold little sound.

'We might have strategic interests,' he said.

35

'Not since the Panama Canal wasn't built through Providencia,' Carpenter said.

'You still read history?' the consul asked, unpleasantly.

'I'll trade my secrets for yours. You first.'

And the consul settled down, loosening his absurdly wide tie. 'Gold, if you want to know,' he said. 'Even though it sounds like Rider Haggard or John Buchan. In fact I'm not sure John Buchan wouldn't have been ashamed of using simple gold.'

'Gold and strategy.'

'Suppose,' the consul said, 'that there were to be major trouble in South Africa – just suppose. Blacks walk out of the mines, mines can't trans-ship, mines are sabotaged, maybe. Or the West has an access of moral fervour and puts the screws on Pretoria, and the Boers just stop exporting gold.'

Carpenter listened politely.

'Then we all know what happens,' the consul said, shaking his head. 'Only one power can fill the gap, and that's Mother Russia. Millions in hard currency flow into Russia, Russian economy survives and thrives, Russians all over the place buying the high technology they can't make for themselves. Not a very helpful thing.'

Carpenter wondered how much these junior Foreign Office men ever knew of the world around them, a world they were so admirably equipped to put down on two sides of paper.

'So all of a sudden, the marginal gold producers look interesting. Especially any that might – what is it you say? – come on stream in a short time.'

'Bonanza,' Carpenter said.

The consul looked surprised. 'Yes,' he said, 'the Bonanza mines, among others. Perfectly workable, we're told, and abandoned only because fixed price gold didn't pay against South African competition. Then when the price was set free, the country belonged to the Diaz family and the mines were too far from Leon for them to notice.'

Carpenter said: 'I almost believe you.'

'You were out in Bluefields, I gather? Looking at some site or other? You can't possibly expect me to believe your bank would put money into some grandiose piece of public works in Providencia – you know as well as I do where the money goes. All that earthquake relief, and not a building that's new in Leon.

36

World Bank poured in millions – I've seen the books. Public Housing Project this and Public Housing Project that; sometimes, there were even plans. But Public Housing Projects all came in as authorised cheques and went out in Vuitton suitcases, straight to Switzerland or wherever hot money hides nowadays. The Diaz clan are like that.'

'So people tell me.'

'You know the *paquete* story?' the consul said. He was settling into his lecture, mercifully forgetting what he was meant to ask. Carpenter encouraged him. 'Just so you'll know who you're dealing with,' the consul said.

'There was an earthquake, you remember – conscience of the world aroused, Leon in ruins. Place looked as if it had been ploughed. So Diaz appealed for earth-moving machines, and the Spanish sent them out of Latin solidarity – set up the credits, arranged the loans, sent the goodies. Issued a dozen or so press statements which talked about the glories of Spanish heavy machinery. Naturally, because they knew Diaz, they gave him twenty per cent of the loans. A kind of finders keepers fee.' The consul's face had a way of falling a little out of focus as he drank his beer, growing a shade redder and plumper.

'Naturally,' Carpenter said.

'Twenty per cent for the privilege of losing money by lending it. Because this is what happened. Diaz couldn't get to the money, but he did get to the equipment – brought it ashore, lost it for a couple of years on one of the Diaz ranches. Finca Esmerelda never looked better – all ten thousand acres of it. Meanwhile, of course, the Government of Providencia is paying off the loans from time to time, and eventually Diaz can't make the machines work any more, so he sells them – sells them, mark you – to the Providencian Government. Diaz got cash, of course, plus another twenty per cent for finding the Government such wonderful equipment. The Spanish didn't get paid any more. Nobody wanted to talk, because it was all too embarrassing.' The consul swallowed. 'The Spanish *paquete*, they call it. Ask anyone.'

A secretary came to the door and said the consul was wanted. 'Can't just run when they whistle,' the consul said. 'Gives the wrong impression.'

Carpenter looked at his watch.

The consul clattered to the window, back to the room; it was the position he always took for saying things he'd later deny if anyone bothered to ask.

'Keep an eye out in Providencia, would you?' he said. 'Booze, drugs, politics, girls, boys – anything. It lets London know I'm making my living and we're keen on feeding the Americans tidbits at the moment.'

'I thought they knew it all,' Carpenter said. 'They've been there almost a century.'

The consul said: 'Ah, but they don't get it all, do they? Old man Diaz throws his money around in America, a quarter of a million to help LBJ in 1964, a couple of Congressmen on the payroll. But you see our cousins when they want to get the Providencian army out on joint manoeuvres – strength of the shield against Communism, that kind of thing. Diaz won't budge. He's far odder than they know.

'I'll tell you another story.'

There was an odd anxiety in his voice, as though he needed Carpenter to stay – to feel he was doing substantial business, like a proper diplomat, not slipping out to fund some lost hippy's return to London, or tell an irate businessman to pay a traffic fine.

'It's the 1930s,' the consul said. 'The country's rife with smallpox. You can track the thing, and it's headed straight for Leon. Old man Diaz, who is Anastasio's grandfather, is terrified of death, and terrified of coping with thousands of dying in the streets and being blamed. So he sends to Sears Roebuck, from the catalogue, and he orders Christmas tree lights – all red and gold and white and green. You know the kind of thing; all the little lights he could find. And he takes them out in great ropes and puts them over the roads into the city and he tells everyone it's magic and the pox can't come into the city.'

'And did it?' Carpenter asked, distracted.

'For Christ's sake,' the consul said. 'He also shot anyone trying to get into the city from the infected towns.'

Carpenter made his excuses and set off for the street. Behind him, he heard the consul shouting: 'Whatever you're doing in Providencia, don't bet your future on Diaz.'

★

38

Mercedes did what she always did in her first hour back in Manhattan: called John Grey III. She stood by tall windows that looked out on crowns and towers like a Christmas window. She worked through the mail, which her maid had sorted on the old social principle of the weight of paper, and she dialled Grey's number.

'You had a good time?' she asked.

'Puerto Rican,' John Grey said. 'Waiter actor model.'

'It sounds like an orgy.'

'Just a career that hasn't happened yet.'

'If you didn't like boys, we'd be the perfect couple.'

'For Christ's sake,' Grey said. 'That's why we are the perfect couple.'

It had been like this all the years she'd been in New York. When she felt marooned in the Essex House, she'd called her friends – New York Brahmins, almost English to the ear. Their daughter had been at la Rosée, sent away to become marriageable, a state she resisted, she said, because of her gorgeous, glamorous brother, John Grey III. Her parents had the decent certainties of old families, and they saw Mercedes in trouble, Vico no longer in Switzerland (the full scandal had not yet emerged); they invited Mercedes to stay.

She was grateful, but not happy. She lacked the social antennae to tell how long she would be welcome, and what role she was meant to play; she suspected she was indulged because she was black, something exotic. But the house was big and made of chocolate stone, and John Grey was beautiful and blond, and irritatingly remote in the manner of an elder brother with a sister's friend. She didn't always feel like an act of charity.

It couldn't last. There was a dinner party at which Mercedes was spectacular: borrowed jewels, a frock bought on Vico's money and her own flowering. Next to her sat a matron from Connecticut, one of those dowager-bright women who play social events like tennis; she decided to be agreeable.

'Such a lovely dress,' she said to Mercedes, fingering the stuff like a tailor. Mercedes had nothing to say. A little later, the woman decided to notice the scatter of diamonds against silver, a rope of grey-white light at Mercedes' neck. 'How clever of you,' she said. Mercedes was beginning to feel like an animal on show.

And now the woman was desperate for some remark that would make this strange young black girl bridle, or smile. 'Your hair,' she said, 'so original.'

Mercedes stood. They were between duck and sorbet, and for a moment nobody saw anything strange. But then Mercedes took off the jewels and threw them down on her plate, glints in a mess of orange gravy, and she took off her shoes and slapped them onto the table, and to the silent horror of the party, she slipped her dress over her head.

'There,' she said to the dowager. 'That's all you're having dinner with. You don't need me.'

And she stormed out of the door in her shift.

The Brahmins could find no words of annoyance or reprimand; it was simply obvious that she had to go. In the hall, she stood shivering. A maid came, puzzled, and she demanded a car.

'But Mr John is taking the car –'

'Get me a coat,' Mercedes said.

John Grey came out to her, grand in his blond athlete's way but no longer patronising. 'Nobody ever did that to Aunt Grace before,' he said. 'Nobody had the brains or the guts.'

Mercedes smiled, carefully, in case his words didn't mean what they seemed to mean.

'I can't stay here, can I?'

'Probably not. You can move in with me for a while.'

'Your sister will be jealous,' Mercedes said, calculating.

'My sister,' said John Grey, mysteriously, 'knows me too well.'

In the car Mercedes said: 'I want to dance.'

'I thought you'd never ask,' John Grey said.

His apartment was a set of decks and turrets on top of a grey tile battleship of a building in Greenwich Village. Mercedes was impressed, and tried not to be. She snuggled back into a sofa and worked her long, brown legs like an exercise class. Her silk shift rode a little too high; John Grey noticed.

'You want some coffee?'

They settled in the kitchen, sometimes brushing against each other like cats.

'Why are you staying with my parents?'

'I couldn't live with my father any more. My adopted father.'

'And who is he?' John Grey had the social habit of the catechism, the prime marker of his class.

'George Vico,' Mercedes said.

Grey let the glass bowl of coffee crash onto the floor and explode in a black fountain.

'You know him?' Mercedes said, innocently.

John Grey looked at her like a child who's been just too clever. 'They brought back a headline for him,' he said. 'Fugitive financier. Nobody's been that for years. It's like a movie.'

'Probably,' Mercedes said, primly. Movies meant nothing to her; they'd been an unreliable school for manners.

Grey cleaned the floor and she perched herself on a stool, legs wound around the chrome. When he stood up, he kissed her directly on the lips.

'I like you,' he said.

Mercedes sprawled on the sofa, and perhaps she didn't mean the silk to shape her so exactly. Perhaps.

'You must have come from somewhere,' Grey said.

'Not like you do,' Mercedes said. She had seen how the Grey family had a tangible past in books, in closets, in picture frames; they kept dates like jewels, dates always earlier than other people's dates.

'I don't belong to my family,' John Grey said. 'I work on Wall Street. I'm a crook.'

Mercedes giggled. 'Like George Vico.'

'I walk down the Street,' Grey said, 'and there are all these great tall castles, all with guards and towers and battlements. They even hang out flags – the Brown Brothers Harriman flag, the Chemical Bank flag. Men come out and joust. There's a street market where you can eat. It's like a mediaeval war.'

Mercedes suddenly found him too close. She looked out of the windows to the Empire State Building which, that night, was a shout of white light.

'When can we go dancing?'

'Not before one.'

'What do we do until then?'

John Grey stretched himself. 'We could make love.'

Mercedes had a serious little smile.

41

'You don't sound keen,' Grey said.

'I never did it before.'

'Nor did I,' John Grey said. 'Not with a woman.'

But the remark did not faze Mercedes; she only filed such remarks.

She pulled her slip over her head and she came softly to the sofa where Grey was lying. He thought of gazelles. He held her head roughly and he kissed her.

It was something she had to learn, and perhaps use; she thought of it quite coldly. It was only a little barrier in the body, and John Grey was like all those strong, blond boys her schoolmates had desired. She went exploring under the stiff fabric of his shirt. She liked the touch of skin, and she tried the taste of it; she licked his bare chest, lightly. She said: 'I like you.'

He scrambled out of his clothes, and she lay across him. She could feel her skin coming alive against his, as though it was rasped a little. And he reared up, and began to lap at her nipples, licking and nipping, and she was losing herself. He put his big, broad hands at her sides, and shucked off her pants.

She couldn't lie quite still; she was aware of nerves and muscles she didn't know. And he measured the shape of her, the firm, high breasts, and then he pulled her forward and buried his head between the lips of her sex. She was impatient, and she was delighted all at once.

She was across his thighs now, the hot wet of her sex teasing at his hard cock. She chose a moment, and she looked down his body and settled herself abruptly onto him.

He felt her take him in and he felt the little flesh barrier break away. He began to move inside her, a whole life inside her, as though he was reaching up towards her heart. And above him, she moved to make him touch her exactly as she wanted; she looked down into eyes that were filled with her reflection. She was shivering, he thought, and she shivered with her whole body; she clung to him. And the trembling was suddenly not an itch but a fire, and she flung her whole body back like a runner at the end of a race, and she was gloriously there, coming and coming.

She fell forward, soft and wet and loving, and they lay for a while in a sort of sweet shock. They nuzzled and stroked; they didn't separate. He could smell the flowers of blood.

He turned her, when she didn't expect it. She felt almost trapped under him, and he used his weight to hold her in position, and when he began to move again inside her the first movements seemed to pull the skin. But then she began to move with him, and she was grunting, whimpering, and lost. She shivered again, like a storm.

They showered, and they went dancing at Studio 54 under the huge crescent moon and the pillars of starry life, and they gloried in their energy and life. They didn't think of anything as debilitating, as demanding as love.

The next morning, Mercedes went shopping. She was on the up escalator at Macy's thinking about coffee and denim, and she was dimly aware of a middle-aged woman, neat in powder blue, staring at her from the other escalator. The stare was alarming, from a face that had been tightened with knives. And then, there were shouts and confusion. The woman was racked with excitement and she was trying to scramble back up the escalator, battering through the stodgy shoppers with their bags and parcels. She brought down a square man with a bag of pots and pans; the escalator stopped, jammed with handles; the square man had his hands over his head, and he was saying in shock: 'That woman stole my hair. All my hair. She stole my hair.' But that woman was still cantering on, awkward in a hobbled skirt. Mercedes began to run.

Security stepped in Mercedes' way, and from far behind she heard the woman screaming: 'Listen. Just listen to me. Did you ever think of modelling?'

The woman caught up. Security still half suspected that the black girl was up to no good, but they also knew the middle-aged woman.

'Mrs Lincoln,' one guard said, respectfully.

'Yes, dear,' the woman said. 'I'm Lincoln.'

'Oh,' Mercedes said. The woman seemed motherly enough in a modestly bossy way. But she couldn't catch her eye.

'Of the Lincoln Modelling Agency.'

Mercedes didn't know what the woman meant, and she had a reader's knowledge of the world's wickedness from books passed in the dormitory at night. She thought of: white slavery, a lesbian pass, a movie director's talent scout, a movie star's procuress. She thought of vampires.

'There's always one exotic,' Mrs Lincoln was babbling. 'And you, darling, you are it. The only thing you can be is a star.' She pressed a card into Mercedes' hand

'This woman,' Mercedes said, 'is bothering me.' But the guards would not help.

'Call me,' Mrs Lincoln shouted, and Mercedes went quickly away through the island of dresses until she was sure she was out of sight.

She went down to Wall Street in more panic than she liked to admit. She passed through the brawling dealers' room and into John Grey's office. He was glad to see her and unsympathetic.

'Take the phone,' he said. 'Call her now. Apologise.'

'But I don't like her –'

'She runs the biggest modelling agency in New York. And what the hell else do you think you're going to do? Be a lawyer, a doctor, the Pope? A party girl? For Christ's sake, she'll make you a star.'

Mrs Lincoln delivered – *Vogue* covers, catwalk work for Yves Saint Laurent, ads for tricolour toothpaste, designer jeans when they were hot. She doubled the sales of a down-market line of sports gear and salvaged a déclassé white rum. It was true the blonde white girls stole most of the grandest endorsements, but the camera loved her and saw no substitute. One of the Rolls-Royce soap operas kept calling and calling. She could be a wild woman loose among their old money, new money, bent money.

And for some eighteen months, she slept famously – with a raw-boned, soulful man (the new James Dean, the flaks said) who mixed raucous physical glamour with a private life that only enhanced the look (nothing was denied, ever). His turbulence made Mercedes even more visible, made her known as sex and glory enough for such a man. When he died, there were rumours that stayed alive of their own accord, and turned into legend: how he'd died in some esoteric act of love, how he'd killed himself over some fancied infidelity of hers.

She had his money. She had what remained of Vico's allowances. She had her career. She put her name on the invitations to art benefits, although she rarely went, and gave summer beach parties with assorted curators (writers fought for admission to the charabancs out to the Hamptons). When she appeared at the clubs, however plain the dress, the floor parted; she was more needed and more livening than amyl or the best cocaine.

She heard John Grey at the door, and the maid walking across to answer. She nerved herself to admit she was going to Providencia without explaining.

John Grey said only: 'There's an opening on Thursday. Palladium.'

'I said I'm going to Providencia,' Mercedes said. 'You're supposed to argue me out of it.'

John Grey said: 'It's two days in another country. What's the problem?'

'The invitation is from Tomás Diaz.'

'Fine. I didn't think it was from the World Council of Churches.'

She glared at him. He was meant to fight, start the evening's adrenalin; she needed the rush. But she also knew that he disappointed her out of only two things: perversity, which was always possible, or worry.

'I'm going,' she said defiantly.

'I need a drink,' Grey said. He was helping himself almost before he spoke.

Mercedes said: 'You had a hard day at the office?' That did it; she made such a perfect parody of a sitcom wife, Grey was laughing at last.

'We have some problems,' he said. 'I think.'

'You can tell your partner.'

'You thank God you're not a partner, at least not on paper.'

She was startled. 'Things are that bad?'

'We seem to be running out of paper,' John Grey said.

Mercedes sprawled on the sofa, loose like a sleeping cat, but her eyes were sharp. She knew Grey's business; in a way, she invented it. All the time the columns made Mercedes and John Grey an item, and the night-time people knew them for the best of friends, they didn't any of them know the half.

Grey was a serious man, numerate, a patrician who had been fascinated by computers as a kid and long before three-year-olds learned to babble Fortran and alarm the grown-ups with their powers over number. He had worked on major projects; he had seen their flaws. He helped put together the programs for FedWire, the electronic net that shifts money, three deals a second, between the banks of America. He'd sorted out basic troubles for a Manhattan bank that counted on electronics to keep the awkward, bumbling, demanding public at a decent distance. But that work was a few days of furious stimulation and then weeks of boredom. He had no counter-culture inclinations to take him off into the wilds; he wanted to fill the hours and weeks between the highs.

He had numbers. He also liked seduction. That put him logically into the money business, somewhere. He'd talked one night with Mercedes and she'd said his family could plant him in a bank or brokerage, and both of them knew he did not need that anonymity or respectability.

'Tax shelters,' he said.

Mercedes knew about such things. Her own accountants proposed billboards in Ohio, a field planted thick with windmills on a bluff in California, a share of a herd of cattle. She was her mother's daughter; money was the walls of your castle, a shield. And she was Vico's daughter: she read what accountants wrote.

'Something like movies,' John Grey had said. 'I like that idea. Except you can't do movies any more. You have to have a partnership, you have to have a risk, and you have to have punters who just put up a fraction of the risk. Then people write a cheque for $1,000, tell the taxman that's a downpayment on a risk of $4,000 and write that $4,000 out of their taxable income.'

'Which,' said Mercedes, 'at a fifty per cent tax rate means you pay $1,000 to cut your tax bill by $2,000.'

'I'm sorry,' John Grey said. 'I'd forgotten you knew all about this.'

And they had settled in this same room to think of the perfect scam.

'Government securities,' Grey said. 'Trade them – make a loss at the end of the tax year for extra protection. Roll the loss over, year after year.'

'Sell it to cokeheads from LA,' Mercedes said. 'Make it sound exclusive.'

'It's too much like a business,' Grey said.

'You'd have to have traders,' Mercedes said. 'Then you have to be cunning to make the loss on time –'

They were good American children, talking with the television on. A bell rang, a dwarf appeared in a forest, and shouted, 'The plane, the plane,' and the credits ran for *Fantasy Island*.

Mercedes gawped at the screen, and Grey caught her sightline and the idea was born. They never knew which one of them first thought of it.

'You could,' Mercedes said, never taking her eyes from the flickering screen, 'just get the paper. Just get a computer to print out the trades. Don't put them through the market, just the computer.'

John Grey said: 'We'd need cover. Nine to three, they'd have to deal straight. Then I guess we could do it all out of the *Wall Street Journal*. We'd be so hot –'

'The taxman gets the papers, the clients get the tax break, and the clients can't touch the assets because that's the nature of the partnership, and who's to know?'

She grinned, innocently.

'Of course you couldn't really do it,' she said, not meaning it for a moment.

And it was a wonderful joke against a clan and class, one that John Grey delighted in. By early evening all the bawling riot of the dealers' room was a calm, children's play place – where deals were decided by dartboard or I Ching, and the floor was littered with old papers. They wrote the market more frenetically, more alarmingly than any novelist could, with death-defying risk and sometimes fearful losses, and a curious talent for balancing everything out on just the negative side of the ledger. And the idea sold itself – two lunches at the Russian Tea Rooms with a West Coast composer who fancied himself, very loudly, clever with money and they had a waiting list of Hollywood clients.

It was not such a triumph for Mercedes. She looked at John Grey with real love – a man misleadingly like some cowtown blond come to Manhattan for a brief career based on a cleft chin, a tight body and a brain blank as paper; behind that model's look, there was a mind and mischief. But they'd settled into such a companionable, uneventful life together; they almost kept each other away from adventure. And Fantasy Island was now a business to be run, not an adventure. And somehow the city was changing too. Her Manhattan had been a place where all the lines crossed, and sparked; but now it was too easy to go to places where you felt comfortable. Nice, rich people danced together; the energy of the gay places had been dampened by disease, and institutions like Studio 54 went down to tax and drugs; there were too many suits where once there had been anarchy. The city was coming like a Saks Fifth Avenue window.

And the ambitions changed in these self-contained worlds. The kids were too young, too know-nothing, too flirty and pert, even though they were barely seven years her junior; they wanted to be small stars in a closed world. Mercedes began to be nervous that her fame might trap her where once it had freed her.

All this was in her mind when she said to John Grey: 'You could just fold the whole thing.'

Grey finished his drink. 'You can't mean that.'

'Listen,' Mercedes said, 'the punters need their taxbreaks. They don't dare ask questions. Pay them back ten cents on the dollar and they'll keep quiet.'

'The Internal Revenue Service won't,' Grey said. 'Classic time for a major audit.'

'But you've got the paper, so far.'

She was impatient with him. She wanted him just to cut away from games that had turned dull or problematic, to keep moving. If the momentum died, they died; she was sure of that.

'My supplier's got nervous,' Grey said. 'And you know the scale of the deals we say we do – we need paper to cover millions.'

'You'll get it.'

'Maybe,' Grey said, 'you could sell the business to the Diaz family. Get them to take the rap.'

Mercedes said: 'Sell it to Citibank. That would be more fun.'

Their talk was all at a tangent, not connecting.

Only in the early afternoon did Aurelia set out the papers and read them. A Providencian wife, of a certain class, could not

48

seem too keen on knowing things.

Mario had the *New York Times* a day late. Mario knew what was proper to a family of the old guard – the patricians who clung to their mansions in the hills, aloof from the whole Diaz circus of quartermasters and horse-thieves, at least until they needed favours. And Aurelia's adopted Mama approved of Mario in turn. Aurelia was bound in the gentle net of their mutual approval.

Mercedes was the headlines. She was announcing some new perfume, at a gallery opening on a receiving line which looked like royalty and was mostly Rockefellers. Aurelia looked at the pictures with a child's intensity, trying to work things out.

'Papers,' said Mama. 'You'll dirty your hands.'

There was the smell of gin, the expensive, imported kind, and a lush perfume; Aurelia saw teeth perfected by Dr Vogel in Los Angeles, skin maintained by surgery and spas in Miami, a face that never went naked or undefended. This woman had trained Aurelia to be a daughter, just as a maid is trained – but for the special job of marrying right, producing children, managing the books and perhaps ending with the lonely and absolute power of the matriarch. She taught how to make simple things last so that nails could be a career. She explained nothing, and particularly not birth; she had decided birth was a distasteful business since it was denied to her.

'Your father, unfortunately –'

That phrase had echoed through Aurelia's adolescence. Mama had been so certain about her social position, what's right and wrong, what can or can't be done; but she was sure, too, that all those certainties didn't add up to a life.

'I suppose,' Mama said, 'you'll go to the Diaz party?'

Aurelia waited for the disapproving lecture, and it came.

Ian Carpenter dressed for the night – black tie even on this foetid evening because the Diaz clan had manners as American as their accents. He wanted to be correct.

If he came back to Providencia so often, it wasn't the intrinsic interest of the Diaz clan but their intrinsic worth. The old man had a billion stashed around the world, where his Park Avenue wife could not find it nor his family kill him for it.

49

That left a fortune which required management, and Carpenter amused himself by edging towards that job. There were a hundred more pressing things, but he had a mind precise enough to settle those. This was the one elusive idea, and it was worth a fortune.

He climbed into the rented car and for a moment the whole landscape blazed at him – a blood-orange sun that smeared light between the black trees and caught mirror brightness in the lake. Cats went up walls in pursuit of their private demons. Above the volcano, the plume of white steam had turned crimson. A phrase kept niggling at him, refusing to leave his mind: 'This place is a riot of cheap metaphor.' Which was true on the drive to the Tomás Diaz house. You climbed past the official buildings of Leon – the InterContinental, the secret police, the Presidential Palace, the army barracks and hospital, the American Embassy – by climbing a dead volcano with a black lake in its crater that the soldiers used for swimming. Sometimes, the volcano seemed to shiver a little, though all its buildings were supposed to be proof against earthquake.

There was a brief stretch of freeway down from the volcano, which was all politics. The line of the road zig-zagged to stay on Diacista land, and where the Diacistas had more land, there were the frames of suburbs.

The lights were against him at a crossroads. He saw a man with a rifle, in khaki that didn't quite match the colours of the National Guard. He hit the accelerator hard.

Tomás Diaz had set his house beyond the last suburb and surrounded it with barbed wire, steel gates and Guardsmen to check invitations. Beyond that careful barrier, there was the sweet resinous smell of old pine and a low house that was glamorous with lights.

He saw Aurelia at once, standing with her husband. She wore a dress like property – showing the assets, but showing they were guarded. She acknowledged him, Mario was magnanimous, and they might even have been friends, casually talking. Girls in grey uniforms went by with trays of canapés, anxious to get things right, and there were dour Indian servants, their faces blank.

'They all talk about their children,' Aurelia said.

50

'That leaves us out,' Carpenter said.

'There's even been a fight on the terrace. Someone asked a vice-minister where his son was and the vice-minister got furious.'

Carpenter looked blank.

'Because we're all afraid of the children now,' Aurelia explained. 'People send them away if they can. Or the children go off to the bush or to Costa Rica and come back as guerrillas. The kids are like consciences.'

'Troublemakers,' Mario said, predictably. 'All they have is a kind of graduate seminar in revolution, and they're careful to keep it out of the country. All Althusser and no guns.'

'Then why –' Aurelia stopped herself, and smiled most sweetly. 'We shouldn't be talking politics,' she said.

She squeezed Mario's hand, and Carpenter felt dismissed. They had all that long, protected intimacy; he had only forty-eight hours to remember.

He went out to the terrace. There were mosquito coils burning, sinister little worms with red tips, and the gentle heartbeat rhythm of a merengue and a big woman, arms like pistons, working to a beat no one else could hear.

'Get me a drink,' she shouted to the crowd. But her partner ignored her. Her accent was south of Virginia, her walk a sashay compounded of gin and would-be sensuality. She came up against a squad of servants.

'Drink. *Comprende?*'

The servants looked embarrassedly at her partner, who was shaking his head.

'Drink. Gin.' And when none of the servants moved, the woman hissed: 'At least in my country we had the sense to kill the fucking Indians.'

The crowd lost only a beat. The woman was certified important, property of the American Ambassador, and so what was intolerable in others had to be found eccentric, even refreshing in her. But the woman's own attention strayed at once. She stood pointing like a gundog, transfixed by a slim, bare-backed figure standing away from the dancers.

'My God,' she said, 'it's Mercedes Zenon.'

She barged her way through the dancers, two gins past civility and her minder tracking her. The fuss caught Carpenter's attention and he turned.

She was Aurelia: black and Indian and Spanish and ambiguous, like Aurelia, and the same moves, the same legs, the same cat's face graced with life. He couldn't tell why she wasn't Aurelia, except that she'd chosen to live inside a spotlight and Aurelia was decorous and masked.

The minder had reached the Ambassador's wife, and led her away. 'I only wanted to meet the bitch,' the wife was bawling.

The boy by Carpenter's side watched with exasperation. '*Por favor,*' he said, 'this is my country. May I speak my own language? Sir?'

Carpenter's belly was beginning to warm with rum, and he found one of Tomás's girls – soft like eiderdown and tinted an unlikely blonde. She pressed herself against him as he danced, and he reacted with an automatic hard-on; he was at a private party all his own, far away from passions or drunks, even Aurelia and Mercedes. And the terrace lights had been dimmed so that hands as well as feet could move.

The evening was hot, kind, jovial at last. Dancers slipped between shadow and shadow, a frieze of skirts and neat, fluid movement. There were splashes, and a brief, derisive cheer, and Carpenter assumed that someone had been pushed into the pool.

And then he heard the splashing again, and he knew it was wrong. It came with a rattle and it spat the pool water high, like machine-gun fire. It ran like a jumping creature over the black and white paving stone.

Drink and the time made people slow to react; they were safe in the warmth of the music. But Carpenter's girl was sharp like her kind, and she let out the scream of a monkey in the woods. Then, all comfort was gone. People fell against each other, scrambled for shelter behind sofas in the house, hid behind unfilled planters, legs still visible. But they could not tell where the guns were. They seemed to be across the pool, on the other side of the house. They even seemed to be inside the house.

And nobody shot back. Carpenter realised that even before he thought out what it meant. If this was some friendly drunk, shooting up the night for the hell of it, he'd be on the terrace now, answering to Tomás Diaz, or he'd be shot. You don't

52

indulge fools with guns when there are guerrillas in the bush. But if this was serious enemy fire, then where were the guards? When the submachine-gun stopped, and the frogs and cicadas were still silent, there was no friendly fire.

Nobody deserts Tomás Diaz. In Providencia, there's nowhere else to go. If there were Guardsmen in place, they'd be shooting and hollering just to prove they'd tried. So someone had silenced the guards.

The big girl curled and pushed against his thighs like an animal in panic. He had an inconvenient rush of blood. But he tugged at her, limp as she was, and put her across his broad back and crept into the house, as low as he could go.

In the first room, a couple still clung in one of the pits of artfully unlit sofa. The doors to the hall, the heart of the house, were swung shut.

Carpenter tensed himself. He'd never fought in a war, never knew from body learning what to do when the guns opened up. He could only guess that the centre of the house must be more secure than the outer rooms with their walls of glass. He swung himself up, felt his thighs tense under the weight of the girl. He barged into the door.

He saw military boots. He felt steel in his ribs. He raised his head with difficulty and saw a man's face masked with a bandanna.

'Get down,' the man said, startled.

Carpenter said: 'The girl. She's passed out.'

The gun was up against his heart.

In the hallway the lights had been dimmed, and he could see two dozen of the guests, men and women, crouched in the centre of a starburst of elaborate tiles under a grandiose electric chandelier. It was like a surprised church. Neat men spoiled their dinner suits and matrons rasped the knees of silk stockings, praying for deliverance.

Carpenter dropped slowly down, and let the girl slide off his back.

There were six men prowling about the congregation. From Carpenter's head-down position, he had to crane to make out the specifics. He could see Aurelia's husband, curled up resentful and dismayed, and Aurelia sitting as serious as an athlete

53

thinking out a race. And across from them, he could see Aurelia's shadow, Mercedes, who sat neat and cross-legged, watching the room with a cool, intelligent interest. He could see the puff-ball Minister of the Interior and hear his unstoppable nervous belching.

'The guards,' a woman was saying. 'There must be guards. There must be.'

For answer, one of the six gunmen opened a clip of ammunition into the mirrored walls, shattering glass and making shards out of all that the prisoners could see. He threw down the gun for inspection. Silently, the Diacistas could recognise the same Israeli automatic that the guards had carried.

There was a stifled quiet, broken only by a middle-aged woman who had begun to rock and keen like a mourner at a wake. She was bleeding above the eyes, and the blood and tears sent her black mascara running; her face looked like a bruise.

One of the guerrillas called them: *'Compañeros.'* They couldn't quite tell who had spoken. They didn't dare move for fear of guns and splinters of glass.

But Carpenter could see that the tallest man was talking, a dandy from the look of his uniform, whose bandanna seemed to hide a sparse beard.

'You keep your heads down,' the man said. 'You keep quiet. You are prisoners of the Amadista Front of Liberation, and you're not in danger – not if Diaz does as we say.'

'Never,' the Interior Minister said, automatically. His belching spoiled his defiance and his wife told him to shut his mouth.

'Up,' the man ordered.

He seemed very young and very sure. Carpenter looked round and he could not see Tomás Diaz.

'Up,' the guerrilla said again, and the congregation found unsteady feet.

Two of the soldiers ripped the tablecloths from the buffet tables and tore the cloth to make blindfolds. The hostages formed a rough line, cuffed into place, and they were roped together and then blinded, looking like a store window taken from storage – tied dummies, wraps and dinner jackets all dusty and spoiled.

Carpenter felt claustrophobia first, a panic because the world

54

now ended at his blindfold; and beyond that there were men with guns. But he was calm with surprising speed. The world wasn't his responsibility any more. For the moment, he had to do as he was told.

'Move!'

The line shuffled forward like a drunken conga, each step needing concentration, all dignity set aside in the hope of not cannoning into the man in front. Their shoes had gone; Carpenter felt the glass slicing at his feet. Suddenly the night air broke on their faces hot and wet, and the sounds of the dark were back. Everything shrill, everything loud seemed shocking, an intrusion in this tiny world of blindness. And everything might move some nervous trigger finger.

They had stopped, on command. One by one, they bundled up into some kind of truck, shoved from behind if they couldn't climb. Then the truck was moving. Carpenter tried to guess how far, how fast, but all he noticed was the odd absence of gear shifts in a hilly city, and the cold metal that cut him when he was thrown against it on corners.

No sight. No watch, therefore; and no sense of time from sun or dark. Just the noise of the truck, the sense of pointless motion. He hoped for little clues from smell or sound; two dozen people could not remain a clinical, silent body. He felt vulnerable as an egg, but oddly strong; nobody could want to kill him in particular.

He tried to think out what you do in times like this. Keep your head down. Follow orders. Don't make the guerrillas nervous. Hope that there'll be some chance to bust out of this captivity, and thank God all this is not happening in a pressurised shell at 35,000 feet.

The truck stopped, and thirty people fell against each other warmly. They stayed together a moment too long, but nobody complained; it was warmth, and besides, the next man on the rope might be a Diaz or a Minister, someone you need. Fear and deference were keeping people still.

The six guerrillas had no names or faces. They might be the children, the ones so awkwardly discussed on the terrace over serious drinks. One day the kids were shame and the next they killed you. But they were better than the Diacistas liked to say.

55

This was no graduate class in revolutionary theory, when the six could break open the most closely guarded part of Leon barely an hour before El Maximo himself was expected. And they knew what they were doing. El Maximo would be a lousy hostage. He was the one who had to act.

'Move!'

The guerrillas said enough to make the line shift, not enough to give a sense of direction. Their voices circled confusingly. But only those voices made sense of the world, and the line went forward, crumpling and tripping as they came down from the truck, and setting out across what felt to tender feet like bare ground.

Carpenter tried to keep himself upright and centred. Sooner or later he'd have the evidence to work out what to do. They'd have to reveal something. He wondered if any of them would die.

He could feel the cold of airconditioning run too high. They must be close to Leon, for reliable power. He was aware of other people grumbling faintly, as though they could already see, and then the blindfolds came down.

The light was pink. He thought at first it must be some trick of hurt eyes, but he looked again. The room was huge, all plush and rosewood, like a Jayne Mansfield movie. Blankets hung on the walls, nailed in place, must be covering windows. The air-conditioners masked any outdoor sounds. They were pampered, isolated, and lost.

He thought it was like some game – the random cut of intersecting lines. Here were the kids with their patricidal gag; there were the Diacistas; and he happened to be standing where the two met.

He looked for Aurelia. She smiled at him, but a faint smile, and she cradled her husband's head. Mario looked blank. Carpenter wanted to wash her face and comfort her, at least to talk. But if anyone said anything, the guards slapped the talk down like a conspiracy.

Throughout the next hours, people began to sleep. Suddenly, white light came on. The guards arrived with a mess of food, the remains of the buffet in a muddled heat of chicken and fishes and marinated things. They left it in a corner.

It ought to be morning, but Carpenter knew it could not

be – not yet. He looked for his watch but it had gone. Evidently the guerrillas were serious about taking time away.

Around him there were the sour, intimate smells of a shared night – sweat, perfume gone stale, drink taken hours before and now souring the air with fear. Carpenter felt raw and fuzzy, like after too much drink, which made no sense. He didn't move to the food.

Aurelia was awake. In the night, she'd moved to Mercedes' side. Their faces changed and echoed each other like one of those strange Japanese postcards where a change of angle makes the picture smile. Aurelia's neatness, Mercedes' glamour, were lost in a tangle of loose and open clothes; they seemed primed for action.

But what action was possible? Carpenter could see no way to break the doors or windows; they must be guarded. And there were always at least two men in the room with guns. They couldn't plan or signal, and they'd have to take out two men at once to have a chance. Even then –

A door opened and shut, fast as a sleight of hand. Aurelia nudged her husband and Mercedes sat straight. The tall man, the dandy with the beard, had come back.

'*Compañeros*,' he began.

They grumbled together, nobody's comrades.

'You have a right to know what's going on,' the guerrilla said.

Carpenter realised with a shock that these were the terms of their lives, nothing less. The room paid attention.

'We've told Diaz to release seventeen political prisoners. They're to be given a plane and safe passage to Costa Rica. When they're safely on the ground, you can go.' The dandy looked up from his paper like a schoolmaster moving off the textbook. 'And we want the release announced. The people will want to express their support for their imprisoned comrades.'

The Interior Minister, sallow and soft like the puffball he resembled, rolled up to his feet with that precise committee man's instinct for the moment to speak. But he said the wrong things.

'Diaz won't agree,' he said. 'No surrender to international Communism in this hemisphere. We would all rather die.'

The dandy had only to look around the room and the

Minister's bluff was called. 'You think it's such a great thing,' he asked gently, 'to die for the honour of Anastasio Diaz Sacasa?'

'We know who you are,' the Minister said. He'd used that line before, and it always chilled the enemy. To be known and exposed was to live at risk; these people couldn't tolerate such risk. Knowing names was his power.

'We're all around you, old man,' the dandy said. 'We're everyone.'

'The hour after we leave here, you're a dead man.'

'If you leave,' the dandy said.

Women shivered.

The Minister puffed himself up like a lizard that inflates its throat for a fight. 'Give you sods a book,' he said, 'and suddenly you think you're the people. You think you know it all, and it's all out of a book. And who wrote the goddamn book, then? The Communists. The Marxist-Leninists. They wrote the book in Moscow.'

The dandy said: 'And where did they write the book for Diaz?'

'We know who you are,' the Minister said, flatly.

The dandy circled him. He had his hands at the back of his head, ready to tug at the bandanna. Carpenter thought he saw shock on Aurelia's face, as though she wanted to warn the guerrilla.

'Would it surprise you to know that I don't give a damn?' And the dandy took down the bandanna. 'José Mantica,' he said, 'at your service.'

'We'll know where to find you,' the Interior Minister said.

And Mantica put his face very close to the Minister's face, so the man could hardly focus and had to pull back for the pain in his eyes.

'We know who you are,' Mantica said. 'We know where to find you. We found you tonight.'

The Minister subsided.

'You have to hope,' Mantica said, 'that Señor Diaz will be reasonable. We don't want to harm you. We want you alive for the courts.'

'The courts,' the Minister sniffed.

'When it's our turn,' Mantica said, 'there will be something like justice. You'll see.'

The Minister spat.

'Afraid of justice, are you?' Mantica said, and he marched himself out of the room like a fury.

Some of the women had edged over to the mess of food – olives and broken fish, cheese beginning to melt over long-cut papaya – and they stuck their hands into the mess and fed greedily. Last night's manners were set aside; they no longer clucked at how their menfolk ate.

There was very little talk. Aurelia and Mercedes sat back to back, the warmth of their bodies talking for them; they seemed very strong and private, like one being. Across the room, a matron stirred in the crumpled heap of her black dress and began shaking her head. She glared at Mercedes; she made the sign of the cross. She seemed angry with the tangles of her dress and beat it into place. When she stumbled to her feet, her legs were bloodless and too weak to hold her. She fell, and blamed Mercedes, and on the second attempt she crossed the room.

The twin women sat quite still. The matron didn't even acknowledge the douce and proper Aurelia but stormed at Mercedes. 'You came back for this,' she said, first speaking and then shouting. 'You came back just for this.'

Mercedes did not respond. She was used to the old, lost, mad or envious who shouted in the streets; she had the strength of Aurelia, too.

'You,' the woman said, crouching on big thighs and pressing old breath into Mercedes' face, 'you came here just to be taken prisoner. You're one of them.' She was rolling side to side like a wrestler looking for an advantage. 'Nobody wants you here, girl. Nobody but these dirty –'

A friend tugged at the black dress, but now the woman reckoned she had finally made sense of her predicament and would not be silenced.

'Bitch!' she shouted.

The guards came scurrying.

'See,' the woman bellowed, 'see how they look after one of their own.'

The guards put a gun to the matron's side and for one moment it seemed she wanted martyrdom, but she backed away into a corner, growling.

Mantica slipped into the room. He walked towards the matron and she spat with great deliberation.

The room was dead except for the constant racket of the airconditioning, and that was so constant they no longer heard it.

'Zenon,' Mantica said. 'Mercedes Zenon. We need to talk.'

And they took Mercedes out of the room, leaving the matron to glare in her corner. The floor was suddenly very hard beneath them all; the room had contracted. In her corner, the matron was murmuring some comfortable form of words to bring down her anger.

Together, they'd felt oddly safe. But anything that broke the group made that sense of security fade.

'They'll kill us,' the Minister said, 'one by one.' His stick legs could hardly support the bag of his belly. 'After all,' he said, 'it's their turn.' And then he realised he'd said too much.

The Amadistas' turn. Tanks in the streets, perhaps, or guerrilla armies. The guards said nothing and they stopped the hostages guessing out loud. Diaz might let them die. It was unthinkable that their guarded world had been disrupted; now nothing was unthinkable.

'I wish I took playing cards to parties,' a man said; the room laughed.

They all needed the kindness of the guards, watched those lean young faces with apprehension, wanting to do the right thing. They depended on the guards for food, water, a chance to go to the bathroom – for a place to be alive. They were learning to be grateful even when they stumbled against the sink and toilet bowl, blindfold again.

They wanted to know Mercedes was all right.

Even the matron in her corner, now calmed and serious, considered how useful and vulnerable a famous hostage might be, one who came so far for the Diaz family. Diaz couldn't afford to lose her; the guerrillas were bound to exploit her.

Carpenter caught Aurelia's eye for a moment. He wanted something to do, some way to break out of this impasse. But even the guards were looking down, half tired and half embarrassed. There seemed very little honour in simply being a prisoner, or a guard.

★

60

In another room, Mercedes sat opposite José Mantica. She wasn't entirely surprised to see where they were. But now she knew, she wondered if she could ever go back to the group.

'Thank you for coming,' Mantica said.

'It was a party,' Mercedes said. 'I might have come in any case.' She was nervous about their intentions and even their seriousness.

'We need your help.'

'I was afraid of that.' She decided on a lawyerly manner, which she could adopt with surprising skill after years of negotiating a price on her services. 'There's nothing I can do,' she said. 'For the next three years, I'm not even a person. I belong to Mercedes Zenon Perfumes Inc., a subsidiary of –'

'We need to know about diamonds.'

'You don't understand,' Mercedes said. 'I have to behave, keep myself clean and looking good. I can be fired for falling under a truck. It's that kind of contract.'

'Just these diamonds,' Mantica said. He spilled the stones out onto a kitchen cabinet, a still fall of ice that the light made lively. He put away the little velvet bag in which they had come.

'I don't know about diamonds,' Mercedes said.

'Tomás Diaz had these. I guess he'd just bought them. Something portable in the event of trouble. But we don't know how to sell stones like this, or what we'd get for them.'

'I don't know. I really don't know.'

'But you'd know someone, surely? You and your money. You know George Vico. You know about things like that.'

'I don't even play the stock market. People play it for me.'

Mantica sniffed. 'A dealer,' he said. 'Just a dealer.'

'Walk down 47th Street. There are hundreds of them. Look for the men in the broad hats with the ringlets and the kaftans and the pale faces, and the cases.'

'You could be serious.'

'I am serious.'

'About Providencia?' Mantica asked. 'About this country that you come from.'

'I came from here a long, long time ago.'

'And the man who killed your father? Diaz, and the dwarf Chamorro? You don't care that they still have power?'

61

'It's in my contract,' Mercedes said. 'No major revolutions for three years. The minimum of guerrilla activity. I can't even put on weight.'

'You want to know why I asked you to come?' Mantica said. 'Because now you're here, the whole world will hear what we did to Diaz. It'll be a scandal. And he will have to give in.'

'He hasn't agreed yet?'

But Mantica sailed over her sharp question. 'I'm grateful,' he said. 'But I wanted to ask something more. This seemed like the only way we could discuss it, face to face.'

'Listen,' Mercedes said, 'I came. Going to the wrong parties isn't in my contract either, but I came here.'

'I knew you were serious,' Mantica said. 'I thought you'd be serious about a billion dollars, too. All the money Anastasio Diaz Sacasa pillaged from this country over the years, from your father and my father – the reason the city looks like a wasteland, why people die of dengue fever still. We need that money.'

Mercedes said: 'Diaz does, too. I expect he has it guarded quite well.'

'He doesn't dare let his family know where it is, in case they steal it. He doesn't dare let his wife know, in case she divorces him and demands half. Only Anastasio Diaz Sacasa knows.'

'You want me to seduce the man? Ask him for the combination on the safe when he's about to come?'

'That money has to come home.'

Mercedes crossed her long legs with a model's precision and all at once the sheer elegance of her body was there, even in tired clothes. Mantica noticed; he couldn't help noticing.

'I don't argue with you,' Mercedes said. 'I just see no way at all to do it.'

'You know people in that world, Vico, for instance. We won't get far if we stay inside the law.'

'You think I might break the law?'

'You might ignore it. You're strong enough and clever enough.' Mantica stirred the diamonds. 'There could be a percentage, of course. And national pride, and the excitement. It's the biggest game there is.'

'You think so.'

'Buried treasure. A billion dollars.'

'I find treasure by lending my name to a smell. That's enough. I don't need so much fortune.'

'Say something else,' Mantica said, gently.

Mercedes stood up. 'Can I go back to the others now?'

'No. That won't be possible. You know where they're being kept.'

'So what will you do with me?'

'Reason,' Mantica said. 'For example, ask you if Tomás paid cash for these diamonds.'

'How would I know?'

'You know about diamonds. Do people usually pay cash?'

'I suppose so. Mostly, yes. It's money in the pocket, not the till. That way, the taxman doesn't need to know too much.'

'So the deal's done – no cheques that might be stopped?'

'Probably not. Unless he has a credit account with some dealer.'

'Then we could sell. You could sell.'

Mercedes felt a little dizzy. She had a world of light and clubs and friends and, in the end, settledness. She had a respectability guaranteed by contract; it chafed. It paid the bills, but it couldn't hold her.

But this – this was an absurdity, an absurd temptation.

'Why would you trust me?' she asked.

'We trust you.'

'Because of what happened to my father? That was a long time ago. I've had to forgive.'

'I don't believe anyone forgives a murder like that. You'd have revenged him if you could.'

Mercedes wondered for a moment what Mantica knew. She remembered the dory in the lagoon, and the bloating corpse of the Captain tugged behind.

'You could sell the diamonds in New York,' Mercedes said. 'I mean, I could take them to a dealer –'

'Thank you.'

'I didn't say that I would do it. I just said it would be possible. For a start, how do I get the stones out of Leon?'

'You'll see,' Mantica said.

And he began a roll-call of the other hostages, pulling one out every few hours, leaving the congregation nervous each time the door moved.

Carpenter felt alone. Mercedes had gone, and the Interior Minister, then Aurelia. Aurelia's husband had come over to talk, but the guards suspected conspiracy between two of the younger, more fit men. The mess of food was beginning to smell sour.

He heard the guns like firecrackers at first, but then he realised the firing was close. The room jerked to life like puppets when the curtain rises. Women crossed themselves and laced into a cat's cradle of defensive poses.

Aurelia was back, her make-up cleaned away and her dress loose. She said she'd been to the bathroom. She didn't understand the guns.

Then Mercedes came scrambling into the room, bright-eyed with alarm at the guns now talking outside.

Carpenter worked his muscles, to be ready, but no guards came into the room. Maybe the firing meant they were too occupied outside. There was the sound of an engine roaring away. If the Amadista guerrillas were somewhere fighting for their lives, then no life in this room was worth a shit.

'No, no,' the wife of the Interior Minister said. It was as though she had always known where braggadocio would end.

And then there was a quiet, profound when it came. Nobody had died; it was an anti-climax. Carpenter edged towards the door. It would be well to be ready when someone came, whoever came in this unkind stillness. There were no guards to question any more. He pulled aside the blanket that must cover the door. He tried the handle; of course it was locked.

That left the windows. Beyond the blanket was only glass and wood, and the blanket would catch the shards of glass. But there might be outside shutters; there could be steel security bars.

Mercedes seemed to be warning him off. He didn't understand it. He hardly knew the woman and yet she seemed to anticipate his pent-up energy and his need to move.

So he defied her. He took a run.

The window was wood-framed, by a miracle, and he broke through in a leap and landed awkwardly with the rough blanket keeping him from the bits of glass. Somehow, he'd thought it would break like those spun-sugar panes they use in the movies.

And because of his fall, he was the last to see where they had all been held prisoner. When he looked up, the others were staring; some of the men seemed angry.

They saw, ahead of them, the house in the cool hills where they'd been to Tomás Diaz's party. Their whole captivity had been a few yards away, in a guesthouse close to the main gates.

Carpenter stood, brushed himself down and went round to open the doors. He watched the others walk out into the sunlight, baffled. Somehow, this was not even proper captivity in a dark, dangerous place; it was a joke that threatened their lives. The goddamn Amadistas had known how to deny their victims glory.

He saw Mercedes and Aurelia, in black and in white, standing at the door hand in hand.

Mercedes told the Interior Minister she had to get back to New York 'for a shoot'; he looked startled. 'For *Vogue*,' Mercedes said.

The Minister nodded. 'Of course,' he said, but in his bothered mind he saw Mercedes out with gun and net, stalking Vogues in their fearful jungle.

Outside, there was only the detritus of a party; the hostages the last to leave in their assorted cars, with outriders to make a shabby little procession of their journey home.

But the roads also felt like the hours after a party. Down sidestreets there were still groups of people talking, held back from the main road as the hostages passed. There seemed to be confetti. Carpenter fancied he heard the echo of cheers.

All the cars went to the same barracks, and there was an awkward half hour while the police decided they had nothing to say and that the people waiting were too important to be questioned at once. They took in only Mercedes Zenon, without explanation; the gossips said it was because she had to go back to New York. They only wanted a statement, any clues they could piece together to cover their shame.

Aurelia shrugged at Mario, who was tired and cross. 'Take him home,' she said to Carpenter, who nodded, surprised.

'You'll come with us?'

'I'll call you.'

And since Carpenter wanted only a good jag of whisky to close off the whole incident, he agreed. Mario was pompous and fractious; it was a relief to be rid of him.

At his house a thin scatter of mail was waiting for him, a letter in Jill's writing and an invitation from Mexico City that was hopelessly out of date. He tore open the envelopes and waited for Aurelia to call.

Mid-day, she still hadn't.

One o'clock, he needed lunch. His housekeeper had gone and he didn't want any elaborate social contacts. He took himself to the barbecue place by the swimming lake in the volcano, and sat in the shade of a tree with a beer and a piece of beef.

Everyone was talking, and not about the hostages. They were talking about Mercedes Zenon, how the cops thought she'd walked away with diamonds that belonged to Tomás Diaz, how they'd held her and searched her, how even when she got to the airport they still followed her, bothering her, and insisted on another interview.

Carpenter thought for a moment. There had been something odd when Mercedes came back from talking to the guerrillas: she had a purse. It was a little bag of velvet, a tiny thing, but not something that could have survived the siege. It was the kind of bag he'd seen used to carry gems.

He put the idea aside. Mercedes Zenon had too fine and registered a name to turn to amateur diamond theft in her own country. Besides, he thought, she would do it better; she had Aurelia's intelligence.

He returned to the house. Nobody had called.

At three the phone rang. It was Mario, anxious about Aurelia.

At three-thirty, she called.

'We didn't know where you were,' he said. 'Mario was worried and we heard that Mercedes was being questioned –'

'You sound like Mama,' Aurelia said. 'I spent the day with the police. I even met the dwarf Chamorro.'

She sounded so matter of fact. But it couldn't be that easy, to see the man who burned out your father's eyes. She wasn't the forgiving kind.

'Come and see me,' Carpenter said. 'when you can.'

Aurelia laughed a little. 'I've got a wife's duty' she said. The line went dead.

That evening, at the InterContinental bar, Carpenter ran into a journalist acquaintance. They talked about the siege; Carpenter obliged with some details and feelings. And the journalist obliged with Mercedes' story.

She'd been questioned, then gone to the airport and been there for hours, waiting for a plane. She refused the VIP room; she'd stayed in sight, a glittery, spoiled presence, all the morning. Finally, they'd shoe-horned her onto the first Air Providencia flight that was leaving for Miami. Then they'd decided on one more search before she got away and taken her to the VIP room. The cops had come back, tails between their legs, and some woman had been assigned to do the search. That wasn't usual; it was deference.

And now there was terrible embarrassment. After all, Mercedes Zenon was the guest of Tomás Diaz. The accusations had got out of hand. The cops urged Mercedes through to the Customs and immigration area where she couldn't phone.

In that empty hall, she'd stood for a moment. Then an airport official said he'd seen her slip through a side door that might have taken her to the ladies room but actually went out onto the tarmac. She slipped along the fringes of the airport and through a hedge of bougainvillaea and stone. He'd lost sight of her there.

'Weird, isn't it?' the journalist said. 'I tried to check if she actually got that flight but nobody seemed to know. Or rather, nobody was saying. The cops were embarrassed and they didn't want loose talk.'

Carpenter went home very thoughtfully.

All that unaccounted time when Aurelia was with the cops; and her late return home just after her twin sister failed to catch the Miami flight for which she had so elaborately waited; that was something to think about.

He imagined that Mercedes had slipped out to the airport much earlier, taken the first flight out, perhaps arrived back in Miami in a white dress with a load of diamonds sewn into the hem. And Aurelia, from some point in that confused and exhausted morning, had been Mercedes.

Mercedes who had tried to warn him not to jump the window. That must have been Aurelia, he decided.

He had a whole fantasy elaborated before he slept.

★

'I got an early flight,' Mercedes said to John Grey III from Miami Airport, 'to avoid the Press. Aurelia covered for me.'

'Did you have a nice time?'

'You know they give you a rose with lunch on that flight? And then they put the rose through the microwave?'

She giggled, and John Grey knew from experience she was up to something.

·TWO·

He was coming back to enthusiasms in Providencia – to Aurelia and the Diaz billion. Besides, it was better to be away from the board in London, to be distantly accountable; and home was too cold and complicated. He wasn't a domestic animal.

He recited all that like a silent creed as he entered the bunker.

Passing the door was crossing some moral line. The volcano opened a tiny vent and you walked into the clammy cold of neon light – busy cubicles, uniforms stalking back and forth with the noise of boots, pictures of Diaz with the Pope, Diaz with the leaders of something called the World Freedom Covenant, all hand-tinted and propped against file cabinets. The place jostled with nervous life.

Diaz had retreated here since the guerrilla raid. He had occupied rooms in his bunker, a place usually reserved for cops and victims, and imported taste from Miami; the arrival of the bath-tub had been a minor scandal. And now he was settled on a pink sofa between a scatter of 8 by 10 glossies for visiting supporters.

Outside the final doors, tall, carved wood contraptions, Carpenter waited. Tomás Diaz made himself an excuse to pass by, a reminder of some obligation owed, although Carpenter couldn't imagine what.

'If you could get the old man to make sense of his affairs . . .' Tomás said.

Carpenter looked blank, artfully. 'I don't know what you mean.'

'Everyone knows what I mean,' Tomás said.

And when the high doors opened, Tomás barged ahead to grab a little of his father's time.

Carpenter settled in his armchair.

'– if you must,' he could hear Diaz saying. 'You go to Geneva, people will think we're running. You've already handed me a defeat –'

Tomás dropped his voice, and Carpenter couldn't make out his words.

'My business is my business,' the old man was bellowing. 'My business. Just that. '

Tomás was louder now. 'You're not immortal, you know. You could stop a bullet any time.'

'But I won't stop your bullet,' Diaz said. 'Not while I'm the only one who knows where the money is.'

'For God's sake, make sense. We're talking about death and a billion dollars.'

The old man said, coldly: 'I don't talk about death.'

Tomás stamped his way out of the inner office, shut in a cloud of fury, in no mood now to acknowledge even potential allies.

But his father was different. He had calmed himself with surprising speed, as though his anger was just a form of giving orders. Carpenter saw strong, unused hands: a perfect manicure. The suit corseted a body grown a little too fleshy for its owner's macho. Diaz was resisting middle age, and showing the struggle.

'I am so glad,' El Presidente said, 'that you can be in Providencia. As you know, we are a family that likes to leave its mark –'

Carpenter said he'd been impressed by the plans for Blue-fields. Of course, it wasn't his decision.

'Of course,' Diaz said. His accent could have been New Orleans, since that was the city where he'd been sent to lose his virginity, and his mother to learn sewing.

'There will be some very complicated questions of collateral,' Carpenter said. 'Questions we should discuss later.'

'Collateral,' said Diaz, sharply.

'We are not the World Bank,' Carpenter said. 'We invest to make money, and when we lend money, we like to be sure we won't lose it. That't the nature of bankers, after all. So if you could suggest –'

Diaz was caught between annoyance at such talk, alarm and a more constructive thought: offer something solid, get the loan, take the profit. What could it matter if they foreclosed on a million if he'd already banked ten, or twenty?

'It is possible,' Diaz said, 'that we could find something.'

'We'd prefer something like US Treasury Bills,' Carpenter said. 'Something negotiable, easy to value and in dollars. That's for the early stages of the deal, of course.'

'I take it,' Diaz said, 'this seriously interests you?'

Carpenter nodded. There was always the scintillating chance that Diaz would take the bait, put up some of his own fortune and leave just fingerprints or traces on the collateral so that Carpenter could guess the scale of the hidden fortune.

And the two men, crudely bluffing each other, smiled.

Diaz knew Carpenter must have some motive for being here beyond this particular piece of business: Providencia's credit had not been good for years, but a handful of Congressional investigations had almost killed it. Commercial banks lent against deposits, and nothing less if they could help it; or else against the final guarantee of Uncle Sam, who could never let Providencia fail. They didn't just talk about collateral.

Carpenter knew Diaz would, by reflex, steal whatever was loaned to Providencia.

And yet the two men were wonderfully agreeable, discussing the fishing on the lake – freshwater shark, Diaz said proudly – and the beauties of the mountains where the coffee grows, and where to have dinner in New York. Conversation was exactly like tennis: an evasion of the real issues, but a test of character.

They respected each other.

'We must talk again,' Diaz said. 'Besides, there are some private matters – we seem to do business well.'

A sprat to catch a mackerel. The two men, knowing it, each played the same bait.

Carpenter didn't look too eager. That would never do. 'Of course,' he said, 'if the bank can be of any service –'

'Dinner,' Diaz said. 'If you would come to dinner –'

Carpenter left the bunker and was grateful for natural air. He walked to the edge of the parade ground as the National Guardsmen began to shuffle into ranks. White light snapped on, drowning the evening pinks and greens; the square was like a football ground. And onto this stage, Anastasio Diaz Sacasa

71

cantered, brisk and formal, smarter than his men.

Carpenter stopped to watch for a moment. This was a famous ritual: the evenings when Diaz met his men and acted like their friend. He promised action to one who felt slighted, gave a bundle of notes to a man whose child needed an operation, and let it be seen. It was like some criminal family, its Godfather dispensing patronage, which is so much stronger than fear. These men arrived with empty bellies, no standing, no names; now they had power. But it was the personal power to gouge money or run a chain of girls, not the power to join together against Diaz; his kindness kept the guard divided.

The men broke ranks, and Carpenter drove home. He called Aurelia but reached only the silly girl who ran the place in daytime. The Señora might call him. Yes, he could leave a number. The girl never spoke for the Señora.

'Of course not,' Carpenter said.

'I don't have to make people happy,' Mercedes was saying, and she threw down the silk dress she was holding. 'They all know the game. I put my name on the invitation, they've got what they want.'

'But you're going,' John Grey said, gently.

'I'm going,' Mercedes said. 'I don't seem to do a damn thing except go to parties. I can't even put myself in front of a camera for three years, except for the perfume. They own me.'

'They pay you. And the maids, and the apartment and –'

'I'm allowed to work,' Mercedes said. 'I have to work.'

John Grey rolled to the floor and began to do press-ups.

'You don't take your shirt off dancing any more,' Mercedes said, tartly, and went to the bathroom.

John Grey was sprawled across her way.

'Remember,' he said, meanly. 'Other men may see you naked. But only I know your net worth. Remember that.'

When she came back, she had changed: but not into some semblance of afternoon glamour.

'I have an appointment,' she said.

Grey said: 'Fine. But I thought we were having lunch.'

'We could. If you'll just walk me to my appointment.'

'You're a big girl. Take the car.'

'I'd really like someone with me.'

'New York finally got to you?'

Mercedes went to a drawer and pulled out a little velvet bag. She tipped it onto the mirror-surface of a low table and released a string of blue-white fire.

'I have to see a man on 47th Street,' she said.

'I didn't know you were in the loose gems business.'

'You know where these are from,' Mercedes said. 'Or you can guess, because you're bright. They're from Providencia.'

'They're yours? Of course. A present from the President.'

'In a way. He doesn't know he's given them away though.'

John Grey stared at her. 'And you're working for yourself, Mrs Raffles?'

'Don't be dumb.'

'Listen,' said Grey, 'if I'm supposed to be accessory before the fact, I'd like to know.'

'I'm doing a favour,' Mercedes said. 'For some friends. Just a favour.'

John Grey sighed deeply. 'You're an urban guerrilla? For real?'

'Do I look like a guerrilla?' she said, and turned in her best catwalk manner.

He was a little more easy when they reached 47th Street. He liked the shops selling light, the iced, broken, blue-white light from stones. There were men carrying cases of light, but dressed in the enveloping, scruffy black of Hasidim. They bustled, seeing only one another.

There was a discreet brass plate between the shouting slogans 'YOU MUST SELL GOLD' and stairs to a third-floor office. Mercedes looked out of place between the dull cream paint and the faint disinfectant smell of the stairwell.

The door was locked and locked again, with spyholes and grey steel. It took a little while to be admitted, and the locks went off like percussion. In a little room with unpainted pipes, a man called Solomon sat at a table.

'Good day,' he said, neither sorry nor happy to see her, but a patient listener.

'I am interested,' she said, 'in something more portable than paper investments. After all,' she crossed her legs neatly, and sexlessly. 'I am a widow now.'

'If you say so.'

'I want to arrange a sale, some fine stones. And I want to know about buying stones.'

'That is my business.'

'You can tell me how to set about buying.'

'First,' said Solomon, 'you think again.' He was a pale man, born for a back room, with very black eyes. 'Bonds are better, I promise you. You want to beat inflation, I give you a fine Rembrandt, a nice house in Connecticut with maybe a pool, a pile of ten per cent Treasury Bills. All these things are good.'

'I want something portable,' Mercedes said.

'Or you buy something pretty, something you love. Something you don't keep in the bank because it scares you.'

'I am talking quite serious money,' Mercedes said.

'You forgive me,' Solomon said. 'I don't know what money is serious to you. Perhaps these stones you have to sell – if I could see them –'

A frazzled, middle-aged man arrived with a pile of pastrami sandwiches and a cardboard cup of lemon tea. Solomon let him lay the packages on the desk, and let him out, and watched the meat cool with manifest regret.

'If we can talk privately,' Mercedes said, insisting on her point.

'Talk,' Solomon said.

Mercedes brought out the little velvet bag and poured the stones onto the table. Solomon took up an eyeglass.

'My friends say you can handle stones like this,' Mercedes said. 'Of course, if they're too fine –'

'They are not too fine.'

'Then you understand –'

'But I do not buy these stones. I am not a fence.'

Mercedes stared at him. She'd come with the most respectable of introductions, and with the most careful presentation of credentials.

'I don't know why you insult me,' she said.

'I don't insult you,' Solomon said, putting down his glass. 'I know these stones.'

'I expect you deal in stones like this all the time.'

'I mean, I know these particular stones. I sold them three weeks ago.'

Mercedes felt her heart turn over. Of course, if Solomon was one of the few big-time dealers prepared to do business with outsiders – not family or friends – then it was logical enough that he should sell to Diaz. Logical, but not foreseen.

Think. He must have alarms. He must be able to summon the cops if he needs them. What deal, what story could convince this man, who is most precisely honourable in his own terms and owes nothing to Mercedes Zenon?

'This is,' Mercedes said, 'a matter of private business.'

'The President makes a present to the lovely lady,' Solomon said. 'Oh yes, that is a good story of private business. But these stones are stolen, the President says so. Did you perhaps disagree after he gave them to you. Is that your story?'

Think. A story that would make sense to this man, disarm his suspicion without triggering whatever most offended his moral sense.

'It isn't always easy to move money,' Mercedes said.

'For the President, who pays me in cash here in this very office, I do not think it is difficult.'

Think. Would a dealer like Solomon care about insurance companies? Dealers handed gems only to dealers, or only when they had cash. They didn't take risks to insure against.

Try it.

'It isn't easy to move money,' Mercedes said. 'But if an insurance company has to pay out when gems are stolen –'

Solomon looked at her, with that studiedly neutral eye that neither judges nor approves.

'The money is urgent,' Mercedes said. 'The Diaz family would be happy to shave the price –'

Solomon picked up the phone.

'You won't mind if I call them?'

She froze. The unworthy thought kept pounding through her mind: days into that perfume contract, where I must be more pure and thin than dreams, this man could have me arrested for grand larceny.

'It might not be discreet,' Mercedes said, trying not to be too quick. 'You know that phone calls can be monitored –'

Solomon looked interested.

'– and it would make your position look a litle odd. After all, you say you know the gems are stolen.'

Solomon put the phone down. He was enjoying this match.

'And who do I pay, if I do business?' he asked 'You?'

'An account in Costa Rica,' Mercedes said, 'with a cheque to bearer. The money can't go to Leon.'

'That would be asking for trouble,' Solomon said.

He took up a single stone between his thumb and forefinger, turning it as though touch would tell him what to do.

'A commission of twenty,' Mercedes said. 'And your expenses. And a quick sale. They are fine stones.'

She watched Solomon. He owed Diaz nothing in particular. But he might feel he owed the law everything.

He said 'Thirty per cent.'

She tried not to show relief.

'And as for your buying – let me tell you things. Your money, it's marginal to me. I don't turn it away, I don't go round the world for it either. You buy gold, young lady. Gold has a price. If it's pure, it's good. But these things –' he picked at the stones '– they are worth only what someone will pay. Diamonds are individuals, they're flawless or worthless or they're maybe fine. Maybe this year in fashion, worn by Miss Zenon, and next year – who knows? Maybe it's a nice setting or a terrible one.'

'But they have a price. They always have a price.'

'That changes. One time there was de Beers and it has the mines, it has the markets, the stores – it sets the price. $66,000 a carat and rising. And you know what de Beers forgot? When the money's that good, anyone goes scratching for diamonds. The Russians do, and the people in Zaïre, and suddenly there are too many diamonds. It's not a rigged market at $66,000; it's an open market at $14,000. You should think on these things when you buy stones.' He opened his carton of tea. 'And you sell to me, or someone like me. You can't sell on an exchange. The one time they had a thing called the Diamond Exchange in London, there's a man sells diamonds – pretty things, in a box with a certificate. And each week, he tells the papers how much diamonds are worth. But who's buying, who's selling? Always

76

it's the same man – Mr Diamond Exchange. And he's not in the game to make a loss.'

'You're teaching me a lot,' Mercedes said.

'Sometimes,' Solomon said, 'it's easier to move money.'

'But you'll do business?'

Solomon sighed. 'Young lady, I don't want too much of your business. It's too exciting for an old man, too much drama.'

She smiled.

'God go with you,' Solomon said. When she looked at him more closely, she reckoned he meant it.

Overnight the rains came hammering down on Leon. The dust was sticky now, and turning viridian. Mud glissaded in the way of the trucks on the all-weather road. Out in the bush, the rivers were rising and very soon there'd be no way through the swampy land: it would take you down, neck-deep, and hold you until death. El Presidente announced the guerrillas had retreated (he called them 'roaches'); other people said they were next door to everyone. The city was full of rumour just as the gutters brimmed with rain.

Carpenter didn't have long, he knew that.

Aurelia was waiting at the house. 'I never liked the rains,' she said and later, in bed, she shifted her leg along Carpenter's leg. 'I'm glad you're here again.'

'I don't have anything to do here any more.' He felt grateful for the shipwrecked safety of this great white bed

'I'm here.'

He turned to Aurelia and he said: 'I love you.' Saying it made him hard again.

'I only have the afternoons,' Aurelia said. 'Only a few days, a few afternoons.' The light in the room was the grey-green of an aquarium. 'You won't stay, anyway.'

'That matters?' He thought she looked such a kid.

'I'm a wife in Leon,' she said. 'That's my job. My career.'

He put his arms around her and she didn't bother to struggle.

'That's not enough,' he said.

She pushed him away and dashed for her clothes.

'It's my life,' she said, half-dressed, a slip muffling her voice.

'I'm sorry,' he said. He could hear that she was crying.

Aurelia threw the white silk over her body, like a cloud blotting out the sun, and she said: 'Sorry. You're always sorry, sorry, sorry, sorry, sorry. Sorry won't do. Sorry isn't it.'

The silk vanished under a blue dress. She tugged on stockings so fiercely that one tore. She was running from the room before he could bring himself to move.

He heard her car start, cough, die and start again in the drenching rain. Then he could hear only the rain.

He would not just wait in a drowned town. He went down to the porch and tried the phone; water gusted through the screen and forced the house lizards inwards. The phone had died.

He had to do something. You stay put, you rot in mind and heart, and maybe if you make yourself a life of waiting for a woman you can't ever have for yourself, then you drink, you indulge in self-pity, you begin to stage your emotions like a melodrama. He would not tolerate that.

He clambered into the car, still in jeans and slippers, drenched to the skin, and went skidding down the driveway into the suburban streets. He was within a block of Aurelia's house when sense returned. The rule is: to be a wife is a job, and the same woman can't be one man's wife, another man's mistress. Aurelia couldn't leave, Carpenter couldn't stay, they couldn't be together: unless they were prepared for a cataclysm in both their lives.

He felt almost brave enough for that, but he also felt stone sober. He parked opposite the house. Her husband would be home, of course, a weak man all tangled in a trough of papers; they'd face him down.

And the daytime housekeeper would be there, dancing her sad child's dance, without music, with a mop and bucket in the hallways.

And Aurelia, confined to that long barracks of a house.

He couldn't sound the horn; she was expecting nobody. He thought for a moment: maybe she didn't go home. But where could she go in the tiny town of middle-class Leon, and what could she be doing?

The house door moved and the screen kicked open, and Aurelia stood there in a gaudy summer dress and high, teetering heels. He sounded the horn once, but she couldn't hear him in the drumming rain. He watched her scamper to her car, the dress

78

clinging to her in the wet. She spun fast out of the driveway.

He wondered where she was going. He wondered if he, the lover, was only her alibi.

It took him a minute to turn the car, and then he had to follow her as closely as possible. She could vanish any moment behind the black curtain of rain.

She was heading up the flank of the volcano, into official territory. There was the military base, the cliff above the lake, the army hospital. She was running downhill towards the InterContinental.

Someone else, Carpenter thought, someone staying in the Inter-Continental. Another transient. But he knew that couldn't be.

She swung right and he followed, but only a little way. Even through the rain he knew this road and where it led: the bunker.

He couldn't follow without a reason. The guards didn't let you through. And it was not a healthy place to wait, not with nervous guns trained on any passing traffic. But Aurelia passed the gate as though she was expected, and was gone into the thick dusk of rain.

He wanted to wait and challenge her, but the guards were already stirring out of their command post in the middle of the road. He took himself quickly back to the main street, and then drove cautiously so as not to seem hurried by nerves.

Aurelia must have some innocent business in the bunker. With the man who had her father killed. With the man who killed her father. With the cops who harassed her sister.

Think again.

They knew her at the gate as though she had some long relationship with the Guard. As an informer is known.

He stopped the car by his house. There was a crack of lightning and the world went blue-white for a moment.

She had dissolved before his eyes, and now he could not be sure of her shape, her nature, anything about her. But she was inside him, in his blood, like an infection.

Matters of money couldn't be further from his mind.

'You can't be serious.' For once John Grey was alarmed.

'They asked me to help,' Mercedes said.

'But how can you help? There's a billion dollars somewhere.

You can't even find it. Diaz's wife can't find it, with the best divorce lawyers in the world.'

'There has to be a way,' Mercedes said. 'Things the family knows and doesn't even know it knows. Clues from the old man. Things Vico knows.'

'You'd go to Vico?'

'Of course I'd go to Vico. He's my adopted father still.'

John Grey walked to the window and looked down on the clogged streets. 'You liked the risk this morning, didn't you?'

'I felt alive,' Mercedes said.

'Maybe some of us don't have the energy for risk any more.'

'Don't get dull on me.'

'It isn't dullness,' Grey said, and he turned to her with a painfully open look, eyes naked. 'It's self-preservation.'

'But you can help. There can't be so many places in the world where Diaz could hide money. Where would he start?'

'You don't understand,' Grey said.

'Just tell me,' Mercedes said, because she was beginning to understand and she needed to rekindle his mind.

'Tell you,' Grey said. He sat down heavily. 'Listen, people used to hide money in Switzerland. Nazis hid it, Jews hid it, everyone hid it. The whole of Central Europe got its money out through Liechtenstein in 1947. Those are the traditional places. In Liechtenstein it's illegal even to reveal a company has been formed, so that's still secure, but the Swiss have let the American cops in once too often – even for technical offences like insider trading. Switzerland makes people nervous now.'

'Then where do they go?' She knew she must make him concentrate: she had a feeling he was worried by more than his paper problems with Fantasy Island.

'Anywhere,' he said in a shrug of a voice, and then felt ashamed of being so dismissive. 'Not anywhere,' he said. 'Not Frankfurt or Montreal or Kalamazoo. But he could be in Hong Kong or Panama or the Netherlands Antilles – or washing his money through the Caymans, or keeping it in a numbered account in Budapest. You get twelve per cent in Budapest.' He seemed to be summoning energy that was elusive. 'Or the Bahamas, of course. When Switzerland began to leak, a lot of respectable money went to the Bahamas to join all those

Canadian millionaires and the old friends from rum-running time who are now,' and Grey managed a flicker of wickedness, 'into other businesses.'

'There aren't so many places,' Mercedes said.

'Listen,' Grey said. 'All those places know how to hide and obfuscate and mystify. That's their business. You don't have a name to start with, except the name of Diaz and that's not likely to be slapped on his accounts. If Diaz just has nominee accounts, and he could have those in London, you're in trouble. If he just put his money in fiduciary deposits in Switzerland –'

Mercedes had the bright focus of a girl at a seminar. 'What,' she said, 'would he do with fiduciary deposits?'

'Give his money to a Swiss bank, who invest it in their name in some big bank in London or New York. That way, only the Swiss bank knows who really controls the cash, and the Swiss don't take withholding tax – negative interest, as well – because the money's really invested outside Switzerland.'

'And Liechtenstein?'

'Is a maze. No public records worth the name. You don't have to say who gets the benefit or who owns the shares in a foundation, or an *Anstalt* which is the same kind of thing.'

'It's like a maze.'

'Worse,' Grey said. 'Because if someone has a Liechtenstein foundation which owns a Panama company which runs nominee accounts in the Bahamas which make investments in the Caymans which have fiduciary deposits in Switzerland –'

'It will be more difficult,' Mercedes said.

'And suppose you tracked down the money,' Grey said. 'How would you get your hands on it, even with Vico's help? Old man Trujillo put some money in Switzerland and his family was in court fifteen years before the bank was told they didn't have a right to a cent. Eva Peron went off on the Rainbow Tour and squirrelled away fifteen million in Switzerland and forgot to tell the bank who got the money when she died. So the bank got the money, which is Swiss law.'

'We wouldn't work inside the law.'

She sat beside him and pulled his hand to her lips and began to bother his fingers, softly and wetly.

'O God,' he said, but then he pulled his hand away. It seemed such a brisk, unfriendly gesture that she was alarmed. She stood up and paced the room; and pretended she hadn't noticed that he rejected her.

'The money,' he said, vaguely, 'it could be in Uruguay, too. That's why they have all those fancy condominiums – money from Argentina and Brazil, running away. Or maybe he just has bearer bonds under his bed. Or –'

'Where would he go in Switzerland?'

'The Swiss don't have as much sense of morality as they like to pretend. Latins used to go to Geneva, not Zürich, and mostly they got screwed. Peron got screwed, Trujillo they wouldn't do business with and still he got screwed. But the private bankers wouldn't touch him.'

'Then who took the money?'

'A man called Muñoz. He scooped it up, bought a lovely old bank in St Gall and ended up in jail. In the end, all Trujillo's bastards paid Richard Nixon to sue the family for the money; it didn't work.'

'So Diaz,' Mercedes said, 'could have gone to Muñoz.'

'For as long as Muñoz was there. But he isn't, any more.'

'Someone took over,' Mercedes said. 'Someone always takes over.'

'There's a bank in Geneva, Rombauer et Cie. Rombauer never made it to the inner circles in Geneva – never got to the Club des Terrasses, or even the Groupement, which is the bankers' association. So he never caught morals from them when they had a little attack over Trujillo and Co.'

'So that's where the Diaz money must be,' said Mercedes triumphantly.

John Grey looked and sounded like an exhausted man. 'For Christ's sake,' he said, 'drop it. It doesn't make sense.'

'It does make sense,' Mercedes said. 'It's a hunt, it's a risk. It has to make sense.'

'I told you,' Grey said. 'I'm frightened of risk.'

'Not just because you have some trouble with paper? That wouldn't worry you.'

Grey said: 'I don't want to explain.' She went to hold him but he pulled away. 'Don't touch me,' he said.

She looked down at him and wondered what could possibly have terrified him into this maddening limpness.

'I'm going to go visiting,' she said. 'I have to start somewhere.'

He seemed half ashamed of his reactions. 'Where will you go?'

'To the old lady,' Mercedes said. 'She used to invite me to her lunch parties.'

'The old lady?'

'Señora Augusta Diaz Torres,' Mercedes said.

'Who is –'

'Anastasio's aunt, and the book-keeper of the clan.'

'Good luck,' Grey said.

She knew him far too well to risk asking what was wrong.

Tomás Diaz had business that day in a town that wasn't much – wood shacks in a cluster at the end of a potholed track. Fields were tucked in around it like rugs. The only sound was trucks as the soldiers rattled and crashed ahead.

He took position. The sun was low by five, and it was then, with a scenic instinct, that Diaz began to pour mortar fire into the town. Houses caught like torches and blew outwards in shards of straw and plank. Women and children were shocked into hiding, then shocked out by the fire, then ran in a screaming confusion. One group let a great white sheet go billowing in the wind, like a flag of surrender. The sheet caught fire.

Tomás Diaz stood on a hill like a teacher, and watched his lesson.

Men in the fields heard gunfire and saw the flames and they came pelting back, shouting as their women screamed, but perversely trying to move out of sight, dodging between the tall clumps of sugarcane.

Diaz gave the town a lull. His task was to cleanse it of guerrillas and he must do so thoroughly.

He set the trucks to roost round the little valley like carrion birds.

When the men were all in the burning town, trying to stamp down and wet down the fires, Diaz gave the last order. This time, he added napalm to the mortar fire. The breeze-block church, sturdy through the first assault, was now caught in an orange glow, its windows filled with the shadows of people. The last refuge burned among the new charcoal of the streets. A man ran out dressed in black, trailing flame.

Diaz heard a single note, higher than pain, of women mourning for the wrong of being born.

He ordered the whisky bottle from his jeep and took a swig. Smoke blacked out the sunset and left only the smudged orange of the fires.

'Shit,' he said to his second-in-command with evident satisfaction. 'All we need now is the girls.'

Mercedes nodded to the elevator man and she was hot like a thief in a violated house. This was enemy territory; she was inside.

She was glamour, success, Providencian culture who'd been brave as a hostage in Leon and said nothing later to embarrass the Diacistas; she was welcome, all the more now her name was everywhere in the glossy papers and her face signed a new perfume. Señora Augusta liked a certified, marketed success.

'Doña Augusta,' Mercedes said.

'The other young people have come,' said Augusta with a distinct sigh.

Mercedes followed her to an alcove of chintz.

'We haven't seen each other for such a long time,' Augusta said. After all, Mercedes was famous enough now for her presence to be a favour.

Mercedes held her hands.

'So nice to see friends,' Augusta said, 'especially in these difficult times.'

She was a stack of blue rinse above a thick, wattled neck, and then the body of a sharp-elbowed market woman wrapped in budget Adolfo; and she held court in a nightmare of sentimental Capo di Monte, a family history, pale and crowded, bought by her decorator.

The meal was all inhibitions. There were older guests who no longer trusted the young, and the young were chilled by the dragon presence of Augusta. She was, after all, in some unspecified way, the one who controlled the money. When they'd eaten, Doña Augusta took Mercedes away for coffee.

'It's so difficult,' she said, 'to know who to trust nowadays.' It sounded oddly like an invitation.

84

Mercedes looked at the older woman. She was broad and functional, and she shoved for room, but she covered that peasant strength with manners. Minute to minute, either side could show. Mercedes had an odd sense that she was Augusta's memory, the girl Augusta once wanted to be.

'To be honest, my dear,' Augusta said, 'I have a little business.'

Mercedes smiled. She would love to be confidante to the bookkeeper; she must not seem over keen.

'There are papers the lawyers say I must sign,' Augusta said. 'I'd like to go with a friend. Someone who doesn't want anything.'

In the limo, Augusta babbled. She'd been concerned for everyone in Leon. She thought Anastasio should crush the guerrillas, end the whole affair. He'd done it before.

'He is not,' Señora Augusta Diaz Torres said, with the full force of her name, 'the man his father was.'

They came to a bank on Madison Avenue and the limo stopped.

'If you'd come with me?' Augusta said, a little sadly. 'I feel a little nervous in New York.'

Mercedes couldn't imagine what made Augusta nervous. She was sharp enough to see all manner of possibilities in the invitation – a test of honesty, to see if those diamonds had really left Leon with Mercedes Zenon; a proof to anyone watching that the Señora's business could not be so very important if she did it with a distant friend.

The Señora talked with a bank official in a little office away from the banking floor. Providencia money, Mercedes thought, and tried to hold the thought; whatever the Diaz family has, it stole from Providencia.

The bank officer jotted numbers, argued very seriously, then wrote something else on a pad and handed it to the Señora. Evidently she wanted something he did not. It must be a withdrawal, Mercedes decided. It was something she needed to know.

When the Señora had finished, Mercedes followed her briefly into the bank officer's cubicle. While she was here – 'Miss Zenon, what a pleasure,' the bank officer glinted – she would just like a note of the day's money market rates. The officer scribbled and handed her the paper. 'If there's any way we can be of service . . .'

He must lean hard on his pen. Mercedes put the paper into a pocket of her suit.

'My dear,' Augusta said. This time, she said she was going to her lawyers', and that was a question rather than a statement. Mercedes said, graciously: 'Of course.'

She sat in a conference room with magazines and coffee, and waited for Augusta to emerge and make sense of the discreet silence.

'I have to go to another office,' Augusta said. She sounded apologetic, but Mercedes knew perfectly well this appointment must have been planned. In the car, Augusta confessed as much: she had a deposition to give, some money case.

'They are talking about serving papers,' she said, with great dignity. 'But they can't do that while I'm giving my deposition. Oh no. They can't do that there.'

And Mercedes waited again. Her presence puzzled a junior partner who tried conversation; Mercedes thought she might recognise him from dancing, somewhere, some time ago. She smiled.

And Augusta came out.

'I didn't say it,' she said to her own lawyer.

'Never mind,' the lawyer said.

And she snatched at Mercedes' arm with fingers strong and hard as a bird's talons. 'Please,' she said, 'we have to go.'

They pushed into the elevator and Augusta pressed '2'. Mercedes thought it must be a mistake, but at floor 2 the old woman stepped out into the corridor, waited for the doors to close, and then started at a fine jog towards the women's room.

She slammed the door. Mercedes stood by the washbasin, fascinated. Doña Augusta had a substantial bag with her and she began to tug things from it.

'Hold the door,' she shouted to Mercedes.

And the decorous old lady pulled and pushed her way out of a striking, brick-red dress and left it in the corner. Off with the dress came the thatch of hair. The dragon was almost bald.

She scrambled in the bag for jeans. She moulded herself into them, broad as a continent; she pulled on a thin sweater and put

86

a crumpled linen coat over the whole suburban mess. She shifted money and credit cards to her new pockets, and finally she took out a matted, lurid thing which she planted on her head.

She looked in the mirror and petted the strands of her cheap red wig until they settled down a little.

'There,' the Señora Augusta Diaz Torres said, perfectly changed into a veteran of the shopping mall.

'They'll recognise me,' Mercedes said, afraid she was also expected to make some awful transformation.

'They'll follow you,' she said. 'You go first.'

Mercedes was struck by the woman's sheer, imperious cheek. She simply assumed she would be served, not second-guessed, and that the law would never touch her while she had her wits about her.

Mercedes did go first, and looked in the great marble lobby of the building for anyone who might be a process server. There was a middle-aged man fidgeting with the express elevator controls, a black messenger with a stack of huge envelopes. Or maybe the writs could not be served while still in this building, or on the forecourt. She looked out to the street. There was a man in pinstripes, sitting on the wall in the pale sun; he seemed to be smoking a joint. There was a cab.

But nobody dressed in henna and polyester came out of the elevators, or down the stairs. Doña Augusta had vanished.

Mercedes walked to the kerbside and wondered whether to take the Diaz limousine.

She asked the cabbie to start the meter and wait round the corner, where she could watch from the back. There were two exits of course; she hadn't allowed for that. But probably Doña Augusta would wait a while, and certainly she'd brazen out from the front of the building. Being caught had not occurred to her.

Mercedes took out the scrap of paper from the bank. She held it to the light and could just read two sets of figures impressed there – '045 2 X 178' and '7641290. A dollar amount doesn't start with a 0, she thought, nor is it punctuated with an X. That number wasn't money. But maybe it was an account. '045' would fit, too; it was a bank sorting code.

The other number was much more hopeful. Maybe it was the balance on 045 2 X 178: if so, it was $7,641,290.

It wasn't a billion, but then Augusta didn't control the billion. But it was what John Grey had said was impossible: an address for some of the Diaz money.

She was congratulating herself when out of the building came the vast red and gaudy bulk of Señora Augusta; she piled into a cab.

'Follow,' Mercedes said.

Augusta's cab went down Park Avenue like a fairground ride, stopping at greens, starting at reds, weaving down to throw off anything behind and in that spectacular progress making the rogue cab obvious as a ferret among elephants – obvious because of everyone else's anxiety.

In Herald Square, it stopped by Macy's. As Mercedes paid off her driver, she wondered if Augusta thought her cab contained the process servers. What law case could possibly be worth this absolute loss of dignity?

But Doña Augusta had gone running at the revolving door. On the floor Mercedes could see the dead thatch of red. Out there, on the shopfloor, a bald fat woman was running for her money.

Mercedes began to laugh so much that the security guard asked if everything was all right, and when he recognised her, fell quiet. She was giggling under a vast, Alpine picture of herself: a glowing, rather Egyptian woman visiting a Swiss mountain with a curious look that seemed to encode a whole romantic history.

The maids had let John Grey into the apartment.

'Take this,' he said. He'd drawn and signed a cheque and he pushed it into her hands. 'It's your share of Greystoke. Your investment. We're going to go under, soon.'

Mercedes wouldn't touch the cheque. 'You can't do that,' she said. 'We named that scam for Johnny Weismuller and Tarzan.'

'Heartfelt tribute,' Grey said. 'At the time.'

'I'm counting on you,' Mercedes said. 'Look, I found seven million of the Diaz money. I know which account, which bank, what name, and I know Señora Augusta wants to withdraw it. All I have to do,' she had a child's sunny way, 'is withdraw it first.'

'Like Fantasy Island,' Grey said. 'All I had to do –'

'Are you trying to alienate me?'

'I'll go out with you tonight,' Grey said, 'if that's what you mean.'

She looked hard at him. This wasn't drink; Grey never had abused his finely built body with the cocktail of coke and Ecstasy and sniffing heroin and crack and ethyl and the rest. This was fear. And John Grey III was not a man to be afraid of a failure; everyone had failures, and the game was how to recover and how briskly. Something more fundamental had happened, something which he was keeping private from his surrogate sister, and his sometime lover.

She tried to hold him, afraid he'd push her away again, but this time he was passive in her arms, grateful for the warmth. She set him to sleep for a while.

In the limo, much later, they talked themselves up to celebration. They stepped out in a block of raunch by Union Square, a street of human litter where welfare men came out to score dimes and sense, and hustlers who were boys with breasts, women with cocks, muscled for a good position to find a john. Out of this parade, shabby even in its rhinestones, rose the square monument of an old movie theatre. Tonight, the theatre was besieged by crowds whose arms went out like claws, and cops in line, and greeters who chose who would or wouldn't pass the doors. Searchlights crossed in the air and picked at windows accidentally in the nearby condominiums. And there was a tide of night people, with cards and hope, washing over the streetlife and washing it away.

Mercedes and Grey rode such a wave to the barricade, and were welcomed cursorily by a thin, painful man who smiled like a break in his face. They passed up a staircase of lights into their eighties wonderland.

But why did all this seem de-natured, without the energy that had long kept such places tolerable? It was hung with certified art, selected by a 1960s authority who had encouraged Warhol and including nobody who hadn't shown at Boone or Castelli. The people were neat, nice, rich and dressed down. There were proper designers, and one more improper in red with earrings of dollar signs; there was the proper list of socialites, some of whom wrote columns, and columnists, some of whom would sidle into each other's copy for want of better subjects. Models looked like prom queens, and there were men in Wall Street suits. In a corner, there were night faces – Boy George, Grace Jones and Marilyn – but they seemed toned down from old glories, like a sepia print from a coloured past.

John Grey said: 'I want the scam to end all scams.'

'That's it,' Mercedes said.

They went for drinks to the Impresario Room, with lace and candelabra and forty feet of Haitian primitives.

'When I worked on FedWire,' Grey said, looking around, 'I left a trapdoor. Enough to swallow up all these people and their money. Boom!'

Mercedes said: 'You can tell me.'

John Grey looked sideways: 'I don't know if I can. Sometimes I don't think you're entirely honest.'

Mercedes kicked him. A pale, thin, blond Texan, busy running hands through his hair, noticed and winked elaborately.

'You see,' John Grey said, leaning forward confidentially, 'there's a system that moves almost all the money in America – moves it out of the banks in the morning, puts it back in the evening. In the middle, around noon, there's three hundred and fifty billion dollars in limbo on that wire. It's too slow, you see, it can only handle three transactions a second. We asked for more; they wouldn't do it.'

He sipped his drink. 'Imagine if that system just stopped. If there were three hundred and fifty billion dollars that just dropped out of the world. And it's worse than that, because big companies just access the big computer and don't even tell the banks, and half the time they take daylight overdrafts – pay bills in the morning because they know they'll be paid in the evening. Nobody knows how much that is. Some people say it's thirty times all the assets of all the banks in America. Think of that.'

Mercedes said: 'And you could stop that dead?'

'It's not just the system, just FedWire. It's banks and business in America. You know the banks lost a ninth of their assets just when they had to clear foreign deals at five in the afternoon instead of next morning, when they could no longer park other people's money on their books overnight. Well, this little trapdoor makes that change look insignificant.'

90

Mercedes pulled him to his feet and they went exploring. They went to the basement loos which had been surrounded by a funhouse madness, and they went to the balcony and looked down.

'Look down on the dancers,' John Grey said. 'Watch the others perform. The eighties.'

'This isn't a metaphor,' Mercedes said. 'It's a club. You want to dance?'

Together they moved out of the cavernous crumbling vaults of the old theatre and down to where people danced. She was stiff at first, regretting the old flurries of the lovely and the weird who now were reduced to the pavement people shouting outside. But for old times' sake, and for the music, she began to loosen, until the music caught her like a wind. She stepped as neat as chess, the moves that look like a colt's impatience at first, and then she broke. She was unfussy, exact; and she brought the balcony people to the rail.

From above, a set of battlements and wonders came down, and then a bank of video screens that showed a single image, a vast vulva, and then the cleverness hemmed the dancers in too much and they began to disperse. The audience stayed for the sets.

'It'll do,' Mercedes said.

They looked private; even the most determined flak kept his distance. Mercedes allowed only a couple of the obligatory column pictures; in one, she looked oddly stranded by the flashbulb, distant from the scene.

'I need you,' Mercedes said, 'brother.'

They stayed only an hour.

In the car, Grey held her hand. After mid-town, he said: 'A friend of mine died.'

The lights careered past like ribbons of glitter.

'He died of AIDS.'

Mercedes said: 'I'm sorry.'

'I knew other people, of course – not close friends, but faces on a dance floor. This was someone I loved for a while.'

Mercedes could give him only her warmth and her seriousness.

'It's strange,' Grey was saying, 'how everything seemed so

91

innocent, so obvious – only a few years ago. It takes one virus to change all that. People get scared of sex, scared of each other, scared, scared. I thought I wasn't scared. I thought I was sensible enough, healthy enough.'

She held him.

'Our time,' he said, 'it's over, isn't it?'

Aurelia also came to dinner with the President. Her husband was away in Kansas City, fretting over some computer course which would tell him how to answer questions if he could ever formulate the right ones. So Aurelia was invited here. Perhaps it was Tomás Diaz who had arranged things, thoughtfully, the better to win Carpenter's friendship. Perhaps it was the old man, whose cops had their way of knowing things.

Dinner was in Tomás Diaz's quarters, on the edge of the Presidential compound. There was talk, and no music, and a bucket of Margharitas dispensed by an unsmiling Indian girl who was deadly scared to get things wrong.

El Presidente brought his showgirl, a leggy blonde from Las Vegas, past her best, whose flashier body parts served him as worry beads in bad moments; close to Diaz, you could see why the Duvaliers of Haiti, Papa Doc himself, had found the man a social embarrassment. Tomás Diaz seemed to be on his own. He showed anyone who'd listen the various military matters on the walls – General MacArthur accepting the Japanese surrender, Clausewitz torn from a book, Simon Bolivar, a widescreen Victorian version in steel engraving of the battle of Flodden, a Nazi helmet and a pile of military music on old records. It was indiscriminate, politically innocent; a child's collection.

Carpenter moved close to Aurelia. 'Do I have to get through this whole damn party without touching you,' he said.

'Yes,' she said. There was no explanation. He understood that just as they could be lovers on particular afternoons, here and now it was as if they had never been together. He fretted over what he had learned to accept.

And he was disturbed by the dwarf Chamorro. He was just a sea creature of a man, stranded on a stool, with a huge, square head; a grotesque. But he followed people with his eyes, not to find evidence but to tell them what he knew.

92

Everyone drank too much, because it was a joyless evening. And Carpenter found himself fancying some link between Aurelia and the dwarf. It seemed he fascinated her – made her curious, made her dream of a child who could fuck her, roused some messy fantasy that was better left fantastical. Or so he thought, because she seemed to be moving for him as though she was a show, and once she whispered something that made the dwarf start and then look up expectantly.

Carpenter struggled through the evening. He managed to promise no favours, take no cocaine and avoid pointed questions from Tomás. It was a minor achievement. When the party collapsed for simple lack of energy he waited in his car for Aurelia to come out. If Mario was away, he could take her home. They would have a night at last, like Bluefields.

Cars pulled away in a brilliant mist of rain and light. He wondered if Aurelia had seen him leave.

After twenty minutes, he reminded himself she had no other way to get home.

After thirty, he was beginning to be annoyed. She knew where he was; she knew he was waiting; she should be with him.

Thirty-five. He took off in a pig's squeal of tyres, self-righteously furious that he had ever thought of waiting.

The dwarf. It was a vicious, out of focus, pornographic thought.

In the house, he was suddenly afraid for Aurelia. He heard his heels clatter on the tiles and tried to drown the sound with a record. He was too aware of shadows, the flicker of a lizard running the wall, like nights when you can't sleep for drink.

He had to wait in the house, because where else would Aurelia find him?

He drank. His belly turned ominously. There wasn't much time; he couldn't be here for much longer. He wanted time with Aurelia.

He fell asleep on the sofa and the whisky spilled on him.

It was the wrong evening for John Grey's pain. Mercedes tried to hold and warm him but she had nothing to say. She was full of the shapeless preoccupation she'd once thought meant Aurelia was in danger, or trouble. Aurelia's feeling was in her body, setting aside her own circumstances and drowning her.

John Grey said: 'We'll shine.'

She said: 'Aurelia. Oh, Christ, Aurelia!'

And Aurelia had never been this close to the dwarf before. Oh, he played with words a little, tried some clumsy gallantry, but he had what no man of normal size could have: the power to make women curious. Matrons gossiped about the bull cock on the tiny body, and they knew his power had no limits. If Chamorro had your body in the cells of the bunker, he owned it, and could dispose of it in the most literal sense. To make love with him would be to take that power, but still to have the great luxury of absolute surrender. The women didn't want hurt, but they didn't want responsibility either.

'I never went to the Tropicana,' Aurelia said.

'Nice girls don't,' the dwarf said. He guessed this was the invitation.

'I'd like to see it.'

Chamorro's eyes were big and greedy. She was such a fine lady, such a triumph.

'I could join you,' Chamorro said. 'A little later.'

She sat in the back of the taxi with a mind just as blank as the night and the rain. She couldn't turn back. She had never done anything like this before. It was like a parody of sleeping with Ian Carpenter. She had done nothing like this before.

The cab left her under a rough plastic awning. There were rows of cabins all around, some in discreet cul-de-sacs. In the reception room, Guardsmen were playing dominoes, slapping the stones so the girls in the waiting room flinched. And Aurelia saw the girls: not formed yet, but tricked out in fishnet and lace for very tired desires.

The wind had risen: it fingered the trees and made shadows scuttle in the pathways between the rooms.

A big man, in a white tent of a shirt, produced a credit card and was sent to shop among the children. One had lipstick smeared on her face; it made her look as if she'd lost teeth. She hitched up her skirt and he poked roughly; her smile seemed to hurt her bones. But she wouldn't do, and so she dropped her skirt. She started to handjive with the girl next to her.

Aurelia couldn't feel anger, or pity. She had to go to the desk clerk. The dwarf had made the call; she was shown to room 16.

It was a lifeless place. All that lust and fantasy should have left traces in the air, but instead the place was void: a TV set long unplugged, a lamp with three red bulbs, a big bed with thin sheets and a bathroom beyond. She could hear boisterous talk through the walls, a romp of college boys who'd taken the room with girls. She heard shouts and laughs. She was grateful.

She stretched. She turned back the sheets and checked the window locks. She wondered how Chamorro would want her – gloved and decent, or perhaps abandoned. She didn't know why the dwarf hadn't come.

The rain and the airconditioner gave her a little privacy, but the walls were mostly shaving-thin. She set the shower running, for the sound. She looked at the door locks and reckoned they wouldn't matter; the door was flimsy as card.

She wondered what kind of meeting the dwarf had, to keep him. But that was the one thing she must not imagine.

At the dressing table she looked at her face. The young matron, properly masked; the mask, in red light, could as well be the face of a whore.

But she wanted to get on with the show. She thought she heard a knock on the door, first tentative and then fierce, and she gave a pretty little cry and looked through the spyglass. He was too short to see; he held up a rose and a bottle of champagne.

He called her 'Señora', which told her which game to play.

'You are very lovely,' Chamorro said. She was a wife, of the right class; fucking her would break his own slim moral code. That was the kick.

'I really don't do this sort of thing,' she said.

'Drink,' he said, solicitously. He had glasses in the pockets of his overcoat. 'Such a pretty dress,' he said, and sat down heavily on the bed. 'Don't tear it when you take it off.'

She wanted to be drunk. She couldn't imagine what she was doing in this room, a hand away from the man who burned out her father's eyes. There must be some way of turning back, even now.

But nobody leaves Chamorro, nobody who has been under suspicion even for a moment. She had to go through to the end.

She wriggled her shoulders and her dress began to slip; she put her hands back to tug at the fastening. The little man's eyes began to water.

She let the dress fall to the floor and stepped out of it. Her slip clung to her, outlining her buttocks as she pretended to check her face in the mirror, daring the dwarf to make his move.

He sat reading her body like a map, and then he lunged. She looked down on a blocky, oiled head that struck her belly and almost winded her. The dwarf went up under her slip and tore it; his tongue was busy.

He was grunting 'Sweet fish, sweet fish' and she stared round the room like a furry thing in a trap, praying her body wouldn't now betray her. She felt the edge of his tongue, working inside her.

The bottle was close to her hand. She fancied she felt spittle inside her, on her lips. The huge head was working furiously and soon he'd look up, wanting to see and hear whatever reaction he expected from his fantasies, wanting her to get it right. She could do no more. She picked up the bottle and she cracked it down hard on the dwarf's head.

He slipped away from her, eyes wide.

She picked up the glass by her head and threw it against the wall between rooms. It broke with a high sound that cut through the rain and the roar of the airconditioner.

She brushed her torn slip. She wanted to wash but did not dare leave the square little body in case the dwarf woke. She was afraid he was moving, his big head shaking.

She flung the door open to the rain, and in came the party from room 17. She went immediately to the bathroom and began washing her body and hands.

There was a tall woman at the door. She said she was Nora; she came to comfort Aurelia. She saw the frantic washing.

'Thank you,' Nora said, and kissed her. 'Without you, we'd never have got him alone.'

'I did it,' Aurelia said.

'You can go now? They'll know you were here.'

'I was obvious,' Aurelia said.

Nora took her hand. She still wore a sodden white cotton glove.

When the dwarf woke he began to kick reflexively. Four men each took a limb and hauled him into the air where he could only buck and spit. His short legs gave him no leverage.

Nora handed Aurelia an alarming razor, brilliant and open.

'For all the ones he killed,' she said. 'For your father.'

Aurelia held the razor. The light made it seem blooded already. She watched Chamorro struggling and hoped he would stop shouting soon.

'For the Indians,' Nora said. 'The ones he took up in helicopters by threes. The first wouldn't answer, so he threw him out. The second took too long, and he was thrown out. The third always talked.'

Aurelia couldn't do it. Revenge had been so simple and immediate on the lagoon; but this was long planned and somehow arbitrary. She began to question what right she had to be an executioner. She did not see how the act of taking this man's life could save or return her father, or her life. And she knew something worse. She was making Chamorro wait, torturing him as surely as he tortured others. Even now he was helpless, he could compromise her. Either she killed or she tortured.

The blood came up in her eyes like a physical curtain, and she jabbed the razor into the dwarf's neck and tried to drag it through the pipes and sinew. It was harder work than she'd expected.

They set a towel to blot up the blood and curled the body under the sheets. It looked as if the dwarf had slept on while his mistress crept back to her proper home.

The phone rang.

It couldn't ring. Nobody was supposed to know where Chamorro went, unless it was his closest aides. And his aides ran the National Guard who ran this motel.

She picked up the phone. She pretended to be breathless.

'I'm sorry,' she said. 'He's in the shower. I could take a message –'

She put down the phone and said to the others: 'They knew there was going to be trouble. And they knew he was here.'

'We're going,' the woman said.

Aurelia didn't mention what she most feared: now they knew she'd been in the room with Chamorro when Chamorro died. Or at least they'd know that in the morning.

They bundled out of the motel rooms in a boisterous gang, the men mobbing Aurelia and the other women so they looked like trophies carried off for the night. Outside the gates there were battered popular taxis waiting, the ones that ply fixed routes, and they climbed in; they changed cars at a suburban villa.

Aurelia was shivering. 'I knew I'd have to go. I just didn't think it would be tonight.'

Nora said: 'You'll be back in Leon when we're all back. A heroine of the revolution.'

'Yes,' Aurelia said.

She was empty of that great political purpose she sensed in the others. She wanted to see Ian Carpenter again, but she feared they'd despise such a personal need. She wouldn't see the man now until some indefinite, remote date.

She said to Nora: 'If we can stop a minute. The papers I need – at a house, near here.'

'We've organised papers.'

'But I have to have these. I have to.'

She was desperate for Nora, who seemed so cold and efficient even in her comforting, just this once to sense a need.

'Stop,' Nora said to the driver. 'You have five minutes. Two comrades with you in case there's trouble.'

'I've nowhere to run,' Aurelia said, for an instant thinking herself the prisoner.

She left the car and was soaked in a moment, and the two men running by her had drowned eyes, and condoms pulled over their rifle barrels, in case. They slipped between the houses and up to the weak door of the porch, and through into the drawing room.

Carpenter came awake with a gun in his belly.

'I'm sorry it's like this,' he heard Aurelia say. 'I have to go away. You'll hear why.'

He could hear the phone ringing. He wanted to answer the phone. He half-assumed these figures in the dark were shadows and not real, whisky ghosts. They were stopping him from answering the phone.

He tried to stand up. The men with the guns looked to Aurelia and she nodded.

'I have to answer the phone,' he said.

'Go ahead,' Aurelia said.

He opened the door to the hallway. The phone rang with a clean brilliance between the tiled walls; it hurt him.

'Yes?'

'This is the office of the President,' a voice said. 'The President asked if you'd care to join him. Drinks and perhaps some company. He has something to discuss.'

Carpenter said: 'But –'

'There will be a car in perhaps a half hour.'

'But I have company.'

There was a very little silence at the President's end.

'Company,' the voice said. 'But you will be here, of course.'

'I will be there,' Carpenter said, weakly. 'In an hour.'

He put down the phone, and Aurelia was watching him.

'I wanted to say good-bye,' she said.

The men with guns were already impatient, hissing that they had to move on. She hugged Carpenter and she slipped away, out through the porch into the night.

He closed the porch door and tried to see where their metal or their clothes might catch the light as they cleared his garden. He saw nothing.

A car passed the end of his driveway.

He went back into the house.

And then five cars passed the end of the driveway, one after another, fast as a chase. He was startled.

Someone was chasing Aurelia.

And Aurelia came to visit him with men who carried guns, and said this was good-bye. It didn't make sense to him. He felt truculent with the Scotch and mystified. He would follow.

He could hear the cars far away in the quiet of the night. He started his own car and set out to follow the noise.

He could see lights moving out on the motorway where usually there would be no traffic at this time of night. He went that way, and as he drove he puzzled at this evening. Aurelia with the dwarf Chamorro, whom she must hate, and Aurelia being chased; Aurelia with armed men, going into hiding. Aurelia at the doors of the security police, and Aurelia running off with the Amadista guerrillas. Aurelia as baffling as winds.

99

Ahead, the convoy of five cars had suddenly stopped, screeching into the forecourt of some low concrete building and forming a star of headlights onto the façade. Carpenter didn't know the building. He slowed down so as not to draw too much attention to himself, because he didn't know who was there, or on which side.

Or even what the sides were, he admitted to himself.

He heard doors slam. He fancied he heard guns cocked. He sat in the still road, just out of sight of the building, and he knew that would not be enough. He closed the car door quietly, locked it with an absurdly conventional gesture, and sprinted close to the boundary of the lit forecourt. He moved in the dark between the bushes.

There were no lights in the building. There was one car parked apart from the other five, but he'd never seen the car Aurelia was travelling in and it would surely not be her own. He could see a door along the shadowed side of the building; he ran to it and sheltered there a moment.

He could hear running inside the building. He could hear someone's boots crashing on gravel, someone coming round the building. They were men with guns, in a panic, hunting people, and he was in the wrong place. He had to try the door.

It seemed stuck, not locked. He put his weight against it and was in a little ante-chamber, much like a shed. It felt cool.

He looked around. A torch beam cut through a window, and in the light he could see a doorway – heavy steel, with a portentous lock. If he could push that door ajar, he'd be where Aurelia was; he might warn her, save her.

He tried the door. It slid a little, silently, and he walked through. Inside, the air was cold, not cool. There was steel shelving up to the ceilings, and on the shelves, plastic packets that were soft to the touch. He could see the layout because there were lights criss-crossing as though carried by men on the hunt.

He heard the shed door pushed open behind him. They'd have to cover every exit, he knew that; but he knew it too late. He saw the light go tracking between the tall library shelves and pressed himself against the wall, unsure where safety lay. If there was safety anywhere.

He could shout out 'Aurelia' but how would he save her? She

100

had guards for that, men with rifles. He sank down and worried how he'd save himself.

In the criss-cross of torchlight, he saw feet, a woman's feet, running over steel. If light could reach her, the guns could reach her. He heard a spray of gunfire, ricocheting off steel and concrete until it filled the huge room. The steel shelves seem to shiver.

He slipped forward to keep moving because he reckoned a moving target would be more difficult. He was terribly afraid the light would catch him. He didn't know who was shooting, and he guessed both sides would count him enemy.

A machine-gun barked and barked. The sound hung on the air like smoke.

He threw himself face down on the cold steel floor and calculated how he could get to Aurelia. He could be a diversion for her, so that she could escape. He could run –

His hands were out, trying to sense where he was and what was around him. His right hand met something wet and sticky on the floor, something dark. He couldn't make out colour. He moved his hand in the liquid that seemed to drip from the shelves.

White light went on and lit the whole room like a surgery. Carpenter made himself look down at his hand and found it red-black with blood.

Up among the shelves, the ruptured packets sputtered and oozed with blood. He felt it in his hair. He remembered Diaz had a business selling blood from Providencia.

Carpenter carefully stood up. He'd throw shadows in this brilliant light; he would be seen.

She stood at the end of the room, still in that white dress but splattered now with blood. She was framed by the tall shelves. She saw him briefly; she seemed to freeze and then run on.

The guns sounded. But whose guns – the guards or their pursuers?

He backed to the door of the shed. Through there, he'd be one to one with an armed man; in the blood bank he was confused and surrounded by an army. He moved the door.

And the lights died again.

Through the maze of shelves, he could see the torchlight

101

moving and something being dragged, something in white.

He couldn't see who was tugging Aurelia out of that place. He remembered blood in falls, and the smears on her dress. He slipped back into the shed.

He felt dull pain on the back of his neck, a blow that seemed to go deeper and deeper; and he knew nothing. He remembered a second of being grateful.

He raised a heavy eye in the bunker. He knew it was close to Diaz's office; he remembered the corridor. He was lying on a patched sofa and all six blonde feet of the President's showgirl sat at his side.

'You need a drink,' she said.

He recognised the bunker. He remembered he was bidden to a late party, more relaxed and raunchy than the formal dinner and a diversion to keep the banker's attention. He had an odd sense of being in the middle of some Western brawl, with memories of blood, a wrecked saloon and the showgirl tending his wounds.

She gave him warm Scotch. 'Everything's fine,' she said.

He sat up, sore and baffled. Diaz came stomping out of his office, his grin broad. 'Thanks,' he said.

The evening was already like a kaleidoscope, gaudy pieces all in sight but changing their pattern minute by minute.

Diaz pulled at his wrist and dangled a gold Rolex. 'For you,' he said. 'Take it. If you hadn't said you had company –'

That elusive pattern in the kaleidoscope was seeming darker than before. 'Why are you thanking me?' Carpenter asked.

'You know as well as I do,' Diaz said. 'It's a good watch.'

The showgirl saw the agitation in both men and said, as though to soothe them, 'Really, everything's fine.' She was edgy as a fine horse that smells fire.

'But I have company . . . ' Carpenter remembered his words. Minutes later, cars chased past his house, out to the bloodbank. There couldn't be a connection.

He gulped his drink.

'Maybe,' the showgirl said, 'he should go to bed.'

'Everything's fine,' Diaz said. It was an order.

Carpenter heard himself saying, over and over, 'But I have company.'

He saw Aurelia in white and blood, being pulled from the

102

building. He remembered the terrible echoing of the guns.

'I think,' he said, 'I should go home.'

He woke soon after dawn. The rains had broken for a moment and the sun was bright like knives. He roused his hangover, showered and shaved and dressed, and his brain shuddered like an oyster at a touch of lemon.

The phone. The goddamn phone.

'But I have company . . .'

It was Aurelia's husband, calling from Kansas City, setting his teeth to be grown-up.

'My wife,' Mario said. 'Her car's gone, the maid hasn't seen her, the bed hasn't been slept in and there's no message. We're both adults, for God's sake. Is she all right? Where is she?'

Carpenter said: 'I don't know.'

'I wouldn't bother you, but in these times –'

'I really don't know.'

'You never know what happens to people these days,' Mario said.

'What happens to people these days,' Carpenter thought. It was as though Mario wasn't afraid at all of what guns and bullets might do to Aurelia, but rather of what Aurelia might do. He didn't know her, and he knew that now.

Carpenter had nothing to tell Mario, only what he'd seen; and he couldn't make sense of that. He saw light, a woman in white, blood. He didn't want to think he'd killed her with those careless words on the phone.

'If you hear anything –' Mario said. He was full of bluster, and still pathetic.

By the afternoon there were stories like the shocks of an earthquake, spreading and shifting. Chamorro was dead. He'd been killed at some Diacista orgy, by the wives of men he'd killed. They'd found him with women's knickers tied over his face. He'd been castrated and thrown on a dungheap. People savoured the details, and panicked at the consequences. Because Chamorro was the President's man, the President wanted action and bodies, now. But there was also talk that Chamorro had shared his information with the Americans, been the contact for the CIA: and how would the Americans take his death?

The city gossiped to stave off terror.

103

Tanks rumbled out of the barracks. The minimal airforce –
Diaz kept it small lest the pilots turn against him – was out of its
camouflage and on the runway at the airport. On the main roads
there were trucks so heavy laden that they lolled and panted like
tired dogs. But in that city saturated with guns, nobody knew the
shape or the face of the enemy. The enemy could be your wife,
your mother, your child.

Carpenter called the airlines. There was nothing left for him in
Providencia; the game was done. Diaz was under serious threat.
Diaz might be falling.

And Aurelia was gone. He could not yet make himself accept
that she was almost certainly dead, just that she was gone and he
could no longer find her when he came back to Providencia.

The stories never stopped. They said the President's showgirl
worked the balconies of the old Presidential palace as if she were
playing the supper show, high-kicking and shouting that nothing
was wrong.

He drove out to the airport and bullied his way onto the long
flight out – Miami by way of San Salvador and Belize. He stuck
close to a pair of German diplomats heading home; protection
could help.

Diaz paged him, and wished him well, even said he might
value some advice. There seemed to be no questions about why
he'd been in the middle of that grotesque shoot-out, only
gratitude.

By Manhattan, he had almost stopped hearing his own voice
saying, over and over: 'But I have company . . .'

·THREE·

'Just a little help,' Mercedes said. She wanted John Grey to start fighting and laughing, like before.

'All you know is that the old lady wanted to move some money. And you're guessing that.'

'I think,' Mercedes said, 'she said she wanted bearer T-bills.'

'She can't buy those if she's a US resident. You have to swear you're not subject to US income tax and then you can have them without giving a name. Very convenient.'

'But if she couldn't get those, she'll have to find some other way.'

'They'll stall her while they sort out the residency question. They'll expect her to hide the money. That's the only point of bearer T-bills.'

She watched him, hoping he was back again to life.

'So they're expecting her to draw out her millions,' Mercedes said. 'If we could simply find a way –'

'If,' John Grey said, unkindly.

The maid appeared and said she had a message. 'Man called Solomon,' she said. 'Your deal's been done. You can see him when you want.'

'What if we bought diamonds?' Mercedes said.

'How? With Doña Augusta's money?'

'If the money were transferred somewhere they don't ask questions –'

'The Russians in Zürich,' Grey said. 'They need the currency. Wozchod Bank.'

'Thank you,' Mercedes said.

'But you still have to move the money.'

She kissed him. 'Trust me,' she said.

She took a cab to 47th Street and saw Solomon in his mean cubicle of an office.

'I wondered,' she said, when she had taken, examined and pocketed the cheque, 'if you would do a Zürich buy for me.'

'You still want stones?'

'I want to make an investment. Seven million.'

Solomon raised an eyebrow. 'Such a plunger,' he said. 'I think that used to be the word. Before your time.' He coughed. 'But why don't you buy in London?'

'Because,' Mercedes said, 'I'd have to buy at a sight in London, wouldn't I – from de Beers. They give me a bag, I take it or not. I wouldn't be good at knowing if I had the Hope Diamond or a bag of glass.'

'De Beers does not sell glass.'

'But if we buy from the Soviets,' Mercedes said, 'we can fuss over each stone. I can get my money's worth.'

'You would want me to go to Zürich? To examine these stones?'

'On one of your Antwerp trips,' Mercedes said.

Solomon sighed. 'It would be possible,' he said. 'You realise I couldn't take delivery in Zürich? That has to be at Swiss customs, at a port. And the Russian diamond brokers like pre-payment. They take orders under code, if you want.'

'I'll have the money in Zürich,' Mercedes said.

'And the code?'

She thought for a moment. 'Brilliant,' she said.

Out on the street, she took a deep breath. Downtown now to one of those gigantic islands around Wall Street on which a bank, some civic art, a subway entrance and a tower block all crowd together. The bank was a Manhattan giant where names are nothing.

She'd called ahead to arrange an appointment. It didn't matter much with whom; the key was to pass the guards who kept the barrier between the public marble and palms and the inner offices in the tower. She needed only to broach that line. Naturally, a private banker was happy to conduct Miss Zenon's business. Naturally.

She had dressed severely, camouflaged like a practical woman who'd unsex herself for a vice-presidency; she was almost plain.

106

The guards patronised her and called her 'dear'; they didn't snap to attention. She crossed, briefcase in hand, to the elevators.

She wanted to look back, to be sure she'd got this far. She was rehearsing in her mind what she had to do. If only the money got to Zürich, it would be private there – protected by Swiss law and, much more, by the Russian passion for dealing. It was Moscow, after all, which invented the Eurodollar market, Moscow that plunged into London property in the 1970s, and not with a subtle motive of undermining capitalism. The Russians like games, and dollars.

The guard had given her a little card to clip to her lapel. She looked at the other plain and serious persons in the elevator; their cards had photographs. She wondered whether it was better to lack a card or have the wrong one.

Twenty-five floors up; humans were particles loose in a chamber of concrete and Calder stabiles, the corridors were long and grey. She went to her private banker.

A transfer to Costa Rica. A banker's cheque. A nominee account in Costa Rica, yes. No, she would not be passing the cheque through an account. She would be happy to pay whatever commission was appropriate, by cash or cheque.

The banker was a little troubled. Most manoeuvres were meant to be recorded on paper, most of the time. But he was easily persuaded. Miss Zenon was money, and chic, and introductions; you never said no.

Mercedes was back in the corridor, a secretary guiding her to the elevator, even threatening her with the private, express elevator which would take her right past the floor she needed. Mercedes smiled, but would not be steered.

On the twenty-second floor, she got off the elevator. She took off her visitor's tag.

The corridors here were bleak and grey. They opened into outcrops of beige carpet and grey cabinets; people put small, tenuous pictures of their kids on desks to warm the place a little.

A messenger was cantering down the corridor.

'Wire transfer room?' Mercedes asked, briskly.

She knew to ask messengers. They are too far down the hierarchy to question questions.

The messenger pointed.

The wire transfer room was a shuffle of paper, hemmed in with terminals and telephones. She stood by the first clerk and peered over his shoulder. He'd punched up a transfer order, office number to office number, and filled in details.

Upstairs, she'd had her banker make the transfer in front of her. She said it was urgent, could not possibly wait. And she'd watched very carefully to hear and see the numbers that he used.

'Office number' was 371.

She had the telephone authorisation code. She had the interoffice settlement account number. She wasn't entirely sure which was which, but she had a note of two strings of numbers.

She said to the clerk: 'Check the interoffice number for me, would you? I've got a client coming in who likes to see the bank working.'

The clerk shrugged.

'Read the screen,' he said, and went back to his slips of pink and white and flimsy.

She made herself track slowly down the corridor. Oh, but it was beautiful and simple: they never guessed she wasn't entitled to know what she seemed to know, so they confirmed it. All she needed now was a telephone.

So far, it was a gag. Now, it was theft.

Stolen money, she told herself, stolen back, and in the process, punishing the thief.

But she didn't know the wire room number. She had to call the operator, and an uncivil voice added with actual malice: 'Have a nice day.'

She dialled.

'I have a transfer for delivery in Zürich tomorrow,' she said. 'The interoffice settlement account number,' and she gave it; that would take the money out of Doña Augusta's account and into the pile of money ready to be dispersed around the world. 'The code,' she said, and gave it. That would authorise movement. Then she said: 'The paying account is –'

'Sorry, hon,' said a faintly campy voice. 'Not today we don't.'

'I don't understand.'

'The interoffice settlement number. Wrong. You'd better check it. It changes at noon.'

She repeated the number.

'Sorry, hon. It was good ten minutes ago, but not now.'

She was in a bare corridor, in a big bank, with a hustle of substantial security men; she held a dead phone.

She needed time to think, and she went to the women's room. She washed her hands three times.

Bluff, she told herself. They give you what they think you're entitled to have. Half the time that just meant not rousing their suspicions. But the wire room wouldn't help again and she had only her visitor's card. She had to find someone to phone.

She went back to the corridor and nerved herself. There was a secretary now at a reception desk. Mercedes demanded a phone number, for her private banker. The girl obliged and pushed across the phone.

'New here?' the girl said.

Mercedes only frowned, a chilling vice-presidential frown meant to say that any question was impertinent. She needed the suit and the mien to get her through.

She talked to her banker's secretary. She carefully didn't give a name. She just said the Costa Rica transfer was held up; he'd given the wrong number. Could he give the new one, please.

She found she'd crossed her fingers. She must not show any anxiety.

The secretary in the corridor watched her with interest. New, they wanted to act like monuments; they hated to be overheard when things had gone wrong.

But the secretary was giving the right number now, and Mercedes noted it.

'They've got you running about, haven't they?' The woman sitting before her only meant to be friendly, although there was an edge of satisfaction in her voice.

Mercedes shrugged. She went off down the corridor.

'Other way,' the secretary shouted. It wasn't a kind shout; it was more a reminder.

Mercedes went back into the wire room, still trying to stop herself seeming at all out of place but acutely aware that she had no plastic identification tag. Surely they'd notice and challenge her. Maybe the girl in the corridor, who'd had such good reason for doubts, would challenge her.

She fired the numbers over a clerk's shoulder. The numbers

tallied; it was routine. She ordered a transfer of seven million dollars from Doña Augusta's account, through interoffice settlement to Wozchod in Zürich. Code-name Brilliant.

She hadn't used the phone to the wire room because she'd suddenly realised how much that might matter. John Grey had said they recorded every call. There'd be no record of this transfer, only the suggestion that her private banker had done some private deal. And she didn't give a damn.

She had to stop herself smiling, make herself walk the harried, proper walk of the new officer. She saw the secretary on the phone and didn't care. She felt the visitor's card in her suit pocket and took it out, ready to be official again once the elevator came.

The elevator didn't come. She turned to see the secretary, and the secretary was talking to two men who had broad shoulders and alert muscles. She knew they were guards.

The secretary was flirting, of course. Just flirting. Or she was making some report or complaint that had nothing to do with Mercedes Zenon.

The secretary was pointing.

The elevator did not come.

The two men straightened, as though they'd made a decision.

She looked side to side. There might be emergency stairs, but to take them would mark her as a refugee and that would make her situation worse. Her smile was fixed.

The guards came up on either side of her as the elevator doors opened. She went to step inside, to join the few distracted people standing in the pool of white light; the guards came with her, as discreetly as they could. Nothing would dissuade them.

She turned to face the doors, anything to avoid the guards' faces. I can't pass security, she thought, without surrendering my visitor's pass. But if I show that pass, then these twenty-second floor guards will know I had no business in their territory. They'll believe anything the secretary said.

She sighed, without meaning to, and a short man by her side looked up. She thought of the screens and numbers that, she almost believed, were taking Doña Augusta's money and turning into tangible, luminous wealth a continent away. But she still had a trace of her mother's instincts – for what you can touch

110

and put away. She knew, but she didn't feel, the link between those green screens and money for Leon.

'Miss Zenon.'

She hadn't noticed who stepped into the elevator at each floor. They were clerks, messengers, assistants, the kind of people who left their personality at the door with their lives. Now she blinked and looked around. She half-knew the face, some trace of memory from that Diaz party in Leon. A sizeable, amiable man.

'How nice to see you,' she said. She could get out with this man. She could worry the guards.

Ian Carpenter said: 'I didn't expect to see you here.'

The elevator doors opened and shut again, and the little box was crowded. The guards had to move very close to Mercedes; she could feel their breath.

Carpenter sensed what was happening. He saw Mercedes distracted, and embattled; he thought of Aurelia. He thought of little else.

'These men,' she said quietly, 'are bothering me.'

The guards looked awkward, but they didn't move.

Carpenter said: 'Miss Zenon is with me.' He said it with such authority that the guards did not question whether he had authority at all.

'Sir,' one of them began.

'Yes, yes,' Carpenter said, and Mercedes moved herself closer to him for shelter. 'But I'll be responsible.'

'Sir, I'm sorry. If we could talk privately –'

The guards looked for clues: his pass, her ID.

'– if you could identify yourself –'

'Ask Mr Leventhal,' Carpenter said.

The elevator seemed to stop at every floor until the eleventh. There the doors shut for the last time and it went into express mode.

'Mr Leventhal,' Carpenter said drily, 'is your chairman.'

And the doors opened on the marble and palms of the ground, and Carpenter swept Mercedes out of the elevator and up to the bank of guards.

He said, very quietly: 'You do have a pass?'

Mercedes retrieved her square of card and handed it to the

111

guard, who said: 'Honey, I hate to let you go. You just lose your pass next time, you hear?' Mercedes smiled. Behind, the twenty-second floor guards came charging to the desk, bumped into each other and stopped short. They were at their limits.

But they heard what their colleague said, and they rounded on him.

'You better learn you don't talk to ladies like that,' one said. 'Not any more.'

'Sorry, I'm sure,' said the deskman. He knew something else was bothering his colleagues.

They stood and watched Mercedes through the revolving doors. The reflections stopped them seeing her sidewalk dance, a bright, triumphant spin.

Carpenter looked at her much more directly than she wanted, as though he knew her and had a right to answers. He almost thought he did. 'What,' he said, 'were you doing? Exactly?'

'I went to the bank,' Mercedes said. She couldn't stop smiling.

'And the guards were there to protect you?'

Mercedes said: 'Those men were guards?'

'They were guards,' Carpenter said. He hailed a cab and pushed her unceremoniously into the back. He had been so infuriated with Aurelia's wilfulness, her other lives; he would not let it happen again.

'They hate it when you go to the bank,' Mercedes said. 'All bankers do. They'd much rather play with your money on their own.'

'You can tell me,' Carpenter said.

Mercedes looked anxious for the first time. She was glad to be clear of the bank, glad to be speeding north, but she did not know this man.

'You can tell me where we're going,' she said.

'Lunch, I guess,' Carpenter said.

'Do I have a choice?'

She wanted to look angry at the affront in this offhand kidnap. But she was thinking of seven million dollars, of Doña Augusta's fury to come, of the money for Leon; she was complaisant, and then she was giggling.

He said: 'Maybe I shouldn't have said your name out loud.'

'We can go to Bar Lui,' Mercedes said. 'I like that.' She settled herself in the corner of the cab, long legs stretched out and stroking against each other; she felt good. She couldn't stop herself running a hand against the silk of those legs, for the sheer joy of it. By shifting a little, her douce skirt parted and she could feel the leather of the seat against her thighs. She laughed out loud.

'You did something good,' Carpenter said.

'I know you,' Mercedes said. 'I don't know who you are.' She felt hot enough for any adventure.

'We were at that Diaz party,' Carpenter said. 'Hostages together.' He shut the partition between driver and passengers.

'That's like being at school together,' Mercedes said. 'Did you see Aurelia since then?'

Which was when he gave himself away. Until then, he'd held the advantage; he was the one who knew. But when the name of Aurelia came up, the concern in his face wasn't casual. Mercedes could see a geography of feeling.

'I saw Aurelia,' he said.

Mercedes leaned forward, very serious. 'What happened?' she said. 'I knew something had happened. I felt it.'

'I'm not sure,' Carpenter said.

'I thought,' Mercedes said, 'she might have gone underground by now.'

He almost laughed at how appropriate the phrase was, a broken-back laugh. 'People do that,' he said.

'I think she was an Amadista,' Mercedes said. She wanted to see his reaction; she couldn't tell if he'd chosen a side in her particular war.

'Maybe,' Carpenter said. 'A lot of people are.'

'You wouldn't be,' Mercedes said. 'You're a banker. A banker who can do business with Diaz. There aren't too many of those.'

'I don't know,' Carpenter said. He was fascinated by the glitter of her, by the way she held her body like an invitation. And he felt at once disloyal to Aurelia and loyal, because this, after all, was her mirror.

At the end of lunch he made himself say: 'I heard she'd been injured.'

Mercedes said: 'I felt it. We're sometimes like one body; what she feels, I feel. I felt a terrible loss.'

113

Carpenter didn't quite know what to do with such openness. He said, defensively 'I don't know anything more,' and then he was annoyed with himself.

Mercedes shrugged.

They waited a moment for coats. It was an odd moment; he could have held her then, and she would have responded. They both knew it. She was glorying in whatever she'd done, lit up by it; he was seeing Aurelia.

'I won't tell anyone you were there,' Carpenter said.

'There's nothing to tell.'

He didn't believe her. He didn't see why she would lie to him. She knew him, didn't she, if she was truly one body with her twin?

'Then if I mention to Leventhal that you were there –'

She slipped into her coat. Who the hell was this man to blackmail her, to come so close to her, and what would he want next? 'I don't know what you want,' she said. 'Give my love to Aurelia, if you see her.'

And she walked out, her style so cold it kept away intruders.

He watched her go. He saw an Aurelia who'd calculated a face and nature for herself, a star, a woman outside any moral or social scheme he recognised. He also saw a body that made him ache: the same grace, the same dark eyes, the same kind, small breasts.

He couldn't leave it there.

The Señora Augusta Diaz Torres said: 'You lie.' Then, for emphasis, she screamed it.

The bank official said: 'But the transfer was made three days ago. Seven million dollars.'

'You tell me who said this? Where did it go?'

'Unfortunately –'

'You take the money, you tell me nothing?'

'There is some delay,' said the official, 'in the paperwork.' He meant confusion.

'But no delay in taking my money.'

'This was a properly authorised transfer.'

'I did not authorise it.'

'The bank can accept no responsibility –'

Doña Augusta put down the receiver with elephantine grace and hurled the phone against the wall. She stood with the ominous out-of-place quality of a duchess in an alley.

A black thought occurred to her.

Perhaps somebody she knew took her money. Perhaps the bank that couldn't tell where money went couldn't tell who gave the orders either.

She had a theory at once. She'd have killed Tomás Diaz that moment if she could have found him: scape-grace, light-fingered, always begging and tricking for the money his father wouldn't give. A little here for an emergency, a little here for family duty, a little more because of some embarrassment. She loved him so well she knew he'd steal from her.

And so she called Leon. But Tomás was away, she was told; in Geneva.

They had banks in Geneva. She'd see about that.

El Presidente's Sergeant-Secretary had found a number for Ian Carpenter in New York; he was a patient man.

'El Presidente,' he said, 'apologises. The night of the incident he foolishly made you a present of a watch. He would be grateful if you could return it –'

'I don't understand.' Carpenter resented the intrusion.

'It is very important,' El Presidente's secretary said.

The President must be losing his mind, Carpenter thought, because what could a watch matter?

'Naturally he would pay –'

The man must be sitting in his armed trap, waiting for the next humiliation.

'I don't know what you're talking about.'

How could Diaz remember one present among all the hundreds he distributed, all calculated at the time, all forgotten quickly: like the expenses of a business.

'The night of the incident,' the sergeant-secretary shouted against the static on the line. He had been determined to sound reasonable. 'You were in the Presidential offices –'

'I don't like the idea that I steal,' Carpenter said, obstinately. 'I'll send him a watch if he needs one so badly.'

115

'No, no,' the sergeant-secretary wailed, losing to the fizzing of the line. 'There is no question –'

'Tell your President,' Carpenter said, 'I see no point even in talking any more.' And he put down the phone.

He didn't think Diaz gave any object sentimental value. He never risked that much. And besides, Carpenter had everything to think about, everything except watches.

That day, ordinary as it was, he'd come to a conclusion: or rather, the conclusion came to him, fell like a shutter in his mind. It was impossible to deny and impossible to live with.

Aurelia was dead. He had tipped off her killers. He was responsible for her death. These things were now fact to him.

He had never betrayed, never caused a death; he could say better things in his favour, but those were a start. Aurelia's end was outside his moral scheme. He'd cut people out, played corporate games as hard as any man, and in those games there had been losers; but not victims. He knew how to set traps and bait them, then walk away from the caught. But that was only calculation, its consequences not profound. Aurelia was dead, and he'd done it with four words.

'But I have company . . .'

He needed a drink. He poured too much Scotch into a glass and drank it neat.

'Company . . .'

Killing with words was a kind of magic, and he had no magic in his mind. It was such a small cause, such a terrible effect, like a spell. He had to do something, and he did not know what.

Burn a candle. Not in his church, which in any case he had long ago left. Offer a confession. Make an offering.

He saw it was ten. Checking the time made him wonder where he'd put that goddamn Rolex, the one that Diaz wanted so badly. It must be in the bathroom, he thought. He poured more Scotch.

He looked around at the dead, careful taste of the place, the quite new copies of the *New Yorker* lying on a beige ground; and he knew he needed space and brilliance. A shock of coke would help, an hour up, but that was not provided in this corporate apartment.

He found himself thinking about eyes in the cab downtown, eyes in the glass of the windows, Aurelia's eyes, when they were painted and when they were bare; Mercedes' eyes, drowning him. He imagined rooms where all the light was broken and made into colour by the refraction of those eyes.

It was his fault. But he did not know how far guilt should extend. He didn't pull the trigger. He didn't knowingly betray the woman. He had rushed to save her, but found nothing he could do.

The whisky was getting to him. He thought, in a maudlin and undisciplined way, of a child crushed by a drunken driver. He thought of the firm that made the drink, the bar that served it, the friends that bought it, the driver that consumed it, the ill luck of the driver that consumed it, and why the child was on the streets at all in the path of the car. Whose fault, whose responsibility?

Oddly, it was comforting to hide in those thoughts.

The cab left him outside Odeon, first in a line of cabs which seemed to land and empty like a shoal. He saw her at once.

She was bare-shouldered, in a sketch of chiffon, and she smelt giddy. She saw him, but she passed him, looking.

He watched her go. She was with some big, blond man who looked like a model. He felt sick.

Cars slipped by in the rain. He didn't need Odeon now, or dinner or the night. The long steel hull of a truck cruised by. He felt dazed.

He tried walking, as though the cut of the rain would wake him. Or punish him, he wasn't sure. There was a bent man in a doorway, in a knitted hat, hissing: 'Smoke, sense, ludes . . .'

He needed chemical life. He turned down a vial of crack; he didn't want to smoke. He sniffed up a dime of coke, and the dealer watched him walk away. Only a casual score; no reason to warn him.

Carpenter was up and edgy now, sure about things but startled when a steel door rolled up a wall and in the grey light two men stood still by a truck, like a diorama in dry ice.

The rain was sharp on his face. He needed some refuge. He passed a building on an unlikely street which had changed from warehouse to condominium, with a lit hallway and lights over each bell.

But he couldn't go in. He had no privilege here. He was wet

and high on a dead street. He wanted to know which way to walk but the drug wouldn't let him have doubts. It tugged him forward.

He began to hear silence, and in that silence a car coming closer. Cars don't chase you. Cars go their own way, down the same streets; they only seem to follow.

But when lights appeared at the head of the street, Carpenter stepped aside into a doorway. He had the strongest sense that someone was after him. The long, low car went softly past.

He felt something soft around his feet. When the car had passed, he struck a match and looked down. A man and a woman were curled against each other in a case of breath and dirt.

He looked out of the doorway and went down the street with exaggerated caution. The sleepers wouldn't trouble him; they were warm for the night. He'd never seen such people together.

He heard a shot.

He told himself it was a car backfiring, or maybe a firecracker in the wrong season or a steel door dropping into place. But when it came again, he was sure it was a gun.

The streets were mazes. He wasn't sure which way to head, and the sides of the buildings seemed to hold him at a distance, not offer him shelter. The rain was beginning to wake him and bring him down, which was unkind, and he could see no way out.

Someone was shooting, and he was the only target in the streets.

No taxis. No other cars to flag down, and besides, how to know which cars to trust. They wouldn't stop for a bedraggled man in a warehouse street in any case. He could see the stars above his head, and he knew any sudden light would blind him now.

He was by a six-lane highway and he could smell the river. Way over the water, he saw the Maxwell House Coffee Cup, huge in red neon, dripping and dripping into the night over New Jersey. He saw piers, and square buildings.

Up to his right there were people and lights, a barstrip beginning to open for the night; to his left, by the river, were the covered piers. None of it looked safe, but he had an instinct to get out of the way, to be safe in the dark.

The first pier was shuttered. Inside, trucks shifted; trucks meant people and he couldn't quite explain himself. He was more tired than he'd thought, and more battered by the past days.

The second pier was promising. Its door was broken down and inside was a great tin-roofed cave with catwalks running side to side. He crawled inside, and he heard his heart working. He could also hear the river as it stroked and sucked the piles of the pier, breaking it down with kindness.

Far down the great empty hall he could see a light flare and die. He was startled until he saw the pinpoint red of a single cigarette.

He sat against a wall on broken wood. He had time to pull himself together. He shivered. As his eyes began to adjust to the deeper dark, he lost his sense of safety. He could see men walking. It was as if the stones became drifters, the metal bones of the pier separated out into figures in blue jeans. His eyes were wide.

The lights hurt. Through some door he couldn't see, a car had come into the body of the hall, and the headlights sent the thin figures scattering.

He watched. It could be the car that chased him, but how could he know, and how would they spot him among all the other figures.

All he could see was light. Against the light, he saw shadows move like warrior ghosts, infinitely tall to the distant ceiling, wide and strong as monsters. Then they were too close to him, far too close for him to run, and his back was against the wall.

One of the shadows grabbed at his arms, held them forward. The shadow tore the watch from his arm and then threw him down. Carpenter saw the shadows diminish into men and vanish into the car. He saw the headlights moving off.

He picked himself up. He had lost a watch, not his life, and his own damned fault for being on the wrong street in the wrong city at the wrong time, without even thinking where he was. He made himself walk. He was shaky at first but he grew confident. A man said out of shadow: 'You OK?'

'I'm OK,' Carpenter said.

He'd get the bastards, he thought. He crossed through the tiny door and onto the street again. There was a set of weathered beams there and he sat down abruptly as though someone dissolved the sinews in his body.

He sat, helpless.

And now the car was back. He could see it coming, see it peel off from the main highway onto this side road which must once have carried the trucks for the piers. The car was coming, and he was out in the open.

He tried to brace himself.

He saw the limo pull to a halt and the door open. He expected the shadows again.

He saw a woman's long legs, and he smelt perfume.

'You don't know where you are,' Mercedes Zenon said.

Carpenter smiled ruefully. 'I could tell you,' he said, 'if I could move.'

'Did they take anything?'

She was supporting him now, propping him towards the car. He tried to make himself strong and straight. He was grateful for the warmth of the limo.

He held out his wrist, which was bloody and bruised. 'They took my watch,' he said.

'Nothing else?' Mercedes seemed surprised.

Carpenter felt for his wallet. Credit cards, cash, all the lifelines of a professional life, all in place.

'They only took the watch,' he said. He thought of the call from Leon and Diaz's sudden worry about his watch. It seemed absurd.

He remembered most how Mercedes didn't comfort him during that journey. She was watchful, and she was matter of fact. She said she'd seen what was happening after he walked away from Odeon. She felt she owed him one.

He felt exhausted and comforted; he slept.

He woke the next morning in a wide bed, in a bright room. He felt across the sheets. Nobody there. He smelt the sheets; he thought there was scent.

Mercedes came in, sleek and efficient, and Carpenter could only manage the blink of an old, sore cat.

'What you're feeling,' she said, 'is pain.'

He tried to sit up. 'I guess,' he said. He looked around. 'Am I in your bed?'

'Yes.'

120

Carpenter laughed. 'It's like that fairy story,' he said. 'A man gets three wishes, but he forgets to wish to remember.'

She sat at the end of the bed. 'You have business today?'

Carpenter thought for a moment. 'No,' he said, 'I've done most of my courtesy calls. I guess I should book a flight back to London.'

'Why did they want your watch?'

'I don't know.'

She was outlined against the sunlight, her long slim legs like shadows in the shelter of her skirt.

'You knew Aurelia,' she said. 'And Aurelia – she's gone because of Diaz, I suppose.'

Carpenter said nothing. Aurelia's death was a secret he had trouble sharing with himself.

'Would you do something for Aurelia?' Mercedes said.

She couldn't know what she was saying – such a casual offer of redemption.

'You knew about Diaz and his money,' Mercedes said. 'Didn't you? Why else would a banker hang around Providencia?'

Carpenter sat quiet.

'That money would help Aurelia's side,' she said. 'Finding it would be something for Aurelia. Wouldn't it?'

'This is like a courtroom,' he said.

'But then you're a banker, aren't you? There's no reason you should have moral principles, not about money. You don't have to care about people in Providencia.'

He stared at her. 'And you? You sound as if you've been rehearsing.' He swung himself out of bed. 'Did you have to learn the lines?'

'I have just one question. What's so hot about that watch of yours? Why do they want it?'

'I have no idea.'

'You don't know?'

'It was a perfectly ordinary watch. Now Diaz gave me a watch in Providencia, but I left that in the apartment –'

'In the apartment?'

And he caught her eye.

'If it matters so much,' she said, 'we need it.'

He caught her urgency and bundled himself into clothes the

maid had pressed overnight. They drove furiously into the corporate East Side and crashed past the doorman of the building.

'Sir,' the doorman said. 'You're 6A aren't you?'

'Yes,' he said, hardly stopping.

'I have to announce you,' the doorman said.

'But I'm the tenant. I mean, my bank –'

'There's been some difficulty,' the doorman said. He was writhing on the point of embarrassment. 'An incident.'

'What the hell sort of incident?'

'The police are there,' the doorman forced out, and turned quickly to work his bank of phones. The elevator came as he finished his call and he bellowed at Carpenter: 'Sometimes the gentlemen want to know –'

Carpenter said 'Pardon me' at the apartment door; it came out like stage English.

'Yeah,' said the senior cop, who was so elegantly built he wore his shirts too tight.

'I am Ian Carpenter. From London.'

He didn't have to be told what had happened. There was little to spill in that blank place, but the intruders had managed. The ripping and breaking had almost brought the place to life.

'You've been burglarised,' the cop said. 'Ian Carpenter from London. Terrible manners these people have.'

Carpenter's briefcase lay open, locks smashed, cigarette lighter (in corporate onyx, of course) used to set the papers alight. Most of what remained was ash in an envelope of sour leather.

'Could be worse,' the cop said, philosophically.

Carpenter went into the bedroom and Mercedes followed. His cases had been flung about and his clothes taken down and slit where they had no pockets. In the bathroom, they had even cut the shaving stick, like customs officers.

'Is it gone?' Mercedes said.

'It must be gone,' Carpenter said.

The senior cop had propped himself against the doorjamb, almost posing. 'We'll make a report,' he said.

'There's a gold Rolex –'

'There are thousands, Ian Carpenter. Don't get me wrong, but

122

it ain't worth the paper to report it.'

'But this watch –' Mercedes said.

The cop smiled, lazily, and stopped flexing for her. 'Lady, you know this town.'

When the cops left, Carpenter asked: 'Why does that watch bother you so much?'

'I don't know who else you do business with, but you do business with Diaz. He gives you a watch, and suddenly people want your watch and attack you or break into your apartment. Diaz just wants his watch back.'

'And you,' Carpenter said. 'While the cops are still in the building, tell me this. What did you want at the bank yesterday that was so unofficial the guards caught you? You're not some penny ante thief, for Christ's sake, and the guards don't follow you for seeing your banker.'

'You helped me.'

'For a minute, in the wrong light, I thought you were someone else.'

'I know,' Mercedes said. 'You did last night.'

The line was left in the air, dangerous only if touched.

Mercedes was puzzled about the watch. Why should Diaz set in motion such an elaborate, risky machine to bring back a simple watch? Anything curious about Diaz intrigued her; she knew so little about where he found his friends or hid his money. She couldn't let Carpenter go until she knew at least why the watch mattered.

Which was why she took his arm as they walked on a brisk morning down Fifth Avenue. The sun made a crisp theatre set out of the shops. She nudged him to Rizzoli's window and looked at a pile of black and silver books – culture in packaging, by the set. She said they should go to the 57th Street galleries, maybe have lunch at the Russian Tea Rooms. Fill his day.

She felt surrounded. It was an instinct first, a sense of discomfort; then it was three substantial men who formed a triangle around them.

Mercedes thought of celebrity freaks, with their unspeakable needs. The day was too bright for the threat to seem real.

And Carpenter was less used to menace. He assumed this was

123

New York manners, and went to shoulder the largest man aside. But the man wouldn't budge.

'We need the watch,' he said.

Carpenter stared into the window. He could see the trap now.

'Nobody's going to help on a New York street,' the big man said. 'Not when we look so much like cops.'

Carpenter caught Mercedes' eye. He nodded minimally, and hoped she knew what he meant.

'Don't make trouble,' the big man said.

Carpenter swung a fist at a hard belly, and Mercedes brought a sharp toe up into a second man's groin. In the moment of consternation, they broke out of the box and started pelting down the Avenue, through the morning matrons about their expensive business, cannoning off pinstripe men and dodging past all the promise in the windows.

Carpenter hung back, to be between Mercedes and the men. He could feel the life and adrenalin come back. He didn't care who these men were. He had a reason: he could save Mercedes. Now he just had to fit the actions to the reason.

'Djinn,' Mercedes was shouting. 'Half a block.'

He didn't understand, but he followed, careering across the Avenue between stalled taxis and running up against a joint-smoking, Walkmaned roller-skater flourishing his muscles the wrong way up Fifth Avenue.

'Here,' Mercedes said. There was a tall glass door, painted black and white and marked very clearly 'By Appointment Only'.

Inside the door was a desk with a pretty, angular girl whose eyes made no concessions, and a tall black man in formal dress who could either be Southern elegance or a karate champion, depending on who came in from the street.

'Good morning,' said the girl, who had been made up to sit in a spotlight. 'May I have your names?'

'Mercedes Zenon.'

'I'm so sorry,' the girl said, not meaning it. 'I have no record of an appointment.'

'You shop here by appointment?' Carpenter said.

'Naturally.' The girl was a Medusa in model's guise. 'If you want to make an appointment, perhaps Mr George would be able to see you. Later today.'

124

Mercedes could see through mirrors that the three bulky men were on the sidewalk outside. They seemed to be debating, which would not hold them long. 'Now,' she said.

The butler was no longer deferential; he was letting his presence be felt.

'Please call Djinn,' Mercedes said.

'He is in Beverly Hills,' the girl said, adding, most unpleasantly, 'unfortunately.' She meant: 'Unfortunately for you.'

There was a wall of Baccarat perfume bottles, one full, and a set of the famous in Lucite – Frank Sinatra, a Kennedy and a Saudi Prince, all 8 by 10. There was no easy escape.

'Miss Zenon,' a soft voice came from behind the bottles, 'but what a surprise. We have nothing organised, nothing laid out. We do not have the gentleman's sizes –'

'I need a favour,' Mercedes said, through the bottles to the anonymous, caressing voice on the other side. 'Would you get me out of sight of the street immediately?'

And Mr George emerged, said 'Naturally' and quickly led them past the wall. There was a room of wardrobes and a white stair curving up.

'I had no idea,' George said.

'You could show us shirts,' Mercedes said.

George was nervous, but he was also the perfect salesman, and the routine allowed him to seem calm.

'Egyptian cotton,' he said, presenting a pile of shirts, 'naturally. Woven in Switzerland, made up in Carrara.' He looked at Carpenter, a little unsure. 'Carrara, Italy. Naturally.'

Carpenter looked at the shirts. They were ordinary, if good shirts, at $300 a time; the distinguishing mark was a single coloured button. If you wore a tie, Carpenter reflected, it was a $300 secret.

Mercedes was more tactful. She praised a tapestry hanging from pegs. 'The chapel of Louis XVIII,' George said, adding with the mechanical need to make distinctions, 'a private chapel, naturally.'

Carpenter felt a little like a kept man.

A buzzer went. George peered over the balcony and saw the butler blocking the way of three determined and large men.

'Dear, dear, dear,' George said. 'Dear, dear.'

'They were following us,' Mercedes said.

'How terrible,' George said. It wasn't clear whether he meant Mercedes' plight or the thought of thugs fisting down the wall of Baccarat.

He pushed them into an inner office. There was a white marble desk and lighting like Heaven in a 1950s movie; there was now a single star in Lucite, star of stars. Carpenter saw it was Cary Grant.

George brought forth from a drawer a mink-lined box in which lay a Colt revolver, tricked out in gold.

'Mr Djinn designed this,' George said, unnecessarily. 'If the gentleman is competent with a revolver –' He fussed in a concealed closet and brought out a heavy overcoat, black astrakhan. 'This is bullet proof,' he said. 'Since Mr Reagan's incident –'

He broke off his pitch to answer his phone, and returned smiling. 'I think,' he said, 'your troubles are over. I have an appointment at twelve with a gentleman from the Arab world and his bodyguards are arriving now. You'll forgive me if I leave you –'

Mercedes said: 'Is there some other way out?'

'Yes,' George said. 'Oh yes indeed. And you must not think me presumptuous,' he was blushing, 'but perhaps, if you could tell nobody that you were received at Djinn without an appointment.' He looked beseeching, like a labrador in need of love.

'Of course,' Mercedes said, and the straightness of her face was heroic.

They were sent through cutting rooms to a basement and then through corridors to a service elevator which came up in an unlikely building on Sixth Avenue.

'They don't have the watch,' Mercedes said. 'They still don't have it.'

'I don't have it either. I was sure I left it in the bathroom.'

She looked at him with sheer exasperation.

'Call me,' she said, 'if you find it.'

*

He settled into his boardroom chair and dusted off his mind. It was an organ he felt he'd neglectd in the past forty-eight hours.

As he waited for the others, Leventhal's secretary bustled in. She was a wonderful shield of a woman, big and kind, and she was obviously concerned.'

'Mr Carpenter,' she said. 'Oh, I'm so glad you're here. You must have left this in the men's room when you were here yesterday. It has an inscription and everything, so I knew –'

Carpenter took the watch from her.

'You're very kind.'

'Not at all,' she said. 'I'm just glad you have it back. Mr Leventhal will be here in a moment.'

He put the watch under a light. It wasn't new. It was gold, certainly, and solid. The date was at the top of the dial, in working order, above the words 'Rolex, Oyster Perpetual, Day Date' and then 'Superlative Chronometer, Officially Certified'.

But that was what any Rolex said, he thought. Diaz couldn't need the watch back if a photograph would serve.

He thought it must have a serial number, and he fumbled with the case, it tiny handle and the edges of the dial.

'It has an inscription and everything . . .'

He was teasing himself. He turned the watch over, and saw: a plot of lines, like a maze, with a cross-hatched square at its heart and the words GoTo Boca Raton.

He held the engraving up to the light, trying to see some subtler pattern in the lines.

The words. GoTo Boca Raton was like some Chamber of Commerce reward, some inspired promotion; but the slogan was curious and a Rolex is an expensive advertising medium. And the maze, or the plan, meant nothing. Perhaps it was something in Boca Raton, a house or a garden; but it could as well be the gardens of Vauxhall or the Metro system of Toronto.

At least a watch has one singular thing: its serial number. And there would also be a model number. Together, those could be some code: an account number perhaps. They say when Sanjay Gandhi went down in flames, the family cried for the loss of his watch – which carried the numbers of their Swiss accounts.

Leventhal saw Carpenter playing with his watch and assumed

a rebuke. 'I'm so sorry,' he said. 'Trouble. From your part of the world, too.'

Carpenter said: 'I was just looking at this watch.'

Leventhal threw himself into a chair. He was a man of great physical elegance, a perfect patrician whose father, as it happened, dealt in smoked fish on the lower East Side; but sometimes the energy burst out of him.

'This'll amuse you,' he said. 'We have a client who says someone's taken seven million dollars out of her account, without her say so. Naturally, she's cross. Impossible, of course; but you can't prove things are impossible, not nowadays. It must have been wonderful when the clients had to look into the eyes of some senior book-keeper and be silenced by all that honesty.'

'This is an Englishwoman?'

'God, no. I meant your adopted part of the world – Providencia. It's some silly, catastrophic book-keeping slip, a computer blip. We'll have it sorted before you leave the building.'

'Seven million,' Carpenter said. 'That's bad luck.'

'If it ever happened,' Leventhal said. 'The woman who's complaining is one of your Diaz clan, and you know how reliable they are.'

Carpenter snapped open a file and changed the talk like points on a railway; he didn't want to seem too fascinated.

'– and we'll confirm,' he was saying, 'that we manage the European end of the syndication. But we'll need to sweeten the terms. The Europeans don't all think they've got a duty to the world economy to save Brazil – they'll need a few points of interest as well as guilt.'

Leventhal said: 'You know your market. But we're stretching it, even now. We need the Brazilians to keep the payments up – if they defaulted on a salvage loan –'

'We think,' Carpenter said, 'you won't get the money without those extra points.'

Leventhal made notes on scrap paper and pushed them across the table. Carpenter read the figures and nodded.

'Then we can live with that,' Leventhal said. 'God knows they need the money fast, and so do we.'

His secretary whispered through the intercom and Leventhal excused himself for a moment.

128

Carpenter set the watch on the table. 'GoTo Boca Raton.' A maze. A model number and a serial number, maybe some other inscription in some less usual corner. For the moment, he wanted to solve the mystery, but much more he wanted to know what the mystery was about – why he'd a sore arm and a cut head, why this information was worth a mugging, a burglary and a daylight assault. Why was it so urgent? And why did it start mattering only when he refused to send this particular watch back to Leon?

'I didn't mean to keep you,' Leventhal said when he returned.

'No, no,' Carpenter said. He realised he must seem abominably rude. 'I was just looking –'

'It seems,' Leventhal sighed, 'that seven million really has walked – gone to Zürich to talk to the Russians. Now we just have to find out who gave the orders.'

'To the Russians?'

'Wozchod,' Leventhal said, 'which probably means gold or diamonds – they have their brokers in Zürich. And your Mrs Diaz says she didn't send the money off.'

'She might have done,' Carpenter said. 'The Diaz clan seemed pretty edgy when I was last in Leon.'

'Oh, she'd been talking about pulling out her money. Talking about bearer T-bills, apparently, until someone pointed out she lived in America. I don't think she'd quite grasped the idea of tax.'

'In Providencia, the Diaz family don't pay taxes. They levy them.'

Leventhal said: 'I just hope the world doesn't get wind of all this.'

'You're lucky,' Carpenter said, snapping shut his briefcase. 'If there's one family on earth that never talks about money –'

And Leventhal nodded, a shade too keenly.

'I need to see the watch,' Mercedes said.

'Then you come here for drinks,' Carpenter said.

She didn't want to seem too eager, too dependent.

'I might have time. Tomorrow.'

'Tomorrow I'm going back to London. The morning flight.'

'That's impossible.'

'Listen, you need the favour –'

'I don't beg.'

'Just be here. Six o'clock.'

She came at seven.

'I have other things to do,' she said.

'So do I,' Carpenter said. 'I have a wife and bank in London. But you wanted to see the watch, so –'

He put it on the table in front of her. She looked at it closely, like a jeweller without the eye glass.

'It's an ordinary Rolex,' she said, after a while, 'except for the words and the marks on the back. And they don't make any sense.'

'I hoped you'd be able to decode them.'

'There's the serial number, of course. Numbered accounts.'

'You know where the serial number is?'

She ran a nail under the join between bracelet and case. 'If you take the bracelet off,' she said, 'it's usually engraved between the locks. At six o'clock.' She picked at the watch with a strong nail and handed Carpenter the dismembered dial.

There were six digits carved on the side of the casing: 2 5 9 1 3 5.

Carpenter shrugged. 'That could be anything, anywhere,' he said. 'Or just the number of a watch.'

'No,' Mercedes said. She held the watch closely and defied it to hide a secret from her; but it offered no revelations. 'It means something,' she said.

He thought: this is the only thing we have in common, except for Aurelia, and Mercedes is not Aurelia. The thought shocked him. He'd been a little mad about Mercedes.

'Where do we go from here?' she asked.

'We?'

'You're interested,' Mercedes said. 'They hit you. You were in Providencia hanging around Diaz. And you didn't send the watch back, did you?'

Carpenter stood up. He felt strong again, and he was annoyed. He would not let her back him into some absurd, illegal, hopeless scheme. He said: 'You know the old woman Diaz? The one who lives in New York.'

That hit home. She looked startled for a moment, and then

dissolved into a column item. 'I know almost everyone,' she said. 'That's what the papers say.'

'You know she's just lost seven million? Disappeared the day you were in the bank and the guards were chasing you. That's quite a coincidence.'

'Banks lose millions every day.'

'Señora Diaz lost the money, not the bank. The day you –'

'I heard you.'

She was sitting like a schoolgirl now, alert and nervous.

'I'm surprised,' he said. 'I saw all those pictures for Parfum Mercedes Zenon – all those pristine Alpine scenes. I'd have thought you'd signed a contract to stay pure.'

'I have a life to live, outside the pictures.'

'But only the life the company allows.'

'It's a standard contract,' Mercedes said. 'And what the hell do you know about modelling contracts?'

'Enough,' Carpenter said. 'That's the advantage of being a banker. You know a little about everything. Not enough to confuse you.'

'The perfume launch has started,' Mercedes said. 'It can't stop now.'

Carpenter shrugged. 'I thought you might have just a little trouble,' he said, 'if you were in jail.'

Mercedes said: 'This is where I say – you can't prove anything. Or am I meant to say – you got me bang to rights? I don't know the phrases. I never read the books.'

He stood very close to her. She could feel his warmth, smell tweed and cologne and sweat: she was under attack. She tried to keep as precisely calm as she had been.

'Don't say anything,' Carpenter said. 'I'll just call Leventhal at home –'

'You don't have anything to tell him.'

Carpenter said: 'It'll be a start. The guards will remember a woman called Miss Zenon if they're told to remember.'

'Then they'll remember you,' Mercedes said. 'You'll be implicated.'

'I doubt it,' Carpenter said. 'I just did twenty million in underwriting commissions with John Leventhal. Why would I bother to steal seven.'

131

He was relishing his power, and some kind of male authority that went with it. It was seductive like a woman.

'I did it for Aurelia,' Mercedes said.

He wasn't thrown this time; he expected her to say something similar.

'But who gets the money?' he asked. 'Who profits?'

'The money goes to Costa Rica, eventually. To the Amadistas' accounts. It buys guns or food or medicine or whatever they need. It's for Aurelia's people.'

'For your people?'

'I didn't quite say that. It's been a long time.'

'And you think some American court would acquit you because the money's for some bunch of Commie terrorists –'

'Listen,' Mercedes said. 'This isn't my war. It was Aurelia's war. That's why I got involved.'

'You did it for the kicks. For the rush.'

'I did it because I am a serious person, although you won't believe it. I care about Providencia, sometimes. I remember the people who killed my father and I want them out before they steal a whole country and take away all its hope. That's not much to ask.'

'It involves a revolution.'

'Letting them stay, the Diacistas, is a worse thing. It involves tolerating thugs who prey on people. It's like saying you won't use police to get rid of muggers on the street.'

'They're a government, not a gang.'

'You never lived with them, or under them. You were just their guest. You got the women, the drink, the drugs, whatever you wanted – I'm sure. Why should you see anything else?'

'I took a watch,' Carpenter said. 'That was kind of an apology because the National Guard had just knocked me out and dragged me off to the bunker.'

Mercedes stopped in her flow of rhetoric. She said: 'They did that to you?'

'Yes.'

'But how did you offend them?'

Carpenter was tempted to spin himself a hero's story but he was virtuous. 'You don't need to know,' he said. It was a bluff that made her speculate furiously.

'Do you know what happened to Aurelia?' she said quietly.

'I think,' he said, 'Aurelia is dead.'

His sense of power ebbed away, and instead he watched Mercedes' face like a book, trying to read her feelings.

'You knew her well?'

He didn't know how to answer. In a way, he knew her very well out of a few afternoons, a night or two; or at least he knew her intimately. But he did not have information, except on his skin. 'I knew her,' he said.

'Would you do things for her now? *In piam memoriam?*'

'I am a banker,' Carpenter said. 'I have no more interest in Providencia now. I have no interest in revolutions.'

'You could teach me things,' Mercedes said. 'Teach me how to find the money. You don't have to tell me how to take it away from Diaz; I can think of that.'

'You don't know what you're saying.'

'I do. I know you want to avenge Aurelia. You need to settle your heart.'

But how much did he owe to Aurelia? He had no answer now, any more than he could decide in the cab to Odeon. He knew he owed something to the bank, to himself, to some standards on which he'd prefer not to be cross-questioned; but not to a wider world. Serve something that wide, you have no basis for decisions, no possibility of action; morality is about who and what you serve, a choice among possibilities.

'I suppose,' he said, 'we could talk about the Diaz money. In general. I don't know anything in particular.'

'You'll tell the bank what you know?'

'You could tell me how you did it.'

She explained, immediately; confession loosened his grip on her, made his knowledge less remarkable.

He said: 'You're bright.'

'I had some help,' she said.

'Who helped you?'

'I can't confess for other people,' Mercedes said. 'That's called informing.'

She'd timed it right. He now had a vision of a rival, and that vision would turn him.

'Ask him,' Carpenter said. 'Why ask me?'

'Because you know about banks round the world,' Mercedes said. 'I need you for that.'

She made it clear she needed information, clues, perhaps expertise: he had something to offer. But that wasn't what he heard or saw. He saw a part of Aurelia that might slip away.

'Switzerland,' he said. 'In the 1950s. When Anastasio Diaz Sacasa started shipping out money, he'd most likely have sent it to Switzerland. Later –'

'He could have gone anywhere.'

'In principle,' he said, but he was warming to the problem. 'The Swiss sent Trujillo away; they even decided that officially. But they took Somoza's money and Diaz was everything they like – big money, hidden money, with an owner who's always a long way away.'

'He could be with Credit Suisse,' Mercedes said.

'He could be,' Carpenter said. 'But try to think like Diaz. He's hiding a stolen fortune, and he needs to keep it very safe – somewhere his wife and family can never find it. He's not going to walk in off the street with a billion dollars in a suitcase. He's going to go somewhere his friends go, a bank whose name he's heard at least in rumours. A specialist.'

'There used to be Muñoz,' Mercedes said.

'You're well informed. And after Muñoz, there was a successor – the bank for dubious Latins, no questions asked in Spanish. Diaz would have heard of it.'

Mercedes looked proud and expectant, sure she'd found the right ally.

'Rombauer et Cie, in Geneva,' Carpenter said.

'Good,' Mercedes said. She kissed him. 'That's where we start.'

134

·FOUR·

It was like a haunting. There she was, smiling on some late-night TV talk show, and he glimpsed her while changing channels; she was a colour picture across two pages of his evening newspaper, seducing a million registered readers and him; her signature folded out, white on black from the heart of a glossy magazine. She even arranged an invitation to the launch of Parfum Mercedes Zenon at the Dorchester, a pale affair of flaks and models, the awful energy of salespersons outnumbering buyers six to one and unofficial lines of good cocaine in the bathroom of the suite.

But he didn't go. She was a dream, like the impossible idea of finding and seizing the Diaz fortune. He had slipped back into the shape of his organised life, back to living at a distance with his wife and sometimes loving her warmth and kindness, even though he shared it with the world. Friends started dinner parties at once, like a carousel lit and starting to turn. He read memos on the operations of the bank, not just the deals and flurries that he stirred on his travels.

And yet, on that predictable round, there was always the face of Mercedes and, through her, Aurelia. He wanted to remember her on a threadbare bed in Bluefields, or painted at a party, but he kept remembering Aurelia when she was blooded and in a white dress, being pulled away for anonymous burial. He couldn't lose that image even though it was more dream than memory.

The night he went to Oxford, he was sure he had escaped. It was the gaudy for his year, *gaudeamus igitur*, a shuffle of men in middle age all half way to recognising and liking one another and themselves. They checked on marriages, success, ambition in a sentimental way, as primates pick for lice in an act of friendship.

'I saw your picture,' said a don, 'in some newspaper. With that extraordinary Zenon woman.'

'Yes,' Carpenter said, unhelpfully.

'Bankers really do lead such exotic lives.'

Carpenter drifted on. It was a soft spring night, full of stars and the smell of new flowers; the earth smelt fresh. He acquired the stories of the others, one by one – the shaggy, donnish man who had spent twenty years on half a dozen children and a single volume of some county history; the aesthete, painfully preserved, and the rugby star, now bloated, still together after all these years; the student hack who now hacked for the heavy Sundays, telling himself one day he'd do some important, worthy thing. They were all what they'd promised to be.

And the drink pulled back memory like a tide. He was realistic, he imagined; he'd been gawky and inept as an undergraduate, far too eager to buy other people's time and love, but still working harder than the others thought. His life looked like a fixed course, as though he'd never chosen but always accepted thankfully what presented itself.

On the wide lawns of the Fellows' Garden, he walked and remembered – a Republican revenge on some monarchist dining club, a London affair and the conspiracy to make it possible, summers on the river. He drew on the past and it made him feel absurdly bold.

His little knot of friends came to the wrought-iron gates of the Fellows' Garden and looked through to the wide lawns and the garden front of the college. Carpenter waited for his eyes to become accustomed to the light; he wanted to see the great weeping beech and the groves, the roses that would be opening.

As he watched, the weeping beech was suddenly lit with arc lights, and from within, then dimmed until it had a lively evening glow. He stared. He remembered the annual ball, and girls in long dresses drifting over the lawns to the private world that lay, screened by branches, round the tree's trunk. He remembered the smell of their skin after dancing.

The garden front, that range of Victorian buildings, were dusted with soft light that made the creeper shine a dark, strong green. He smelt stocks on the air.

136

And the don in their company said: 'Unfortunate. We agreed to allow some film crew –'

The middle-aged men in their tuxedos gathered to watch with all the intent and fascination of children.

The gate to the gardens opened, a shadow against the blue-white light, and a woman came through, her hair like an aureole from some pre-Raphaelite vision. She walked softly over the lawns.

The lights died.

The men in tuxedos thought of cars, brandy, home or hotel beds, but they could not nudge Carpenter into moving.

The lights came up again, this time only on the weeping beech, and the woman walked. She stopped to pick roses, and the don tut-tutted. She came to the trailing arms of the beech, pulled them apart and walked through; the tree closed behind her like a curtain.

'God,' the hack said, 'I need a brandy. It's chilly here.'

When she reappeared, she had all the ghostly glory that a million-dollar media budget can provide; he knew he was watching an illusion that had been calculated into life but he didn't care. Mercedes had haunted him for weeks; he was not at all surprised that she should be walking in the gardens here, just a step through this gate.

She was all professionalism, looking neither to right nor left, back in position at the garden gate.

'I must go round,' Carpenter said.

'Oh dear,' the don said. 'Yes indeed. I rather think we have a contract that they are not disturbed. I don't quite approve of this sort of thing, but it buys the central heating.'

Carpenter would not be dissuaded. He walked through the familiar quadrangles, the open spaces by the hall and then the elegant arcades beyond, until he came to the back of the tall, smoking lights. He had to make Mercedes something more than a ghost if he was ever to feel at peace.

She saw him, and she showed no surprise. 'We have technical problems,' she said. She had a man's coat thrown round her shoulders against the evening breeze.

'You don't seem surprised,' he said.

She shrugged. 'I'm working,' she said. 'Surprise is not what

I'm paid to show.' An assistant brought up a canvas chair and she sat; a make-up man came with paints. 'This is the romantic part of the campaign,' she said and then, as an afterthought, 'what are you doing here?'

He told her. He also said: 'Will you be in England long?'

'I go to Europe next,' she said. 'Department stores and parties. Paris, Amsterdam, Geneva. Then we have the last pictures to do in Italy.'

'You're going to Geneva?'

'It's on the itinerary,' Mercedes said. 'I have a few days off there before Italy.'

'You'll do – what?'

'I might talk to people,' Mercedes said, and they both knew what about.

'I'll be there,' Carpenter said, impulsively.

'We might overlap,' she said. It sounded less than an invitation.

The director shouted for quiet and action, rehearsed the lights and summoned her out to drift again through the soft black night on the lawns. She turned into her own public image, brilliantly.

In the foyer of the Geneva hotel, it was the image that hid her. She took the public spaces like a star, followed by an entourage of cases and cameras, and people asked no questions. They knew her name, her face and why she was there; there were people paid to make sure they did.

But when she came out of her suite, she had a choice. She could come out into the spotlights as Mercedes, or she could move quietly and alone, anonymous. The only Mercedes the city expected was the star.

She'd learned the trick over the years. Posing at airports for the hungry agency photographers was part of the job, the marketing of Mercedes; but once inside a city, that same fame was like a shield. When she came downstairs she could take a cab to the rue de la Corraterie without attracting attention; people knew she couldn't be Mercedes Zenon.

She stood in the brisk afternoon at the doors of Rombauer et Cie. She felt close enough to the Diaz money to taste it; but still did not know how to check where it was, or how much, let alone how to take it.

She walked around the bank like a burglar casing a potential job. It was one of those heavy merchant's houses with a mansard roof and an ungenerous door, domestic but also private as a vault. Through the door, she could glimpse a kind of drawing room, all rosewood and crystal, and sense its antiseptic air. The bank was a nursing home for money, where it went to be private or retire; and visiting hours were limited.

She could be a customer. They'd respect the money she was rumoured to have. She could be an investor, maybe. They'd remember that she was the daughter of George Vico, and while they'd fear that, it would also fascinate them. Or else she could claim to be the ambassador for old man Diaz, his trusted mistress. She just had to think of the trick.

She had looked through the list of banks in the phone book – banks, banks and even banks in liquidation (on rue de Lausanne). She had stood down by the river and looked around at the signs of banks, the brass plates and the neon boasts. And still she was sure the Diaz money must be with Rombauer.

She took a tram back to the hotel. The woman ahead was looking, sadly, at a spread of Mercedes in a fashion magazine; she'd broken the snap sample in the ad and the smoky, winy smell of the Mercedes perfume was in the air. But she didn't notice Mercedes; Mercedes would never ride in a tram.

She sat for a moment in the hotel lobby before she recognised Tomás Diaz. He was quarrelling with a girl at the reception desk, very straight with self-righteous anger, and the girl was sweet and efficient.

Tomás in Geneva was intriguing. He must be here to talk about money, or maybe arms; nothing else made sense. Maybe Tomás ran errands for the old man, ferrying the suitcases full of used notes, or maybe he, too, was in the dark and planned his own hunt for the family hoard. She thought it best not to approach him. After all, there had been that suspicion over diamonds in Leon; she was not sure how he would react.

He was at the door and waiting for a cab. He stamped his feet although the day was not yet cold; he was tense as a strung wire.

She went to the house phone and ordered her car, hoping

Tomás would have to wait a while. It came in time. It was worth the risk to chase him, to see where he was going and who his contacts might be.

He might go to some advocate's studio in a building full of lawyers, or he might go to some ordinary bank for a dull transaction – money for a skiing weekend perhaps. She told herself not to expect too much. But still she urged the driver to dodge and weave behind Tomás's cab, which he did with almost too much verve, hiding in the lakeside traffic and keeping close.

They turned along the river. Past rue de la Monnaie. A turn into rue de la Corraterie.

She had crossed her fingers so tight they'd turned white.

His cab stopped at the door of Rombauer et Cie.

She sat right back in her seat, telling the driver to go straight past the bank and up to the top of the hill by the Protestant Memorial. There, she got out and thought. Japanese tourists came milling past the long white wall with its rack of waterlilies at the base and took diligent pictures, looking puzzled. They asked her, with firm smiles, to get out of the way.

In the car again, she decided to go back the way she'd come, to pass the bank again, just in case.

She was lucky. There on the sidewalk, stiff with fury, was Tomás Diaz.

She told the car to stop. 'Tomás,' she said, and beckoned. Tomás Diaz stomped over, his petulance hidden by a soldier's manners; he almost saluted her.

'Can I give you a lift?'

Both of them thought the coincidence extraordinary; neither wanted to say it. And Tomás had another reason for disquiet. Ever since the party, and the hostage-taking, Mercedes had been a bad omen for him.

'I didn't know you were in Switzerland,' she said, brightly.

'I knew you were here,' he said. 'From the papers.' He seemed to disapprove.

'I'm selling perfume. It's surprising how much work it takes. I get so bored.'

She smiled, but he refused the cue.

'We should have dinner,' she said.

'I'm just visiting,' Tomás said. 'I won't be here long.'

140

'I was brought up here,' she said. 'I know where to eat.'

At the hotel Tomás sprinted ahead, clutching the sizeable briefcase he'd taken to the bank and still moving as if the case was heavy. Mercedes watched. It made no sense for him to be drawing money in Switzerland, not from a personal account.

He must have been refused at Rombauer's.

But they had seen him at Rombauer's, and he had an appointment grand enough to make it worth carrying a sizeable pile of money. She wondered whether he'd come here to smoke out his father's money or to arrange a future for his own. And the money in that case: was it even now on World Bank books as 'Housing Project 56, Leon' or some such thing?

She saw Tomás lugging his case and she had an inspiration. Suppose he'd made an appointment simply as Diaz and they'd seen him, even welcomed him, because they'd reckoned it must be the old man Anastasio? It would explain why he'd been admitted, with his sack of cash. It would also put the Diaz money in that particular bank.

He'd been turned away. Maybe they found him too small fry, or too unrespectable. Or maybe he'd tried to put money into his father's account and they'd seen that gesture for the scam it was.

She knew these things, she decided, although her evidence was only a hunch that the case was full and the expression on Tomás's face. And she was right; Tomás Diaz was in his hotel room, full of humiliation, puzzled that his hefty load of money could not buy him information, or friends.

He looked out to the *jet d'eau* pissing against the wind in the lake. He put on the television set and there was a news bulletin in some goddamned dialect he didn't understand: people he'd never seen before except for a sudden card of his father flashed on the screen. Then there was stock footage of guerrillas posing in mud. It was gone, and he was none the wiser.

He sat by the window and slowly surrendered to a great, luxurious rage. He picked up the case he'd tended so carefully and tipped it out on the bed, a flood of green. The bills were old and oily and scattered around or else came in tight, virginal wads. He threw them all, put his hands under them as he might have done under leaves in a northern autumn, and made the money fly.

141

The maid came to turn the beds and put a chocolate on the pillow; that was her job. Nobody had answered when she knocked.

She was a little woman, in her fifties, and when she saw the man dancing in a cloud of money, she blushed.

'We ought to see lawyers,' Ian Carpenter said, although it pained him, and although he knew that his wife would smile and take his hand.

She did. 'We can't be friends if we do that,' she said sweetly. 'People always fall out when they're getting divorced. It makes them enemies.'

'But that's what you want,' he said, reasonably.

'I just think we might be apart for a while. We are, anyway. You have the bank and I –'

She was so warm, so balanced that she could not even register the need for change.

'I suppose it's up to you,' Carpenter said. 'I wouldn't marry anyone else.'

'Exactly.' She beamed. He wondered why he was indifferent now to her sweet smile, and her generous breasts, and all the things he'd once loved.

In his office, he looked out of the window at a skyline that was sad and second-rate, where the Wren churches had been cut out by sprigs of unambitious towers, sometimes trying to claim importance by sheer bulk and sometimes so self-effacing in their toned and mirrored skins that they seemed to vanish, having appropriated all the sky and city they could reflect.

It wouldn't do any more. He thought at first he wanted just to be back on the road, with all the problems and chances that involved, but it was no longer that simple. He remembered Aurelia; he knew Mercedes; things were out of kilter.

He made some calls. After all, if there was really Diaz money in Rombauer et Cie, it would help to know everything about Rombauer.

Besides, it wasn't possible, the whole game. He knew that. So asking questions was just an indulgence, not a commitment.

He called a journalist friend who lived off being a consultant of some unspecified kind.

'He's not in the Groupement', he was told. 'He's not in the Club des Terrasses, not that he's strapped for $20,000. He could afford to join, but they wouldn't have him.

'But he's a proper banker. A proper bank, by Geneva standards. He's more than a *gerant de fortune*, just sitting on the money there; he has to do something with it. Of course what he mostly does is put it out in fiduciary deposits and lose it in his own schemes. Usual thing.

'Nobody really knows who his clients are. After all, even the second-tier grandees do their brochures in Arabic now, although the real grandees are still horrified at the idea of putting their name on the door. He's supposed to have lots of suspect Latins, like Muñoz did once, but suspect Latins have got the Caymans and the Bahamas and Uruguay as well, so God knows what he really has . . .

'And he has business of his own. Not much, but expensive – development, something he calls the new Gstaad. It's up a working-class mountain outside Lucerne, at the end of a rack and pinion railway. He'll need a lot of luck . . .'

Carpenter could see the man: a chancer in an Armani suit, a hustler. He'd be neat but expansive. And he still lay behind the formidable shield of Swiss law, where even asking for the books is industrial espionage. To get inside, to find out what really happened at Rombauer et Cie, Carpenter needed something more.

It came quite accidentally. He had talked to colleagues, saying he had problems syndicating the Brazilian loan (which was true) and needed some time in Geneva (which was dubious) and did they have anything they needed done?

There was someone: a partner who was mired in fighting a Wall Street merger in the oil business, where huge fish ate huge fish like a Balinese painting. Part of the defence was a suggestion of insider trading; and the way the insiders had traded was through nominee accounts in Switzerland.

'Fine,' said Carpenter

'The bank,' said his colleague, 'is Rombauer et Cie.'

'Really.' He wished he had the affectless 'really' of New York in his register.

'Small outfit, privately held, private bank. I don't know if we'll use the fact publicly, but it might help with the British

143

investment managers. They don't like impropriety when they have no cut.'

Carpenter ordered the tickets and looked out again at the skyline. It had a certain evening romance, he thought; it had possibilities.

If Rombauer et Cie was warehousing shares for corporate chiefs, Rombauer et Cie was in trouble; it was the kind of offence on which, for appearance's sake, the Swiss were happy to invade the occasional bank and pry out its secrets. But once that had happened, Rombauer et Cie would be no longer a perfect haven, and clients like Anastasio Diaz Sacasa demanded perfection. Their survival might depend on it.

'Since I'm going to Geneva anyway,' he told his colleague.

'Give her my love,' the colleague said, 'whoever she is. I loathe Geneva, anyway. And put the fear of God into them, will you?'

'Cheerfully,' Carpenter said.

On the plane, he had a fitful dream about a white-suited, straw-hatted gentleman thief, after priceless jewels and wonders, passing dogs and walls and steel doors and cobras trained to strike, and swinging finally, balcony to balcony, jalousie to jalousie, to freedom with his solid, glittering spoils. Money was something different, an abstract on a green screen, all codes and electronic impulses without apparent romance.

He jolted awake. 'Jalousie,' he muttered to himself. 'What is a jalousie?'

The middle-aged woman sitting at his side gave him a curious look, and he stared through the window at the night.

Money did have a romance. Money was in the mind, a network full of shams and games. Everyone took it for granted, but if you looked at it with an innocent's eye, it seemed terribly fragile. You had to be careful, stealing a billion, not to upend the whole illusion.

It was three-gin philosophy and he felt ashamed of it as he went through Customs. But still, he had a magic watch, a secret code, and he knew that somewhere was a treasure trove.

It must be in Rombauer et Cie. He had the number; he knew the bank.

And he had the first flicker of how to set that money free.

144

There were no dogs or cobras to outwit, but there was the limitless pleasure of screwing the Swiss.

They came down out of a sky blue as paint into the still white of the Alps. It took Mercedes' breath, as it always did, the moment when you begin to see the colours – cold, blue, brilliant colours – in the white. She stepped down from the helicopter smothered in fur and Rombauer followed, like the stop at the end of a sentence.

He bounded. He twinkled. He spread his arms expansively across all the Alps, and he said: 'The new Gstaad.'

She saw the mountain with her own eyes. There were a few concrete platforms, snow blown against them like lichen on a wall, and a blue crane that looked almost dainty under the morning rime.

'– the chalets,' Rombauer was saying, 'a hotel to match the Palace at St Moritz –'

It was a lovely dream, but it lacked fundamentals – no charming private railway to bring the rich but a rack and pinion and an awkward cable car; no horses for sleighs at this inaccessible height; no movie stars to pull the papparazzi and guarantee the ranks of guards who are proof of real celebrity. Rombauer had no past to sell, and the grand Swiss places all have a century since the English came, eccentrically, to sketch and ski.

Rombauer scuffed at the snow with mirror brilliant boots. 'The first thing we built,' he said, 'was a helicopter pad.'

Mercedes said: 'It must be expensive here.'

He was torn. He needed this woman for her black glamour, her power to bring a new generation up to his new Gstaad; but why should she? He also needed money, and he didn't want to understate the profits. There was Mercedes herself, who'd come into a sizeable estate, and behind her was George Vico.

'It's wonderful,' she said, 'after New York. All those crowds.' She looked out at the spires and hooks of rock, all under snow, an alien world which man left at night. 'All those yuppies crowding in who can't quite afford the city, and all the poor pushed out so soon there'll only be pretensions, and nobody wild on the street and nobody to clean or audition or amuse.'

'New York,' said Rombauer, hopefully, 'is not a home.'

145

It was her home, of course, but she was working well, nostalgic for her dubious Swiss roots.

'This would,' she said, 'be a fine investment.' She left it open whether she was thinking of buying a chalet or some shares.

'We are fully financed, of course,' Rombauer said.

'Of course,' she said.

In the helicopter she snuggled against him like a cat, so he could feel her warmth. 'You know,' he said, 'we might still arrange an equity position – if you were interested?'

'You'd really offer me something like that?'

'You'd be invaluable.'

Mercedes knew her worth, and she could guess Rombauer's. He was fully financed to buyers, but eager for more finance. He talked grandly about building his new Gstaad by helicopter, but nobody was working in the mountains, and this bird was hired and had to be returned rather promptly.

'You wouldn't want me,' she said, disingenuously. 'I have my name on so many things –'

Rombauer reckoned she must need some arrangement and he improvised. 'If we just knew you were interested,' he said, 'perhaps if we had pictures for the Press – it would help your investment.'

He was truly hungry; he had cashed the cheque already in his mind.

'It will have to be discreet,' Mercedes said. 'I have a contract with Parfum Mercedes Zenon – they own me for the next two years.'

'But you can go on holiday,' Rombauer said. And he was excited again, brimming with certainty about his schemes; and that excitement had everything to do with the smell and the warmth of Mercedes. He thought of Amazon armies, of life on some soft corrupt plantation, of glorious women –

'I never want to come down,' she said.

But when they had landed, she teased him for tea at the Club des Terrasses, which was malicious; he had to tell her how dull the Club was, how full of bankers who only warehoused money, how he, too, had the right townhouse and the right drawing rooms for doing business. She could see he was hurting, afraid that this pigeon, too, would fly off to be courted by some other bank in some other jurisdiction. Thirty years ago, the world's loose change was his living; now that living had drifted away to distant islands which hardly had banks or laws when Rombauer started out. He needed Mercedes.

In her hotel room, the flak from the perfume company was waiting. She made him open the wine and sat with one long leg drawn up under her and the other thoughtlessly stretched out.

Rombauer was in trouble. She was inside the bank. She was full of the exhilaration of the mountains and the chase.

She was impatient when Carpenter called. He sounded self-important with his news when she had discovered so much, knew (she was sure) where the Diaz money was, and that its guardian was in trouble. She told him to be more discreet on the phone; they might have a drink later.

It was her mission, her scheme.

And Carpenter, disconcerted, wondered why she suddenly sounded like some unconcerned business contact.

'We could have dinner,' he said.

'I have to see Tomás Diaz,' she said.

She didn't calculate the effect but it was formidable. Mercedes didn't know Tomás well; she didn't like him at all; certainly, she wasn't likely to collaborate with him. Yet both of them wanted to know where the Diaz money was.

She wouldn't do anything stupid. He was almost sure.

He went to bed with a grievance, like a boy.

'I'm afraid,' Rombauer said, his stub of a body stiff with anger. 'I cannot even listen to these questions.'

Carpenter shrugged. 'Then the American authorities will have to be told,' he said. 'That doesn't do any of us any good.'

'We have fiduciary deposits with your bank,' Rombauer said. 'Millions of our clients' money. We will simply withdraw them –'

'But not as fast,' said Carpenter, 'as your clients will leave you if they hear the police have been reading your books.'

Rombauer sighed, involuntarily. 'I have no reason to suppose that any client of mine is engaged in any illegal activity. If I did, I would not be allowed to do business with them. You know that.'

'I know the law,' Carpenter said. 'I also know you can choose exactly what you know.'

The two men were fiercely alert, but sitting in decorous chairs across an old partners' desk; they could have been an advertisement for the bank, except for the pressure each put upon the other.

Rombauer would not concede. 'If you have a warrant,' he said. 'Or a subpoena, or the authority of the Swiss police or even some legal instrument from the United States –'

'I am trying to save you all those things,' Carpenter said.

He calculated how far he dared go. He had to intimidate Rombauer but not infuriate him. They must keep talking.

'The accounts,' Carpenter said, 'are these.' He pushed over a list of the nominee accounts and added, at the foot of the paper and in ink, the numbers he'd copied from the Diaz watch.

'I don't see –'

'Nominee accounts. Fiduciary deposits. So we can be sure these are not Swiss clients, can't we. No reason for a Swiss to leave his money here and have it deposited in some foreign bank in your name; he's not subject to negative interest?'

Rombauer said: 'I know the system.'

'Unless, of course, he's a Swiss crook.'

Rombauer coughed.

'So we can take it these gentlemen are overseas,' Carpenter went on. 'And we happen to know who they are.'

'I can't comment,' Rombauer said.

'They're trading shares in their own company. Either that stops and you confirm what happened, or the US authorities are in here with warrants.'

'If I confirm this,' Rombauer said. 'What guarantee do I have that you won't simply tell the Americans?'

'Why should I? I don't want you to pull your fiduciary deposits with us. I don't even want you to have trouble. I just want to win a takeover.'

He could read the calculations on Rombauer's face, and he didn't want the man to have time to make a decision, yet. He said, kindly: 'I'm sure we can sort things out.'

The list of numbers lay before Rombauer. He wouldn't look at it, or even acknowledge it was there. 'There is no reason,' he said, 'why I shouldn't call the police. Under Swiss law –'

'Under Swiss law,' Carpenter said, 'we all have our problems. They tell me you've been visited by the bank inspectors, again. Their ideas about capital reserves –'

'That is confidential.'

'But they seemed to think you were living off cashflow, just that, which is eccentric for a bank. Of course, frankly, I'm always grateful I don't have to cope with Swiss law.'

But he did not mean that, and Rombauer knew it.

'But you do,' Carpenter added, very quietly. 'And the Swiss don't like what they call laxness in the books, and they like the occasional scapegoat. One bank down, the others are safe for half a decade. Isn't that the way they do things here?'

It was a gamble, a mess of gossip and assumptions, but it could work. Rombauer showed his nervousness because he had not yet raised the phone and called the police despite Carpenter's outrageous request. He could easily have Carpenter treated as an industrial spy, seeking to break the bank secrecy laws. But he hadn't done that. He must be afraid of investigation. And perhaps, if he was afraid, he would recognise the melodramatic history that Carpenter softly spelled out.

'Don't rush things,' Carpenter said. 'Take a day. I'll be at the Hilton on the lake.' He rose from his chair and the illusion of equals and colleagues fell away; he loomed over Rombauer. 'But if I don't hear from you,' he said, 'then you can expect the Feds.'

Rombauer said: 'It was good of you to call.' Carpenter thought for a moment that the man was being sarcastic but he was sincere. 'It would be better if we could settle this man to man,' he added. 'Between ourselves. Between banks.'

'Of course.'

Carpenter allowed Rombauer to throw open the tall double doors to the waiting room, and nodded to him as though to some higher servant.

And he saw Mercedes.

She sat like a fashion plate on the sofa, immaculate. He smiled at her but she did not acknowledge him.

Why did she have dinner with Tomás Diaz? Why was she here today?

He was determined to catch her eye. 'Miss Zenon,' he said. 'How nice to see you –'

'Have we met?'

Rombauer frowned. He disliked the slightest sense of social impropriety; he cared about appearances, and manners, despite looser ideas when it came to money.

'Miss Zenon,' he said, 'I am so sorry we have kept you waiting. But business –' He spread his white little hands.

She smiled at him and walked into his office without even acknowledging Carpenter. And Carpenter was left to move down the corridor, from one pool of golden light to the next, past the heavy wood and anonymous oils. He smiled at the secretaries and they nodded.

At the door, he walked into the damp cold afternoon, and felt nervous. He should never have left her in the bank alone. She didn't know what to do, what to look for. And if she produced the same numbers that he had produced –

He hailed a taxi and went directly to the hotel. There, he had room service bring a large envelope, padded, and wrote a brisk note.

He took the Rolex watch and put it onto the hotel Xerox machine to have a reminder of the patterns on its back. Then he packed the watch, carefully, into a box and into the padded envelope. He added the note.

There was a billion dollars at stake, after all. He didn't want to lose his chance at the money.

He called a courier service that was prepared to go to Leon. He addressed the envelope to Anastasio Diaz Sacasa.

Clients never visited so often, so Mercedes could not be a client, at least not an ordinary one. She came, she saw M. Rombauer, she was left in a pleasant room where clients rarely went and she made phone calls, wrote letters and made lists. She was helping with the new Gstaad in some unspecified way.

'I need somewhere in Geneva I can think,' she'd said to Rombauer. 'Somewhere that isn't a hotel.'

He said: 'I'm sure we could find you an office at the bank.'

And the arrangement was pleasant enough. She had another week before she must go on to Italy; she would spend it here. If she could, she would discover things.

She made sure Rombauer knew if she fixed a lunch, and on one day she took the high-spending wife of a Hollywood schlock producer up to the Alps on a mission that Rombauer gratefully took to be salesmanship when actually it was an alibi for the wife. If she brought him only prospects, he was grateful.

Inside the bank, though, she had half expected to stumble on information; and that did not happen, not at first.

She couldn't be anonymous in the corridor, not when she was a stranger; they always knew when she was coming and behaved as they would for the boss, the clerks and secretaries. She never saw the workings of the place, only its official look, and that seemed far removed from money. There was a teller, but under occupied in a hallway cage. There were the grand rooms, and then, like a history of fashion, she went from rosewood to taupe and chrome, to the modern functional rooms that seemed all struck out of one mould.

She couldn't dawdle in those rooms. She had to have some reason for being there. Sometimes it was information she needed – a phone book, a plan from the new Gstaad, the name of a good messenger service when her borrowed secretary was away from her desk. Her problem was that all the bank staff wanted to placate and serve her; her presence was so curious it must matter.

But she did sometimes go to the back rooms. She found herself following a clerk who bustled ahead with files. He dropped one and Mercedes helped him pick up the contents; he was grateful, but puzzled that she bothered. Indeed, he was suspicious; he looked carefully around the floor to see nothing had been missed.

The clerk flurried on, and Mercedes unfolded her hand. One slip of paper remained: a deposit slip. Five million dollars and change, newly arrived from a New York bank called Security National for the credit of an account called COBA.

It was ordinary. She wondered what she'd hoped for.

But the file clerk had turned into a little room where she knew, from earlier expeditions, there was a shredding machine and bags that went immediately to the incinerator. It was Rombauer's touch of reassuring melodrama.

The date on the slip was yesterday. Already, the slip had to be destroyed.

She walked back along the main corridor and went to talk to Rombauer's secretary. The pretext was thin, but the woman was far too polite to question M. Rombauer's guest.

And she listened. 'You just deny receiving the money,' she heard Rombauer say. 'That's all. You deny it. They had no reason to send it. Union Bank had no reason to pass it on to us so it didn't happen. They'll accept the denial. They'll think they just lost the money.'

A clerk was saying: 'But sir –'

She thanked the secretary for some trivial favour and returned to her own office. There, she called for a car and decided she did not need to tell Rombauer she was leaving.

In the hotel, she thought of calling Ian Carpenter. But she'd gone to such trouble to avoid him, to allow no connection between the two of them. Besides, she remembered John Grey III, and the faint, persistent fear she'd seen in his face; she had been too frenetically involved in perfumes and treasure hunts even to call him. She ought to call. He should know what she needed to know.

'Do you have any friends in the computer rooms at Security National?' she asked.

Grey said: 'You know they monitor every trans-Atlantic call? They have this machine that picks out key words and –'

'There might be something up,' Mercedes said.

'They call it Tinker Bell,' Grey said.

'Maybe there's a five million payment to a bank in Switzerland – out of Security National's own funds, I guess, and going through Union Bank.'

'You sound like George Vico's daughter.'

'I'm interested,' she said.

'He was always interested. Any information, any intelligence would do – it could always be used.'

'How do you know so much about –'

'I read the book,' John Grey said.

She lay, expectant and contented, on the wide bed and listened for the phone. Of course that piece of paper was significant; of course it fitted Rombauer's conversation; she was on a roll.

She could see the long lines of her body in a mirror. She shifted appreciatively. It was body enough to fascinate others, even bankers in Geneva, even Englishmen with clues, even –

The phone rang.

'It's not a fuss,' John Grey said. 'It's a panic. Their second major loss in a few weeks.'

'What happened?'

'A cable out of the wire-room to Geneva, to Union Bank. It went straight through and Union Bank took five million out of Security National's account. No reason not to. And then the money just disappeared. It was supposed to go to some Geneva outfit but it never reached there.'

'Did anybody mention Rombauer?'

'Oh, I see. No, nobody had a name.'

'Thank you,' Mercedes said. Almost as an afterthought she added: 'Are you well?'

'Yes,' John Grey said. It was a very serious answer to a casual question. 'Yes, I'm well.'

She didn't hear that mix of relief and gratitude until the phone was down.

She had her story now, she was sure: enough to blackmail Rombauer, enough to use him. The best that slip of paper could do for his bank was fill it with investigators before he had time to obfuscate; the worst was to break it.

She should tell Carpenter. He was her ally after all; he even had the clue to the Diaz account. But what use was that now? Rombauer would have to tell her what Carpenter knew.

She thought maybe Rombauer had learned her tricks at Security National, how to waft money out so quickly and simply it was never questioned, never traced. But that pride didn't last until morning. When she woke, she wanted to use the slip before Rombauer arrived, to make that clerk she'd trailed produce new clues.

'Something's missing,' she said to him.

He looked blankly polite. She wasn't authorised to know things; Rombauer had said nothing but she seemed to be a friend. They said she was George Vico's black daughter, which gave her a certain cachet even now. The clerk liked the word 'arrangement'; maybe this was one.

'I know it's missing,' she said, 'because I have it here. A deposit slip for five million dollars.' The slip lay face down on her desk; the clerk took comfort in thinking it was something else.

'I don't think we should discuss –'

'But Rombauer et Cie says it never saw, never wanted five million. This piece of paper says the money did arrive.'

The clerk looked flustered. He didn't know whether she was an insider, entitled to attack him, or an outsider impugning the bank. And since he didn't know, he could only stammer and bluster.

'My job,' he said, 'is to file and –'

'Hiding evidence,' Mercedes said. There was a word in English like 'misprision' but she couldn't remember it in French.

'It could be a police matter,' Mercedes said.

'But nobody knows,' the clerk said. 'You were the one who found the papers –'

Mercedes sat back sharply. It hadn't crossed her mind that the clerk would assume she was some kind of accomplice, her complicity to be defined later. He thought she was bawling him out, as Rombauer might.

'The bank,' Mercedes said, 'expects better.'

Her senses were raw. She had to hear everything, be sure this conversation was not overhead. And she had to press her advantage.

'I need,' she said, 'the COBA file.'

The clerk said: 'Of course. Will that be all?'

He came back and sat opposite her, arms round his body like bindings.

She took the file. She had asked for the one that didn't fit, the one whose name she could remember; she did not have the number for the Diaz account. She opened the pages and saw a thicket of rough figures, pencil marks, payments in and out. There was white-out, thick on the columns of accounts. She wished she had learned more thoroughly from George Vico and John Grey.

The clerk watched her closely. He had made a mistake in dropping the file and he was not used to making mistakes. He wanted to be sure this was not another.

COBA was registered in Panama. That was a start. COBA had

154

received a payment of five million two days before, which could be the money, vanished from Security National, that Rombauer denied he had received.

He wouldn't do favours like that for friends. People were bound to ask questions; he could be required to give answers. This was something he was most likely to do for himself. He was desperate enough to think of such a theft.

She thought, and she sensed the impatience in the clerk. She couldn't ask questions; she didn't know the right ones to ask, and the wrong ones would give her away.

Vico had talked about Swiss banks doing business in Panama. She remembered, vaguely, from talk heard through half-open doors and over dinner tables where she was patronised. This was a tax ramp for the Swiss, she thought. If you're foreign, your money maybe goes out in Rombauer's name to some grand London bank and that is legitimate; but it is not always possible. And if you are Swiss, then you pay withholding tax on money in a Swiss bank. It's cheaper if the money goes abroad to live.

But Rombauer didn't pay Rombauer interest, so the question of withholding tax did not occur. Why would he put five million he'd so riskily acquired into a Panamanian company meant to save his clients from tax.

To repair it. She was sure of that. You pour in cash from time to time so the books look good to the auditors and the clients get their interest cheques on time. And otherwise, you drain away whatever you need – for some new helicopter or new crane on that dazzling impracticable Alp.

She had the intuition, but she lacked the proof in these figures. There were payments in from various sources, and payments out, some to numbers – which might be numbered accounts. But she couldn't be sure if the company was in deep trouble, or just operating.

She didn't notice Rombauer at the door.

'Working early?' he said.

The file clerk turned and bridled. He couldn't complain and he couldn't explain, but he knew he was wrong, quite wrong.

Mercedes made herself cold and brisk. She took a sheet of paper from the desk and laid it in the file.

'You can take that now,' she said to the clerk.

155

Rombauer stopped the clerk on his way to the door. He took the file.

'I didn't know,' he said, 'Miss Zenon was interested in the files?' And he was no longer indulgent. 'I should have been told.'

The clerk looked down, like a holy martyr in the face of temptation, although he was tempted only to howl.

'And I'm surprised,' Rombauer said to Mercedes, 'that you abuse hospitality —'

'Really,' Mercedes said. 'I asked for some stuff that might help with the new Gstaad and I got this file which means —'

'I hope it means nothing to you,' Rombauer said.

'It is the wrong file,' Mercedes said.

The clerk could see the deposit slip still on her desk, a pool of marked pink on the polished wood. The clerk could focus on nothing else. He was bound to mention it, to absolve himself if he could. Mercedes picked it up casually, made a pencil note on the back, and slipped it under a blotter.

'We don't need you any more,' Rombauer said to the clerk. He slammed the door.

'I don't know what you want,' Rombauer said. 'But what you've done is against the law here. You can go to jail for it.'

'I really don't think a simple mistake —'

Why is he so sure? she asked herself. He was puffed like a fighting pigeon, and the same alarming purples, a man of forty suddenly betrayed by his heart. He was furious, but righteously so; he thought she did not understand.

'If this is to do with Vico,' Rombauer said, 'he might have picked someone more clever. I thought his men were good.'

She said: 'We are.'

Rombauer snorted. He was wrapped in all the certainties of a Swiss, an honorary man of substance, a husband and a father; he was everything a man is meant to be. From that security he could defend himself if need be. He could, he told himself; his brief defeat at Carpenter's hands was only a matter of bad timing, bad luck.

'I think,' he said, 'it's time you left.'

She only stood up from her chair, but she had the air of some Amazon, painted and fierce; he remembered his less wholesome, more friendly dream of Amazons. She seemed very strong, and very hard to fathom; she could be power, or cunning, or only their shell.

'You can call me at the hotel,' she said. 'Or you can find me in Siena. Or New York. I'd like an apology before I leave for Italy.'

He stared at her. She'd held the COBA file, somehow; those were secrets that even an auditor must never see. She was either lucky or informed. And yet she did not know enough to give the *coup de grâce*; perhaps she did not know enough to interpret what she'd seen.

'I expect,' Rombauer said, 'you'll want to ring for your driver.'

And he pointedly flourished her through the door and left her in the corridor. With immense dignity, with the habit of a hundred catwalks, she stretched and brought her body to life and marched into the hallway. The teller in his cage had never seen her look so fine.

She thought in the car that she would never see Rombauer again, or the inside of his bank; she'd done something remarkable, although she was not sure what, and then been unable to finish the job.

She would call Ian Carpenter.

He wasn't in his hotel. His bank wasn't listed in the phone book. She didn't want the complication of seeking out wherever he was working that day, whatever he was doing. She left a message and called her friend the producer's wife; and they went to spend serious money.

She lifted a string of fire with a glassy dial at its centre which was only a diamond watch; it was a lovely thing. But lovely things were no longer absorbing. She'd not known precisely what to do with the COBA file but her sense of disappointment went beyond that. For a second, in that office, she'd been afraid – not of the small pouter Rombauer, but of scandal. She had a contract not to be scandalous, only to appear it in double-page spreads. She'd taken four million for a kind of respectability, and she didn't want to lose it.

'Aaron will love it,' she told her friend absently.

He took the little hotel envelope and he slit it open in the elevator. He pulled out a deposit slip.

'*Huitième* . . .' the liftboy said.

He stepped out. The flimsy paper wafted down to the floor and he retrieved it.

There was also a note.

She'd explained what she knew like a telegram, and like a telegram it did not entirely make sense. She said she was going to Italy early. He wondered why she didn't want to face him.

He threw himself down on the bed.

If only he'd had this scrap of evidence before, he might have asked the right questions and made the right trouble. Five million by computer fraud to Rombauer's Panamanian company – that was the kind of deal the Mafia and Tibor Rosenbaum used to pull in the sixties. It was an old-fashioned deal, the kind an old-fashioned man pulls in panic. It was imitative, not clever; it required only one wire-room accomplice.

It was just the kind of scam that Rombauer would try.

He wished he had held the COBA file, seen the white-out and the scrawled figures that Mercedes mentioned in her note. That missing five million sounded like desperation; and if it meant Rombauer's and other people's money had been confused, that was the unforgivable sin. Things had to look precise for the Swiss or they shut the bank.

But he hadn't seen the papers, and Rombauer could not be pushed into producing them; he was already at the outer limit of the questions a Swiss banker dares tolerate. If only he'd known, he might have controlled Rombauer. He might not have sent that all-important Rolex back.

But it was too late to change tactics now.

A mirror by the bed reflected an empty space; she should be there, alongside him. He thought fondly how she'd bluffed her way to devastating information, and with anger how she'd wrecked a brilliant opportunity. He wanted to confront her, shake her.

The game was getting to him.

The voice on the phone could have been some plantation owner, raucous and aggrieved. 'You better have some ideas,' it said.

Carpenter lay half awake in a darkened room. It took him a moment to realise he was talking to Anastasio Diaz Sacasa.

'I thank you kindly,' the voice said, 'for the watch. Now why in hell you didn't just send it back from New York –'

'It was a gift,' Carpenter said. He was awake enough to justify himself, sleepy enough not to know when to stop. 'You –'

'It had sentimental value,' Diaz said. It sounded unlikely.

'I'm sure,' Carpenter said, trying not to sound sarcastic. He had to order his wits; he had to work this conversation for all it was worth. 'I'm just glad you got it safely.'

'I saw you there in the offices,' Diaz was saying, 'victim of the guerrillas, I knew I had to offer you some kind of apology from the people of Providencia –'

He must be persuaded to talk money, but not too quickly.

'And this other business,' Diaz said. 'This other business you mention is most disturbing.'

Diaz had the habitual and almost pathological discretion of a man whose life is all locked boxes. It was hard to know how to broach some delicate subject.

'You may need to find an alternative,' Carpenter said. He hoped to God the vagueness in this conversation wouldn't totally deprive it of sense. 'Another safe place.'

'I don't know how to do that from Leon,' Diaz said. 'There's no possibility of my leaving here now, not until we've won this war against the Communist –'

Carpenter said, quickly: 'You could let me handle it.'

The static welled up like a tide. Diaz hated allowing others to inspect his life and his assets; it was bad luck to share information. But this man had volunteered that Rombauer et Cie was about to be in trouble, and he had returned the watch. His interest lay in doing business with Diaz, not harming him. Diaz tried to reach an uncharacteristic sense of trust.

'You say in your letter,' Diaz said, 'that there is not so much privacy as there used to be?'

The code infuriated Carpenter, and he tried to be direct.

'The Swiss Central Bank knows who has each numbered account,' Carpenter said. 'And when there's a major case of insider trading, or fraud, they often tell the American authorities.'

'The Americans,' Diaz said, 'are not discreet.' The static came and went on the line. 'But I had an arrangement,' he said.

'Monsieur R.' – Carpenter fretted at the boy's secret code – 'made arrangements with another bank. M. R. had the power of attorney.'

That made sense, with a little interpretation. To get around the Central Bank's insistence on knowing who owned each numbered account, an outfit like Rombauer's would open its own numbered accounts in some other Geneva bank. The client gave Rombauer the money and Rombauer put it in a numbered account elsewhere, with a single copy in some office safe of a power of attorney which linked the client to the money. The computer in Berne knew only that Rombauer's had put money in another bank.

That was not good news for Carpenter. It meant Diaz had his money safe from the American investigators, who would never be allowed to see the power of attorney.

But he had no reason to say so.

'Sometimes that works,' he said.

'You mean it doesn't always work?'

'I mean sometimes it works. I don't want to pressure you.'

'You have to understand,' Diaz said. 'The Americans have made some extraordinary accusations against me over the years. They have no discretion.'

Again, Carpenter wished he was fully awake. Diaz must be referring to the time Congress investigated what became of the millions in earthquake relief sent to Leon by the US Government and various relief organisations. Leon had never been rebuilt, but the suburbs suddenly blossomed with Diacista development, and Mercedes-Benz cars marked a new upper class as surely as they do among the coke-rich nouveaux of Colombia. And some of those millions simply disappeared. Perhaps this numbered account was filled at the time, and perhaps the Americans would find out; that must be what Diaz feared.

'You can't keep the Americans quiet,' Carpenter said. 'And once they're talking, everyone knows.'

He meant: your wife will know. She can rest her Park Avenue life on alimony, not silence.

'I can't talk about it,' Diaz said.

'You can always move,' Carpenter said. 'Find another bank for the time being. Or move out of Switzerland.'

160

'But if I tell Rombauer to do that, there'll be a record.'

'Not if you instruct me,' Carpenter said. 'You organise a power of attorney to over-rule his mandate, and I shift things to another home.'

'And why should I trust you?'

'Because I want your business,' Carpenter said. 'I don't want your money for myself. And I'm the one who warned you.'

'I don't trust honest people. Everyone sounds honest to start with.'

'Then give me a percentage,' Carpenter said, half joking. 'Buy me off.'

'I will not –'

'I mean,' Carpenter said, 'move the money to the Zürich office of my bank. You can always move it again afterwards.'

'You shouldn't have said "money",' Diaz said. 'They listen to these calls.'

'You just have to give instructions. Tell Rombauer what to expect. Give me the power of attorney. Who else can you trust if you don't trust me?'

That struck home. Diaz was marooned in Leon while his son prowled Geneva and his family were out hunting for the money. Any crack in his hiding places was an emergency. And he had no banker in Switzerland to whom he could turn except the suspect Rombauer. Like Trujillo, Diaz was one of the very rare victims of Swiss morality.

'You know me as well as anybody,' Carpenter said.

Diaz said only: 'We'll see,' and ended the conversation as though he needed to know he was in control.

Carpenter drew back the curtains on a grey, cold morning. A mist had curdled at about a man's height above the black lake water and the birds were still. He shook his head like a wet dog.

He'd threatened Rombauer. But he'd done so carelessly. He'd given the number to identify an account that might well be empty, long ago siphoned off to another bank. Supposing Rombauer was suspicious now about how much Carpenter really knew?

It didn't matter, he decided. All that mattered was that Diaz was scared, and had nobody to trust. That way, Diaz could be persuaded to steal his own money. It would be interesting to see how much remained in Switzerland after all these years – how much Diaz had learned about the alternatives. After all, he could have a savings account in Austria with no name or code, just a passbook to identify him; he could have money at twelve per cent in Budapest. Perhaps he was a traditionalist. Perhaps he was truly clever.

Carpenter went walking after breakfast, along a concrete jetty that curled out into the lake past swimming stations, a town of concrete shanties and changing rooms. A few workmen shuffled in the cold: the black lake water seemed to smoke. He felt the brisk, damp air.

He was delighted with the watchwork precision of his scheme. He used information to scare Diaz, soften up Rombauer and gain control of the money; it was elegant and neat. He even admired how far Mercedes had gone, and wished she'd understood better what she was achieving.

The path came to a little park, a few trees in the middle of the water; their bare black branches were beginning to show a sheen of green and silver life. He stood and looked back at cold Geneva, its gardens and statues absurdly like some English seaside town.

There were footsteps behind. He turned too quickly, still bothered by the Manhattan troubles, and saw Tomás Diaz. The man marched in the cold morning like a soldier rehearsing for his squad.

Carpenter said: 'Bonjour,' but Tomás stared and cut him. Tomás had his own troubles. He was afraid his father would lose and he'd be left with nothing except a name and a lack of mercy, neither quality any longer in demand. He had an absurdly forlorn look in the cold: a little soldier, lost.

Rombauer left messages at the hotel proposing a morning meeting; Carpenter rang to accept. It was an awkward balancing act, seeing Rombauer now. He needed to do what his own bank required and clean up the details of insider trading so they could be used; he needed to know if Diaz had panicked yet; and he wanted to see how Rombauer was bearing up. He also wanted not to be arrested.

Rombauer was waiting for him at the partners' desk. He treated him like a client, with coffee and polite conversation, as though the subject of money was both too grand and too vulgar to be broached. And when he had exhausted his politeness, Rombauer said: 'You suggested there had been some trading in American stocks through nominee accounts at this bank. There was.'

'We know that,' Carpenter said.

'And you mentioned names,' Rombauer said. 'I can't confirm, obviously, but you would not embarrass yourself by mentioning those names again.' The sentence struck Carpenter as baroque, the product of a morning's work on its curlicues.

'Thank you,' Carpenter said.

'There is one account on the list, though, that does not quite fit. The last number on the list you gave me. I can tell you nothing except that we have no account with that number.'

'My information –'

'– was obviously wrong. And now, since you have the facts you required –'

'Of course.' The elaborately polite Rombauer turned, coldly dismissive. 'Naturally,' Carpenter went on, 'you'll let me have the full record of share transactions here?'

'Of course.'

Carpenter turned the typewritten pages that Rombauer had prepared. The pages were plain and had been left carefully unheaded; the lists of deals seemed, so far as he could see, to match those he'd been given in London, and the names confirmed all the bank's suspicions. It was less than proof, but enough to embarrass the hell out of those American oil executives who were now so keen to preserve their jobs.

'Then,' Carpenter said, 'let's hope you can be spared the trouble of an investigation.'

'That is the point of this information.'

'I know.' Carpenter slipped the papers into his briefcase. 'But of course, it's out of my hands now. So many other forces are involved.'

Rombauer composed himself with visible effort. 'I do hope,' he said, 'there will be no trouble.'

Carpenter found more messages from Diaz at his hotel, messages which had come at half-hourly intervals. He knew the difficulty of getting international lines out of Providencia; those half-hourly calls must represent trying almost continuously.

He placed a call and looked again at Mercedes' note. She'd retreated early to Florence, she said, on her way to Siena. She had left the address: a minor villa behind the Boboli Gardens and at the city walls usually loaned by the Italians to passing artists. There was no phone number, and no invitation.

After three hours he made contact with Diaz, who had a hungover, sour tone in his voice, compounded with something close to hysteria.

'I don't want them to know anything,' Diaz said. 'You have the power of attorney. I've fixed that. You can go and take the money and put it where the bastards can't find it.'

He didn't need to be exact about which bastards; for him the term bastards covered everyone else.

'Fine,' Carpenter said. 'I think it might be wise.'

Next morning the paperwork arrived and he went to Rombauer's for the inevitable confrontation. At first Rombauer denied any possible connection between his bank's private accounts in other banks and some remote figure in Providencia. Then he was angry.

'What game are you playing, Carpenter? What are you up to?'

'I don't play games,' Carpenter said. 'These are instructions from a client.'

'Yesterday you just had an account number. Today you have a client. You planning any other mischief before you go?'

'Don't protest too much,' Carpenter said. 'It's unseemly.'

Rombauer glared at him. 'You're stealing clients,' he said. 'You're doing it with stolen information. You want to explain that to the police.'

And Carpenter lost patience. He could no longer be bothered with Rombauer's stalling; he had other things to do, other places to be. Arguing with the man was like listening to a beached fish argue it hadn't yet been caught, not fairly.

'I don't think,' Carpenter said, 'you'd want to do a great deal of explaining. Your nominee clients have anything to do with COBA, did they? And the five million that went into COBA –'

Rombauer was white with anger. He couldn't focus on danger; he could see only the awful failure of everything that held his

164

business together. 'Slander,' he said, and then for emphasis he shrieked the word like an uncertain tenor edging up to the highest note. 'Sl-an-der,' he howled.

'Is it?' Carpenter said. And then he added: 'I presume this account of yours is in good order. The books can be seen? This paper says I have power of attorney, so I want to be sure.'

'I will tolerate this no longer –'

'You will tolerate this,' Carpenter said, 'until we've finished doing business. After that, I don't give a damn.'

'I don't tolerate this,' Rombauer said. 'I do not. This is Geneva. I am an established bank. We are protected by Swiss law. You have no right –' But the fine phrases had degenerated into splutter.

'I will ask for the books,' Rombauer said.

He had changed, physically, his shoulders forward and his muscles slack. Carpenter took no enjoyment in the sight.

The file came, and the arrangements were made. Rombauer gave an account of how the money had been used; Carpenter agreed to ask no unnecessary questions. The account became Carpenter's and Carpenter ordered the money transferred. It was done, an anti-climax, in an hour or so.

'I like old-fashioned paper,' Carpenter said, fatuously. 'So much more convincing than electronics.'

Rombauer signed the last sheet and said: 'I have other business.' He might be boasting, or telling Carpenter to get out, either way the phrase sounded empty.

Carpenter stood at the doorstep for a moment. The air caught him and he was stiff as a proper banker, in his dark suit with his briefcase clutched against him. He was a model of propriety. He took a step down the road and all its grey discretion was suddenly nothing more than a backdrop. He began to smile, and to laugh, and then he broke into a jog and a full, loping run, pelting down the rue de la Corraterie, dodging the traffic and down to the river. His eyes were wide and happy, his breath like a dragon in the cold. He wanted to shout.

It wasn't only victory, either. It was the sheer, overwhelming pleasure of being alive and the luxury of not having to hide the feeling.

He was running along the lakeside paths. The train to Milan.

The train to Florence. A taxi to the villa. A whole world to share in a big bed.

He jumped high and then had to slow himself, still grinning, to stop from cannoning into a brown-veiled matron, a late Lollobrigida who was watching him closely. He wanted to fling his arms around her; she would have been glad; but the damp judgmental air put down the moment.

Before he left, he was methodical. He checked the Diaz money had been delivered, and cleared, was truly out of Rombauer's control. Then he called London. Rombauer had admitted everything, he reported, and they could act against him now. All they'd needed was the confession.

That left the other facts, which were luxuries now. He knew a little about COBA, and he had some proof that Rombauer stole five million from a New York bank. He couldn't use either fact against Rombauer any more, because he had no more use for Rombauer. But he could inflate the Rombauer scandal when it came and make sure the Diaz money had no way of running home when this crisis was over.

That was business, and justice; they could be the same.

The Swiss would like to know about COBA. Leventhal at Security National would like to know about that five million dollars which vanished from his vaults. They could both be obliged. He made the calls, sent Leventhal the deposit slip and packed together a copy of the slip and a brief note in a hotel envelope and sent them anonymously to the Banque de Suisse.

It was the end of Rombauer.

·FIVE·

'Damn stones,' she said, picking her way on high heels across a square of mediaeval cobbles.

'They're the original stones.'

She only snorted at him. 'Why do you like old things? I don't like old things.'

Carpenter thought she was curiously nervous, as though the old made her wary. Her family had no kind past.

'The towers,' he said, gesturing at the great façades of the Piazza del Campo set around its cockleshell of pale brown stone. 'It's extraordinarily grand –'

'Grand,' Mercedes said, 'like Disneyland,' and reached the smooth surface of a paved road with obvious relief.

Across the square they came to lanes which ran up and down the hills, steep and narrow. Some were half-lit, in a net of shadows, and some ran off into blind ends; but some were full of loud white light. There were blue dolphins standing out from the walls in cardboard, and each lamp was a cluster of white bulbs and the lanes were so saturated with light that shadows had disappeared until the very top of the buildings. Down the middle of the street was a line of tables laid with white cloths and a procession of wooden chairs.

'The set,' Mercedes said.

The entourage was there already, and they clustered forward to protect and calm and prepare her.

'It's not a set,' Carpenter said, with his old sense of fact. 'They always celebrate like this. It's the quarter of the town that won the *palio* –'

'The *palio*,' Mercedes said. She sat straight as a schoolgirl, mocking him with her attention.

'Which is a horse race,' he said, 'twice a year. They race round the Campo and every quarter enters a horse and rider –'

'And rider,' she said, as though noting and learning.

'For God's sake,' Carpenter said. 'You're sulking.'

'I'm working,' she said.

A camera crew was setting up at the foot of a hill, where two lanes crossed. Out of it bustled the director, who called Mercedes 'darling' with automatic feeling and said she wasn't called for another hour and a half.

'Walk around,' he said. 'Enjoy the city.'

Mercedes looked at Carpenter bleakly. She'd counted on all the apparatus of her job to keep her occupied, and reassured. Carpenter made her nervous.

'We could have dinner,' Carpenter said.

'I don't eat before I work,' Mercedes said.

'You don't get nervous, do you?'

'Not nervous. But it's better not to eat or drink.'

'You'll get cold –'

'That's none of your damn business.'

The director, a lanky, quiet man, had lost his taste for calling people 'darling' and was edgy to get back to calculating shots.

'Take her for a walk, would you?' he said to Carpenter.

'You see,' Carpenter said. 'It's official. I'm your minder.'

'Don't you have a home to go to?' Mercedes said. But she stood and allowed him to wrap his coat around her shoulders, and they walked down the brilliant lane.

'It's like a Fellini film,' Carpenter said.

'That's not a compliment.'

A small, round woman scuttled like a chicken down the side of the street, followed by an older woman, square and dignified. Behind them both came a man walking with a stick.

'She's the mistress, and he's the husband, and the one in the middle –'

'Or, he's the priest, caught *in flagrante delicto* by his housekeeper –'

'– with the rich old lady who owns the street –'

They giggled and the worst of the tension was over.

'What happened at Rombauer's?' he asked.

'I found things out,' she said, 'and then I left the rest to you.'

168

'Rombauer's finished,' Carpenter said. 'And I've got a power of attorney over the Diaz money.'

'You never told me how much money.'

'We'll know exactly in a couple of days. But it's around fifty-six million –'

'Is that all?' She was shocked and she froze. 'You're telling me we only found fifty-six million dollars – when there's a billion out there –'

'You didn't think it would all be in Switzerland, did you?'

She said nothing. But that was exactly what she had hoped: that this treasure hunt would be easily compatible with where and what she had to be, a diversion.

'You want to go on?'

'I said I'd do this,' she said, 'for Aurelia.'

'You're doing it for yourself, too. You want to do a proper job.' He put his large hands on her shoulders and she resented the pressure. 'You're a serious woman.'

'Don't patronise me,' she said, but she let his hands lay.

'Poor Rombauer. He's finished, of course.'

'I don't give a shit about Rombauer,' Mercedes said. 'He made a living like everyone else. I just wanted the Diaz money.'

'For Providencia, of course.'

She glared at him. 'I didn't want some English banker controlling it,' she said. 'Some banker who likes to make friends with people like Diaz –'

'You wanted it for the Amadistas,' Carpenter said. 'I make you a present of it – all transferred to Costa Rica, whenever you want.'

'You're crazy,' she said. 'Your bank would never stand for that.'

'I have the power of attorney. I do things at my own discretion. And Diaz is in no position to check.'

'But he will be –'

'I thought you liked risk.'

She shook herself free and walked on. A tight side alley led up to a wider street which was flanked with towers; and in the towers there were high gates and courts dimly visible beyond. The cars ran at the hill and walkers kept aside.

'I have a job to do,' she said.

There was a small restaurant, beginning to fill. The menu offered truffles with almost anything, and Carpenter said he was hungry.

'I could eat a little,' Mercedes said.

They sat at a tiny table, cramped together, over a dish of pasta with specks of black truffle and Parmesan.

'We're getting there,' Carpenter said, raising his glass. Mercedes didn't puzzle over what he meant, but Carpenter began to.

She picked at a dish of spinach *arrabbiata*, with chillies, garlic and oil, and at a salad. She sipped a little wine. She seemed to restore herself as she ate.

'We could walk back slowly,' she said.

Carpenter looked at his watch. 'You're due back in a half hour.'

They wandered along the streets and looked down the lanes between buildings that were no more than gaps between stones.

'We could –'

And Mercedes led the way into an alley that was lit only by lights from open windows. In the shadows, tiny cats scuttled to safety. Underfoot there were falls of wood and rubble, as though nobody passed this way. A radio played disco, and the air smelt of rot.

'I don't think this leads anywhere,' Carpenter said.

'I want to see where it goes.'

On a side wall there was a sign: Vincolo degli Argentieri. 'Must have been the silversmiths' alley,' Carpenter said.

'You think of history, don't you.' There was suspicion in her voice.

'I read a lot.'

She tugged him on into the alley's half-dark. It turned slightly to the right and then back again, enough to block any casual view.

She stopped and he butted into her. She didn't move away.

He kissed her very lightly on the neck, where the skin barely covers the nerves, and she shivered. A light went on, high above them. She settled back against the wall in the comfort of his coat, close as a skin to him.

'You just want an accomplice,' he said.

170

'What do you care? Don't tell me you want love.'

'I don't just want –'

She put her hand into his shirt, opened it deftly and scorched his chest and belly with her nails.

'In an alleyway?' he questioned. 'Standing up?'

'That's how you think of me,' she said.

'For Christ's sake, why –'

'Because I'm nervous,' she said.

She took his hand and brought it under her slit skirt. He knew she was dressed for the pictures, for the teasing of other people's fantasies. His hand felt the tops of stockings, and he stroked the sensitive skin inside her thighs. She had stopped smiling.

She could hear every tiny sound, each catfoot and each velo passing in the distant street. She could make sense of none of them.

'Here?' he said, as if they had a choice any more.

He pulled at her briefs and his hand was clumsy in the bush of her sex, stroking, feeling for the clitoris.

Old stone sheltered them and the brisk air on their bodies, part clothed, part bare, woke up an alleycat's lusts. People might pass the alley, might come to windows, any time. Footsteps might come close. Any moment, any moment now.

She was pressed back against the damp stone, and he slipped the crisp white off her shoulders. The weathering of centuries was imprinted now on soft, brown skin, and she was hot like fever. His hand still moved urgently under her skirt; he bent and separated those firm small breasts with his tongue, and then cupped her nipple in his mouth.

She pulled away, and she threw up her skirt. In the tent of their clothes, he rushed into her.

Footsteps. In this tight alley.

He was inside her, up to the heart and rising, and there were footsteps: they were caught. They couldn't tell on which side the feet were moving. They were trapped in the thrust and give of making love, and now they struggled to be silent. Breath was a sound too many.

The steps came closer. Lights flared behind the wall which seemed to close the alley off.

Carpenter's eyes were blank now; he couldn't stop the furious pressure. If he stayed still, he felt he was tearing, and Mercedes could not let him stay still. They turned empty eyes to the lights and the footsteps.

What they'd thought was a wall in the dark began to roll slowly up.

Mercedes watched. She was fascinated, aware of every movement, waiting for watchers. She didn't want them to go away. She wanted everything, everyone.

Out of the wall came headlights, and then the sound of a car engine.

They were spotlit now, dressed in fragments of respectability and furiously involved. Their breath, forced and smoky, hung in the lit air. Ian Carpenter had never hung so long on the moment of coming, until Mercedes began to move, and together they were lost.

The car sounded its horn. They pressed against the wall, and the car went out of the alley with surprising speed, careering into the town. The lights in the garage died.

Carpenter leaned against Mercedes and for the first time the cold night air cut bare flesh instead of teasing it. And they laughed, a little like children, pressed together. She licked companionably at his lips, his cars and his closed, tired eyes. They pulled their clothes together, regretfully.

The door began to roll noisily down.

They were tidy again, and they pulled apart as though their skins were sticky.

The door snapped shut.

'You all right?' asked Carpenter.

She shook her shoulders into her white blouse. 'That was an accident,' she said.

'I know.'

He turned away a little, out of a late decency, and went to look at the door. It was an ordinary steel garage door, with a window to one side which lacked glass. It smelt like a dormitory for cats.

He stood on tiptoe and could just see through the high window. A cat in refuge there gave a startling growl and jumped away.

The lights went on again. Carpenter could see a garage with oil on the floor and brick walls, a mess of tarpaulin and rope, and the vaults he associated with some mediaeval room. He saw a man come through a door and move to the pile of tarpaulin and pull away the first layers.

Under them was a man, tied and gagged. Carpenter felt Mercedes come up behind him and put her arm around him; he motioned to be quiet.

The bound man was pulled upright. His legs were bloodless and dead; he stood with difficulty.

The other man took out a gun and put it to the man's head. There was a dull sound, muffled; and the bound man fell on his wounded side.

The gag and ropes came off. It was like some tenpenny peep show, a poor view of something monstrous.

Carpenter saw that the bound man was Rombauer. He turned, grabbed at Mercedes, put a hand over her mouth to stop even the slightest sound and went scrambling with her out of sight of that lit window. It was like an eye, like a vigilant, remorseless eye. He couldn't breathe until he was out of sight of it.

Mercedes looked startled, but she didn't argue. She lifted her feet high over the rubble in the alley and ran like a gazelle. She knew not to make a sound.

They came back to the main street and stopped.

'What did you see?' she asked, breathless.

'I can't tell you.'

'You have to tell me. We're partners –'

'You have to get to the set,' Carpenter said. He looked her up and down, straightened her skirt. 'I'll tell you later.'

They walked apart, down to the brilliant streets where the crew was waiting in a knot of admiring kids. The blank tables were crowded now, and there were great green bottles of wine set out, with bread and knives and salt. The street began to live with a buzz, and the shadows of people.

'I'm late,' Mercedes said, defiantly.

'You're fine, darling,' the director said. 'Just get into make-up.'

Make-up was a pizzeria backroom, still smelling of yeast and tomatoes. Mercedes disappeared to be remade.

Some time before the cameras first rolled, the director had shifted Carpenter out of view: too clean, too quiet. A raucous, winy streetful of men had assembled, waiting at their chairs for the entrance of the star.

Carpenter sat in the pizzeria itself, at a little round table. The owner, assuming he was important, brought coffee and a piece of panforte; Carpenter thanked her.

He couldn't believe what he had seen. To see a killing was bizarre enough, something you might imagine from a late night on Third Avenue or a war zone, not a backstreet of a city at peace. But to see the killing of someone you knew, so close and so implacable; that was appalling and impossible. Impossible, he kept telling himself. Besides, he had no intention of going back to check.

The people – the men – in the car. Had they seen faces or just bodies when they swept past down the alley? Carpenter remembered, with a sharp feeling in his belly, how he'd turned his face into the light. At the time, it seemed hot.

And why Rombauer? It was highly unlikely that the banker was in Siena simply for the art or the culture; he had no time for art or culture. If he'd come south, it must have been for a specific reason, and the only reason that occurred to Carpenter was walking now to her place at the head of the street feast. Rombauer must have followed Mercedes.

Whoever had a grudge against Rombauer for failing would have a grudge against anyone who had forced Rombauer into failure.

His stomach turned again.

He rehearsed what he had seen. A pile of tarpaulin, a man, a gun, and then a shot. He was sure of all that. But perhaps he had imagined the man's face and it was not Rombauer at all, and far from shooting, perhaps it was just a question of moving out some bum who'd come to sleep under the tarpaulin.

He saw Rombauer killed.

He tried to imagine the heaped tarpaulins again. If Rombauer was alive under there, he'd have struggled, surely, or rolled, or manoeuvred somehow to be free of those thick, smothering sheets. Even his ropes wouldn't stop him. Rombauer couldn't stand, either; he had to be propped.

Maybe Rombauer was already dead when he was shot. But somehow that was almost more disturbing, more grotesque, than what he had first thought. And he had no idea how to tell Mercedes. If it was somehow an illusion, then he had no right to

174

alarm her, but if it was not, then there were unknown men in this town who hated Rombauer enough to kill him. And Rombauer's state as victim might be infectious.

'OK,' the director was shouting. 'Everybody quiet. This is where Mercedes walks down the street and you look back at her, one by one, admiringly. OK. You got that in Italian?'

And he could see through the pizzeria door that Mercedes was glorious, her whole body alive and sinuous and her eyes dark; and she was walking the street like a goddess. She stopped where two old men, bent and not shaven, sat side by side at the table and stood between the two; one took her hand and kissed it. She smiled, a professionally enigmatic smile.

And the director bellowed: 'That's a wrap.'

And his assistant echoed: '*Basta così.*'

The lights didn't die in the street as Carpenter had expected; instead, the men began to relax and pull at their wine, and their women came out to join them. The crew retreated, and the street filled up with a proper feast, with pasta in steaming vats from first-floor kitchens, and sauces that perfumed the whole quarter with tomato and oil.

Mercedes came in through the door and sat down. She let her face go quite blank for a moment, then shook her head and smiled.

'OK?' she said, in her universal language.

'OK!' a pair of spare electricians said, with enthusiasm.

'OK,' Carpenter said, and made himself grin at her.

She sat down beside him and said: 'What happened in that alley?' She was very close to him, as though they were in bed together. 'You have to tell me. Now.'

'I can't tell you,' Carpenter said, 'I'm not sure.' He was almost being honest.

'Something in that garage,' Mercedes said.

'Something I probably imagined.'

'We're supposed to be partners.'

She flounced into the backroom where make-up were waiting to undress her and remove her professional face, leaving him disconsolate in the corner. Nobody quite understood his standing so nobody spoke to him.

She offered him a ride to the hotel in her limo as though that was a favour; and she said goodnight abruptly. He watched the elevator climb out of sight in its cage of wires.

And he went out, immediately. He felt used and frightened, an unlovely combination he had no wish to share. He sat on the Campo in the dress circle of that great square and looked down on the palace and the tower of the Mangia. It was a glorious place, a place of harmonies and light, a grande finale to a city of tight streets he had loved since he first came here as an impressionable boy. But now it looked full of shadow.

He sat only for a few minutes. He felt his stomach turn again, and he thought of Mercedes at risk. At risk, like Aurelia. If he'd been faster with Aurelia, if he'd known –

This time, he knew, or at least guessed that there was menace. He had no idea from what direction, but a banker like Rombauer must have enough clients who would resent, to say the least, the revelation of their affairs. Some day, perhaps, he'd answer the real question: why Rombauer came to Siena. But for the time being, he'd better assume it was a sinister journey.

He paid for his drink and strode back through the night streets. He kept to the middle, remembering those Manhattan shadows that had caught at him.

At the hotel, there were two bulky men standing close to Reception.

He didn't want them to go upstairs. He would wait like a dog to block their way if they showed any signs of going up.

They might be cops. They might be guests. It wasn't that he was sure, or even strictly rational; but he was determined not to be wrong.

He asked for coffee and a reluctant kitchen brought it to the entrance hall. He shuffled the papers. His Italian was just good enough to allow him the headlines, and sometimes the gist of a story; he read about minor scandals, was puzzled over some political story which seemed full of abstract nouns, and he tried a review of a new Steven Spielberg movie. He kept looking.

At midnight, he went up to the floor where Mercedes was staying and sat on a windowledge where he could see her door. He hadn't quite calculated what he would do if anyone came out and asked what in hell he was doing. He was still in shock.

He let his mind run, half sleepy, on Rombauer in the garage.

He wondered whether he had seen the moment of death itself, and if he had, what that might mean. He thought of the smell a body is meant to have, if opened while being killed: a sweet and intimate smell, the horrific flowers of death. He shook himself awake.

He could hear the elevator pass in its cage, and sometimes he could hear footsteps on tiles. He saw shadows coming up the stairs by the elevator: two shadows. They seemed enormously tall.

The two men from the lobby turned the corner and walked towards Mercedes' room.

He tensed himself. He was ready for anything that was needed, ready, although tired and full of grappa, for anything that would save Mercedes.

But the two men looked curiously at him and walked past Mercedes' room to their own.

He sighed.

After a moment he felt his whole body relax. He walked to the elevator. It was time to sleep.

He woke to the chic zebra grid that bright sun and closed shutters had thrown on his ceiling. He stretched, picked up the phone and asked for Mercedes' room; there was a grudging reply.

'I have things to do today,' Mercedes said.

'We could have dinner –'

'O, for Christ's sake,' Mercedes said.

He lay in bed and wondered how he was to protect a woman who wouldn't see him, or cope with a one-night lover whose moods seemed to shift so alarmingly. It never crossed his mind that she, too, might have a new secret.

He went down to the street and he walked.

With Mercedes, he felt constrained; it would seem pretentious to enjoy the streets, even go to some gallery. He didn't understand why. She was no philistine; she was for ever invited to art benefits in Manhattan, fascinated by the paintings between the dancers in clubs like Area. But the old baffled her. She lived in the moment, he supposed. But if she lived so much in the moment, why did she care so much for revenge?

He wandered into a courtyard garden where a single cool tree shaded the walls. He drifted up to the Duomo and across its mystical and bizarre mosaics that honoured prophets unknown until mediaeval times. He fidgeted in the Library, with the fine Pinturicchio panels, looking at a saint visiting an oddly Mediterranean Scotland with lochs like seas, and hearing a German travel guide boom out her explanation of it all.

Coming out of the Duomo, down the steps, he thought he saw Mercedes. If he did, there was no point in alarming her. She'd probably some assignment to be photographed and looked at; that was her occupation. He could be furious at her occupation, sometimes.

He climbed the white stairs in the National Gallery, past the wishy-washy Sodomas like storybook pictures for Edwardian children (with sadistic interests, like most children) and up to the Simone Martinis. He remembered them from adolescent trips through Italy: the brilliance of their red and gold, the strangeness of stories told in one space but more than one time – so that a baby was at a window, falling, and miraculously saved, all in the same canvas. He was absorbed.

A professorial man, broad-shouldered and a little hunched in an old tweed jacket, came up alongside him. Carpenter shifted immediately. He didn't like to feel badgered; he liked to be lost in a picture. And the older man smelt of pipe tobacco and must.

In the next room there was a panel of a single saint, all pale and golden. He looked at the face for the strength he associated with Martini; and the professorial man was there, again.

'Signor Carpenter,' the man said. 'You will forgive this rather curious melodrama, but it is as well to avoid unseemliness.' The man smiled, a crooked smile with yellow teeth all exposed to almost film star limits.

Carpenter said: 'I don't think I know you.'

'You know friends of mine. We know you've been involved with Rombauer et Cie, for whatever reasons, and we know Rombauer et Cie is in great difficulty. This is not convenient. You will not pursue this, or make further trouble.' And the professorial man changed tack immediately, forming a few platitudes about the painting; then he slapped a copy of the morning paper into Carpenter's hand.

'Enjoy your stay,' he said.

And he walked easily away. Carpenter felt as though he'd shifted worlds – from the logic and clockwork mechanics of his ordinary life to this looking-glass existence of being witness, victim and the one who is menaced. A barrier had gone by and he hadn't noticed, and now he was in another place.

He walked to the stairwell. Down the white stairs he could hear the echo of sensible steel tips on heels; it must be the professorial man. A guard asked if he could help.

'No,' Carpenter said. 'No, no.'

And he walked softly down the stairs.

If people were going to make threats, he'd at least know who they were and what they meant, precisely.

At ground level, he saw the professorial man crossing the lobby and out through the glass doors. He walked faster. The man now turned and walked up the hill towards the Duomo. Carpenter followed, grateful for the first crop of tourists who hung, a little pale and flustered, around the crossings and souvenir shops. He dodged through them, and kept the man in sight.

He came to the Duomo, which is a candy affair of green and white opposite the worn brick mass of Santa Maria delle Scale – the old hospital which starts high and tumbles down a cliff, storey by storey. He thought he saw the professorial man turn into the main entrance of the hospital. He couldn't be sure.

He sat on the cold Duomo steps and looked at the newspaper. A story was outlined in Magic Marker, luminous and red; he couldn't miss it.

'Death', he read, and 'Swiss banker'. In the story he could make out words like 'mutilated', 'animals', 'tragedy'. Somehow, the story lacked the name of Rombauer but it had everything else.

Rombauer had died here. He had died here last night. Therefore, he had died before Carpenter's eyes. He had seen what was intolerable to see, and fascinated him just because it represented the last taboo to break.

He folded the paper.

The body had not been found in the town but out on the road

to Poggibonsi, in an olive grove. He gathered from his minimal Italian, it had been – Rombauer had been, he had been – 'ruined'. By animals, they said, but what animals run wild through olive groves near Siena?

He shivered, and kept his handful of facts circling in his mind, like a man does before sleep on a bad night. He remembered that, a little while ago, he had seen Mercedes go where that professorial man had gone: into the hospital building.

It must be like a maze inside, storey after storey of mediaeval rooms and spaces, all forming a kind of wall before the cathedral square. He didn't know where to start.

He thought he knew which entrance Mercedes had used. He went there now. There was an open wooden door, and nobody moving; the long, grey corridor, barrel-vaulted, had been floored in rubber so that footsteps were absorbed. It felt like walking on blotting paper.

The corridor was blind; no rooms or other corridors led off it. It turned sharply to the right and there were steps; then, when it seemed to have come to an end, there was a small door set off to the left. Through that, there was an ante-chamber that smelled of candles, incense and old robes; and through that, there was a tiny chapel.

A priest with a senator's middle-aged face neither acknowledged Carpenter nor ignored him. It was as though he were part of the chapel itself, with its cramped low space and wildly gilded altar. The room seemed very small.

'Father,' Carpenter said, in experimental Italian.

The priest looked at him, expecting either everything or nothing by way of confession; the man did not look comfortable in a church, and he looked troubled.

'Was there a woman here? A young woman, black?' Carpenter asked.

The priest turned to a row of candles burning on the altar. He reached up and snuffed them, one by one.

'A woman,' Carpenter was saying. 'A black woman.'

The priest turned, still waiting for what the man truly needed to say. Then he decided there would be no barriers broken that day. 'You have the wrong chapel, my son. She is in the other chapel.'

180

'And how do I get –'

The priest gestured. 'There is a passage that goes that way,' he said. 'Or you can return to the Piazza and there is another door –'

Carpenter bundled through the door the priest had shown and along a corridor with high carved screens of wood and glass. He came to a door and peered through the glass.

The second chapel was a high-ceilinged place with air that grew hazy with dust close to the topmost windows; at one end, a whole wall was painted, and an altar stood like something on a stage. The place was sparse, the black pews dwarfed. It was cool and empty.

Except that, at the end of one of the pews, a woman sat. She was dressed like Mercedes; she looked like Mercedes. But she wore a veil and was sitting beside a man in a wheelchair: a man who was a rack of bellies suspended on a ruined back. They were talking very confidentially.

He was baffled. Siena was far away from the worlds Mercedes inhabited. She had said nothing about knowing some elderly man in this hospital.

Carpenter tried the door. It was locked and he didn't want to draw attention to himself by rattling the handle.

He couldn't even see their lips, let alone read them. He saw Mercedes stand very quickly, but he could read no anger or alarm in her face. The man in the wheelchair shrugged.

He saw the priest again. He drifted down from beside the altar the length of the aisle, past the couple talking urgently. Mercedes did not acknowledge him; the man in the wheelchair was dismissive; and the priest went by, dreaming of changes and confessions.

Mercedes faced the altar. She bowed, made the sign of the cross. The man in the wheelchair watched her. She brought down her veil and slipped past the chair, out to the side of the chapel where there were a few candles burning before a painted Saviour. She lit a candle.

And the man with the wheelchair came up suddenly behind her. She was startled. He seemed to be brusque. He signalled to the priest, who came scuttling to the door by which Carpenter stood.

181

He could have moved; he decided to stay put.

The priest pushed the door open carefully.

'*Permesso*,' Carpenter said. 'Let me help.'

The wheelchair rushed the door as though the man in it had not even considered the possibility of obstacles. Carpenter thought he knew the face; but there was shock in seeing such a man bound to a chair. This particular man should have untramelled, unapologetic power or be the centre of a conspiracy. He couldn't be caught this way.

Carpenter stood by the side of the door. As the chair passed, he said: 'George Vico.'

It seemed the chair would not stop, but a little down the corridor the heavy man applied the brakes.

'No,' he said, and then Carpenter was sure. 'Not as far as you're concerned, whoever you are. George Vico isn't here.'

And the chair rushed on into the passages of the hospital, and the priest, with an apologetic smile said: 'The way out, *signore*, is through the door to the Piazza –'

Mercedes had paused by the door. She was properly dressed for such a meeting, Carpenter saw: in pristine black, and veiled. He wondered if he really saw her; she was so unexpected in this world of candles and priests.

But she was waiting for him. 'I didn't want to tell you,' she said. She seemed very sobered, almost cowed; he saw no trace of either the petulance or the passion that he seemed to incite in her.

She came out into the sunlight and threw back her veil. 'I should have told you,' she said.

They walked across the square and down into the city. She tripped a little, as though her stand was unsure, and he supported her. He turned her towards the first of the restaurants they passed, for the sake of a chair and a drink.

'You know who that was?' she said.

'George Vico,' Carpenter said. 'Your adoptive father.'

'George Vico,' Mercedes said. She had a glass before her and she emptied it of wine.

'You don't have to talk now,' Carpenter said.

'Oh, but I do,' she said. 'There isn't any time. I have to talk and talk.' He saw that she was breaking a breadstick, again and again, until it was a kind of buff dust on the cloth. 'Vico says they killed Rombauer.'

'I know,' Carpenter said. 'The papers –'

'They killed Rombauer,' Mercedes said, 'because of what we found out about him. They, they needed their privacy and suddenly Rombauer couldn't provide it.'

'You have to tell me who did this.'

'Vico says it was some Italians. They have a kind of Masonic lodge – generals and bankers and politicians – and they like to keep their affairs private. They thought Rombauer had given them away.'

'But he didn't do that.'

'They paid him to keep a lot of secrets. When he didn't, when the cops were in the bank, they got very nervous. Apparently Rombauer came here to ask Vico's help, and the next thing he knew Rombauer was dead.'

Carpenter did not explain what had happened in the alleyway of the silversmiths.

'And now,' Mercedes said, 'Vico says they'll be after us. You and me.'

'He knows about me?'

'He always knows. It's his talent. It's his business. He sits on his island, and he can't be a player, so he knows what other people play.'

'I thought,' Carpenter said, 'he was exiled in the Bahamas, that he couldn't leave.'

'He has an Italian passport. This is the one place he can come, and nobody asks questions or checks the files.'

'And he's sick?'

Mercedes shrugged. 'A man in a wheelchair in a hospital chapel. That doesn't look extraordinary. He needs to be anonymous.'

'He could be anonymous in a suit.'

'Not George Vico,' Mercedes said. 'He either flaunts himself or disguises himself. He couldn't bear not to be recognised.'

The stars of money were much like the stars of Sunset Boulevard when they faded, Carpenter thought.

'So there you are,' Mercedes said. 'He knew which hotel you were in. He had the police tell him where you were registered, and he said in another couple of days he'd have the credit card record. He knows.'

A waiter brought a plate of antipasto and set it between them. It smelt oddly rank.

'He says we're at risk,' Mercedes said, 'unless he helps us.'

'He's not some Mafia *capo*. He can't offer protection like that. He can't even be anywhere except Italy and the Bahamas. Too many people want to jail him.'

'But,' Mercedes said, 'there are these people –'

'How do you know they're real?'

But he remembered what he had seen through the eye window of the garage, and he knew the least they faced was a man who would kill. If the gun, the tarpaulins and Rombauer had been a show, it was extraordinarily effective: as good as life.

'I don't know where to go,' Mercedes said, 'except to him.'

Carpenter held out a hand but she did not take it. 'I'd protect you,' he said. 'I will protect you.'

'If you can,' she said.

The waiter hovered as though to encourage them to the antipasto. Carpenter waved him away.

'Why does he frighten you?'

'He doesn't frighten me.'

But at the very least, she'd remembered things, including the time when Vico had ruled her life. She remembered the father who touched her.

'He can't do anything.'

'But these others –'

'Come,' Carpenter said. He settled the bill and took her out into the sunlight. As he hoped, a matron recognised her and started a little roar of whispered names. She responded, as she had to; she was glamorous again.

But on the way down the street, she said: 'It could be any one of them. Any of them. They killed Rombauer. They found his body somewhere by a road. They –'

'You want George Vico to be involved in this.'

'Perhaps he could help. Perhaps he would make it all possible.'

Her eyes saw streets in the sun; her mind was full of a jumble of distracting memories.

184

'I guess I have to,' she said.

'Have to – what? Go visit Vico in the Bahamas? Sit here and let him give the orders?'

'He knows things,' Mercedes said. 'And you said there wasn't much of the money in Switzerland.'

'We can start there,' Carpenter said. 'It's what we've got.'

At the threshold of the hotel, she came close to stumbling. 'Damned heels,' she said.

George Vico sprawled indoors, a blubbery sea creature stranded on a kind of stuffed beach chair. He could see the hedges of bougainvillaea in the spring sun, all mauve and russet, and the hibiscus flaring everywhere and the red candles of ixia. Beyond, there was the sea: a picture postcard water, emerald and turquoise with a faint white line where the reef broke surface. He was living in a goddamned resort.

He felt cold.

Pain in his back nagged him. Pain in his chest frightened him. He felt his body had been wrecked and he wanted someone to blame.

But there was, as usual, nobody: nobody who couldn't be bought, and therefore nobody worth knowing. He had bought German Cay because, across the Gulf Stream, he could just make out the Florida coast. He went down each morning and looked out, and he railed at America that had put him into exile; he shouted about revenge. But by afternoon, and a few whiskies, America seemed to taunt him. He could see home but he couldn't go home.

He was a kind of American hero, he always imagined. In his sparse study he had a few photographs in wood frames: Vico as a kid in a New Jersey garage, greasy; Vico as a young man posing with a line of products when the garage became an oil business, of sorts; Vico in a suit, in Wall Street offices, already looking comfortable as his company went public. There were no pictures of the times Vico discovered he liked paper and money more than products, nor of the day he realised that other people did not have his nerve. Nobody thought a single man could buy the world's largest mutual fund, strip its assets and hide them and then escape prosecution. And because nobody believed such a

185

thing would happen, it happened easily.

He had a headline tacked to the wall. 'Fugitive Financier in Drugs Probe,' it said. They had brought back that phrase 'fugitive financier' for him; it virtually belonged to him.

Above his head, an old and gaudy parrot watched attentively. He'd bought the bird in Providencia, thinking it would be a pet for Mercedes on the long journey to Switzerland; but somehow the bird had always stayed with him. It was loyal, but it had a judgemental eye. If he had the muscle, he'd dispose of it. But at least it was a kind of company.

He pushed himself off his chair, with difficulty. He could walk all right, even run if he had to, but moving between the horizontal and the vertical seemed to involve dead flesh. He glared at the parrot and walked to the window.

Besides sea and flowers, there were little planes. They came and went, the timetable of his days. Sometimes they brought cocaine in from Colombia, and sometimes they shipped it out in crocus sacks to Florida, to be dropped north of the Everglades. There were supplicants who arrived, asking for capital or advice; and there were the troublemakers, too. He liked anything that made those bastards across the water remember him, respond to his name.

But he was also trapped. He could go occasionally to Italy, but only with great discretion. Otherwise, there were warrants everywhere. For all his interests in the Bahamas – thirty per cent of this bank, of that newspaper – he was not welcome if he left his own island. He was an embarrassment, a chronic issue. And in the kingdom of his island, his house was temporary and bleak – the whole cay not much more than a garden. It was as if his mind still functioned perfectly in a body ruined by a stroke.

It angered him. He needed agents in the world outside to achieve the simplest things. In America, those agents had to be carefully disguised; elsewhere, there was only fixing to be done, no true dealing. It was a distinction that he valued, and which trapped him.

He watched a Cessna Caravan come into land, a workhorse plane. He wondered whether Mercedes had come.

But it was never Mercedes, never a reminder of his glamorous past, always Anna, the too-broad daughter of a marriage that

186

seized up more than ten years back. She loved to walk the airstrip, all in the heat of the loaders' eyes; her little son trailed on her arm.

'Gramps,' the boy said. Vico swept him up and held him high, ignoring his look of terror.

'I think they're watching me,' Anna said, ambiguously.

'You show yourself off,' Vico said.

'I mean the Feds,' Anna said.

Vico shrugged, and bundled his daughter and grandson into the house.

'They're talking a lot about you, Papa,' Anna said. 'It isn't easy for me.' She took a drink from him. 'I have to live in America; it says so in my divorce papers. I can't take the boy away.'

'Papers,' Vico said. 'Fuck papers.'

'I'm an American,' Anna said.

They smiled and watched the boy roll side to side into the garden, looking for something to play with; he walked like a sailor. When he was out of sight, they switched off their smiles like lights.

'On the news they said it's drugs now,' Anna said. 'We see the news. Everyone in the area sees the news. The boy hears it, and the kids at school hear it and they beat him up. They said his grandad did business with the Cubans.'

'Change schools.'

'You could tell me what you're doing. I can't keep changing places like you can.'

'You take care of the boy,' Vico said, 'I take care of my life. That's fair.'

'It's not fair on the boy.'

They were growing tired of their own arguments and Vico knew it. He needed fire.

'Mercedes is coming,' he said. He waited for a reaction.

'After so long,' Anna said. 'Why?'

'Because she's got guts. She's not some suburban Mama who's scared what the neighbours think.'

'You don't need her.'

'You say you're not happy coming here, not happy helping.'

'She never helped you before. You think she'll stick around if things get difficult?'

187

Vico shrugged.

'You can't go on wandering,' she said. 'Dealing here, dealing there. You'll run out of countries.'

'Oh Anna,' Vico said, with maddening condescension. She shamed him with the easy assumptions of a life that he'd long ago thrown away.

'They did make up about the drugs, didn't they?' she asked.

The boy had wandered back to the house from the empty garden. He walked past his mother and his grandfather and crossed to a bare room with a toy train laid out. He sat astride, waiting passively for the engine to whistle and chug away.

'There,' Vico said. He lumbered over and he began to push the train, grunting and whistling with the effort.

Anna said from the door: 'She doesn't have a baby. If she did have a baby, it wouldn't be your grandchild.'

Vico pushed the train. The boy looked serious.

'I don't want things to go wrong,' Anna said.

He made a circuit of the track and straightened up laboriously. His back clicked and complained.

She'd gone, which infuriated him.

'We'll find Mommy,' Vico said to the boy. The kid fixed a face he'd learned from TV, where you love Gramps.

'Find Mommy,' Vico said.

He went pounding through the bush like some great lost herbivore, the breath roaring in his head. He stopped where the white sand started.

She was standing on the crescent sweep of the beach. The day was too brisk for swimming; she stood facing into the wind.

Everyone betrayed George Vico, he thought – ran away, lost interest.

'You want money?' he shouted down to Anna. 'You need anything?'

'I don't need money.'

'Then what the hell are you doing here?'

'I came to see you, Papa.' Her arms were stretched out like some limp martyr on the sands.

'You've seen me,' Vico said. 'Now fuck off.'

She didn't want to be watched any more, which gave away the strength of her feeling.

Vico stomped back to the house and lay down on his beach bed, puffing.

She'd come back, if he needed her. Women always came back, and that was all she was: she had nowhere else to go. And besides, he had business.

He kept his visitors waiting a precisely insulting amount of time. There were two of them, a patrician Italian with brilliant, shocking blue eyes and an indeterminate Levantine wearing a tiny pectoral cross.

'What brings you here?' Vico asked, all innocent, as though the guards would have allowed them to land without stating their business in advance.

'We have a problem,' said the patrician.

'Don't we all?' Vico said.

'We've been interested in buying Stingers. We can't find a seller.'

Vico said: 'You don't want 'em.'

'It would make all the difference,' the patrician said. 'We're serious men. We're happy to pay. It's just a question of supply –'

'You can't use 'em,' Vico said. He had a knowledge made out of deals and catalogues and it suited him to lecture on it. 'They'll blow you away. Half the time the missile doesn't leave the tube, and the other half you've got to hit the target straight on. One kilo explosive charge and no proximity fuse.'

His visitors were patient.

'And then,' Vico said, 'there's all that wonderful infra-red heat-seeking crap. You fire 'em over water, they chase clouds. Over desert, they go hunting sand. Military planes all have heat flares. You want to hit anything, you're sitting on the runway, somewhere cold, and you know the flightpath.'

The men said: 'But the US won't admit that. You point a Stinger at one of their planes, they've got to act scared. Point it at the Presidential helicopter –'

Vico roared with laughter. 'You're going into a new business? I thought you were the ones who reckoned you'd make things hot in Italy so the world would want a law and order government in Rome – a new Mussolini to sort out the reds.'

'We have different enemies.'

'Besides, how are you going to explain how your Autonomistas, or whoever, are bringing down planes with American missiles?'

'There's a market,' the patrician said. 'Anybody can buy. You know that better than anyone.'

'You don't think I have principles?'

'Mr Vico,' the Levantine said in a buttery English, 'please don't misunderstand my colleague. We would be most grateful for your help –'

'It's big money,' Vico said. 'Stingers are politically sensitive. The Pentagon's officially terrified they'll fall into terrorist hands.'

'But through your contacts,' the patrician said, and he seemed to hiccup over the rest of his sentence, 'in the – substance business.'

They amused Vico. His business wasn't arms so much as knowing people who wanted to buy or sell, a broker's role. A missile, a bank, a sack of cocaine; it was all the same. It was an offshore game.

He said: 'Something could be done.'

The meeting became a fidgety affair. The men had nothing more to say, and no great wish to be polite, but still they had to wait for their plane back to the mainland. They tried small talk.

'We were very disturbed,' they said, 'by M. Rombauer's troubles. Many people must have been glad about his death.'

Vico beamed.

'It was nothing to do with us,' the patrician said. 'But it was fortuitous. He must have been in Siena to see somebody –'

'Maybe he came to see the Duccios,' Vico said. They were fishing for information he didn't want to give. At the same time, he didn't want to seem innocent. The appearance of guilt would help his credibility. 'I sometimes go to see the Duccios.'

They didn't believe it, of course. If they'd needed him less they'd have sneered at the southern vowels that slid into even a three-syllable name like Duccio.

'We're grateful,' the patrician said. 'Of course, it's too early to know what the investigators will find, but the idea that our private business –'

'Yours as well,' Vico said. He'd give them that, and let them calculate its meaning on the flight home.

When they'd gone, he sat with the whisky bottle on the table. The little shit Rombauer screwed up; he was gone. He couldn't have mattered that much to anyone, unless that anyone was a vengeful, irritable man who needed to prove his power from a distance.

'There,' he said aloud. The drink and the evening dimmed the light.

He heard the helicopter coming just as the sun was at its briefest green and gaudy glory over America. It came in low, a racket followed by a great wind that set the palms dancing in silhouette against a sky that was suddenly a dark, velvety blue.

He went to the window. The bird came down neatly, and as the blades stopped, he saw a woman at the top of the steps. She was cold and exact, like a *Vogue* picture; she'd put away all the fear she'd shown, for a moment, in that Siena church. His word for her was 'bandbox'.

'You don't have to pose,' Vico said. 'There aren't any photographers.'

Mercedes stood on the doorstep and drew off long white gloves. 'It's the wrong time of year,' she said. He circled her, nagging like an old dog that wants love; she wondered for a moment if she was being too cold, showing her confusion that way. He still had some power in his eyes.

'I'm glad you came,' Vico said. 'Shows you have some sense. You know you need me.'

'I couldn't leave things,' Mercedes said.

She saw that her picture hung on the wall. She wondered if it had been brought out specially for her visit.

'It's been a busy day for an old man,' Vico said. He relished the smell of artifice and flowers that clung to her; Anna had smelt of soap and purpose.

'You could get me a drink,' Mercedes said.

The whisky burnt her stomach pleasantly. She complimented him on the house and on the island. She said she looked forward to seeing it.

'You running away,' Vico said, 'or are you starting something?'

'Why would I be running away?'

'Because there's a gang of right-wing Italian thugs who hated to have their neat little Swiss bank busted up. They shot Rombauer first.'

'Why was Rombauer in Siena?' Mercedes asked.

'How should I know? I imagine he was after you. You were very noticeable in Siena.'

'I was working.'

'I'd have known you were there anyway. I'd have found the hotel registers, or the credit card slips, or the phone accounts –'

'I know,' Mercedes said. 'You know things.'

'So he must have been after you.'

'And it was pure coincidence that you were in Siena?'

Vico finished his drink. 'No,' he said. 'I came to see you.'

'It's a long way to come, after such a long time. You never came to New York or –'

'I couldn't come to New York. You know that.' He seemed to be trying to make himself vulnerable, the old turtle sloughing its shell. 'You haven't been to Italy often,' he said.

Mercedes shrugged. 'It's an old country.'

Vico threw himself out of his chair. He would not be seen struggling to rise; he would do it in one bound. 'You must,' he said, 'see the rest of the sunset.'

It was almost too late, but from the beach there was still a faint line of green and red wash along the horizon.

'I don't know what you're doing,' Vico said, softly. 'You fool around with Rombauer, people tell me you were asking questions about his Panama companies. Then suddenly everyone wants to know about the Diaz money. Is that what you're after?'

She took a deep breath. It was very seductive to stand here, in the cool evening, with her one-time father; she could say anything in the dark. If she could trust George Vico, she could pour out all her hopes and her alarm. If . . .

'You pulling a scam?' Vico said. 'Or are you planning to be a hero of the revolution? I never know with you nicely educated middle-class girls.'

'I'm not middle class.'

'Never say that. You'll alienate America.'

'I come from a place where there isn't a middle class.'

'Your father had a store.'

'A tiny store. A wretched little store.'

192

'You giving the money away or keeping it? If you find it?'

'Diaz stole that money from Providencia,' Mercedes said. It was odd how much easier courage was in the twilight. 'That money goes back to Providencia.'

'I thought I raised you to be more sensible. They got lobster for supper. I hope you like lobster. They always have lobster.'

'I'm serious,' Mercedes said.

'You're serious, little girl. I hear you.'

'You're just jealous of anyone with any purpose. Or a place to live or a place they come from or anywhere they can stay.'

'Go ahead,' Vico said. 'Daddy understands.'

She turned to him furiously, but in turning she recovered her composure. She summoned a sweet social wraith of a smile. 'It's for my mother country.'

'You've hardly been there. You never even see your own mother, which –'

She said: 'I need a shower.'

He watched her with the pig eyes of a man who scents real weakness.

'You see your mother often?' he said.

'If we can't talk sensibly, I've got a helicopter waiting.'

'He won't want to fly at night,' Vico said, reasonably. 'And besides, I run the planes and the helicopters and the boats. People go when I say they go.'

'You can walk from one of these islands to the next.'

'There are no boats on the next island. No planes, no helicopters.'

Before dinner, she came back from the shower and sat before him with her legs crossed neatly. She saw specks of blood in his fierce green eyes. She wondered if that was heart, drink or temper.

'You shouldn't wear stockings,' he said. 'Not here.' He couldn't stop watching her.

'If you're so good,' the plantation voice accused, 'then tell me how to hide the American companies. If anyone saw the Rombauer papers –'

Carpenter was fascinated by Diaz's worries. He had reckoned it might be time to return to Leon, to see the man sweat. El

Maximo might be all too happy to transfer a few more assets, reveal a few more clues.

'That bastard Rombauer,' Diaz said. 'So fucking stupid.'

Carpenter had left Mercedes at Milan airport on her way back to America. She wouldn't say exactly what she planned but he was sure they were both safer out of Italy. He had still not told her that he witnessed Rombauer's killing. He did not have the words.

In London, he spent a morning in the office and an evening with his wife. She'd chosen to go with friends to some basement in Notting Hill Gate for tricolour salads, pastas with floury sauces and too many bottles of dry, white Orvieto: with her was the man she talked about. He was a writer, of a theoretical kind, who looked like a squirrel, alert and fussy. Jill smothered him in her downy warmth. He'd always think he made her happy. Everybody did.

The squirrel wanted a fight. If Carpenter was capitalism, he'd be socialism – on memories of two weeks in Cuba, courtesy of some progressive firm in Huddersfield. How could Ian associate with Fascist bastards like Diaz? It was like General Motors and Hitler, where the Nazis just happened to inherit one hundred million dollars worth of tank factories. It was war crimes.

Carpenter watched Jill. She was lovely; she had a way of smiling that was between motherhood and having your cock sucked, and this night she wanted the men to fight over her like bulls. He knew he wasn't interested. Being manipulated by a good person is still being screwed.

The squirrel was more sure the more he drank. He was amiable enough, but he had the faith – a litany drawn from a smokestack, Victorian Europe and now refined until it was as demanding and useless as any schoolman's creed, then transplanted with remorseless certainty to other people's countries. The squirrel liked his revolutions just before they succeeded, when they were raw and bloody and untouched by expediency. He played politics like Tarzan.

Carpenter excused himself. 'I have an early flight.'

'Off somewhere?' said the squirrel with suspicion. He seemed to think sudden travel was an affectation, at least out of term.

To be difficult, Carpenter said: 'The Bahamas.'

He saw at once that the Bahamas were gratifyingly incorrect.

'It's a working-class resort off Florida,' he said. 'Particularly liked by American blacks.'

But he could see that they knew better. They didn't have to go.

'Is there anything we have to settle?' he asked Jill.

'Nothing,' Jill said. 'Let's send it all to the lawyers.'

He left, glad she'd decided at last to sort things out. It was what he wanted. He was tired of a safe, constant, meaningless marriage that had dried out and died.

After he left, the squirrel said: 'Nice man. Does he have a drink problem?'

But Carpenter was away from them all, rushing to America. He felt, for the first time, crammed into the plane, in a metal envelope where he didn't control his destiny.

In Miami, he tried to find a number for George Vico in the Bahamas. Nobody seemed to know. Bahamas Inquiries, once the 809 operator raised them, had no record, which he knew was odd; the Nassau book has everyone from Niarchos to Paley. And having gone that far, it seemed indiscreet to ask for the number on interstate calls or private calls abroad. The name of Vico was interesting to all those listening machines.

But he did want to know whether Mercedes had gone to her father. He needed to know what she planned.

Someone had passed the word. He was taken aside for drinks, propped in the first four rows of the plane to Leon with a Vice Minister. He kept smiling at a sweet-smiled, wet-lipped girl who brought the drinks, and she kept smiling at him. She leaned generously toward him; she smelt of bread and sweat.

'We have to evacuate the plane,' she said.

He didn't believe her. He thought it some elaborate joke to test his reactions, that she'd laugh if he stood and began to move.

'We don't have much time,' she said. She'd taken his glass.

He stood and looked back down the plane. People were restive at the sight of the privileged rows now clutching their hand baggage and preparing to get out.

'Move,' the stewardess said.

He ran down the steps of the plane and after him came the whole human cargo, stripped out of the plane like pulp from a fruit. They were all tumbling against one another, frantic. Some were shouting; most were determined to move out of range. It was as though they all had the memory of gunfire.

At the door to the terminal, the ground staff said: 'It's probably a false alarm.'

But the plane was towed out into the green wasteland beyond the runways. They could see it go, its gaudy yellow and red tail clearly visible in the distance.

Carpenter stood by the windows, waiting. He half expected the plane to explode in a mess of smoke and fire; he began to see why Diaz was nervous. Even in Miami, the property of El Maximo – this plane, these people – was no longer safe.

He went off with the Vice Minister for yet more drinks.

'Technical trouble,' the Vice Minister said, lying.

In an hour and a half, they climbed on board again. This time, everyone was subdued. The stewardess with the wet lips passed by, but her smile had become an automaton's, something on a doll. The life had been scared out of her.

'Ladies and gentlemen,' the pilot said, 'we're sorry for the delay –'

The plane shuddered a little in a patch of turbulent air. As it moved, a woman at the back began to scream.

The sky shook through the window and then grew calm again.

Diaz had sent the Presidential Lincoln, a stretch affair that could have taken a swimming pool; even the Vice Minister was impressed. Carpenter settled in the back. He found the machine obscene, he realised, shocked by his own sudden access of morality. He found its progress, gleaming, through the *barrio* streets vile and also absurd. He wondered how many times the Government had paid Diaz so that he could ride this way. He thought the car a sentimental view of power.

Through the darkened windows, when the car was once forced to a halt, he saw the kids scrambling. Diaz used to drive through the *barrio* very fast, throwing coins through the window. The kids crowded close because of the cash, yet had to hold back or die; that was the sport, the pain in those faces as they waited.

He shifted on the leather seat. He never liked to think too closely about the exact morality of what he did; that was not how

196

he was paid to think. But here, the moral questions could become suddenly overwhelming, like one of those tropical stenches which comes out of a river. He was stifling.

Diaz was delighted to see him. That was startling enough. He pushed a list of companies into Carpenter's hand, names and corporate headquarters.

'I don't know any more,' he said. 'Some of these were held through Rombauer, some weren't. They're all in America. For Christ's sake get them hidden.'

Carpenter wanted to ask why Diaz was so sure his regime was foundering. He wanted to ask, not because he needed the answer. He wanted to see Diaz squirm.

'If my wife finds out –'

In the middle of revolution, the fall of a dynasty of thieves, he was thinking about alimony. It was not even an unreasonable thought: probably, it would shape the rest of his life.

'Divorce,' Carpenter said, 'is no fun.'

'You know?'

'I know. I saw the lawyer before leaving London.'

'Of course,' Diaz said, 'I should divorce her for desertion. But a gentleman does not divorce a lady.'

'A gentleman,' Carpenter said, with mock feeling, 'just pays.' This community of trouble seemed most promising.

He shuffled the list of names. One sounded like a horror movie theme park: perfect for managing cashflow. There was a fish-packing business and a real estate business. Carpenter frowned at the real estate. That company would have tangible assets of the kind that require a buyer before they have real value. He didn't see how Mercedes could use even the plushest of Miami condominiums in the short term.

'Stick around,' Diaz said. 'They're all nervous like cats. You'll find it amusing. And,' he said, 'I want to know what else I have to do.'

Carpenter had almost reached the doors when Diaz said: 'That list. I wrote it myself. Nobody else gets to see it.'

'Bankers are like priests,' Carpenter said. 'Trust me.'

'Like priests?' Diaz said, the memory of an outraged bishop brandishing his mitre over a body in a public square. 'I hope to Christ you're not.'

197

And he waved Carpenter on and out.

In his room at the InterContinental, Carpenter turned on the airconditioning. Nothing happened. He could look out of his window at the back road which led into the bunker; soldiers lived up on the hill, with women and children, goats and guns all promiscuously bundled together in wood shacks. There were no lights.

He rang reception. Reception apologised. 'A temporary difficulty,' a heavy voice tried to say. Falling apart, Carpenter thought. The idea did not comfort him. It was one thing to have Diaz safely distracted in Leon, fighting an invisible enemy, dependent on others to manage his affairs; it was quite another to have Diaz pitched out of his country and ready to take back control.

Carpenter stared out of the window as the soldiers walked and stretched.

A few more weeks, please God, and then he could hand all this to Mercedes, a present for the memory of Aurelia. He could walk away.

On the hill he saw a soldier pushing a woman and some children into a battered Ford, and adding luggage. On the back of the car was a refrigerator. They were running.

Just a few more weeks.

Mercedes lay on her bed in a cold, neat room. She reached out her arms for some warmth, some uncompromised affection. Lust would be nice.

There was nobody, just her appetite.

She swung out of bed and stretched. She'd come to be protected and she felt stifled. She was annoyed with herself.

The morning was already glittering off the sea. She pulled on a dressing gown and walked through the house to the porch. She ordered coffee as if she was at home and settled in a shell of a chair. A mocking bird sounded off, like chipping stone; a humming bird stood in the air.

'Boo,' Vico said.

She turned to him. 'Good morning.'

'You look younger like that,' he said, happily.

She drank her coffee.

198

'You ought to go swimming,' Vico said. 'It's warm enough.'

'Not for me.' He was always a little too close; she didn't feel she could shift out of range.

'You want to talk about what you were doing at Rombauer's?'

'Who told you?'

'Never mind. I'm just interested why you want the Diaz money. You turning into a daughter of mine, or playing heroes?'

'Heroes,' Mercedes said. She moved away from him to the screen of the porch and basked in the light of the proper, almost tropical sun.

'You think the guerrillas will win?' Vico sounded interested. She shrugged.

'You think it will do your people any damn good?'

She did not move.

'You go to Cuba some day,' he said. 'I know them. I do business there. The blacks still cut the cane; they just get paid less. Nobody speaks above a whisper. The *commandantes* know everything. The food's lousy. It's like under Batista except Batista never said he was morally right and inevitable.'

'Nothing changes. Is that what you're saying?'

'Right.'

'The children live,' she said. 'They don't get diseases any more, and if they do, there are hospitals. They have schools. Most people work, which they didn't under Batista. Nobody's actually hungry.'

'You think people care?' Vico said. 'People don't want just not to be hungry. They want chances.'

'It helps if you survive.'

'And your Amadista friends will do all that, will they? Make a better society? And you'll be what – Ministeress of Haute Couture and Culture? Unless someone thinks you're too young, or too female – or too black?'

'I'm going for a walk.'

'And then what happens when the Americans decide to intervene? They've got the gunships, the missiles. They had Puff the Magic Dragon in Vietnam, you remember? The gunship that flew over a forest and left it looking like a ploughed field.'

'Then the Amadistas will need guns.'

'You're funny about America, are you?'

Mercedes turned to him. He'd expected anger in her eyes but there was only an insulting, professional calm.

'I'm funny,' she said, 'about Providencia.'

And she went through the porch doors, down onto the cool, damp morning grass.

Vico watched her go. It had only been a few years and he was quite unsure whether she was sincere or faking. He hadn't expected that.

Half a dozen men had come from a nearby island to tend the beaches. They went walking with brooms of twigs, flicking the black seaweed away from the white sand, a picturesque procession. She walked a little ahead of them.

She didn't like what exile had done to George Vico. He had nothing to get on with, no daily meetings; he was isolated and he was sour. He was drinking too much. He depended too much on anyone who passed through.

She would call John Grey III. In all the flurry of tripping and posing through Europe, she'd almost forgotten to call him. Something about his seriousness before she left New York had upset her profoundly; there was too much mortality in his mind.

In the house, she negotiated for a line.

'Why do you need anyone?' Vico asked. 'We haven't seen each other for so long.'

'I have some work to do,' Mercedes said.

'I could help you.'

'I know,' Mercedes said. 'I'm not sure I'd like the price.'

'You have to radio,' Vico said. 'You use Nassau.'

'Then help me do it,' Mercedes said. 'At least help me do that.'

The day grew edgier, and the sky darker, in perfect unison. She found the obviousness funny.

And when finally she reached John Grey III, she was struck by how unflippant he had become.

'I'd love to come,' he said. 'For a day or two.'

So she'd have her family together for a while.

She ate supper alone; Vico was somewhere in the house, or out between the lifeless white lights of the airstrip with some special cargo. All she cared was that he was somewhere else.

The servants offered coffee with a parody of manners, bowing too much.

She sat on a long pink sofa for a while, listening to the night sounds: frogs, cicadas and the electronic din of natural things. Then she walked very slowly to her room.

She hated to be alone, this profoundly alone.

She came to the door of her bedroom. Something flickered at the foot of the door. She bent down and saw a lit candle, a sturdy red affair. It had a nail driven through it.

She picked it up. She prided herself on having no unnecessary memory but she knew this thing. In Bluefields, you call it badlamp and it is a curse, because a life will end when the candle dies.

She shielded the flame most carefully and put the candle into the bathtub where it was best sheltered from draughts.

She'd come for help but she'd not been complaisant enough. Vico wanted her to know there was a price for help.

She walked to the bathroom door where she could watch the flame play and echo between the white tiled walls.

There was a queue outside the American embassy, jostling and manoeuvring, people who couldn't pull rank on one another because all were equally important. Each wanted a visa for America, even a few weeks in America. Old hands remembered the last days of Batista in Havana and wanted to be ready.

Carpenter cruised by them in a borrowed car. He recognised dinner party faces, even a Minister, all fretting for the certainty of being allowed into America. They'd settle for a one-day visa to Miami.

It was a sad sort of justice. He drove down the hill and turned onto the city's one stretch of wide motorway; he pressed the accelerator. The speed was exhilaration and escape; the difficult world went out of focus for a while; there was only the road and the volcano up ahead with its plume of silvery steam.

Then the traffic stopped dead.

He sat between the high sugar cane on either side and turned the radio on. Boys were out already with plastic bags of Coke and ice, peeled oranges, even a tired stock of red velvet roses with an overpoweringly sweet scent.

201

There must be a roadblock. The cars around him were heavy laden, their axles threatening the irregular surface of the road. People were leaving only to find that Leon was under siege.

He wondered whose roadblock this was – Diacista or Amadista. He didn't want to answer questions. He spun the car out of line in a tight U-turn and checked the rearview mirror for the state of the Guards' nerves. But they were far up ahead, their guns down; they were glad if anyone turned back without being threatened.

He had everywhere to go, and suddenly no way to get there. The airport was shut; he'd already discovered that. The roads were blocked. He wondered whether that bitching straggle at the embassy would ever use their visas.

He found himself surprisingly calm; it was the strength of crisis. The only way out was with Diaz so he'd stick close to El Maximo. From now on, the issue wasn't money; it was survival.

At the door of the bunker, the Guards were quarrelling; they made him wait. Inside, the corridors were a muddle of rank and panic. Soldiers who had business there were grateful not to be on any front line, now that Diaz was losing; senior officers fretted beside politicians and merchants, all cross as wet cats and watchful. Some of them might not get out of this place.

They exchanged rumours in voices that were careful and calm; but the details were gaudy. The airport was shut because of anti-aircraft fire. The guerrillas had brought down a Tan Sasha flight with SA-7 missiles. The Americans had tried to airlift supplies and arms but their planes had been beaten back. The Diacistas wanted to think they still had friends.

A woman, tailored like a knife, sat on a hard chair with a copy of *Architectural Digest*. She seemed to be willing herself into its glossy pages.

A National Guard officer stalked by, hands and pockets stuffed with blank airline tickets. He dropped a pile and Carpenter helped him. Since the planes were grounded, Carpenter assumed he was watching the birth of a fraud.

Suddenly the tall doors to the President's office opened and out came the American Ambassador, toiling in a sea of aides. He looked exasperated. Behind him, Diaz had taken a Presidential pose by the mock fireplace.

It was odd, Carpenter thought, that there were no official cars at the door.

The sergeant-secretary called his name and the crowd looked up resentfully. They had only to find the right man, cut the right deal and they'd be safe. But who? Or who might get there first?

The sergeant might never have ordered an evening and a morning of violence in Manhattan; he was brisk and formal.

In the office, the doors closed, Diaz said: 'The Americans have decided that I am no longer viable. They want me to negotiate with the Amadistas. I shall not negotiate with a gun at my head.'

There was something wrong with the man's habitual bluster but it took Carpenter a moment to realise what. His usual meticulous appearance was a little ruffled, the khaki shirt all too obviously engineered to hold in the belly; El Maximo had allowed himself to look ordinary.

'Fifty years,' Diaz was saying, mostly to himself, 'fifty years since the Marines came in and my grandfather ran the country. You know why they came here? Because the country owed them money and they wanted to seize the customs houses to get it back. Money, that's all. And now they'd rather have Communism. Materialism. Atheism. Godless authoritarianism. Those bastards have no principles at all.

'They stopped selling me guns. All these years we've been a bulwark against Communism in this hemisphere.'

'You had business to discuss?' Carpenter said.

'Fucking bankers,' Diaz said, with what sounded like grudging respect. 'One-track minds, haven't you? Don't care about pain or politics, just money.'

'That's probably true,' Carpenter said disarmingly.

'Money,' Diaz said. 'While we've got money, the Israelis will still sell to us. They always sell.'

'You have money,' Carpenter said.

'It's just a matter of time. While I'm here, the Americans can't just boot me out. Can they? They have to keep talking. I won't move out of here until I know –'

He realised the logical slip he'd made, stopped the sentence and tried to claw back his confidence.

'We ought to talk business,' Carpenter said. The man had to stay in panic long enough to talk.

'You do what you want,' Diaz said.

'But if you think you're leaving –'

'I'm not leaving,' Diaz said. 'I will not leave.'

Carpenter gave up a silent prayer that the man would stay sure. That way, he still needed Carpenter.

'I have a bank in the Bahamas,' Diaz said. 'Mercantile Overseas. I don't know what they're like, but you can leave the money there and I'll come for it. If I need to.'

'I'll need the account numbers.'

'You sure?' Diaz asked shrewdly.

'It will help. You want the Swiss money there, and your American holdings –'

'Get onto those as soon as you can.' Diaz couldn't be a supplicant for long.

'You want to move anything else?' Carpenter asked innocently. 'Do you know where you're going if you leave here?'

Diaz looked exactly like a weasel. 'I don't think that's going to be a problem,' he said.

'You may need to centralise. You can always move things round later.'

'In your bank, no doubt?'

Carpenter said nothing. If he was suspected of nothing worse than commercial motives, he was doing well.

'I said, in your bank?'

'Give me the names.'

'And for Christ's sake keep them all discreetly. Nobody knows except you and me.' Diaz seemed to realise at last what a risk he was having to take and he loosened his tie.

'You stick close,' he added, 'until we can get out.'

Carpenter nodded and put papers into his briefcase as if some quite ordinary meeting had just ended. He must not show excitement. He must not attract suspicion.

'Don't leave the bunker,' Diaz said. 'There's nothing left to see out there.'

Carpenter left the office. In his briefcase now he carried all the clues he needed to some sizeable portion of the Diaz fortune; he had Diaz trapped, unable to intervene. But he, too, could not start work. He couldn't call out of the bunker because the Guards watched and the lines were falling. He couldn't leave

204

Leon until Diaz's ego allowed him to acknowledge at least temporary defeat. He was caught.

He was looking at the sergeant-secretary's desk, covered in papers. The papers seemed to shuffle themselves. Carpenter's hair stood on end; he felt, rather than heard, a low encircling sound that went to the bones. A glass fell and broke. The soldiers and the civilians were all still.

The low sound grew into a rumble, then subsided with a sigh. The walls seemed to shiver. Carpenter thought of the still, dead volcano up above them with its ink-black lake, and imagined a cartoon of a volcano with spits of orange fire.

The sound began to die. He realised, but it took a minute, that the walls were still standing. He'd been shaken in place. The air around him seemed thin like a coffin's air.

The sergeant-secretary was alert for trouble.

A senior civil servant, ministry unknown, was saying in a loud didactic voice: 'Very low on the Richter scale. They wouldn't even report in California. Just a seismic shift.'

The voice was lost immediately in anxious babble.

An aide went unannounced through the doors to El Maximo's office and after a minute El Maximo came bustling out. The starch of all his public years was barely holding him together.

'Passageway's down,' Carpenter thought he heard someone say. The room around him let out a communal whine.

Nobody wanted to follow Diaz, so nobody stopped Carpenter. He ran down a corridor linked with the kind of pale, tasteful sporting prints that a bank clerk might buy on retirement, a stage set that finished at a huge steel door. The backstairs of a grand house ending in some incongruous vault.

The door opened and there was a narrow, black iron staircase spiralling down.

Carpenter knew about this place. Down here, the dwarf Chamorro had his operating rooms, and sometimes 'the gentleman' would come to watch. The only way down those stairs was as victim or as torturer.

But it was easy to go down, following Diaz. Carpenter held the rail and watched his footing on the slippery metal.

Below there was a corridor with tall steel doors, each pierced with a tiny shutter. The cells were scrubbed yet they still held the little smells of piss, breath, fear. Carpenter reckoned he could see eyes at one of those little shutters. The place had the look of a machine, but there was pain caught in its airless guts.

The Guards came to rough attention. They were reassured, but not greatly, by the parade of authority.

Beyond the row of cells there was another door, and beyond that, darkness. Carpenter stood by Diaz and his aides and let the light get to his eyes. Out of the blank dark he could distinguish fallen stones. There was some kind of dust in the air that caught at the lining of his lungs.

Diaz only stared at the stones.

'This passageway,' Carpenter began. 'It led –?' And then he knew. The American Ambassador had some private way into the bunker; this must be it. There had always been talk of such a secret access.

'Maybe they dynamited it,' Diaz said wildly. 'They dynamited it so that we couldn't get through. So we wouldn't be a risk. So they could deny everything. So –'

He stooped and began to tear at the stones.

'Help me,' he shouted.

The aides got down among the broken stones, but they could not move the largest ones and the smaller ones only rolled into positions that were just as awkward. Diaz caught himself and stood up again.

'Don't be such damn fools,' he said crisply. He was trying to shoot his cuffs over hands that were stained black, brown and red.

'We will talk later,' Diaz said, to nobody in particular.

In his office he asked Carpenter: 'What else do you need to know?'

And Carpenter took out his notepad.

Vico was amiable in the morning, ready to calm her fears; but she showed no fear.

'I need to go to Nassau,' she said.

He shrugged.

'You sent the helicopter back. I need a boat or a plane.'

'I own the planes,' Vico said and grinned.

'It's time I got back to business,' Mercedes said. 'It's obvious you've nothing to tell me.'

206

'Suppose,' Vico said, 'I had the names of the banks Diaz used in Nassau. Just suppose.'

'Then I'd be grateful if you gave them to me.' Mercedes was running out of patience.

'I could give you an introduction.'

'Thank you.' She was defiant and expectant.

'And you could collect your friend Grey from the airport. You ought to look after your friends.'

'Then you'll find me a plane –'

'But you have to come back,' Vico said, 'for your own safety. You never know who'll be in Nassau, who'll see you.'

'You're bluffing.'

'Maybe. Remember they killed Rombauer in the town where you were. And it isn't hard to guess you'd run to me.'

'You can't even tell me who they are.

'Will they kill you less dead if you're not formally introduced?' Vico belched like some sea-cow's grunt. 'Besides, I'm just giving you a name and an introduction. You'll need me to do anything else.'

'Yes,' Mercedes said.

He hung over her. 'Call me Papa,' he said.

She had a taste of bile in the back of her throat. She said nothing.

'Call me Papa,' he said. 'When you want to.'

And he lumbered out into the garden like a bear. He seemed disappointed.

He provided the plane. It skipped like a stone over the tiny islands, coral fragments in a sea of glittering blues and greens. She looked down on the black sea holes where the sand fell away into an abyss, and on islands which had the manicured green of mansion lawns and others which were black except for a little scrub. They came down into Nassau from the north, over the unlovely bush; and Vico had provided a car. She thanked the pilot profusely, walked out of the terminal building towards the car, then ducked back along the buildings to the taxi rank by the customs hall. She fell into a beige Mercedes and lay back. She didn't want to be seen.

She had a couple of hours before Grey's flight. Vico would expect her to spend that time at the airport, or at Lyford Cay which was close by; he wouldn't think of her making a dash into Nassau. The avenue of tall, bare royal palms went by, and then the sea, the concrete blocks of big hotels, the little beaches fringed with the casuarina trees whose feathery shade killed everything. She hadn't yet made her decisions when the cab was among low, modern office blocks and its driver asking where to go next.

'Mercantile Overseas,' she said. 'It's a bank.'

The driver, huge and blue-black, turned and smiled. 'Honey,' he said, 'every house in this town is a bank. You know which house?'

'I only know the names.'

The driver threw big hands in the air. 'Lord,' he said, 'those names. Every one like every other one.'

She pulled Vico's note from her bag. 'Shaw Building,' she read.

And the driver turned down a narrow street towards the sea. There was a furniture shop and a bridal shop where the too-tall window mannequin lay on her side, knees startlingly apart. There was also a green and white building, pre-war, made of wood; it had wide verandahs and shutters.

'Shaw Building,' said the driver.

She stopped on the steps. She had only a note from Vico, a name, and whatever reputation she carried with her. She had nothing but bluff.

She asked for the manager that Vico named, a man called John Boswell. He was there within a minute, ushering her into a cold, smart room.

'Miss Zenon,' he said. 'What a pleasure to meet you.'

He saw money, glamour, prospects.

'This is,' Mercedes said, 'rather delicate.' She had assumed the grave and downcast look of a widow. 'You should see this letter from George Vico first.'

Boswell took the letter and was impressed. 'And what can I do –?'

'You realise that Anastasio Diaz Sacasa is in no position at present to deal with his own affairs. The situation in Leon being what it is.'

Did he know? Did he care? He was staring hard at her, as

though she was part of the situation, and maybe compromising.

'He has asked me to make some arrangements,' Mercedes said.

'And Mr Vico has told me to co-operate,' Boswell said. 'And Mr Vico controls the bank, so –'

'Mr Vico knows Mr Diaz. All this had to be done most discreetly.'

'I understand discretion, Miss Zenon.'

'We are consolidating Mr Diaz's assets in Switzerland for the moment. Until things are more clear.'

'There is privacy here, too,' Boswell said. 'I just have to tell the Central Bank that an account holder lives outside the country and they don't need a name.'

'This is a temporary measure,' Mercedes said. 'So Mr Diaz is more comfortable.'

Boswell sent for files and statements. 'I'd like to persuade you that we're a serious place,' he said. 'Even for your own money –'

'I don't doubt it,' Mercedes said. 'But for the moment, I'm just running errands. I am supposed to collect the liquid assets and move them.'

'In a suitcase?' Boswell said. 'That's a little primitive.'

'There is no better way,' Mercedes said. 'Especially when it's Louis Vuitton, in the VIP lounge.'

Boswell grinned. He was well maintained, fifty but with fifty years of tennis and boats; he stood back from things. And for the moment, he had an extraordinarily beautiful woman talking money to him and he watched himself with amusement.

The papers came. Boswell flicked through them. 'I suppose,' he said, 'I should have asked you for the account numbers and all that. But if Vico vouches for you –'

'We're old friends,' she said.

'So there'll be no difficulty,' Boswell said, 'although it is a very sizeable withdrawal. Very sizeable indeed. Luckily it seems to be mostly certificates of deposit; we're trustees. So we can sign the paper over to you and let you have the certificates.'

'Not to me,' Mercedes corrected. 'To Anastasio Diaz Sacasa.'

'Of course,' Boswell said.

And now she was nervous. Once, she'd had extraordinary luck and had found the Diaz money almost without effort; then

Rombauer died and she was on the run. The luck couldn't hold. Boswell should not be this casual about so large a withdrawal. And even a banker in George Vico's employ knew the difference between keeping a man's money in the vaults and handing it to his more plausible friends when they came calling.

She longed to ask: 'Why aren't you more worried?' But the question would explode her game.

'There is an account,' Boswell said, 'which carries the interest on these CDs. Naturally, we retain the account.'

Mercedes looked blank.

'You know as well as I do,' Boswell said, 'what this is about. It's about hiding money. I don't mind; Vico wants me to help. But there's a price for hiding money. You pay a fee.'

'Vico will say –'

'Vico will agree,' Boswell said, 'because he has a piece of the bank.'

'Of course.'

And she was shown out with elaborate courtesy.

In the street, she stopped between two shops. There was a window of Lalique, bolts of towels with flamingos and sunsets and duty-free perfumes, all behind white colonnades; it was like a bazaar in Palm Beach. There was a drugstore window with old coloured bottles and the products of Savory and Moore, waiting for the season when the pale white ladies came back. The boys selling powdered aspirin up back alleys did better.

The hotels were a little less than grand, but she chose one – a great pile like pink coconut ice – and hired a room to have a telephone. She left a message for John Grey at the airport, to join her when he could. And she lay back on a narrow bed and arched herself up and howled with pleasure.

This time, she'd done it for herself. These papers, all stiff and serious, were millions; they were the money of Diaz, now in her hands. It was her triumph and it made up for all the nonsense in Switzerland. She'd come out of eclipse.

As for Vico, he'd never believe it. He'd set it up, but he wouldn't believe she had followed through.

John Grey arrived an hour later. He was in a limousine of sorts, the kind of car that Vico would command. The driver wouldn't go.

'Vico had a car for me at the airport,' Grey said.

'Shit,' Mercedes said.

'We could take him to lunch,' Grey said. 'There's a place up on the hill.'

She gathered up the papers from the bedside table and pushed them at Grey. 'Look,' she said, 'what I got.'

Grey shuffled through them. 'Very pretty,' he said.

'Just pretty?'

'Very good,' Grey said. 'You're still determined to find the Diaz billion, are you?'

'You know I am.'

'I hope the rest of it is in better shape than this.'

She frowned.

'There's nothing wrong with these,' she said. 'They're certificates of deposit on real banks in Nassau. I checked the names in the phone book.'

'Try cashing them,' Grey said. 'It'll be easier here than in New York.'

'I will,' Mercedes said. 'We could do that this afternoon.'

Grey looked at her pityingly. 'Let's have a really good lunch first,' he said.

'You didn't explain what's wrong with these papers.'

'You'll see.'

And he was maddeningly silent, superior like an older brother.

In El Presidente's office, the sofa was heaped with unbroken bundles of garish 500-cordoba notes, like some fall of confetti from a generous sky. There were the boxes of the blank airline tickets Carpenter had seen before; the President's showgirl, face prettily contorted, wrote herself a world that went from Rio to Sydney to Anchorage to New York to Tokyo to Paris. Then she couldn't think of any more places and she'd run out of blank tickets to fill.

They were stealing a country. It was simple enough, like stealing from a store if you have the power of signature. They took cheques from the Central Bank of Providencia drawn on dollar accounts in Caracas, Miami, New Orleans, Mexico City; some were blank and some were simply huge. They withdrew cash from the bank and they overdrew the nation's credit on

211

airline tickets alone. Sooner or later, those tickets would come back to the international clearing house, and Providencia would try to pay. Most, Carpenter guessed, would be cashed not used. It was a simple way to carry money.

Outside in the ante-rooms, two whole classes had assembled, shifting and complaining. There were the aristocrats come down from the hills to ask a favour from Diaz, hoping they had earned it by their silence over the years; and there were the senior officers of the National Guard and the Ministries, convinced the Amadistas would prove much like themselves and desperate to save their lives. They had feared or depended on Diaz for so long they had no independent ways of escape. The country was Diaz; he was their flag, their anthem for a day. If they woke from this nightmare in America, they'd get on with despising him.

El Presidente wanted food. Carpenter opened up the office refrigerator. There were tins of Iranian caviar but they'd been stored in the freezer where they turn to soup; and there was no opener. He slammed the door shut.

He heard a clatter of rifle butts on the floor outside.

'You take charge of this stuff,' Diaz said. 'You make sure it's safe or I'll fucking kill you.'

'Yes,' Carpenter said. He'd become clear and cool in this atmosphere of fuss and panic. He had nothing to lose but his life, and he could do nothing about that. He was watching Diaz behave just as Aurelia or Mercedes would predict, and he could stop it. He just had to keep his nerve, and his power of attorney.

Diaz shuffled papers on his desk. There were piles of embossed letters so fine they cut fingers, and between them, boxes of cigarettes and letter openers and a small revolver. He was getting ready to take everything.

'I'm not going to run,' Diaz said. 'I'm not giving them that satisfaction.'

'Of course not,' Carpenter said.

'I don't run.'

The definitions didn't matter any more, except to Diaz. The Amadistas were somewhere out there, maybe on the hill, maybe in the city; they could be on the open road out to the airport. They were inevitable. And the Diacistas had so long considered them roaches and villains and Bolsheviks that they were too

212

shocked to realise the Americans didn't object.

The sergeant-secretary opened the door a crack and slipped through, keeping what ceremony he could. They could hear shouting.

'Sir,' the secretary said.

El Presidente was writing cheques like a star scribbling autographs. It was mechanical, regular work.

'Sir,' the secretary said again. 'There's something you should know.'

'Talk.'

'The National Guard had to torch the cathedral. There were Amadista snipers, maybe an Amadista brigade. They used mortars.'

El Presidente roused himself. 'You want me to see this?'

'I thought –'

'I don't give a fuck,' Diaz said. 'It's not my city any more, they tell me!'

But he followed the sergeant-secretary, with Carpenter walking behind, after a careful moment of tidying himself. The crowd in the ante-rooms looked scared and anxious, like kids in the first moments of a school dance.

'When are we going, Tachito?' a woman said, softly.

But Diaz walked past. At the bunker door, he stood outside and looked down the slopes towards the lake. There, just before the black water, the ancient, heavy towers of the cathedral were lit with a bonfire light, inside and out. It was so distant it could be a miniature, a show in a museum or a cinema. It was so bright, there was nothing else to see.

'I saw it,' Diaz said.

'The Guard is only just holding the town,' the secretary said. 'I thought it best to tell you outside –'

'Where I can get shot at,' Diaz said sarcastically.

'Where there is nobody to listen,' the secretary said.

Diaz raised his fist in the air and shook it at the city, a gesture of indiscriminate defiance. 'We'll get the bastards,' he said. But he didn't shout.

Carpenter regretted scrambling back into the stuffy bunker. He wondered what would happen if there was a power failure and the air and light cut out on this fractious mob.

213

In the Presidential office, he took the last of the cash that Diaz wanted put in Switzerland. He took it in all its various forms and loaded it into his briefcase. He didn't dare count what was there, in cheques and tickets and drafts. He knew he was shackled to a paper fortune.

'Do you think,' Diaz said, 'they'll come today?'

'Bunco money,' John Grey said.

She sat under the wide poinciana by the library tower and pounded her fist on the bench.

'Mercantile Overseas takes the money, pays the interest, but it never gives the capital back. So you can't sell the CDs at a discount because they're not worth anything.'

'You don't know that. Mercantile Overseas is an established bank.'

'You heard what the people at Chase said. Not acceptable either as collateral or as a deposit. They'd learned not to take them.'

'Then we go back to Boswell. We demand the money –'

'He'd laugh,' Grey said. 'Why do you think he gave in so easily?'

Mercedes said: 'I have paper worth twenty-one million.'

'It's not worth a dollar.'

'But they can't get away with it.'

'Depends on the clients, and how much they've got to hide. Usually they'll roll the CD over every five years; if they wanted the cash, they'd have to sue. You don't sue if you don't want to admit you've even got money here.'

A knot of broad backsides from the cruiseships sauntered past, hip to hip in brilliant polyester green.

'I will not let it go,' she said.

'Nobody's going to take that paper.'

'But there must be people outside the big banks. People who don't know enough to be suspicious. We give them a massive discount, they think they've done a deal. They pass it on to some other sucker –'

'You've got the idea,' Grey said.

'Foreign exchange dealers,' Mercedes said.

'They're in the big banks.'

214

'Casinos then.'

'They don't do twenty million for a single punter, not unless they know you very well indeed.'

'They know my name. My face.'

'They can be very straight indeed with people they don't know.'

'They don't have to take the paper. Just so someone takes it, and wants to cash it – someone Boswell can't keep quiet. Someone who'll scare him.'

John Grey smiled at her, warmly and without guile. He said: 'You're really still playing, aren't you?'

'Aren't you?'

'Things change.'

'We're friends. That doesn't change. We love each other.'

Grey took a theatrical pause.

'I've been watching someone,' he said. 'He's been told he's going to die. He's twenty-six, a dancer, and he can't catch his breath.'

'We're alive,' Mercedes said.

'It may be more difficult to live with disease,' Grey said. 'Never knowing, always wondering. Panicking, sometimes.'

'It's not your fault.'

'I wasn't blaming myself. Or the way we lived.'

Mercedes was up on her feet, and her eyes no longer looked tired. 'I am going,' she said, 'and you are coming with me and we are going to give the performance of our lives.'

Vico's driver had trailed close to them and he was hot to run back to the airport and ship them safely to German Cay. When they seemed eager to spend the night in Nassau, he said the plane was waiting. When they wouldn't listen, he drove them to a hotel on Paradise Island, across the narrow bridge, and he called Vico.

'Doesn't matter,' Vico said.

But it infuriated him. She'd come home all dutiful and already she was going against his will.

Mercedes knew how to diguise herself by keeping her eyes down and her body slack, not drawing attention. She also knew precisely how to reverse that process. On the island, she was anonymous until the top of the casino steps. Then, she looked down on the room of dealers and fruit machines, nerved herself, and walked.

The dealers, slack in the early evening, buzzed; she heard her name. Even the matrons at the fruit machines, eyes glassed with resigned greed, turned to look. She heard her name.

'Give them time,' she said to Grey. 'They'll come to us.'

It was management that came first, neat in tuxedos with the brown and blond look of turned professional boys. They offered dinner, a VIP lounge, diversions, anything that could be caught in the clattering blue light of the house photographer. The flashbulbs stopped the room.

She paused at a blackjack table, like royalty. She bought a thousand dollars in chips – the manager ran errands for her – and she watched the run of the cards from the shoe. She bet high; she lost.

John Grey beamed.

'I feel ready,' Mercedes said with meaning, 'for a serious game.'

The manager bustled back with offers of drinks in his office. When he'd eased open a bottle of Krug and poured it, he said: 'There are other games on the island.'

'I wondered,' Mercedes said.

'It's illegal for Bahamian residents to gamble,' he said, 'but the residents are among the richest people here. So they have private games. Of course the casino knows nothing –'

'Naturally.'

'And there is the question of credit.'

Mercedes looked expectant, but not offended.

'Your name is famous, of course,' he went on, 'but the residents like to settle on the night. It's a convention.'

Mercedes nudged Grey and he produced the bundle of Mercantile Overseas CDs.

'This,' she said, 'is my collateral.'

The manager looked impressed. The papers made sense to him because he had something similar, but in thousands, tucked away at Citibank.

'I think,' he said, with a stage-managed smile, 'this would do very well indeed. You'd find it hard to lose that much.'

'I play hard,' Mercedes said.

216

The manager excused himself, and when he returned was obviously pleased.

'A car is coming,' he said. 'It might be more discreet not to use yours.'

'Of course.'

'I never asked where you were staying.'

'No,' Mercedes said, 'you didn't. But we are with George Vico, on German Cay.'

The manager's eyes widened. He'd provided the perfect pigeon for milady; he had done brilliantly.

'Then,' he said, 'if you'll take a little more wine –'

Mercedes drank, and she thought. She was going to an unspecified place for a purpose not wholly clear, with twenty-one million in her pocket and a bellyful of champagne. She stayed watchful.

John Grey said: 'I'm coming along.'

'You stay in Nassau,' Mercedes said, sharply.

The manager was curious. John Grey looked quite like the kind of man who'd be kept, and ordered: he was blond enough, shaped enough. But he seemed too bright.

'I guess,' Grey said, 'I wait in the hotel.'

Mercedes shrugged. She had to seem single-minded about this game; she had to fake a gambler's passion.

'And you can call me,' he said. 'Later.'

'At the hotel,' she said.

Grey watched Mercedes clamber into a Silver Shadow and drive away. She hadn't lost her sense of risk; and he'd been sobered in the past few weeks, not reformed but made more pensive about his life. Risk was something he calculated now; he no longer embraced it.

And Mercedes watched the dark roads pass. There was a beach and palms, a few hotels; they were on the airport road. The car went through a deep gulley that looked cut by a single shovel, and then up a hill. She was alert to every detail, unable to read any of them yet.

There were high wrought iron gates in the middle of nothing. The car swept through and up a long blank drive. She could see no house until they were at the top of the hill; then there was a white pile high above the sea. It must be old money; this was a house built to catch the winds in less favourable seasons, not just as a winter indulgence.

The car stopped. She stood at a brilliant red door, between balconies and the old, twisted vines of bougainvillaea. She rang.

In the sounds of the night, she could hear nothing that came from the house. She'd half hoped to arrive in Lyford Cay where she knew people, discover gaming was the secret vice of some bestseller, some TV mogul or rum baron. Here she was in a world she didn't know.

The door was opened by a little black maid, dressed in starched linen, who bobbed and turned away.

Mercedes stood at the foot of a grandiose staircase, the kind that studios built for stars, all marble and wrought metal; there was cool tiling underfoot and great bowls of lilies everywhere. The house smelled dead.

She didn't know what or whom to call.

She heard a cough from one of the side doors: a woman of perhaps seventy, her face lined and dusty like old velvet. She wore a dress of grey flimsy, and pearls.

'How nice,' the old woman said. 'What a pleasure to meet Miss Mercedes Zenon.'

She swept forward, grand as a duchess, took Mercedes' hand limply.

'This is an extraordinary house,' Mercedes said.

The old woman said: 'You don't know who I am, do you?'

Mercedes paused politely, but she had to say: 'I'm afraid not.'

The old woman smiled. 'I'm very old headlines, and a very old woman. Nancy Proudie.'

The name meant nothing, and Mercedes was sure it should. 'I'm so glad to meet you,' she said.

The woman turned and gestured her into a drawing room cluttered with flowers and plants and volumes of ancient illustrated magazines. They were open at pages of society pictures, all of them; and the plants seemed to slip between, tendrils and stems as subtle as little animals. Wherever she turned Nancy Proudie was reminded who she was.

'They'll have told you I'm mad,' she said. 'Because I don't think as they do. But you're a gambler. You'll understand.'

Mercedes found an armchair occupied only by a cat.

'You look as though you'd rather be somewhere else,' Nancy Proudie said. 'As though you think the old woman is going to tell you the story of her life.'

But she didn't need to. The pictures, the lilies and the emptiness all told their own story.

The maid arrived with a tray of glasses, ice and Bourbon.

Lady Proudie said, 'I go here and there. I go to Maine in summer and back to Nassau in winter.' She poured drinks. 'I have too much money, you see; it makes most sensible relationships almost impossible. The local matrons are intimidated, and I don't fit the expatriates. So I sit here, being rich, on my own, and sometimes someone comes to play cards.'

Mercedes was on the edge of her seat.

Lady Proudie said: 'We will get to the game.' She had finished a tumbler of Bourbon, and a little hectic colour appeared in her cheeks, like painted life.

'Perhaps,' Meecedes said, 'you'll excuse me for a moment – to make a phone call.'

'Be discreet,' Lady Proudie said. 'We're not supposed to play, you know.' She giggled like a girl. 'That's half the fun.'

Mercedes followed the maid to a phone and told John Grey where she was. He listened to her story and began his own calls.

Lady Proudie, he heard, was the islands. Her husband had made so much, built so much, left so much money and expended so much sweat in the building of the place that its shape was not imaginable without him. Lady Proudie had inherited that power, and ignored it. But if she were offended, then she could ruin anyone who needed to stay.

Grey picked up the thin Nassau phone book to look for Boswells in suitably grand areas; but Nassau addresses are post office box numbers. But there'd be snobbery, he guessed, about low numbers that showed you'd been there a long while; he looked for a Boswell in the thousands, not the ten thousands.

'You're John Grey,' Boswell said. 'Greystoke Securities. That was interesting.'

'I'm calling for Mercedes Zenon.'

'You're lucky to get me. The storm washed the phones away last week.'

'You have a problem with the paper,' John Grey said.

219

'Can't it wait until tomorrow? We have guests –'

'Mercedes is out playing poker. With Lady Proudie, no less. If she loses, she's going to hand over those Mercantile Overseas CDs as collateral. Lady Proudie will cash them.'

'She won't be popular, playing with suspect credit.'

'We want the money,' Grey said. 'Real money. Or else Lady Proudie will be the one who finds out all about you.'

Boswell fell silent long enough for Grey to fear the line had died.

'I'll call the police,' Boswell said.

'You want to explain everything?' Grey said. 'Everything?'

'With your record, they're not likely to believe you.'

'They'll know I know what I'm talking about.'

'I can't do anything until tomorrow morning.'

'You'd better do something tonight,' Grey said. 'Before Mercedes starts losing.'

'You want paper? Or cash?'

'Put it this way,' Grey said. 'Suppose you don't come up with anything tonight. Tomorrow morning, we'll have to go to Lady Proudie and buy back those CDs. To do that, we'll need cash or big New York paper.'

'We have a nice line in zero coupon bonds –'

'I'm sure you do,' John Grey said. 'We all do. But what I want is a personal IOU, and I want to cash it tomorrow.'

'She's playing now?'

'She's playing. She's not good.'

And in the drawing room, Lady Proudie had slipped off the rings and bracelets that might clatter in the game. 'We might begin,' she said.

Mercedes didn't want to rush the game. She said: 'You've lived here for forty years?'

'Fifty,' Lady Proudie said. 'But it won't be long now. I'm very old.'

'You seem to do very well.'

Lady Proudie tapped with her right hand on a polished table. 'People your age don't understand,' she said. 'Things stop mattering. That is why I love playing. I can risk again, something.' She was suddenly businesslike. 'I suppose they told you that the stakes are usually high?'

'They did.'

'And for collateral –'

Mercedes handed over the packet of CDs. Lady Proudie grunted, checked, and said: 'I think that may be a little high, even for me.'

'I wanted to show I was ready to play.'

'Yes, yes,' Lady Proudie said. She seemed obscurely bothered, as though risking monstrous sums was her privilege alone. 'You must enjoy the game, too,' she said.

Mercedes nodded.

And then it was too late to stall. Nancy Proudie ushered Mercedes down to a darkened room. It had been shaped into a perfect poker hell, a single bulb hanging over a circle of green baize.

'My husband used to play,' she said.

There were decks of cards, unopened, on the baize, and a packet of small cigars by Lady Proudie's right hand. Bourbon and glasses sat on the table. Both women sat for a moment, like a moment of prayer, each putting out hands into the circle of light while her eyes stayed in shadow. Mercedes saw that Lady Proudie painted her nails, meticulously.

Suddenly the dusty, faded woman had gone and someone sharp and precise had taken her place; the shadow of her shoulders seemed more square and authoritative.

And so Mercedes acted, as she knew how to do.

Lady Proudie lit a small cigar and flexed her fingers. It was a kind of magic, she became her dead husband.

She'll die soon, Mercedes thought, so it doesn't matter to her. But she knew that wasn't true. The game mattered furiously to milady.

But when she bet, she put the counters forward with her left hand. Left, when she used her right. She must be nervous. 'Your cut,' she said. Her voice seemed lower and more strong.

Mercedes stopped herself touching the pile of CDs for luck, and she risked all this remnant of the Diaz fortune on the turn of cards.

They called it the Night of Promises, later. In the bunker, the sounds of fighting in the city were shut out, but the panic simply brewed in its tight quarters.

221

Anastasio Diaz Sacasa was very close to the moment when he had to go. Already, the sergeant-secretary had pushed a paper into Carpenter's hands and told him not to stand on ceremony. 'This might help,' he'd said. 'But if you see a barrier, crash it.'

Carpenter was thoughtful. 'What happens if the Guards –'

'Don't worry about the Guards. They're too stupid to think. And they've nowhere else to go.'

There was no more time to note down the business of Diaz. Carpenter kept alert and saw how the President had shockingly lost his edge – allowed his shirt to billow loose and his braces to slacken, gone in a minute from a martinet to a middle-aged man in some foolish uniform.

He rootled among the papers on his desk like a grazing pig. He sorted, and sorted again.

The phone rang. The bell was unsteady, like an improvisation. Diaz tried to speak, but someone at the other end did all the talking.

'They want me out,' he said when he put down the receiver. 'Tonight, on their plane.'

Carpenter could read no expression at all in the face. It was sunken, olive, with shadows that looked a little like bruises in the harsh light.

The President, El Maximo, El Jefe, tidied himself for his last official hours. He made an entrance to the ante-room.

There was a scuffle in a distant corridor. The sergeant-secretary reached for his revolver; but he had no revolver. Carpenter looked round. The guards had all been disarmed.

Diaz raised his hands for quiet.

'Listen to me,' he said. 'The Americans have put planes at the airport. We fly to Midland, Texas. It's a US Air Force base.'

'They'll let us in, won't they?' a woman asked.

'You go tonight, you're safe. No questions,' Diaz said. They could face the truth when the plane came down.

'And how do we get to the airport?'

'We have an escort. The National Guard, maybe some Marines from the embassy.'

'And what will they do with us in Texas?'

The powerful people were tense like peasants waiting for a full bus, saving their energy for the moment when sharp elbows and

222

sheer mass would get them on board.

'You're on your own,' Diaz said. 'You're alive. You're alone.'

The crowd shivered. They'd heard noise: something different, something outside. The sound echoed a little in the corridors, improper and fearful. There were supposed to be guards to stop those sounds.

They could hold out for a while. The crowd was thinking that. And Carpenter remembered the piles of rubble in the basement; there was no other way out.

'Thirty minutes,' said a practical, lifeless American voice. 'In thirty minutes the cars will be here. You proceed to the airport. If you don't take the cars, you're on your own and the Amadistas are past the cathedral now.'

It could have been a voice from the telephone company.

In time, they filed out like some parody of those state occasions that Diaz very rarely staged. There was a line of limos, all shiny, and motorcycle outriders and a police car screaming in the silver rain; there were no crowds. The city was lifeless, lit by a moon and, down by the lake, the orange and sulphur diorama of a charred cathedral, still burning. Carpenter was crushed in with Diaz, and with a Vice Minister, the showgirl and an elderly woman who was quite still.

He peered through the windows. He saw people along the roadways. He saw a kind of procession coming up from the cathedral, a streetful of marching people. He saw a woman in a white dress: Aurelia.

He stared out, eyes wide as a horizon at the woman. But the cars went roaring past, and he had time only to think about getting out, and keeping the briefcase that he'd locked between his knees.

At the airport, there was no more power. Even the masters and the influential were refugees, pushed into place. They'd closed together so that none of them could take advantage.

But then a plane roared to life on the tarmac and they all began to run, breaking through the deserted immigration hall and into the waiting room by the duty free shops and pressed against the glass doors to the runway.

The plane might be the only plane.

There was a bright black girl standing there, the stewardess

223

from Carpenter's flight down, and she was armed with instructions to check passes and papers before she let anyone past the door. But there were no Guardsmen ready to stay with her and expose themselves to gunfire or anger from either side; she had only her airline smile. She tried not to recognise all the peremptory faces from First Class. She smiled and smiled and smiled.

But she couldn't hold the door against the press of people. Outside, a mechanic stirred and she saw his hand move; maybe it was the signal at last. She bent and unlocked the doors, pushed them open and let the crowd go through, with its awkward bags and cases, its sacks of paper tightly clutched, its ragged, patched possessions and its sense of terror. They all went charging to the runway but the plane had gone.

The clouds had broken, and the night was now star bright. What they lacked was a plane.

'They'll kill us,' a man shouted.

The airport doors were locked behind them and the lights died.

Carpenter looked around. He could see nothing ready to take a mob to Texas except for a lightless DC-9 by the side of the military hangars.

So he bellowed: 'This way' and went sprinting down the runway, round the belly and up to the side where a door stood open.

The others followed as best they could, tripping on the unmended tarmac in the dark and losing shoulder bags. A girl fell and was kicked and started running again, breathlessly. She joined the others scrambling up stairs that were still being pushed into place, and she filled the last seat. When the plane was full, the door shut.

The steps were pushed away and the plane turned; Carpenter could see a couple still moving on the tarmac as it taxied.

Once airborne, the plane banked immediately, keeping perilously low. The night was only faint through the window. The city glided below, lit in moonlight and firelight. And somewhere close behind them came a lumbering brute of a plane, the one whose take-off had broken the last pretence of dignity in the airport building.

He could see the cone of the dead volcano, and then the steam that overhung the live volcano. The moon made the steam into white cliffs.

He saw fire come up from the ground, a splutter of bright steel like a firework. It seemed to be aimed at the big-bellied plane which was flying with its lights on like a decoy; but Carpenter could see the plane was not a simple decoy. Something heavy fell from it, slow as fear, canisters that went down and down until they landed and blossomed in new colours: flame of red and yellow. Across the city where the heavy plane had flown there was a line of fire. And each explosion seemed to catch the DC-9 broadside, as though they were sharing thin air.

Diaz looked down, entranced. Each time a canister burst into flames, he thumped the arm-rest. He was celebrating what he'd do to his personal property – Providencia he'd said, *es mia finca*. He couldn't keep it, so he'd kill and clean it with the fire.

Carpenter heard a sound like speed cutting air, abstract and terrifying. There was something hot like a shooting star, and close enough to scream, which fell away from beside the DC-9. Across the aisle a pretty woman, tiny in red, took out a Bible, and out of that she took the service of Exorcism. She didn't stop reading until Midland.

And now their plane was up against the steam from the volcano. It cut the white cliff, rocked through it and then climbed steeply. There was no more view, only the Pacific below, and there was quiet on the plane until they were high over clouds and the cabin lights came on again. It was like the end of the movie on an ordinary flight. People bickered, queued for the lavatories, stretched as though they'd slept and began to think about drinks.

Diaz beamed. He had seen the fires; he was content.

Some cousin hissed at him: 'If you'd died, we'd have been ruined. We don't know where anything is.'

And Diaz said: 'Maybe I feel safer this way.'

At Midland the plane fell out of the sky and bellied on the runway. The passengers looked out at concrete and iron buildings lying low and harsh in the white light. Their cold future had arrived.

Diaz was gone before they could sense the true bleakness of

their welcome. He had rights, and Carpenter had a British passport and an ordinary visa; the two clipped gentlemen from the State Department waved them through. The others stayed on the plane, their faces a frieze of empty waiting.

'I suppose,' Diaz said, 'you arranged the champagne?'

The men from State had been told to say as little as possible. It was assumed that Diaz would provoke and bluster; it didn't matter; just give the man no grounds for complaint to his bought-and-paid-for Congresspersons.

'We'll talk in the morning,' the senior man from State said.

They drove to an undistinguished motel, close to the airport base. It was a refuge for airmen meeting their girls, a comfortable and private place, and Diaz regarded it with all the horror he could summon.

'You don't expect me –'

'Until tomorrow morning,' the man from State said, trying to be businesslike without offending El Jefe.

Diaz snorted.

'If you could consider the other residents of the motel –'

Carpenter began to laugh. He wondered how often rejected Generalissimos and Jefes and potentates and dictators-for-life had been parked in this quiet motel, all bickering about power and taxes and torture and good times and the Bolshevik threat, rasping on one another like the old in a home; and then reluctantly coming to admit their anger was as fragile as their power, that in the end they needed sleep. Even Diaz might be quiet for the sake of sleep.

'I don't need an escort,' he said. 'Carpenter, I need to talk to you. As for you two –'

The men from the State Department had never looked more attentive, or more blank.

'– I shall leave early tomorrow morning for my house in Miami. I expect you want to know where I'm going.'

The diplomats didn't argue.

'Carpenter,' Diaz said peremptorily.

He felt almost sorry for a man who was so dependent on having power.

On the way to the motel rooms, Diaz spoke very quietly, as though afraid the walkway might be bugged.

'I want the papers,' he said. 'I want the money out of Switzerland. I want the American money out, too. My wife will be talking to her lawyers even now.'

Carpenter was dragging his feet, on the point of exhaustion; but he needed every speck of concentration he could muster.

'Tomorrow morning, first thing,' he said in a parody of an English drawl, topped off with a desultory, 'old boy.'

'I don't have to wait,' Diaz said.

'We're not in banking hours,' Carpenter said.

'Now,' Diaz said. 'I want the papers.'

He looked ominous, like a cornered dog.

'I'm not going anywhere,' Carpenter said. 'Except bed.'

He closed the door to his room. He could hear Diaz pacing on the gravel outside.

He sat in a busted armchair and turned on the television. Some late night monochrome movie appeared, British heroes stuttering and rattling across the screen – wartime endeavour, left-behind ladies, dashing but fundamentally decent pilots (one wasn't) and a death-defying raid. He watched them jealously. They knew how to be heroes. Their war was right, and obligatory.

But he was a banker, sitting in a Texas motel, puzzled by the very grand ideas of right and wrong. So far, he was inside the law, if that mattered; but to remain legal, he had to continue helping Anastasio Diaz Sacasa. And he'd seen too much of the man, and his family; he'd seen people die, and a country stolen.

But it wasn't his country. To surrender himself to the melodrama he was living, he'd have to risk his career, perhaps his survival; he knew already what Diaz would order if even a wristwatch was missing. Diaz had no interest in the law.

He wanted to be sure why he was going to steal that money, why it was right. It was for Aurelia, whom he'd loved; but until the moment he saw her bloodied body, it was a temporary, away from home love, not the remaking of a life. It was for Mercedes, but that was an entanglement as much with glamour and risk and indulgence as with a woman. It was for poor, battered Providencia, for the kind faces of Bluefields and the desolation of Leon. But Providencia was not his country, not his cause. If he'd been some eager radical he would know he was helping the

227

Amadistas because they were history, and right. But he didn't know such things.

He might have fallen asleep, head down on his chest, while the British heroes went to their planes to a martial music that was stirring like a hit of some drug. But he had to decide before morning if he'd give back to Diaz or start a serious larceny.

When would he know he'd gone too far, had no more choices?

The phone rang.

'Don't think of going anywhere,' Diaz said, coldly, and put down the phone.

Decent, ineffectual, liberal instincts all seemed out of place against that man. What he did, what he had been, passed the boundaries of what was tolerable. And Carpenter could do something; he had the miracle of an opportunity. He could help ruin the man's fortune and return it to the people from whom it was pillaged.

It wasn't just the right thing to do. To refuse the chance would be a great wrong.

He called a cab and a hire car company.

Diaz might watch his room, but Diaz had no help here; all his allies were still yawning and sweating on that plane. Diaz would sleep.

Carpenter padded to the reception, very carefully, leaving the television roaring in his room. He left a note for Diaz that he'd see him in Miami; he didn't want suspicion and pursuit. And as a token of some faith, he left a sack of 500-cordoba notes that he'd been given to carry.

He set out on the long highway across Texas. Six hundred miles to Houston, down a ribbon of road unrolling before him. He was driving past a dawn that was orange and red, then blue. He stopped at a diner for breakfast, eggs and grits, and the diner sign seemed made of the sky and the sky of neon.

He didn't know how well he could drive the next ten hours. He had to find an airport, cut the journey. If he could just get to Houston, and out to the Caymans, he had time to do damage to Diaz and return with an innocent look. The man insulated himself so well from his money, he could no longer give direct orders. Carpenter counted on that.

228

He drank another cup of metallic coffee. He watched the diner sign blink. He nerved himself for the day.

The lady was as still as she had been fluttery, as straight as she had seemed bendable. In the single light, across the green baize table, she was formidable.

'Play,' she barked.

Mercedes turned the cards in her hands. She was sure she'd give away her inexperience by how she handled the pack. She was sure that Lady Proudie would be impatient.

The maid arrived with a tray. There were sandwiches, cigars, a new bottle. All were set on the table, and ignored. They weren't for the two players; they were a kind of offering to whatever haunted Nancy Proudie.

Mercedes dealt.

'If you're nervous,' Proudie said, 'you don't need to play. But you drop the cards now, you understand?'

Mercedes flicked the edges of the cards. She flexed her fingers. She knew John Grey would have found Boswell by now; she wasn't sure how persuasive he could be, how long she would have to play.

The cards went down.

There was a perfect silence. The room seemed insulated, sealed off from the house and its life.

'I'll see you,' Proudie said.

And Mercedes had won.

She shuffled the cards. If she won too much, she was stealing. But she was also delighting the old lady, and Lady Proudie was used to the idea that delight costs.

The cards went down.

She was beginning to feel what gamblers feel: the luxurious, black-out moment of turning the cards and knowing you've won or lost, the rush of blood. She could win a fortune, not just compel Boswell to restore one.

'Pair of kings,' she said.

Lady Proudie grunted. She spread her cards on the baize and took chips from the pile.

'Next cards,' she said.

Mercedes was stung by the fact of losing, even though it was what she had to do. Her instincts told her to compete.

'I need a drink,' she said.

Lady Proudie glared at her.

'I don't have time,' she said. It wasn't a self-pitying remark; it was literal truth.

'We should raise the stakes,' Mercedes said.

'Yes.'

Mercedes could see this woman's long and unfilled life, but you can't pity an opponent at cards.

'Go to a million,' Lady Proudie said. Money wasn't real to her any more; she had outgrown it by excess. The two women were spinning a monster out of air.

'A million,' Mercedes said. She knew suddenly they were both playing to lose.

Outside, in the cutting which led to the Proudie mansion, Boswell stopped the car.

'You realise,' he said, 'Lady Proudie can't afford to be caught gambling.'

'She can afford anything,' Grey said.

'She likes a quiet life,' Boswell said. 'Family, flowers. She's famous for the gardens.'

'She likes risk,' Grey said. 'The bigger the better. Why else would she be playing with Mercedes now?'

Boswell didn't speak, but he slid the car back into gear and drove on.

'I never expected to be here,' he said at the gates.

The house was dark except for a porch light that sent shadow creeping in and out of the columns. They rang, and they waited. Dogs barked.

'I'm surprised she doesn't have guards on the gate,' Grey said.

'People wouldn't come here.'

'But she must have some security –'

The front door opened. The tiny maid was there, starched and sleepy all at once. Behind her stood a large man in jeans and a dress jacket, pulled out of bed to do service. He had a gun.

'Good evening,' Grey said.

The maid bobbed mechanically, like a wind-up thing; and security stood stalwart and square, not moving.

'My name is Grey. I've come to see Lady Proudie and Miss Zenon. It is urgent.'

230

The maid bobbed again, making time to think.

Down in the cards room, Mercedes scooped up chips. So far, neither woman had a strong advantage. Yet she couldn't leave one of the suspect CDs until she had lost at least a million. And she was used to prevailing because she was young.

'Next,' Lady Proudie said.

There was a clatter of heels on tiles and the maid arrived at the door, stumbling and apologising under her breath.

'People to see you, ma'am.'

Mercedes heard subservience, as she expected, but also a little spite.

'Who?' said Lady Proudie, studying her cards.

'A Mr Grey. To see you and Miss Zenon. He knows Miss Zenon is here.'

Lady Proudie set down her cards.

'We'll be in the drawing room after this hand.'

And Lady Proudie said: 'You want to go a million, again?'

Mercedes nodded. She had to lose. She saw that Proudie now moved the counters with her right hand, the lady was sure.

'Deal,' Mercedes said. She wet her lips, like a waiting child.

The cards went down.

Upstairs, John Grey and Boswell were installed between the plants and cats and pictures, with the large butler at the door. The maid returned and said: 'In a minute,' and bobbed.

In the darkened card room there was no more time to worry. If the cards went Mercedes' way, she'd won with false credit and they had no hold on Boswell. But if the cards went Lady Proudie's way, Boswell had to panic, soon.

She looked at her cards.

She could have done better. A pair of queens. She looked across at Lady Proudie's face, and realised the huge advantage of old features in which the muscles no longer move the skin precisely. Lady Proudie would look enigmatic if she was happy, if she was ruined.

Mercedes wanted to drum her fingers on the green baize. Instead, she kept her hands flat on the table.

'There,' Lady Proudie said, and spread her cards.

Mercedes looked down at a royal flush.

She must not laugh. She must seem serious, ready to write off her million but not happy. She wanted to throw her arms around the old woman.

She said: 'I'll give you a cheque.'

Lady Proudie smiled. 'Just the paper,' she said. 'That's so much easier. The CD.'

'Of course.'

Mercedes passed the paper across the table. Lady Proudie took it, and she kissed it. It was a sudden liveliness in such a studied woman.

She put on the bangles she had set aside. She allowed herself to flutter again, and to make her way along the corridor in a dignified, elderly bend. She softened.

She turned into the drawing room, and she was the lady again.

'Mr Grey, Mr Boswell,' she said. 'What a pleasure to meet you. What an unexpected pleasure.'

The two men stood like schoolboys.

'This is an unconventional time for a social call,' Lady Proudie said. 'But I expect you have a reason?'

'Mercedes!' John Grey said.

She stood in the doorway, smiling.

'What the hell are you doing here?' he bellowed. 'You know you are supposed –'

'Miss Zenon has been visiting me,' Lady Proudie said. 'Please sit down.'

'We've been talking,' Mercedes said.

Boswell shifted in his chair, a little relieved.

Lady Proudie rang for the maid, and turned back to the room. As she did so, a paper dislodged itself from her lacy bosom and came, very slowly, to the floor. Boswell could see it, but not quite read it; but he knew the shape and the form.

'You lost, did you?' he said to Mercedes.

'I don't know what you mean.'

'You lost money to Lady Proudie.'

'And how would she do that?' the old woman said.

'She knows,' Boswell said, 'that paper is worthless –'

'Is it?' Lady Proudie said, and stooped to collect the certificate. 'But it seems to be drawn on your bank, Mr Boswell. You are Mr Boswell of Mercantile Overseas?'

He nodded.

'Then I'm sure I shall be able to discount this note at any bank in the islands,' Lady Proudie said. 'On your good name.'

The thought stung Mercedes: Boswell could pay off Lady Proudie for a single million. And if he paid Proudie, why should she ruin him? Their scam was fading.

'There is some irregularity,' Boswell said.

Lady Proudie put out her hand to Mercedes. 'Give me the other papers, my dear. The other collateral.' She counted the certificates, and said: 'Are all these irregular, Mr Boswell?'

The banker said: 'If you'd allow me to explain –'

'I expect you want these papers back,' Lady Proudie said.

'I was simply concerned –'

'I think these certificates had better be regular,' Lady Proudie said. 'I am sure Miss Zenon would not attempt to bamboozle me.' It was a wonderful, carousel word that seemed to surprise Lady Proudie as much as anyone.

'This is a banking matter.'

'Yes,' Lady Proudie said. 'It is. And I suggest the banker makes things right. A million here, nineteen there. Now.'

'Would you want to explain,' Boswell said, 'how you came into possession of that certificate? If someone came to ask?'

Lady Proudie turned the paper in her hands. 'I see nothing about ownership here,' she said. 'It seems to be a bearer document. So I don't think I have to explain.'

Boswell took a deep breath.

'I don't like difficulties on the island.' Lady Proudie said. 'I don't enjoy them.'

And John Grey said: 'I could take Mr Boswell back into Nassau now.'

'When you collect,' Lady Proudie said, 'collect for me.'

And the men left, briskly.

'You were trying to lose,' Lady Proudie said. 'That isn't fair. The risk at that table is the only risk I have left.'

'I'm sorry.'

'And you are a gambler, aren't you? Getting your money back on Mr Boswell's useless paper by threatening him. You had to lose big for that.'

Mercedes said nothing.

'You could have played with me,' Lady Proudie said, and

there was tiredness in her voice. 'You could have let me share the risk.'

The old lady, in her greys and laces, was moving towards the door at a stately pace. She was older now, and she found her walk harder work.

'Get out,' she said at the door, very quietly.

In the Silver Shadow that took Mercedes back to the hotel, she felt cold. The sight draft with which John Grey returned was no real consolation, not for the moment. She'd been judged and rightly snubbed.

'Her life,' she said, 'seems so empty.'

'People say that about you,' John Grey said.

'I need New York night again,' Mercedes said.

'You don't,' Grey said. 'You didn't need it when you left, and now you've got something you almost believe in. Hang in there.'

'You sound like a minister. Or a Californian.'

'Things change,' Grey said. 'I don't deny things any more. I can't even deny death.'

Mercedes shivered.

·SIX·

He flew out of Houston on the Money Express – the flight to Georgetown, Grand Cayman, with a handful of tourists, a few men with skinny briefcases, two accountants with garment bags and a cadre of stolid men who wouldn't let go of their weighty flightbags. It was the bagman's flight, in time to catch the banks.

Carpenter kept his feet on a case of money. He knew which bank lent money to Horror Holdings, one of the Diaz companies in Florida that ran a theme park of zombies and vampires, marketed as an aphrodisiac to the one age group that never needs one. He knew to go to a branch of a respectable giant from the colonial past, a kind of widow who'd resigned herself to taking in washing since the Empire fell on hard times. He'd go in with cash, make a deposit, take the account numbers and see what they hid. He'd find all the money Diaz left in the Caymans as security for the loans that financed his Florida businesses.

Everything was simple in his tired brain. Diaz had to hide what he owned, and wash his profits. He'd have the cash taken in suitcases to the Caymans, and he'd borrow against it to buy shares he left in the bank's name so that the Americans reckoned Horror Holdings belonged to a respectable bank. That way he could take what he'd already made, however he'd made it, and turn it into assets whose real ownership was masked by trusts and nominees.

To find it, Carpenter needed only a deposit, and he carried that beneath his feet.

He drove into Georgetown in a sad mess of loose bunting and raw rice. There'd been a royal visit, one of those sporadic attempts to persuade the world that the British not only owned but also cared about the Caymans; royalty had passed like an exotic rumour and left behind a tangle of flags and tinsel. The town had an aftermath look.

He entered the long, pink bank building and presented himself to the tellers. He said he had a deposit, in cash. Within minutes a manager had summoned him to an inner office.

'Of course,' the manager said, 'we take the money.'

Carpenter coughed.

'But there is a substantial penalty for early repayment on a term loan. You know that. Your principals ought to think.'

Carpenter said: 'I just do what I'm told.'

'But your principals – they're not thinking of clearing the loan?'

The manager seemed hot and harassed. He had visions of losing the Diaz money – cash left so the bank could lend it back to its owner and take a ten or fifteen per cent turn on keeping a respectable face. 'There's no reason,' he was saying.

'Circumstances change,' Carpenter said. He opened his briefcase and took out cheques drawn on the Central Bank of Providencia. He shuffled them like cards.

'This is none of my business,' the manager said, 'but we would very much regret the premature end of those loans. After all, they're useful. Aren't they?'

'Of course,' Carpenter said reassuringly. 'But for the moment, my principal is – consolidating.'

'Of course.'

'He wants to clear this indebtedness, and transfer the shares to a Swiss bank. He is worried about security here.'

'There is no security problem here. Why, the royal family just came and –'

'My principal just lost a country.'

The manager rang for files, and when they came, spread them out where Carpenter could barely read them. There seemed to be loan accounts, as Carpenter expected, less than half the money Diaz had on deposit but secured on all the deposits. The money couldn't run unless the loans were paid.

'I suppose,' the manager said, 'I have to accept your deposits –'

And it was done. When Carpenter had more leisure, he'd order the Diaz companies to bleed themselves of cash for the

Cayman accounts; most likely, they were used to such orders. He'd have control of the companies in Switzerland, and he'd have the Diaz deposits transferred there. It would all be discreet and anonymous, in the name of one grand old bank of the Caribbean to a solid London bank with a branch in Zürich. Nothing could be more proper.

Also, it was larceny. But until the papers actually left his hands, he could always plead he meant to hand them over to Diaz. But Diaz would find he no longer owned his companies, or his deposits – his plunder from Leon had gone to release his cash in the Caymans.

Carpenter heard himself explaining: 'This is just the first stage. It's a complicated process. You can't judge it until it's finished.' He was ready to explain anything.

There was a direct flight to Miami and he took it. His mind and body were exhausted now, ready to crumple; and what had seemed simple on the way to Georgetown now began to seem awkward and dangerous. He was remembering that woman in white on the Leon streets, lit by fire, who might have been Aurelia. He was doing this for his conscience and for Aurelia, but how would she ever know?

She would have seen him in the limo, in that shameful procession running from the bunker to the airport. She would have judged him double traitor. She wouldn't want explanations, any more.

He nerved himself to tell the taxi driver that he was heading for the Diaz mansion, out in the exiles' row in Coral Gables. He expected El Jefe would be cantankerous, primed with whisky, and he was right. Diaz was soft, confused, furious; he allowed his spine to bend, his belly to sag. Now he'd lost vanity, he had only bluster, and he was still bawling out his staff for failing to greet him when he arrived unannounced in Miami. The staff had a long habit of deference; they took the blame.

'You know what I did?' Diaz shouted to Carpenter 'While you went off God knows where, I went to New Orleans. I went to a dandy bank and I went to the tellers and I drew out the whole faith and credit of the Republic of Providencia in that bank. I got a cashier's cheque.'

He was stroking a piece of gaudy paper, like a servant tidies a paper for his master.

'I'd better take that,' Carpenter said, busily.

Diaz surrendered the paper without questions. It seemed he had a heart and mind that were too occupied to spare time for thought.

The next morning, diplomats came. They had little time for Diaz; they had been instructed to deliver an ultimatum, in a genteel fashion.

'The political situation,' they said, 'is rather delicate.'

'Yes,' Diaz said, not being helpful.

'It might be better if you didn't take up residence in the United States. Not immediately.'

'Yes.' Diaz was unhelpful.

'It might seem that we were giving some approval to your position.'

'And you don't approve?'

'We might be accused of harbouring you.'

Diaz seemed to understand for the first time, and his response was chilly. 'Forgive me,' he said, 'for my English is not so good. But this word "harbouring" – you harbour a criminal, don't you?'

The diplomats frowned.

'What's it worth?' Diaz asked. The diplomats tried to hide their relief; but it was too late; they had to pretend they didn't understand.

'I'm not going to be angry,' Diaz said, softly. 'But I have permission to live here, and a house, investments, an American wife. An American son.'

'Mr Tomás Diaz surrendered his American passport,' the junior diplomat said.

'And I have friends. In Congress. Friends who think the State Department is all too Red as it is.'

Diaz was beaming. 'So what's in it for me if I don't make trouble?'

The diplomats struggled and blustered, unused to this simple market manner in their world of rights and advantages.

Diaz began to laugh, a stage laugh which was a statement in itself. 'Don't worry,' he said. 'I'll be out in the morning. I need a vacation.' He saw the alarm drain from the officials' faces and

238

decided to put it back. 'I'll drift down to the Bahamas. Like the Shah did. Like Somoza did.'

The diplomats were stirred, like dreamers face to face with some past horror. They composed themselves most carefully.

'It will be best,' the older man said, 'if all this is completed within twenty-four hours.'

'So be it,' Diaz said.

They drove away hurting with all the adrenalin Diaz had not allowed them to use.

'You could be my executor,' Diaz said to Carpenter.

He heard 'executioner'. His nerves were frantic.

'You could settle my accounts. You could sort everything out.' Diaz seemed to grow angry; Carpenter couldn't yet see why. 'You could be here when I die. You could make it worthwhile for them all.'

'I'm just a professional adviser.'

'I will never make a will,' Diaz said. 'They'd kill me if I ever made a will, especially now. They have nothing to lose.'

'You don't even think you'll go back −'

Diaz shrugged. 'The Americans don't want me. And why should I be a politician any more? I was always a businessman. My business was a nation. It only brought me pain.'

Pain, Carpenter thought, and a billion dollars.

'But you don't understand that, do you?'

Carpenter wondered if Diaz was going to live in a bottle from now on, taking the brightness out of the morning with a whisky and passing the afternoon and calming the evening the same way; making it tolerable to have nothing but time and pleasure. But he couldn't smell drink.

'You don't understand. Do you? You think I'm clever enough and enough of a brute, but it never crosses your mind that a single word I say might be for real. Does it? You decided about me before you first met me.'

'I don't operate like that.'

'You all do,' Diaz shouted. 'You all do. You never think there is anything different or curious. You only see the money and you see that through your own morals.'

Carpenter thought there was precious little moral excuse for Diaz; he was even surprised that the man wanted to claim one.

But he listened. He wanted clues.

'You want to know why, why, why? Do you?'

'It never occurred to me.' Carpenter was embarrassed by the man's passion.

'I'll show you,' Diaz said. 'I'll show you treasure.'

He pulled Carpenter out of his chair and propelled him to a velvet desert that passed for a drawing room. He stamped the floor, and when he heard something hollow he fell to his knees. He began tearing at the edges of the carpet.

'Help me,' he said.

'You could ask the servants –'

Diaz gave Carpenter a look of killing pity.

The carpet came up with surprising ease. Beneath, there were ordinary floorboards and then a brass handle. A trapdoor came up as quiet and sweet as though the hinges were buffed and oiled each day. A metal ladder led down into unlit space.

'This is none of my business,' Carpenter said.

He had a sense, chilly and insistent, that this hunt was about to go too far, and into a place where sense was suspended.

'Let me get the light,' Diaz said. He caught a switch.

Below, tall wood cabinets stood, one against each wall. There was a hanging crucifix and in the corner filing cabinets.

'Get down,' Diaz said.

Carpenter went first. The room was stale and tiny. He looked at the cabinets around its walls and he was nervous.

'This is what they ended,' Diaz said.

He opened one of the rosewood cabinets.

Carpenter looked into the glass eyes of the father of Anastasio Diaz Sacasa. He wasn't perfect in death, but he was ramrod straight and neat in his uniform, an image at least as alive as the ones for which people die on medals, or monuments.

'Who is that?'

'My father,' Diaz said, matter of factly. 'They embalmed Peron, you know. He was perfect. Everybody knew the body was perfect. One day, things change, and the body is ready.'

Diaz opened a second box. There was a smell of chemical dust. This time there was an older Diaz, perhaps the one who pandered so well to the US Marines that they gave him a country. A third box opened. This Diaz had taken the country and made it a business, and a dynasty. A fourth: and this was shocking, unlike the men. There was a matriarch in rusted lace, beginning to lose a little shape; thirty years after she died, her body was also dying.

Carpenter thought: 'You can't kill the bastards. You can't kill them dead.'

'Like King Arthur,' said Diaz, with surprising knowledge. 'The leader sleeps. He can always be called back.'

Carpenter went to touch the uniforms, but he couldn't bring himself to touch. He wanted a museum's glass between his living self and these mummified icons.

'My family,' Diaz said. 'My people. Mine.'

'Are you telling me this was all for family duty?'

'Shit, no.' Diaz seemed amused. 'I only wanted to show you. I don't need excuses.'

There were footsteps above, one man walking.

Carpenter took out a lighter. He wanted to see life in the dead glass eyes; he could imagine the bodies still breathed and felt. The woman, especially, had features and a shape to the cheeks and eyes. He watched the flame, and the eyes; he thought of burning up the bodies, ending this obscene dynastic dream.

'Power never ends,' Diaz said, softly. 'It can be transferred or transmitted. You have power while people remember you. You could use my name in a hundred years.'

Carpenter spun around the chamber. It was no place for reason, but he could manage one obvious thought: that here were silent guards for whatever was in the filing cabinet.

'We have a history,' Diaz said. He tugged at the first drawer of the cabinet and brought out big manila envelopes of coins and medals and citations. It was bombast, filed away.

In the second drawer there were books, privately printed and elaborately bound, encomiums of the clan with packs of newspaper clippings and a scrapbook. There were pictures of tiny children on a broad white beach, scampering and laughing. There were pictures of men hanging from trees, their bodies cut. The family needed to hide nothing.

The room was airless, and Carpenter's mind was racing in hallucination. He felt like a child in a flickering church: both alarmed and anxiously respectful. He could see, all too easily, how his real, rational world could be shot through and soaked with other people's myths – with bodies that signified.

'The air will eat them up,' he said. He was afraid of bumping against a casket and bringing down the body inside.

He heard the footsteps stop above. He heard a shout. He heard something heavy put down by the trapdoor, and saw Tomás Diaz peering down.

'Christ,' Tomás said. 'You didn't hear the news?'

Diaz said: 'What news?'

'Bad news,' Tomás said. 'You don't want the *anciani* to hear. They wouldn't like the news at all.'

'Get on with it,' Diaz said.

Something opened above and was emptied onto the floor. Tomás Diaz came to the trapdoor and stared down.

'Play with it,' he said. 'Play with the paper.'

And he tipped down a rain of torn paper, all reds and yellows and blues, some bearing portraits of Justice, some portraits of Diaz: generations of notes for 500 cordobas.

'What the hell do you think you're doing?'

'You could stuff pillows. You could grow roses. You could wipe your fucking arse on this –'

Diaz was down on the floor, under the cold eyes of his fathers, shuffling the gaudy paper, and Tomás was still showering it down, a fall like confetti.

'It's not worth shit,' Tomás said. 'The Amadistas made a new law. All 500-cordobas to be turned in, at banks in Providencia, for new notes. All old notes are worthless.'

Diaz looked up at the leering, crying face in the ceiling of his little burying chamber and he was filled with contempt and fury. 'Boy,' he said, 'you stop that.'

But the sanctity of this little room had blown away in a mess of paper.

'Nothing,' Tomás Diaz said, 'we've got nothing.'

'You shouldn't see this,' Diaz said to Carpenter. 'Nobody should have to see this.' But the sheer force of the younger man's anger seemed to trap El Jefe in his hole; he needed a shield. 'Calm him down, for Christ's sake,' Diaz said. 'Get a maid to clean up.'

'You want the maid to clean down here?'

'Nobody comes down here,' Diaz said. The fathers and grandfathers sat like a court of judgement; he avoided their glassy eyes.

Carpenter scrambled back into sunlight. The smell of air was welcome. But what he saw was no more sane or reasonable. Tomás Diaz was on the floor in a spew of colour, desolate. 'How will we pay the men?' he said.

'Have a drink,' Carpenter said.

'They're souvenirs,' Tomás said, scuffing up a pile of paper. 'Souvenirs.' The energy came back as though a current passed through his body, and he was up on his feet, standing over the trapdoor. 'I spit on you,' he shouted. 'Where in hell do we go from here? You tell us nothing. We have nothing.'

The elder Diaz growled dangerously, kicking the paper into a corner, closing up the cabinets.

'You took it all, you bastard.'

Diaz said from below: 'You will respect your fathers.'

'I spit on the fathers.'

And the older man lost patience. He threw himself out of the hole and landed heavily. He went for Tomás with large, manicured fists that had not recently seen action and he flailed to right and left, threshing air and sometimes flesh. Tomás ducked and wheeled as though he couldn't quite bring himself to strike his father back; he was skilled at evading. But El Maximo wore a hefty signet ring with a cutting edge, and one sideslipping blow cut open Tomás's cheek. The feel of the blood, slick and hot, turned evasion into anger, and Tomás kicked out at his father's head.

Diaz fell. Tomás went to wipe his face and only smeared the blood and sweat further.

From the floor, Diaz said: 'Get out!'

Tomás came to rudimentary attention and marched out like a little soldier.

Carpenter pulled the older man to his feet and left the room. He wasn't meant to see such a scene; Diaz hated witnesses.

He walked in the gardens, looking back from the shade of a ficus to the jumble of the house. A pink driveway curved around it; a swimming pool glinted with sun and chlorine; a little summer house stood down towards the main gates. He made an arbitrary choice and headed for the summerhouse, a solid, brick affair over-run with heavy philodendron and Jamaica vine. He tried the door.

The place had no secrets, and after the morning's melodramas that was welcome. It was cool, and smelt sweet. He sat in a corner chair and let himself relax.

He remembered books he read when a boy, where treasure lay hidden in deep caves marked 'X' on some parchment map. But it was simple to hide treasure, and trickier to hide a whole past, as Diaz tried to do.

Treasure. Map.

He was half dozing in the peace of the summerhouse. He thought he heard footsteps, and his eyes flickered open on a patient, ancient Indian face, a man not sure he'd be grateful for survival. It was only a servant, he told himself.

'Coffee,' he said, and turned in his chair.

The man left.

Ordinary things in extraordinary moments. Why did that damned Rolex watch matter so much?

He was awake. He could remember, roughly, the maze of scratches and lines on the gold case; he guessed, or maybe he knew, what they were. They were the floorplan of this house; the shaded portion, off-centre in the mansion, was the hidden room.

But Diaz wanted others to know where the relics lay. And the relics were not his treasure, not the one he had put in the Caymans, in the Bahamas, in Switzerland.

The words on the watch.

GoTo Boca Raton.

At the very least, those words were linked to this house, or came from the same period in Diaz's life; they'd been put on the same trinket at the same time.

GoTo.

But he hadn't owned this mansion long; he'd said that. This was the Miami house he'd bought as a refuge if ever he needed one. His pleasures he had always taken in New Orleans.

GoTo, just so, not spaced or put in lower case letters.

Carpenter went to the desk in the corner of the summerhouse. There was a telephone, one that dialled ten numbers from memory. He looked down the list. He didn't expect clues so

244

much as a trigger that might make him think clearly. He needed one of those leaps, spark to spark, synapse to synapse; not something mechanical.

Mechanical. Computers. GoTo Boca Raton.

Part of a program of some kind. An instruction to move to another set of data, or manoeuvres.

Ten numbers. Some were in Miami, some in New York. One was in the Caribbean 809 area code; it could be on any island.

New York. Carpenter half remembered one of the numbers; at least, the first three digits were familiar. It was the exchange for Leventhal's bank, for Security National.

He pushed button 8 and waited for the ringing tone.

The servant pushed softly into the room and padded over with a tray of coffee. Carpenter nodded, half embarrassed that he'd been caught at stealing a secret. But the servant had no wish to know.

He put the receiver to his ear only when the servant had left. He heard a low, steady tone. He thought at first he'd left answering too long and been cut off by some officious machine. But the tone was wrong.

He was hearing the access tone to a computer.

GoTo Boca Raton.

There was no computer in the room; he couldn't see a modem. That would be too obvious a clue, perhaps. But his mind was racing with the possibilities. They had found stashes of money that sounded substantial but were nothing against the scale of Diaz's filching over the years. They'd looked in all the obvious places.

What if the big money was not in those obvious places at all, but in a New York bank?

It couldn't happen. Transactions on that scale would have to be reported, to the Internal Revenue Service at the very least. The banks couldn't hide the accounts effectively. Any computer hacker might break in and find the treasure.

Unless GoTo Boca Raton was the key, the only key.

Unless within that security, the bank simply turned a blind eye to the comings and goings of money, overlooking the reports they should make by law. Unless the bank took vast deposits and concealed them even from its own staff.

245

No wonder Leventhal had been amused by Carpenter's courting of Diaz.

But surely no major American bank would simply fail to report to the IRS? Carpenter smiled. There had been a dozen cases, in banks from Boston to Los Angeles, where amounts in the billions had simply slipped off the official books and onto some more private ledger. The banks had paid fines in millions, but that was nothing beside the profits on a billion.

He had forgotten to put down the phone and the tone had cut off. When he replaced the receiver, the bell rang immediately.

'We're getting out,' Diaz said. 'Now. Get your gear.'

Carpenter stretched and tore off the list of numbers from the phone. He could afford a few days before he tested his theory. He'd wait to see Mercedes, share the triumph.

'We're going south,' Diaz said, in the limo. 'Sun, sea and cunt. What more could a man want?'

Carpenter turned away. He felt hollow in the middle of action and achievement, like a dummy. He wanted to feel, believe.

'You'll like it,' Diaz said.

The cabin was stifling, its wood walls scrawled over with numbers, messages, boasts and loves carved or crayoned. Mercedes stood in the enervating heat and watched the phone.

It seemed safer to call from public phones. Outside she could see the tangle of patient, sweltering people, waiting for lines. If Bluefields had phones that worked, they would look like this.

The phone sounded off.

The number was right, at least; the Providencia embassy was still open. And, yes, there was a man called José Mantica.

'I'm glad to hear you,' he said.

She thought of his painful, thin body and the scrub of beard; and the faith.

'I wish I was in Leon,' he said.

She knew she was meant to echo him, but she couldn't.

'Listen,' he said, 'I'll tell you the news. Diaz is out, you know that. We went through the Central Bank, through everything. They left us just $3.4 million, and that's in Caracas and apparently they forgot to clean out Caracas.'

'You said billion, didn't you? Billion, with a B?'

246

'Million, with an M. They stole the whole damned country. Even the blank airline tickets have gone – they could cash those anywhere.'

'But how do you pay –'

'We can't pay doctors or teachers or soldiers or policemen or cleaners or civil servants or – we can't pay. There's a billion dollars of debt to the New York banks and we can't even pay the interest. We can't even pay the postage on a letter to tell them we can't pay.'

'People will help,' Mercedes said. 'The banks will have to help.'

'Help,' Mantica said. 'Maybe they'll help. They don't want us to default – they'd have to write a billion off their books. They'll roll the loans over. And then they'll give the orders – just like Diaz gave the orders when the banks sent in the Marines. It's all the same.'

The line seethed for a moment with static. Mercedes guessed she'd missed something but she didn't interrupt. Mantica needed all the cleansing power of the confession.

'– Houston says the Vice Minister of Planning was in town, trying to cash a cheque for two hundred thousand dollars, drawn to him. A cheque on the Central Bank accounts in Houston, you understand. He said he'd sue if we tried to stop him.'

'The lawyers will know what to do,' Mercedes said, but she didn't believe it. 'There must be ways –'

'Zenon,' José Mantica said, 'if we don't get our hands on that Diaz money, he's stolen the country. The theft of the century, they'll call it. They're bound to call it that.'

'I do my best,' Mercedes said. 'We've found –'

'Not on the phone,' Mantica said. 'And we'll be fine for a while. The Americans still want Diaz out and they want us in, so they won't let anything go wrong. But the first time we disagree with them –'

'I'll do anything,' Mercedes said.

She stumbled out of the phone booth and told John Grey there was no time left. They walked Bay Street, conspicuously handsome among the fat ladies and the heavy Mid West boys, until Vico's driver found them; he was only too happy to drive them to the airport and the plane. It was a duty he should have performed a day before.

'You're very serious,' John Grey said. He was looking down on the sea, how the water danced in brilliance and changed its colour, sometimes where it tugged at weed, or hot and clear over soft sand. He thought it glorious. Nowadays, he was happy to appreciate the moment.

But Mercedes was still rankling, fidgeting, preoccupied with looking for some better world. She was horrified, at bottom. She'd assumed that her leisurely pursuit of the Diaz money would eventually be a bonus to the Amadistas, a revenge on El Jefe himself even more satisfying than a bullet. She'd strip the man of all his certainties and refuges because he needed cash to buy safety. She'd make him vulnerable to all the others who wanted to see him run, and she'd do it for her father, for Aurelia. For what Diaz had done to her family, death was a minor payment.

But now the hunt was urgent, a matter of a country's survival. The personal, the sentimental had become political.

'I come from Providencia,' she said, out loud.

John Grey drew back from the window. 'I know,' he said, puzzled.

'We'll surprise Vico. He won't be expecting us to have real money.'

'Boswell will call him.'

'You wouldn't call your main shareholder to say you'd just given away twenty million, would you?'

Grey shrugged. 'I don't have shareholders,' he said. 'I'm not the type.'

They landed on German Cay, just as a little Piper Seneca went up the sky.

'But there's no welcoming party,' Mercedes said. She was ready either to plead for help or to fight. She didn't care which, but she needed to face Vico quickly.

The little plane was only a busy fly against the clear sky, and the black birds had come back to the crabgrass like a flock of ministers. Mercedes walked through them and they scattered for a moment, and reformed.

'You have a lot of visitors,' she said to Vico, who was sitting in the drawing room before a tray of dirty glasses.

'Some days,' Vico said.

248

'You mind saying who that was?'

'You don't want to know,' Vico said. 'You really don't.'

'We got the money,' John Grey said.

Vico looked scornful. 'Real money?'

Mercedes put the bankers' drafts down before him and he took out spectacles, pince-nez, from his loose shirt pocket.

'Shit,' Vico said. 'Real money.'

'We're doing good,' Mercedes said. 'But we need some help. You promised you'd help.'

'A promise is a promise.'

'You mean you'll –'

'I said a promise is a promise. That's all.'

John Grey sat down and listened like an interested schoolboy.

'You shouldn't wear stockings,' Vico said. 'I always think of you with your legs bare.'

Mercedes said: 'What are you up to?'

'A little business. I just had a customer who's keen on the Galil 5.6 but the Israelis won't sell it to him. You know about the Galil, I expect?' Vico leered at John Grey, sure of his insult.

'Anyone I know?' Mercedes said. 'I mean, if you want to talk about other people's business –'

'It's your business, too,' Vico said. 'Tomás Diaz wants the Galils. He came to persuade me.'

Mercedes leaned forward, very serious. 'Tell me,' she said. 'just tell me which side you're on.'

'I don't choose sides,' Vico said. 'I don't know who's going to win yet.'

Mercedes seemed to crumple into the sofa, no longer sure and ebullient but ragged and loose.

'Winded you, did I?' Vico said. 'You'll be fine. Just don't wear stockings, that's all.' He heaved himself out of the room.

Mercedes looked after him, and she bunched her muscles and shouted after him: 'I'm not your daughter. I'm not yours.'

Vico stood still. He cupped his ear elaborately, smiled and turned. 'Finders keepers,' he said.

She ignored him, and she said to Grey: 'We need Ian Carpenter. We need to know what's happened.'

'I guess,' Grey said, 'we need to leave the island.'

'He owns the planes,' Mercedes said bleakly.

Lunch was a prickle of grievances, mostly unspoken until the coffee came.

'There's no point in our staying,' Mercedes said, 'if you're not going to help.'

'I haven't had time to talk to you,' Vico said.

'We don't have anything to talk about.'

'All these years, all this time – why, I don't even know your young man.' He had the suburban manner pat, the deserted father straining for the love of his daughter. But she knew him better.

'You know all you want to know,' she said.

She went down to the beach on her own and curled like a child on one of the beach chairs. She fell asleep to the faint work of waves against the reef.

She woke, and Vico was standing by her. He was perfectly still, as though he had been there some time, and she had to bring herself fully awake.

'Little Mercedes,' Vico said.

'I want to go,' she said.

'In good time,' Vico said. 'Not now. We haven't talked.'

She refused to see pathos in his eyes. She saw only the kind of gross, suburban monster she'd seen in Chevys on interstates, a man with power of the most unglamorous kind.

When she next saw John Grey in the house, she said, 'He's like a terrorist. A financial terrorist. He operates by making people scared to argue.'

'Don't let him get to you.'

'It was hard enough leaving before,' Mercedes said, and then regretted her frankness.

'Well,' Grey said, with false brightness, 'this time leaving doesn't seem very likely. Until Vico decides we can. After all, he's the law on this island. What he says, goes.'

Mercedes could see George Vico walking down by the beach. He looked insignificant from a distance, another fat man whose flesh hung loosely like a falling tent from the pole of his neck.

'We have no time.'

'It's only a day or two.'

'He's playing games. He likes games. The more we worry, the

250

more he'll be happy to keep us here.'

'Then play with him,' Grey said. 'What else can we do?'

Vico was staring out to sea, across to America.

Tuesday they left Miami, and Wednesday was like Tuesday: the sea shimmered, the little yellow grunts shoaled past, the beaches were hot and tired. And the girls, who weren't quite professional, smiled. They were brown and generous and sometimes they simply stood, magnificent and void, scratching a thigh.

The Diaz yacht, the *Esperanza*, had a history; one American billionaire, one Swedish billionaire, George Vico himself, and now, rebuilt and refitted in Coral Gables taste, its high prow and its tall rigging sat out to sea like a delicately finished monument.

Ian Carpenter didn't have much experience as a hedonist but he learned fast. He kept thinking he should call London, and somehow it was always too difficult; if the radio worked, then there was a girl between him and the radio. If the girls had gone below, he couldn't find the radio. He stood on the deck, flexed in the sun and watched the needle fish make the sea silver and brilliant. He'd found limbo ahead of time, and he loved it.

There was all the time in the world, so he thought. Diaz could do nothing without him, and Diaz was on the yacht, as frantic as anyone over the very young, very kind girls he'd arranged. They wandered, long plump legs and dark-ringed eyes, as though the sun had dazed them.

Carpenter felt an iced can, cruel on his back.

'You like oil?'

It was a girl called Helen. She had blonde hair and a tight, worked body and she smiled a lot. Now she was kneeling beside him and she'd picked up a bottle of oil that the sun had warmed. She put a little on her shoulders; she let it trickle down between her breasts. She looked to see if he was interested.

He propped himself on his elbows. Time and place had been suspended on this dazzling sea; anything was fine.

Her breasts were fine. She'd slipped off the top of her bikini and the oil was flooding down to the broad, flat nipples. She was brown like good bread; she smoothed the oil on her breasts, teasing them, and offering them. The slick, hot oil had streaked her belly, down to the bush of her sex.

251

She turned herself as though she wanted to be modest and she oiled her thighs.

He put out a hand and stroked where the oil was running, on the sensitive skin inside her thighs. She turned up the bottle and let the oil pour down her body and streak the lower half of her bikini. Below, the oil revealed her sex like light shows through wet paper.

No names, nothing that mattered: only this moment.

His hands were working in a flood of slick warmth. He rolled over her, and covered her; he was oiling himself from her skin, growing hard against her belly.

She worked her breasts together, trapping him in between. He was slip-sliding with a sensation that made him roar.

She was teasing him, with the oil and the wet around her sex. Being outside her was painful. He had a flash of anger that she was playing old whore's tricks, and he drove himself into her, eyes wild. Her fingers were busy with her own immediate pleasure, and he held back on each thrust, back until he could hardly bear the waiting and then forward up to her heart, back while she flicked and stroked herself into pleasure, and forward.

She began to hold him inside her, and then to tremble. He could wait no longer. It was as though her body was singing, vibrating with breath and rhythm; he came with violence.

She held him inside her, and she kissed him on the lips. It was surprisingly personal and she curled against him, warm and slippery.

He could see out past the deck rails to the shore: a line of scrub and sand. He heard the noise of an engine, faintly.

He woke up from his drift and heard crashing and barking below: Diaz was preparing for a new day, hampered by last night's tequila and last night's woman. He came panting up to deck in a terrycloth robe, bothered as a wet dog and carrying his hangover like a stone.

'What the hell's that?' he said.

Carpenter sat up and Helen stretched herself luxuriously and smiled at Diaz. No sense in not making all the friends you can.

Carpenter saw a small speedboat running between the little islands and heading for the white castle of the *Esperanza*. He stared, trying to make out figures on board.

252

At the stern stood a woman, sharp in white, her skin black-brown. She was quite still.

He sat up. He pulled on the jeans he'd abandoned on the deck and stood up. He felt half ashamed.

The speedboat was running for the yacht, and Diaz had two men up on the roof of the main saloon with rifles. They kept the little boat in their sights.

Carpenter looked down, and he saw her. In that moment, he didn't give her a name, neither Mercedes nor Aurelia; she was simply the woman who was twisting and shaping his life. But of course, it must be Mercedes. Aurelia was gone, and would never come close to Diaz again; Mercedes must have tracked him down. He didn't know how easy it would be to run his schemes with Mercedes around, always asking questions, always wanting to play her part.

The speedboat cut its engines and bumped companionably against the yacht.

'Mercedes Zenon,' Diaz said. 'This is an honour.'

Helen covered herself lackadaisically, recognising a star with whom she couldn't compete, and went below.

'It's good to see you,' Carpenter said. He wondered why Diaz was so glad to see her; for a nervous minute he thought perhaps she had been working for Diaz, keeping Carpenter observed, and now her job was over. But he knew that couldn't be true. He knew, he told himself.

'It's so dull in Nassau,' she said, when she'd climbed aboard. 'I thought I'd invite myself onto a yacht for a few days.'

'As long as you like,' Diaz said. 'We're going nowhere.'

'Nor am I,' she said. 'Your ship is lovely.' She smiled and took Diaz's arm. 'You must show me –'

Carpenter followed them with his eyes, but he stayed still. There was something wrong and he did not want to move until he knew precisely what. He smelt the air, and he could smell her perfume; he saw the dance of light in the water and he imagined flowers on the shore.

She knew the ship, didn't she? From Vico's day?

He was puzzled by her.

'I don't believe in systems,' George Vico said. He put down his

253

glass and he seemed almost benevolent to John Grey; Mercedes, he had decided to ignore.

'You book seats on planes,' Grey said. 'I bet you even use American Express – or used to.'

'Systems are just thinking slowed down,' Vico said. 'You program a computer, it knows what you knew then. It doesn't know what you know now. Systems are fools.'

Grey said: 'But essential. Your great mutual fund was a system. If it hadn't been, you couldn't have – done what you did with it.' The delicacy sounded odd.

'I didn't say you couldn't play with them,' Vico said. 'They tell me, you'd know, that if you take an ordinary radioactive isotope from a hospital and put it in a computer room, the computer goes down. Fine. Except that you and I know it's a computer, a machine, but to people out there it might be their credit rating, their savings, their medical history. They don't want to know those things are fallible.'

'They have to be fallible,' Grey said. 'You can't design perfect intelligence; we can't even breed it. And if you had the perfectly intelligent man, you could always shoot him. Intelligence isn't enough in itself.'

'You'd make a system that was imperfect?'

Mercedes got up from the table, her look almost sulky. She'd told Grey to engage Vico, not fascinate him; she wanted help from the man.

'I made FedWire less than perfect,' Grey said. 'If it was perfect, someone would kill it. I believe that. So I leave a trapdoor, for superstitious reasons. A little gap, not important.'

'You make my point,' Vico said. 'Most people don't want to think of FedWire as a machine, a system. They think of it as money in America, and they think that's real – something more than electronic impulses. They think there's something you can touch called money.'

'You touch it,' Grey said.

'I can touch it,' Vico said, 'because I don't give a damn about the system. I can reach in and take out something real.'

He shouted for another bottle, and Mercedes said: 'You don't need another bottle.'

'Sit down,' Vico said. 'Either women don't understand this

stuff, or you do and you can listen. Just don't interrupt.'

John Grey turned to Mercedes with an elaborate wink, which she did not forgive.

'This trapdoor in FedWire,' Vico said.

John Grey said: 'People don't want to know. They have a system that's shifting close to half a trillion dollars every day, three deals a second, a backlog of billions. Every big company borrows what it needs for the day, just by a keystroke; the banks don't even know what they lend on daylight overdrafts. You can't have a gap in a system like that.'

'Exactly,' Vico said. 'But there is.'

Mercedes said: 'I don't have time to listen.'

The new bottle came, and Vico cracked it open. 'You have all the time in the world,' he said. 'You're not going anywhere.'

'It's a very simple thing,' John Grey said. 'I guess I'm the only one who can use it, and it's lethal. It's my little joke.'

Vico was quiet, but his whole body asked for details.

'Once a quarter, if the system gets one command, it will stop and encrypt everything in its memory. Everything. All the money in America will be lost.'

'Someone could use that.'

'I don't see how,' Grey said. 'It would be the unforgivable crime. And once it's done, you have an hour to reverse the process. MTBU, that's the phrase. Maximum Time to Bottom Up.' Grey swigged his whisky; the bar-room pose, legs apart, began to irritate Mercedes. 'So if you wanted to blackmail America, first they'd have to believe you could make things right and then they'd have to surrender inside an hour. Otherwise, nada.'

'They might believe you could do it. They might pay you off to stop it.'

'They couldn't possibly believe it,' Grey said. 'You're not talking about a computer, you're talking about money. If that's vulnerable, then there's a basic flaw in everything they manage and manipulate and make.'

Vico leaned forward, the chair pushed back at a dangerous angle, and he said: 'Someone could use all that.'

'It would have to be someone who had no other way to go,' John Grey said.

255

And Vico seemed to recover himself, to put back in place his boozing, boasting self. 'You'll find someone.'

'I'm not selling,' Grey said. 'It's only my superstition.'

'You'll sell,' Vico said. 'We all sell one day.'

Mercedes said: 'I'm going to bed.'

She walked out of the room and Vico nudged John Grey. 'You're not following?'

'Not yet,' Grey said. He was good at macho.

'You keep 'em waiting, then?'

'A long time,' Grey said, and narrowly blocked a giggle.

The two men rambled out to the porch, and Vico drew in the night air gratefully. He also shouted for more whisky, more ice. He threw a hand into the night and brought it round like the arm of a windmill and said: 'All this is mine.'

'It's a great headquarters.'

'All this,' Vico said, 'nothing else. And just across that channel, where you can't see lights, there's the country I come from.'

'What good would it do you to go back?'

'Good? It would only harm me. They'd crucify me.'

'But you want to go back?'

'It's the biggest machine for money in the world. There's nothing like it. More cash, more credit, more stocks, more suckers. Everything a man needs –'

'You have your businesses.'

A little plane had just taken off, lightless.

'There's nothing worth calculating in those,' Vico said. 'You know about calculating. The rush, the working out, the imagining. Who the hell wants to live by an airstrip where the planes come and go, even if they're carrying coke. I only did one thing in two years that's interesting – sat with the Colombians when they decided to bring their prices down. Mass marketing instead of specialised markets. Crack in vials instead of powder, so people smoke the stuff and get hooked. Good business. They could teach you that at Harvard.'

'They do,' Grey said, 'more or less. I think.'

'And if they can teach it,' Vico said, 'it can't be interesting. Like if it's a system, it's over, finished. The only things worth doing are impossible.'

The talk fumed out of him like whisky breath, a little stale and a little hopeful.

Grey said: 'They may prosecute me. Over Greystoke.'

'You can go anywhere,' Vico said. 'Just stay out of the country. Nobody's going to extradite you.'

'They'd send you home, if they caught you.'

'Not here,' Vico said. He fell silent for a moment, and Grey was too burned by whisky to see why. 'But you only ripped off a handful of rich punters in America, the kind that deserve it. The Swiss wouldn't send you home. I doubt if the British would –'

'I always thought,' Grey said, so casually, 'that if anything went wrong I could fall back to the trapdoor in FedWire. I could threaten them; I could get my pardon.'

Vico said: 'Boy, you can do anything. Anyone with half a mind can.'

But his eyes were still fixed out at sea, where he imagined the long, flat coast of Florida.

'You make me think, boy,' he said.

'You tell me all about New York,' Diaz said. 'You tell me everything.'

She said: 'It's fun.'

'Names,' Diaz said. 'Give me names. Places to go.'

'But you didn't stay in America. I thought maybe –'

'They wanted me out for a while. They'll have me back.'

'Then I'll tell you about New York when you arrive. It's always changing.'

She wouldn't help Carpenter with glances, or smiles. She didn't seem to want physical closeness although she spoke to him sometimes. If she was so damned sure that contact with Diaz corrupted, then why was she here? And why did he feel so distant from her that he could not simply shout that to her?

She was immediately the civilising star of the evening. The girls had dressed decorously, and the men had given up their boys together bluster; at eight, they came to the dining room in white that they wore self-consciously, like models in some drink advertisement. And she arrived a little late, and sat close to the head of the table, glorious and untouchable. She calmed them all; she almost froze them.

257

Carpenter felt his heart pounding, a mix of desire, anger and mystification, and he stared at her. Everything about her was familiar, except the person that sat there; he knew the eyes, the face, the smile, the breasts, the legs, the sex, the way she held a glass. He knew; and he knew nothing.

After dinner, she said: 'Let's walk on the deck.'

She didn't touch him. She strolled to the prow and looked back at all the lights and rigging, a fantasticated tree of white light above the practical superstructure of the boat. She said: 'Nothing surprises you, does it?'

'I don't understand.'

She turned and looked down at the water. He could see their faces reflected, side by side, and it was almost easier to read reflections than her real face.

'You don't feel alarmed? Being here?'

'Why should I? I've done a good job for Diaz, so he's happy. And the job is so good we can lift all the money cleanly. It won't be hard.'

'And who gets it?'

'After all we've done together, you think I'd back out now?'

'Don't shout. You don't want to draw attention to us.' And in very measured tones, she said: 'It occurred to me. You spent a lot of time with Diaz, you've got your own reasons for being in this game. You don't have any reason to love Providencia.'

'But Aurelia,' he said, trying to coop his feeling in a steady voice, 'I did it for –'

'Aurelia, whom you betrayed.'

'Who told you that?'

'What did you say on the phone? "But I have company"?'

'I'm not on trial. I've done what I can.'

He felt a pressure on his spine. It could have been the muzzle of a gun; he turned a little and saw it was only her knuckle, pushed into his bone.

'You're in a strange mood,' he said. 'We're in this together, you know that.'

'Are we?' she said.

'We have to be.'

'Then when do the Amadistas get the money?'

'Now you're the one who's talking too loud.'

258

'I don't have a lot to lose any more.'

He tried to understand her words; they were full of a chilly meaning that passed him by. He said: 'We have everything to live for.'

She was a little like a ghost, he thought; not quite in touch with the body she inhabited and the name she bore.

He said: 'Let's go below.'

'You think I'll sleep with you?'

He held his breath.

'You really think I will, don't you?'

But why was she angry?

He said: 'It's up to you. It always was.'

'You have the girls, the drink, the coke, the sun – all down to Diaz, no doubt.'

'Yes,' he said, 'for the moment. To avoid suspicion.'

'And not because you like the girls, the drink, the coke, the sun?'

'All right,' he said. 'Since when have you been such a pure girl? You're only fighting for the revolution because you've got a million a year from perfumes to keep you comfortable. You –'

'You don't know me,' she said. She spaced the words and made them bite; she turned and stalked down the deck.

He watched her go. The walk was so familiar, and so strange. He thought he was confused because he was in love.

In the saloon, a soldier brought messages for Diaz. His son would join him the next day. Tomás had business to discuss.

She was in Carpenter's bed when he went below, but she was unresponsive. She said: 'But I have company. That's what you said.'

'I didn't know what it would do.'

'You didn't do it for Diaz?'

'I said the first thing that came into my head.'

'And you know what happened?'

He looked at her, his eyes wide with tears. 'I even saw what happened,' he said.

She could find nothing to say, but her rational mind kept fretting at her: don't believe him. Believe nobody's defence.

'I saw,' he said, and put out his hand.

259

She hesitated. 'Tell me exactly what you saw,' she said with a lawyer's instinct. She left her gun in its shoulder holster.

'Nobody could do that,' Vico said at breakfast.

'We need your help,' Mercedes said. 'I told you that. You want me to throw myself down and beg for your help?'

Vico ignored her, like a plaintive child. He said: 'That scam, your scam, John. It couldn't be used.'

Grey shrugged. 'That's what I thought.'

'But it's good. Very good. You spoil the whole system, you put them all in fear of their livelihoods. They hate that. I only wish I could do it.'

'You can't,' John Grey said. 'I'm the only one who knows how to use the trapdoor.'

Vico said, unable to leave the subject be: 'Why haven't they found it yet?'

'They're not looking. They look for regular errors, regular blips. They can't look for one extraordinary disaster that hasn't happened yet.'

'But they must have back-up programs?'

'I programmed those, too.'

'Why did you have to make it useless?'

When breakfast was finished, Mercedes followed Grey outside.

'I thought I'd go for a swim,' he said.

She shivered.

'You're too southern,' Grey said. 'Me, I'd break the ice on the Hudson to —'

'You can stop being stupid,' Mercedes said. 'We're out of earshot of the house.'

'I was joking,' Grey said, patiently. 'Jokes aren't always stupid.'

'Do you realise how much time we've got?'

'All the time in the world. All we need is Uncle George Vico and we've won.'

'Diaz cleaned out Providencia. Almost literally. They have a billion dollar debt to the big banks and $3.4 million cash.'

'The Americans will help.'

'We don't know what the Americans will do,' Mercedes said. 'And why the hell should it always be the Americans, always them? Doesn't anyone in Providencia have a voice?'

'It's our backyard,' Grey said. He shucked off his sweater and his shirt.

'Jesus,' Mercedes said.

'Besides,' Grey said, stripping down, 'Diaz is alive, and while he's alive, nobody is going to know where the money is. Except us. The family doesn't have rights, it's all hidden from the wife and only the old man knows. We're winning.'

He stood on the sand, impatient and naked. He was, she acknowledged, looking good.

'But if something happened to Diaz –'

'He's got his guards,' Grey said. 'I guess if he died, there'd be the whole family out with lawyers to find the money. I guess that could be difficult.'

'You don't give a damn,' she said. But he was sprinting away down the beach and would not listen.

She found herself praying for the life of Anastasio Diaz Sacasa, just because his death would complicate their hunt so hideously.

She stared out to America, trying to see what Vico saw; but there was only sea. And then, into her field of vision came a memory: a white, intricate castle of a yacht, gleaming on the open sea, and alongside it, a tiny seaplane landing. She saw Vico's yacht, the one that had taken her from Providencia when she was a child, the icing sugar fantasy of a ship; and she knew who now owned Vico's yacht.

Diaz was out there, miles away. Someone with a telescope might see her on the beach; she could wave. She could wave and they could come for her.

But she did not wave. The almost sickening pull of memory dissolved quite abruptly. It was not her childhood wasting at anchor out there, only a ship. It was not her life, ready to be remade, only a conveyance in which rode Diaz himself.

God, but she would swim there and guard him herself, for the sake of the money and the future; and in the name of Aurelia. The irony hurt her stomach.

John Grey came back into shore at a brisk crawl, elegantly done, and threw himself into towels on a beach chair. 'Some boat,' he said, nodding innocently out to sea.

★

261

Once Tomás Diaz stepped on board from his seaplane, the social sense quit dead, just as there had been no more indulgence after Diaz said: 'Mercedes Zenon! What an honour!' The tensions were like lesions on the perfect gloss of the day.

Mercedes lay on the deck like some queen in old ebony, oiled and black, turning in the sun and preoccupied. Carpenter couldn't talk to her about anything of substance; from time to time she went below.

He heard hammering, then raised voices. Tomás was bellowing and insinuating, one yell after another, the same argument he'd long rehearsed; Diaz was not listening, loudly.

'Why are outsiders here?' Tomás shouted. 'You don't need outsiders. You need your family, your son.'

'I don't need anyone,' Diaz said.

'What happens if the Amadistas come here?' Tomás said. 'What happens? You're vulnerable, and if you die, your whole fortune goes with you? You think that's fair to us?'

'You think I'm vulnerable?'

'You have strangers on board.' Tomás dropped his voice, tried to steady it and make it coldly serious. 'You might die, Papa. You might die.'

'Wash your mouth out with soap,' Diaz said, and seeing the shock in Tomás's face, began to roar with laughter.

The hammering returned.

'Maybe we should be going,' Carpenter said to Mercedes on the hot deck. He felt no urge to move in the stunning sun, but he also felt the embarrassment of a flustered Tomás and a rigid Diaz, battling below decks.

She said: 'I love the sun.' But she went below almost immediately, saying she wanted to rest.

Tomás came up with the girls, and took a dinghy out to a small cay. The girls were happy to go somewhere a touch less proper, even Helen; and Tomás needed the distraction of a tangle of friendly hands and legs.

Carpenter was alone in the afternoon, in the shade with a jug of cold water and a book: his peace became sleep, and when he woke, the sun was down and huge, and the shadows a cheap acid red. Carpenter shook himself. He should go below and see what Diaz was up to, maybe sell him some plan or find some

262

information, certainly check the man's mood.

It was hot below, but it seemed worse in Diaz's office. The airconditioning must be running low. He called out, but there was no answer.

He walked through the office to the Presidential suite. There might be something to discover, something they could use. He fumbled for a light switch automatically before he realised the porthole curtains were drawn tight.

He flicked the switch, expecting white light. But across the bedroom he saw a tangle of lights from some jumble sale Christmas tree – all white and green, blue and yellow and red, knotted round the door to give a dirty light. He stopped short. The lights had the look of a tawdy electric garland for a saint, or the garlands that Diaz's grandfather once strung across the roads of Leon to keep out smallpox. Cheap magic.

Beyond the lights, the heavy glass door to the steam room was propped open. The bath was working furiously; steam hung like clouds.

'Diaz!' Carpenter shouted.

He could make her out through the steam, at the door of the room; she was shiny with oil and sweat. He said 'Mercedes' very softly and was fascinated by her, the gleam of her, the black wiry hair around her sex, the pinkness of her nipples. He walked towards her.

At the door, some of the Christmas lights were tangled in his hair. He was shocked and brushed them away. Inside the bath, he could see columns of bright steam where the ceiling lights shone down, nothing else except white: and the woman standing at the door.

She smiled.

He pulled off his shoes, and his shirt, and walked into the steam. It roared at him like a great wind, and the room was so bright and so white that looking was like going blind. He edged to the side, slipping on the downhill floor, and she held him. She ran a hand across his chest and stopped, briskly, at each nipple; then she looked at him, knowingly.

He wondered if they were alone. Something in the claustrophobia of the steam, the knowledge that he could see so little, made him imagine what else was in the bath.

She drew him in. The door was gone, now.

He stumbled still, bothered by the dip where the drain ran; he tried for the support of the back wall. He felt smothered and lost, as though cut off from air, and she had stroked him, with her fingers and her nails, until he was painfully hard. And then she dropped her hand, and took him into her mouth, and he knew nothing except the warm, benevolent movement in that wet cave.

He could see something. He was almost coming, pitched back against the wall, all his muscles contracted; but he could see something. Across the room, past the next corner, there was some kind of –

But he could see nothing now except whiteness, sense nothing except the surrender of his sex to the kindest movements. The shape was gone.

He was coming, coming for ever.

'Come on,' she said. 'Let's go –'

He could see the shape again, a bulky shape. He kissed her, but he also pushed her gently away. He felt his way along the line of tiles that led back to the door.

The shape was wrapped in a huge, white towel, back against the wall; it had a belly, and a face, whose eyes were blank and dark-rimmed as a lemur's.

She stood very still.

He put out a hand and moved the head. It broke forward like a puppet's. When he lifted it gently back, he saw that the President did not have eyes. There were only powder burns, like the story of long nights.

The body was warm.

She said: 'That is what he did to my father's eyes.'

He felt vulnerable as an egg. He had the pleasant vacuous ease of a man who has just come, and the terror of a man who does not know how and why another man died.

'You never said you'd do this,' he said, hopelessly. 'If Diaz is dead, all hell breaks loose about his money. I could have told you that.'

'If Diaz is dead,' she said, 'nobody can be a Diacista.'

'They'll rally to Tomás. They'll find someone.'

'Only the old man. He was the only one they knew; he saw to that. He never wanted heirs – not to money, not to power.'

264

'What do we do?' he said.

She shrugged. 'We leave the body. Someone will find it. His valet, maybe. His secretary.'

'But we should say –'

'What are you going to say to Tomás Diaz? We're the strangers here.'

'Who will they hang for this?'

'With luck,' she said, 'nobody.'

He picked up his shirt and shoes at the door with mechanical sense and walked out into the corridors. Nobody was moving yet. The sunset made the walkways the colour of cheap cordials.

He said, testing the word cautiously: 'Aurelia?'

'Does it matter?'

'I thought you were dead. I saw you dead.'

'Hurt,' she said. 'You'd see the scars without make-up and careful clothes.'

'I thought I killed you.'

'I wondered if you meant to,' she said.

He said, forcing out words that were determined to lodge in his gullet: 'You think I meant to?'

'I don't think you meant to do anything then,' she said, which was not comforting. 'But now, I think you may be serious.'

She went away to shower and change, and so did he, and they met again at the bar on deck. A decorous, invisible Indian girl made Martinis. Carpenter drank too fast.

Tomás came back flushed and burned at once, the girls sitting almost prim around him. 'Where's my father?' he asked.

It was the logical question; there was no reason why it should disconcert Carpenter and Aurelia. And so they said they didn't know and went on looking at the sea.

Aurelia. Aurelia whom he'd loved, in another country. Only this time, the wench was not dead; she was here, and she had killed Diaz. At least, he was almost sure that she had pulled the trigger; she'd been concerned that he should not find the body. But Aurelia had also killed Chamorro. It had been easier for him when Aurelia simply disappeared after the rumours of Chamorro's death in Leon; he did not have to think how he judged and valued someone who had killed. She might be a soldier, but he knew no soldiers.

He thought: it is a luxury for me to think this way. My

265

judgement is no longer what matters. I am involved in something which is greater, and ineluctable.

But he also thought: in forty years, I never surrendered to a process, an inevitability. Why should I give up my choices now?

He looked at Aurelia. She was impatient, and Tomás believed she must be waiting for his father. Young Tomás didn't count. So he was bragging, about how he'd soon be organising an army to take back Leon, how he knew how to get the arms.

Carpenter could blow her cover with a word. He could silence Tomás, tell what he knew. But what use was a power he lacked the right to use?

'I'm going to look for my father,' Tomás said.

The minutes grated on Carpenter. The girls sat apart in a lovely, fleshy clump, talking about Miami, clubs, Latins, islands and being in shows. It was automated talk, the kind the punters expected; the girls were far too practical for dreams.

Carpenter said to Aurelia, quietly: 'Brace yourself.'

But Tomás Diaz came back calm as steel. He spoke quietly to the servants. He said to Carpenter: 'My father seems to be unwell.'

And that was all he said. It was a brutal anti-climax, and Carpenter was profoundly unsure what to make of it. When Tomás next went downstairs, he followed, and Aurelia after him.

The servants had restored the lights in the Diaz suite, and dried out the smoky cave of the steam room so that it seemed a properly clinical place for a corpse. The yacht was full of lights, but it was silent.

Tomás Diaz covered his father's face, reverently.

He said to Carpenter: 'He's dead. There's no point in telling the girls; they'll only panic. Some Amadista bastard must have got here.'

It sounded like a practised routine.

'One of those roaches.' Tomás spat, with elaborate show. 'We knew they'd get him, sooner or later.'

'You don't seem surprised,' Carpenter said. He really meant that Tomás did not seem either upset or distracted; and yet he should have been. He should have been facing the final disappearance of a billion dollars.

'It'll be fine,' Tomás said. 'We announce a boating accident. Other waters, maybe. There's nothing to say. Don't want the Amadistas to take the credit.'

'Of course not,' Aurelia said.

'They'd glory in this,' Tomás said. 'Bastards.'

Dinner was cold and formal, a parody of style. Aurelia played hostess, instructing the servants, checking the dishes; she had gone back to her perfected manners in Leon. But because the table was full of big, generous girls, she seemed absurdly like a matron in some reform school, and the two men grossly out of place. Only manners kept the table from a riot of anger and awkwardness.

'After dinner,' she said to Tomás, 'we must talk.'

'Must we?' Tomás said.

When the girls had gone to bed and the servants had retired, Aurelia said: 'You have to report his death.'

'Where to? We're in the middle of nowhere.'

'There are islands close by. There must be some police –'

'You want the police?'

'We have to report this.'

If it was her action, it was lost in the secrecy Tomás proposed. But Carpenter wondered whether she really had pulled the trigger, or whether Tomás himself was trying to hide patricidal dreams. Perhaps she wanted the police so that Tomás could be accused and taken off: an obstacle gone.

'Tomorrow morning,' Aurelia said. 'We go ashore.'

They slept fitfully that night, waiting for trouble that never quite came. In the morning, Carpenter went on deck to find breakfast and there was nobody. He pushed his way down into the galleys and looked around: a pot of coffee boiled into syrup on the stove. He looked for eggs in a refrigerator, and in a deep freeze, and in the second freezer he found the body of Anastasio Diaz Sacasa. The familiar face lacked guile or evil; it belonged to a man with no idea of limits. The ice around the features was beginning to turn them purple.

He slammed down the lid.

Aurelia was already at the breakfast table, picking at a slice of papaya. 'We have to report it,' she said.

Very softly, Carpenter said: 'Because you want the credit?'

She said nothing.

'If you want to report it, we have to get to land.'

'You coming with me?'

'I'm coming.'

They took the small launch and ran the moody engine for themselves; for once, it started quickly.

Tomás Diaz ran to the side of the *Esperanza*.

'We don't say anything,' he shouted. 'There is no need –'

In his mind there danced all the prospects of forging his father's name and going out before his death was known to take back what belonged to the Diaz clan. He was sure it was possible. And when it was done, he was sure he would have an army and a chance at Leon. Nobody had stood against him before. Nobody would block him now.

'I'll shoot,' he shouted.

Carpenter and Aurelia had their heads down, close to the steering wheel. They heard the shots, and an uncanny time between the sharp sound and the fall of shot into the water.

Aurelia wasn't by his side any more. He noticed that as he was heading the launch fast into shore and concentrating on the water for fear of some hidden reef. She was standing towards the back of the boat and was shaking her fist at the *Esperanza*, at Tomás Diaz and his father. She was shouting, but he couldn't hear her for the noise of the wind and the engine. She was shouting. He looked back for a moment, and her shout was open-mouthed, slack-jawed. Her stiff, defiant pose was beginning to fade. There was blood on her dress.

He couldn't let go of the wheel; he had to take them out of range, into the side of the island. He looked for a break in the line of whitecaps that marked the reef; he found the gap and went through. He killed the engine only within wading distance of the shore.

There were men with guns on the sand, and others running to join them. He held his hands up above his head. He shouted that he was unarmed, that he had someone wounded. The men grudgingly put their shotguns down, where they could easily be reached.

He took up Aurelia. She was limp like a bolt of cloth; she was black and gold and bloody. He jumped down into the shallows and rolled her body into his arms and struck out for the shore, his legs dragging against the weight of the water. He felt laden and delighted by his burden; he kept imagining that this time he would save her life.

He hit land, and the rag-tag army surrounded him; he stood with Aurelia in his arms, cradling her. He thought the salt might sting her wounds; he wanted to lick away the salt.

Out at sea, the lovely *Esperanza* turned in the water; the sun caught her portholes and made her dazzling. He could imagine the girls on deck, Helen playing racquetball, all assuming that Tomás was simply shooting for shooting's sake. The servants would go softly about their business. The boat was sure and unchangeable as a photograph, and it turned slowly out of its anchorage at the head of a wide white procession of water.

He lowered himself slowly on tired haunches and stroked Aurelia's hair. The armed men backed off; they had a startled look.

The first time in his life, Carpenter had no time to analyse or interpret his situation. He cried.

Mercedes found a magazine, tall and glossy, which read like a family album: George Vico was on the cover, inside there was a double-spread for Parfums Mercedes Zenon. She saw Vico exposed again, pinned down by a telephoto lens bone-fishing on a still sea, and then among a flock of small planes. But a man isn't caught by a camera; only glanced at, for the time the shutter takes to move. The magazine lied with its great spreads of pictures, making the reader feel important.

They liked to make Vico a monster. They said he was running drugs with Cuban money, buying arms for the Libyans, a mastermind. They showed a square silo on his island and said it was packed with cocaine.

Vico must be delighted. He'd kept the magazine, after all. His beloved America, his dreams, had pitched him out like a soured wife and kept him out. He wanted revenge. He wanted to be seen.

There was even a page of pictures from the Amadista triumph in Leon – a kind of child's crusade come to a glorious end in the

269

endless smiles of kids in olive drab, guns across their shoulders.

A servant watched her from the door, only wondering whether to interrupt and offer coffee.

All stars for the moment, Mercedes thought: she stood in the cable car above Pilatus, that enigmatic look on her face, a page or so away from Vico, a pear of a man out fishing on a bright day, and the Amadistas and Leon and Diaz, whose picture had been torn in one of the photographs, burned in another. They had faces and stories that could be contained on pages.

She heard shouting on the beach. Nothing was ever unexpected on Vico's island; she went to the windows.

Some of the loaders, toting guns, were pelting down through the scrub and the seagrapes to the water. She followed, carefully. It ran through her head that if someone could get within range of the island, then maybe she could get out.

She saw the launch, bobbing without anchor in the shallows, turning every time the tide shifted. The loaders and the other men had clustered on the beach round someone who had landed.

She walked down, out of curiosity. She saw Carpenter first and then the woman he was cradling. She saw herself.

'She's all right?' Mercedes said.

'We don't know,' Carpenter said. 'If you could get these guys to help me with her, if you could get a doctor –'

They laid her on a narrow cot in a bare, white room. Mercedes dressed her wounds; she'd been grazed, not penetrated by the bullets, but the grazes were ugly. Mercedes wrapped white gauze around Aurelia's arm and shoulder and she saw other scars from other wounds, a little history in raised, hard flesh. She worked silently; Aurelia shifted a little on the cot but her eyes were still closed.

'She needs something for shock,' Mercedes said. 'I don't know what they give for shock.'

'There are no doctors,' Vico said. 'Not closer than the mainland.'

'Then bring someone in from the mainland,' Mercedes said. 'Someone who won't ask questions. You must have someone.'

'I don't get sick.'

'Then get one of those fancy cancer doctors from the islands – the ones who aren't allowed to practise in America. Get someone.'

270

Vico said: 'Nobody comes here unless I say so. And what the hell was she doing on *Esperanza*?' He had seen the yacht out at sea, seen it turn and move away; he remembered the sound of the engines, the pleasure of free movement, the wind in rigging. He was more desolately jealous than he had ever felt.

'She was with Diaz,' Carpenter said. 'I was with Diaz. You know that. Dammit, you sold the yacht to Diaz.'

'I know that,' Vico said.

Mercedes put her hand on Aurelia's forehead. 'Get her some aspirin at least,' she said. 'Take the fever down. She's strong.'

She spent the afternoon by the cot. When Aurelia stirred, she settled the sheets; when Aurelia spoke, Mercedes smiled and comforted her, and told her not to try talk, yet. Carpenter watched her concentration, which was formidable; nothing existed for her except her sister. What she heard, she heard only as an annoyance to Aurelia trying to sleep; when the servants brought food, she would see if Aurelia wanted to eat.

By the early evening Aurelia was sore and bandaged, but conscious. Mercedes helped her to a couch in the drawing room, and wrapped her in a blanket.

She said: 'I needed to touch you. After all this time.'

'*Compañera*,' Aurelia said.

'You disappeared, like a ghost.'

'Underground,' Aurelia said. 'You say that in English, underground?'

'But there were stories you were shot –'

'I was shot, but I wasn't killed. It was a war, after all. It doesn't matter.'

'And you were on the yacht, with Diaz?'

'I was being you,' Aurelia said. 'I was trying to see if I could be you.'

Mercedes had been warm with concern all day, and other feelings had been driven out. Now, an ungenerous thought was possible.

'You took my name?' she said.

'Diaz wouldn't have let me on board.'

'And why did you want to be on board?'

'Diaz is dead,' Aurelia said briefly. It was a bulletin, not a boast.

271

Mercedes said: 'Dead.'

'Chamorro, the Captain, Diaz,' and Aurelia was whispering the names. 'They're all gone.'

'But if Diaz is gone, then the money – we'll never be able to get to the money.'

'What do you mean?'

'We were getting so close, Carpenter and me and John Grey. And if Diaz is dead, all the laywers, all the bankers, they'll be guarding that money more closely than ever. There can't be tricks, any more.'

Aurelia said: 'We weren't sure if Carpenter was still helping you. Or us.'

'But did you have to be sure? He couldn't report all the time; he was too close to Diaz. We had money in Switzerland; we had money from the Bahamas – we still have that. But we'll never get the rest of it now.'

Aurelia had the modestly defiant look of someone who will not be tripped up by realities. She said: 'But Diaz can't return now.'

'You think that matters? Without the money, Providencia can't defend itself.'

The two women sat opposite each other, mirrors to each other's faces and bodies and furious at the fact.

'You said you were me,' Mercedes said. 'So I can't go near the Diaz camp again. I might even be arrested –'

'Where would they arrest you?' Aurelia asked reasonably. 'I thought you wanted to share the work, and the credit. Diaz was a present to you.'

'But that is our private business,' Mercedes said.

'It was everyone's business,' Aurelia said. She wouldn't listen to the reasonable; she had too much faith. 'You should be proud to give your name.'

Carpenter was there, but not in the eyes or the mind of either woman. He tried to listen to what was under all the love and anger in their voices, what old contradictions had surfaced at last. He half understood.

'You took my name,' Mercedes said, patiently.

'It's not property,' Aurelia said.

'My name is me,' Mercedes said. 'That doesn't stop just because I'm famous.'

272

'You sell your name for perfumes,' Aurelia said. 'It's a trademark, someone else's copyright. I just took it back, for a while.' The gauze rubbed against raw skin; she winced a little. 'This face,' she said, 'we share this face.'

'What did you do when you were Mercedes?'

Aurelia shrugged.

'I want to know what you did. You took my identity.'

'You know enough.'

'I know you killed Diaz. You wrecked the game.'

'It's not a game,' Aurelia said. Carpenter heard a sententiousness that surprised him.

And he thought of the oiled, shiny woman in the steam-bath, who made love to keep him away from the corpse of Diaz. That wasn't Aurelia; it was Mercedes, all metropolitan, aggressive, unscrupulous, decadent and cool as Aurelia imagined her. Someone's fantasy had come to hot life for a moment. He wondered if Aurelia had wanted to be Mercedes all these years.

Mercedes said: 'You're not the only one who risked things, you know.'

'It's very difficult to talk to outsiders.'

'I'm an outsider? We're one flesh and you think of me as an outsider. I feel your pain, girl. I feel your pain.'

'You don't know about pain. You don't know about the forest and sniper fire. You don't know what it's like when the rains make the whole forest floor suck you down –'

'I'm ready to admire you. You don't have to beg me to.'

'I don't need to be admired.'

'I love you,' Mercedes said. 'I know what you're doing, and why and –'

'You don't know why. You know about revenge and you have a bourgeois idea of justice, and that's it. You don't see the politics of it all.'

'I know about righting a wrong.'

Aurelia shrugged as though she'd proved her point.

Mercedes glared at her. 'If you weren't wounded –' She had all the fury of a parent who hits out at a beloved child for daring to get hurt. 'And how did you get hurt, anyway? You were standing up shouting.'

273

'We should talk later,' Aurelia said.

'We don't have anything to say.'

But Mercedes couldn't go. She wanted to reach out and check that the bandages were not chafing her sister; she wanted to kiss her.

Aurelia said: 'I love you.'

'You don't think that's a bourgeois affectation?'

'I love you.'

And Mercedes said: 'I love you.'

But they didn't touch. Mercedes walked out, and Carpenter followed her.

The sky was growing dark and green; there was rain coming out of the mainland in a curtain.

'We have to get out,' Mercedes said. 'She thinks it's all over now Diaz is dead, and it's only beginning – the money, what Tomás Diaz will do, everything.'

'They can't fly a helicopter, that's for sure,' Carpenter said. 'I doubt if a pilot will take off tonight. And it's a bad night for swimming.'

'I can't deal with English jokes.'

'We could walk to the airstrip and see what's moving.'

'You think a pilot would take us?'

Carpenter shrugged. 'They'd make a lot more when they fly for Vico, and they make it every day. They wouldn't want to risk that.'

But they still went to the airstrip, taking a less than casual interest in the machines. For camouflage, a thin kind, Carpenter circled a bright new box of a plane with a single monstrous propellor, asking questions.

From the front, the machine looked bug-eyed and quite sinisterly asymmetrical, with a big air nostril to the left and a smaller one for oil to the right. Between the aft wheels, the sleek shape had grown a cargo pod that trailed half a man's height off the ground.

'New,' Mercedes said.

Carpenter knew enough to ask how the plane compared with the old DC-3, because that was how Cessna sold their new baby. He was told it was fine at 30,000 feet if you were 'on the snot rag', which had to be an oxygen mask at that altitude, and its

274

range was a thousand nautical miles. Inside, he could see the seats set out more for function than comfort, five on each side.

As he walked away, he said: 'It could do Florida, easily.'

'It could do Colombia,' Mercedes said. 'We don't have any idea which way it will go.'

The rain came down, abrupt and tumultuous. They pelted back to the house.

Vico cornered them. 'They have lobster for dinner,' he said. 'You shouldn't sulk.'

The rain was constant like drums; it blotted out all the high notes of frogs and cicadas, but it also hid the sound of any engine moving on the airstrip. They couldn't tell whether their means of escape was already in the air.

Even so, Mercedes talked quietly to Aurelia and told her they'd leave that evening. Aurelia could stay, if she wanted; and John Grey would stay to see that she was all right. Mercedes had organised all this in her mind before she told the people involved, but it seemed to suit them.

At dinner, Mercedes said to Vico: 'You said you'd help us. Me, and Aurelia and the others.'

'They put me on the news again,' Vico said.

'We need to get back to America,' Mercedes said. 'As soon as we can. Now Diaz is dead, we don't have time any more.'

'Few-gee-tive fie-nan-seer. They said all that again. Drugs and Castro. Anything they can damn well throw, a lot of shit against the Bahamians.' He was expansive, but Mercedes detected nervousness; the flecks of red were back in his eyes. 'Americans don't even know this is a country. Come crashing in here, expecting everyone to do what they say. Then when people don't obey, think they're corrupt.'

'You never bought anyone,' John Grey said, teasing.

'I'm in business,' Vico said. 'Like you, boy.'

'You survive,' Mercedes said. 'That's not a business.'

'It's a start. You got anything better?'

'Yes,' Mercedes said.

'As you like,' Vico said. 'We'll get those television bastards, anyway. Set a black Prime Minister with a good libel lawyer on a bunch of white liberals – they're lost.'

He couldn't sit still. Mercedes wondered what exactly had

bothered him so profoundly – the coming of Aurelia, the sight of the *Esperanza* out at sea or something they did not yet know.

'Incidentally,' Vico said. 'I want you to stay for a while.'

'We can't do that,' Mercedes said.

'You can't go, either,' Vico said. 'The guards are on, in case you wanted to know. We don't want people at the moment.' The four of them looked as though they expected an explanation; he shook his head, but he obliged. 'All that fuss about Diaz, the fuss there might be. And the DEA out there looking for drug smugglers – if they're leaking stuff to the networks, they're planning something. And there's the Securities and Exchange Commission and there's the Bahamians who don't like it when their visitors get embarrassing. We don't want visitors just now. No, sir.'

'We just need a plane out,' Mercedes said.

'It's not possible,' Vico said. 'Not now. We don't want any trouble.'

In the courtyard of the house, everything was quiet; the shade of the great ficus dappled the moon which had slipped back from behind the clouds. Mercedes held Carpenter's hand.

She turned the handle of her door.

Something moved inside, something furious and looking for escape, a clawed thing.

Carpenter threw on the light.

It came for him blindly, furiously as though hurt by the light and understanding that the light was his fault: it was some wide-winged owl, a great, white mass of tendon and feather and claw, and it came screaming.

Mercedes stood in its way. She kept whispering: 'Suck owl, suck owl, suck owl.'

It made no sense to Carpenter; he couldn't see why her reactions were dulled. He threw himself across her and pulled her down, covering her with his body, and the bird went hissing out into the night, a stream of fury, and out in the ficus it howled like horror.

Carpenter pulled Mercedes to her feet and wiped her face.

'Bastard,' she said, and she was close to tears.

'I don't see how the bird got in here.'

'He put it here,' Mercedes said. 'He knows about suck owl like

276

he knew about badlamp. He's playing games with me, reminding me about Bluefields, about things I knew when I was a child, before he took me away.'

'Tell me.'

'He left a candle once with a nail through it. That's a curse. The candle dies, and you die. He leaves that bird in the room, all angry, and that's suck owl, the great white owl. The witch leaves her skin, she flies away as an owl, she sucks blood.'

Carpenter held her tightly.

'It doesn't matter if it's so or not,' she said. 'I know it's not so. But when I was a kid –'

'We're going tonight. He can't do anything else.'

'It's the first second,' Mercedes said. 'The very first. You see something like that, your heart turns over. I don't know why he wants to do that.'

'Because you won't stay,' Carpenter said. 'He can't bear the idea of things going away, even a yacht he sold.'

'He'll have guards on the airstrip. And all round the island, in case anyone comes.'

'We'll get out.'

But he sat on the bed, holding her in his arms and quite unsure how.

'That plane might go tonight,' she said.

'They'll be watching it.'

After a minute, she said: 'Not if they think we're somewhere else.'

'Aurelia could pretend to be you –'

'Vico would look for you,' Mercedes said. 'He'd be suspicious.'

'We could take one of the little boats.'

'It's too cold. They'd never believe it.'

'They might,' Carpenter said, tracking her mind. 'We might go there to be alone.'

They took off the flashy tropical whites that were like signals at night, and Carpenter assembled the CDs and their papers in a plastic pouch. They went down to the jetty and slipped the ropes on one of the dinghies; the guards didn't stir. There was water in the bottom of the boat but they lay still there, looking up at a scatter of bright stars.

'Now,' Mercedes said.

The little boat began to drift out from shore, a paper toy on a glass sea. They lay back with the luxury of shelter, heads low.

Mercedes knew small boats from the lagoon at Bluefields. She could sense that the current would suck them out to a break in the reef, and then there would be whitecaps and rough water. Even lightless, the guards were bound to see the boat before then.

'Over the side,' she said. 'Now. The guards will chase the boat, they won't be looking for us.'

They slipped gently over the side. The boat turned very little in its gentle course towards the reef.

They found bottom. They could walk through the shallows, pushing a weight of water, and they came ashore wet below the waist. Mercedes fancied their trail must be phosphorescent from the sea.

They were already in the shadow of the trees when the guards began shooting at the little boat.

They kept low, and dodged through the trees and scrub to the edge of the warehouse. There was a dragonfly flight of little planes, but they couldn't tell which would fly that night, what they'd carry. They needed a flight for Florida, but in a large plane where they could hide, not in some tiny single-engined affair which dropped the crocus sacks of cocaine. A plane that would land, a plane that would go the distance: they had little choice besides the Cessna Caravan. The bug-eyed machine began to look almost friendly.

There were port and starboard doors, plus two up front for pilot and co-pilot. The guards were still preoccupied with the dinghy, and Carpenter could reach up to the narrow passenger door to starboard. It opened, and welcoming steps came down; they could climb aboard like legitimate passengers, and when they closed the door, the steps came up with a lightly oiled creak.

There was light all at once. It had seemed there was nobody moving on the airstrip, but now the ground was blue-white like a football field at night and the warehouse door had rolled up. There was the humming note of an electric engine, perhaps a forklift, heading for the plane.

Carpenter went down for cover under the narrow seats, and

Mercedes followed. They couldn't stay to the rear of the plane; the wide port door was obviously for the cargo that the forklift was bringing. And they couldn't go too far forward in case the pilot was about to come aboard.

Every sound was like a war. And they were suddenly sure they must have left some wet, sea creatures' trail to the plane's door. Carpenter hoped the night wind would blot up their traces in time. He found himself thinking about the sound of breathing.

Mercedes raised her head. The lights outside threw all the plane's seats into silhouette. She wanted to scream.

Every seat had its passenger: metal, and stiff as death. The plane was an armoury. Boxes and guns were strapped into the seats. If anything went wrong on this flight, they'd end like a Fourth of July.

They were crammed under the seats when the rear cargo door went up. Something heavy was put into the plane, something which made it lean for a moment to port.

'You got ignition exciters?'

Vico was out there, prattling. He loved technology so well he could never resist giving away what he knew.

'I guess we'd better get off,' someone said. 'The weather won't hold.'

'Ignition exciters,' said Vico obstinately. The toy was his, after all, even if he did not get to play. 'You got them?'

'Two,' the reply came. It must be the pilot. 'Tough to start turbines sometimes, and you don't want problems in the middle of a swamp.'

'Low operating speeds, too,' Vico said. It sounded like he wanted the pilot to be grateful.

'Very low. 183 ktas. Low wing loading, you see.'

'Great,' Vico said. 'Great.'

'The weather,' the pilot was saying, and he was climbing at the same time into his seat. One pilot; no co-pilot.

'You want to look out for stowaways,' Vico said, chuckling.

Mercedes and Carpenter held their breath.

'Sure,' the pilot said. They heard the engine fire; the doors were slapped by the mechanics. The sounds were shocking in such a secret trade, but there was no need for silence on German Cay itself.

279

The plane came off the ground like tape off a parcel, and they were blind, pressed into the fluff and oil of the floor. Each move was felt; the plane was sensitive as a sprung bed. Still and blind, they had time to feel fear. If the weather did turn sour, the pilot could let the plane buck and leave them concussed or else go high and leave them without oxygen.

It was like being under water. Very high in the side windows they could make out some stars and a moon of alarming brilliance; this flight must be urgent to dare all the light. And from below, the moon echoed from a gunmetal sea. The underlight would die when they reached land; that might help.

They felt the engine, and heard its whine like a vacuum cleaner.

They were no higher than a thousand feet, which was logical. They wouldn't have a flight plan, they'd fly on radio silence; they'd run through radar watch, whether from the surveillance planes who work airport perimeters or the air traffic systems or even the AWACS the Americans sometimes send up to harass drug-runners. They'd have to fly close to the weather because there was no time to dodge and plough clouds; because a safe route is a safe route, even if the weather kills you. As for landing, that was a judgement call.

Mercedes wanted touch while she was waiting. But Carpenter couldn't reach her. He lay with a strut in his liver, a cramp in his left calf. He wondered if they'd live.

The engine note shifted and from the floor they could tell that the plane was tilted down. The tilt was sudden as a stall, but the stall alarms didn't go off. The light seemed to change.

Any minute. They must be coming into land. They had to guess whether there'd be a welcoming party for this valuable cargo, and whether they'd shoot. Invisible flights can always lose their passengers.

They were very low now. At least the flight was brief, into Florida.

He wished he dared speak to Mercedes. But if the pilot knew he had a second cargo, their chances on the ground were slim. Carpenter fancied he could bluff the pilot into landing, but he couldn't bluff the welcome party into letting him stay alive.

He checked the time. There was no more time. They had to

bundle out of the starboard door before the plane stopped, pray they fell safely and pray again that they fell out of view of the ground party.

He swarmed on his belly down the aisle. The pilot would have his mind busy with a night landing, watching instruments, looking out for the subtle mark that would lead him to his landing place.

Mercedes followed, carefully. The seats around them full of inhuman passengers.

The engine cut. The airframe was suddenly as sensitive as skin. He was sure any movement would be felt.

But the pilot couldn't use radio. That would give them a minute or so more, even if they were noticed on board.

The plane seemed to roll a little, to the right. The engine hadn't cut out, he realised; it was simply down to slow speed and the plane was moving over the undulations of the land like a boat on a swell, rising, falling, rising.

He found himself listening for the metal whine when landing gear comes down on a big plane. He'd forgotten there would be no such clue. He raised himself carefully where a seat and a cardboard box blocked the view of the wide door, and could see the bush going by like the view from a carousel.

Mercedes slid quietly alongside him as he reached up to the cargo door, and pulled.

The ground caught the plane's belly. Carpenter scorched his head on the airframe, but he pulled himself upright on bloodless legs and Mercedes unfolded herself beside him.

Not much time. A plane like this can land in two hundred, three hundred yards – five hundred at the most, if there were obstacles.

He moved the door a little, terrified it would open forward against the wind, but it slid along the side of the plane. He muscled it loose.

Each move seemed to shake the airframe, but the ground was treacherous and bumpy, and the pilot too busy to detect his extra problem.

Slow, slower.

He had the door open far enough to jump. The ground was only a few feet below, but it dashed past like speeded film.

281

Mercedes went first, bundled up like an armadillo facing dogs, falling into the cold, wet grass. There were no lights. Carpenter couldn't see how she had fallen, and pitched himself out, hanging onto the door handle for a moment to try to tug it back into place. He was falling, the door slid easily, but his arm jarred. He fell awkwardly, his whole side burning with startled nerves.

The ground was soft as mercy. The plane spun away from them, bumping awkwardly, and Carpenter lay spreadeagled in the muddy grass.

They'd think the door had jarred open in an awkward landing. Wouldn't they?

He pulled himself up and sprinted behind the screen of reeds on either side of the runway. Mercedes eased through the cutting stems towards him, and she was anxious; she checked his body like a child checks a parcel.

Down the line of flat grass they could see light at last, torches held to the ground. Beyond that, there were two trucks: ordinary, red and yellow rental trucks.

The ground under the reeds was soft and slippy as a cream, and there was black water close. Sometimes the ground was unwilling to let them move.

'At least,' Mercedes whispered, 'if they got a truck in, we can get out.'

All the living things in the swampy ground had been driven back by noise; they heard only mechanical things, an engine, boxes being moved. Then a man coughed, very close. They moved carefully through the reeds, but the flicker of the light and then the sudden disappearance of the moon behind land-locked cloud all helped to confuse their sense of direction.

They pushed reeds aside. The view was all too good: without warning, they had come to the margins of a busy scene. The Caravan had its cargo door up and men were dropping boxes carefully from its belly. They moved with an absurd delicacy in their bulky sweaters and parkas, a ballet of Michelin men.

Mercedes and Carpenter stood together for warmth. They were damp still, from the sea and from fear.

The men took orders in Spanish. It shouldn't have surprised them, but their minds were busy: guns for Tomás Diaz, guns for

282

some new resistance, this time not coming from the people but directed against them.

The truck was loaded, and the men went to the second truck, unwilling to travel with volatile cargo. The two rolled away at a stately pace down a track between woods, and soon the engine notes changed as the ground was easier. Then the noise was gone.

'Let the plane go,' Carpenter said.

'They might leave it here.'

'That man's a professional. He won't leave his assets in a swamp. Not where someone in a uniform might find it.'

The air was cold and moist; it seemed to stroke them.

At last the pilot, alone in the clearing, finished his checks. He stood by the cargo door, puzzled, and made sure this time that it was firmly closed. He looked around as if he expected someone to break cover. The thought of illicit passengers made him nervous; he wanted the hell out.

The little plane turned in a broad half circle and lined up for take off. Then it crept up the sky, careful as a night animal.

The silence lasted only a minute before prickly, watchful noises began to break in. Mercedes and Carpenter could step out from their hiding place onto the trodden mud of the clearing, and out by way of a trail so thickly wooded the trees closed over them. The tunnel was as lively as it was dark.

It ended very soon at a fine metalled road, which cut at right angles into another leading away to a fork. A railway line butted up to the road, crossed it and disappeared between reeds. At each junction, like a phantom suburb, traffic lights hung in the sky, flickering green, yellow, red as diligently as on any interstate. But no engine sounded, even distantly. They stopped in the middle of a crossroads watching that eerily domestic display: amber, red, green, in a wild place.

'It's like a town they didn't build,' Mercedes said.

A sign said, all in one breath, 'POISONOUS SNAKES KEEP OUT' and Carpenter tried to make a joke of it.

Around a blind bend, they came to buildings at last: a low cluster with a flagpole and a noticeboard and the open cinder surround which marks somewhere official. The moon was dipping, but there was light enough to read the notices.

283

Carpenter laughed.

'Tell me where we are,' Mercedes said with the exasperation which comes from great tiredness.

'In a conservation area,' Carpenter said. 'Walk this way for the oranges, mulberries, ferns and bitterns. That way for the pelicans. Nude sunbathing prohibited.'

'I don't understand.'

'I was here once,' Carpenter said. 'They run a nature reserve by Cape Canaveral. They can't build condos for security reasons so they have nature instead. Official nature.'

'What a nerve,' Mercedes said, sitting on the steps of a building marked 'Rangers' Office'.

'I don't know. There's no traffic for miles, nobody comes across the Indian River at night; the worst that can happen is someone thinks some teenagers had a party.'

'But security –'

'They weren't here, were they?'

She stretched, and he sat down beside her. 'What do we tell the men in uniform when they come?' he said. 'Whichever men in uniforms get here first.'

'Tell them,' she said, 'our UFO broke down,' and she was asleep.

·SEVEN·

The ranger came in an old Chevy and listened to Carpenter.

'Our car broke down,' he said. 'We didn't know which way to walk . . .'

The ranger beamed. He drove them into town, found them a coffee shop, promised to look for their fictional abandoned car. All the time, he sneaked looks at Mercedes. She couldn't tell whether he knew her face or if some Southern tendency, still alive in Florida, made a black woman fascinating to a white man.

She said to Carpenter: 'You tell me what we do next.'

'New York,' Carpenter said. 'If I'm right, there must be money in Security National – if I'm right.'

'We need to get that money out of Switzerland. They need it in Leon, now.'

'There's no real legal title,' Carpenter said. 'Not until the family get into the Swiss courts.'

'They're not slow.'

'We have to hope,' Carpenter said, 'Tomás is distracted for a while. He has a country to win back.'

'He'll buy it back,' Mercedes said.

They hired a car and while Carpenter filled the forms, Mercedes called Washington. José Mantica sounded exhausted and furious.

'They froze our assets,' he said. 'This morning, some federal judge in upstate New York. Someone was angry their cheque was stopped, so they phoned a lawyer and the lawyer got an injunction overnight. Every account of Providencia's in America, frozen.'

'Jesus,' Mercedes said.

'We wanted to start a case against Doña Augusta, now we

can't. There's a whole rollcall of loans made to the Diaz family by the Central Bank – they weren't secured, nobody ever paid a penny back, they didn't even pay interest. It ought to be an easy case. And now, we can't even get started. They're blocking us.'

'They can't block you. You mean the State Department is blocking you?'

'The FBI told us they couldn't find Tomás Diaz to arrest him – we've given them the papers in a cast iron fraud case. He's in the New York phone book and they can't find him. Someone's turned against us.'

'We're coming,' Mercedes said.

'Don't come here,' Mantica said. 'God knows what happens here next. We need anything you can get in Leon. We can work from there.'

'But in New York –'

'We don't have a bank in New York, not until some little Diacista finishes his law case.'

They drove along the dead straight highway into Orlando and took the first flight to New York.

Mercedes said: 'We have to take everything to Leon.'

'We can do it with computers in New York.'

'I mean it. They froze the Providencian bank accounts.'

'Then they'll unfreeze them. There are loan accounts in the billions, for Christ's sake – nobody can afford to freeze them. Think of the interest the banks would lose. Think of the loans they'd have to write off after ninety days.'

'You're sure that's true?'

'There are things we can do in New York,' Carpenter said, obstinately. 'There are things we may need to take to Leon.'

'Like these?' Mercedes said, tapping the bankers' drafts she'd taken from Boswell in the Bahamas.

'Like those,' Carpenter said. 'Maybe.'

The flight purser stopped by their row and beamed. 'I hope you don't mind, Miss Zenon,' he said, softly. 'I think there may be photographers when we get into JFK.'

'Thank you,' said Mercedes. She looked down at her drowned clothes and her muddy shoes.

'We could try to discourage them –'

'Just use your magic radio,' Mercedes said, 'or your magic

cellular phone or any other magic you've got. Get me a maid when we get on the ground.'

'Very well,' said the steward, suitably dazzled.

And when they had landed, the maid titupped awkwardly into a ladies room with a garment bag, and moments later Mercedes reappeared. Her face was now impeccable, her suit spectacular white. She opened the collar of Carpenter's shirt.

'Glamour,' she said. 'We are going to be so famous for the next week.'

He glared at her, lovingly.

She crackled when she walked into the public spaces of the terminal, and the papparazzi chased her to record her re-entry. She was the announcement of a new season, a picture to syndicate; the flaks had summoned them with a story. Mercedes Zenon, after a European vacation, with the mystery man, the enigmatic, the financier Ian Carpenter. As yet, he didn't know about his sudden promotion.

'You fixed this,' he said.

'The Diacistas think I killed Diaz by now. They think I stole his money. I need some protection.'

'But you'll be on every front page –'

'Front pages are safe,' Mercedes said.

Carpenter was required to say nothing, and he did so with aplomb. It was a flattering change from half-hearted adultery. And he was fascinated by the mechanics of fame, which had more staff than he'd expected. There were men who organised, who accepted invitations and arranged for their issue all without human intervention, who were paid to launch New Jersey ladies as if they were new, but socially acceptable soaps. Between them all, Mercedes was visible.

They put her into a visible lunch with a face-lifted legal fixer who had denied so much in a chequered career that there was hardly anything left for him to do or be; and with a slightly superannuated but still glorious French star; and a twenty-year-old Californian nihilist who wrote novels. Photographers came, and men and women columnists with tiny tape recorders and eager questions. Carpenter felt a little like a company wife.

They put her on the *Today* show, simply dressed and face scrubbed, to talk about Providencia. She did it well, and her subdued manner startled people. There were phone calls of approval, mixed with some red-baiting growls.

And Mercedes was right; they could not have been more secure. People cared and checked if she was five minutes late. If strangers came too close, flaks checked their lists, and people who had paid for the closeness beat the interlopers back. If she walked into a party in a backless dress, barely hung on accidents of flesh, the cameramen wanted angles, and they'd kill trouble-makers.

Aurelia Zenon sat cross-legged, watching the television. She was furious that Mercedes could simply return to her gaudy world when Aurelia had no way back. The quiet life of villas in the hills was all gone now. There was an absence of order, the kind of order on which Aurelia had been trained to think life itself depends.

'. . . her involvement with the multi-million dollar Mercedes Zenon perfume . . .' said the voice from the TV.

Aurelia turned her back. She knew things Mercedes could not know. She knew what it was to throw away everything and only after the act discover why. She knew about hiding in the bush and suddenly learning a rush of love for the people, then seeing the revolution triumph and knowing those same people had to be organised and controlled.

She needed order, and Mercedes was disorder in her life. She wanted people in their places, safe.

'. . . it's a risky business,' the television voice announced.

Carpenter was known at Security National, and he used the fact. He went downtown to their clump of concrete towers and civic art, expecting to ask for Leventhal's assistants.

But as he walked over the marble of the entrance hall he realised he had a choice. One way, there were guards, palms and elevators; the other, to the left, there was the banking hall, with a flat 1960s fountain and absent, disgruntled tellers. And in the banking hall, they had a computer banking show that invited fooling.

He let the recorded programme play through, with its eager copy, and he thought. He had the over-ride command, or so he believed, but he lacked the codewords Diaz must use to identify

288

himself. He wondered what they might be.

E.L.J.E.F.E., he thought.

E.L.M.A.X.I.M.O.

But Diaz was cautious, even paranoid, even when he could not be observed. He'd hardly choose a code so obvious.

The recorded programme was over. He was being urged to use the system for himself – to access the bank computer, bank as he would do at home. It was a device to encourage people to see that real others used personal codes to shift and sort their money.

He'd oblige.

'Identify Yourself Please.'

He tapped in: 'S.A.C.A.S.A.'

The screen faded and came back: 'This Password Not Operational At This Time.'

A bank security guard seemed interested in what he was doing; two very young black girls, braided and brace-toothed, wanted to play with the machine. Carpenter was glad he'd dressed like a banker.

'Kids,' the guard said with an apologetic grin, shuffling them away. He kept his eyes off the private matters on the screen.

'Identify Yourself Please.'

He thought of Leon, of the bunker, of Tomás. He tried to imagine the mind of Diaz: a bombastic, arrogant man who loved titles.

He tried: 'E.L.J.E.F.E.'

He waited. The computer was sluggish in the morning rush. The screen faded.

'This Password Not Operational At This Time.'

Did the system cut out after too many false tries? He guessed it might. But this particular line could not go down. This was not a line from a particular private phone but a general line, open for demonstrations.

He found himself sweating a little.

He thought of the perversity of Diaz, his taste for slapping back vengefully even when the offence was his. Now the point of the hidden accounts was to spite his wife. His wife Hope, whose name was also on the great white yacht, the *Esperanza*.

Could there be a nine-letter password? With or without an article?

289

'Identify Yourself Please.'

He thought: Diaz would think the Spanish was the great barrier.

'E.S.P.E.R.A.N.Z.A.'

The screen went blank.

'Please Choose The Banking Service That You Need.' The screen filled with a scroll of possibilities.

He was in. But he didn't know at which point there could be an over-ride. It might be now or once he had chosen from the menu.

He told himself to take a chance. The worst thing that could happen was a blank screen. Besides, the over-ride was most likely in the main program, something for people other than Diaz to use. He'd proved by one password that he was entitled to access so far; now he'd have to prove he was entitled to Boca Raton.

He tried. 'GoTo Boca Raton.'

The screen punched back: 'Please Identify Yourself.'

He wanted to cheer. He was into the hidden program, whatever it did, whatever it meant. He thought of Esperanza; he thought he might as well try –

'H.O.P.E.'

And again there was a menu of possibilities; he chose the obvious: check balances.

The screen filled up and trailed the possibility of going to yet other screens. There were dozens of numbers, and perhaps even hundreds of accounts under Boca Raton. It wasn't simply a numbered account; it was a private bank, a place to bring together information and money that was scattered throughout Security National to hide it better.

He had to get the information off the screen. He was sure someone would see it, question it. He felt absurdly exposed between the dashing clerks come to cash their paycheques and the ladies with money bags.

He hit one number.

There were thousands. Hundreds of thousands. He multiplied the amount dazzlingly by a simple screenful of accounts – a guess, not a calculation, but an extraordinary hoard.

All the money Diaz skimmed. All the money he decided was

safer in New York – a prudent, old-fashioned, strength-of-the-dollar, security-of-Washington investor, but one who liked not to be seen. It made perfect sense: the whole of Diaz's life was entwined with America.

But how could Diaz know these accounts were truly private? Once on a computer, they could easily leach to a lawyer, a credit bureau, a shopkeeper or some other bank. Each account, too, is supposed to be attached to a social security number. Which number was written on the Diaz files?

Maybe many, he thought. That's how he would do it. Non-interest bearing accounts, in discreet amounts, in other people's names. Then what mattered, the information missing to the authorities, was the link between those many names. For that, you needed access to Boca Raton.

He hit the cancel key. Security National wouldn't want the world to know about a bank within a bank.

A bank officer said: 'Could I interest you in some more details of our –'

'Sure,' Carpenter said. He left with a fan of glossy cards.

In the taxi uptown he had only one dark thought: banks noticed money going out. The job is holding other people's money until you can lend it for profit. So closing the Diaz accounts would be a little firework show.

The money could always be transferred to another account at Security National, of course. But not the Providencian account, for the moment; that was blocked by law.

He sat in Mercedes' apartment, puzzling until she returned from some club of worthy matrons. She had deft manners with such groups: she understood the ones of twenty-two, already pale and masked and ready for the social world, and she humoured their seniors. That day, they were planning a museum opening, and how to take social credit for it; they settled the receiving line, the entrances. Mercedes made the ladies into a mannerly united front.

'It's a trade,' she said, 'like modelling. You talk about décor and never mention art and it's fine.' She sprawled on a sofa. 'They're generous enough. It's just they expect dinner when they give something. It's a reflex.'

'I have some news,' he said.

'Tell me,' she said. It sounded a little patronising.

He drew her a verbal diagram of the treasure he'd found and she was delighted. 'All we need is a computer,' she said.

'It's trickier than that.'

'Then we play a game with Leventhal. He's Security National, isn't he? His wife is on the committee when she's in town, which is only when the polo players are.'

'I know him,' Carpenter said. 'We do a fair amount of business –'

'Then talk to him tomorrow night,' Mercedes said. 'At the museum. You'll see.'

The lists were written and gilded like lists of the saints and prophets in some mediaeval school, and as much discussed and pondered. The committee ate in the museum, their best friends in the gentleman's club next door and their less good friends were invited to drinks after dinner. It was a dazzle of a night, but even parties seem to need *placement*.

'How very nice –'

Mercedes smiled brilliantly and stepped through the kerbside crowd into the lights. She ran the receiving line like a gauntlet.

'How many committees for the flowers?' Carpenter whispered.

'Two,' Mercedes said. 'You don't have to whisper; everyone knows. It's make work for the upper middle classes.'

'And the ficus and the drink –'

'Given. It always is. That's why it's Moët & Chandon.' She steered him around a pot of sand and tree. 'And they had the pots thrown specially.'

'Jesus,' Carpenter said. He was offended by such meticulous fuss.

Among the hundred there were plain tuxedos, a shimmer of silks, two women with orange hair who held hands: ('Perform-ance artists,' Mercedes said. 'They're walking the Great Wall of China next year and photographing it from a satellite.') A whole hierarchy had dressed nicely. It was like a private view, but without the little plastic glasses of lukewarm white wine and the guilt of ignoring the art. The art here was certified, famous and knew its place, turned into décor like the guests.

Mercedes worked the room. She was pecked on the cheek by

292

older men, hailed often and once or twice cut. She did not have the local fame of the ladies; she was too well known to be quite respectable. A very social Senator's wife wagged a finger and said she'd been naughty on the *Today* show talking about Providencia 'when the President knows so much more than we do. Naughty.'

'Oh,' Mercedes said, lightly. 'I've been naughtier than you know.'

The Senator grinned. His wife believed her.

They found Leventhal a few decent minutes before they went in to dinner.

'Mercedes,' he said, with an obligatory peck. Mercedes smiled carefully. Not so long ago, she'd been in the corridors of his bank, stealing; but she was too famous to suspect.

Carpenter grinned at Mrs Leventhal, a formidable fifty, self-consciously wrapped and preserved but with the unnerving sensuality that comes from complete directness.

'They tell me,' Leventhal said, 'the hangings are wonderful. The building is wonderful. To me it looks like a glass cornflake box on top of a glass shoebox.'

'Relax,' Mercedes said, kindly. 'Men don't have to be philistine any more.'

But for Mrs Leventhal, dark and smiling, men always had to be philistine, and Leventhal knew the rules.

'You never had much of an eye,' she said.

'Except for you, my dear.' It came out more hopeful than courtly.

'Really,' Mrs Leventhal said.

Mercedes chattered them an alibi for long absence, from the delights of Switzerland out of season to Italy and the light on buildings and the perfume.

'It's almost too late,' she said softly to Leventhal, 'for Boca Raton.'

'I don't know,' he said. 'This time of year –'

'Your Boca Raton,' she said.

Carpenter glared at Mercedes for making mysteries where none was needed, but he could also see that Leventhal was puzzled. Mercedes skipped aside to greet some newcomer and Leventhal looked like an old man dazzled by a forgotten heat.

'They hung the Klimts properly,' Mercedes said.

Carpenter wondered if Leventhal even knew of Boca Raton. Under managers don't always talk to managers, nor do managers always inform the board; in any New York bank there are a hundred scams and conveniences that the bank will never know.

'You play polo?' Mrs Leventhal asked.

She was called Chloë, and she cut out and tracked a man, briskly and with grace.

'I'm afraid, no.'

Polo. He saw her, the lady condescending to the grooms; except that polo players were far more grand than that – the new mercenaries.

'But you have such strong hands,' she said.

He was amused. It was obvious, and she knew it; it was an old-fashioned, jewelled flirt.

'– such an interesting idea to invite some artists –' A plain woman passed in white lace, talking shamelessly.

'You really care about this stuff?' Leventhal asked.

'Yes,' Mercedes said. 'Like you do.'

Leventhal looked carefully towards his wife, but she was occupied with Carpenter. 'You always looked at paintings?' he said. 'Even in your mysterious past?'

'It's not a mysterious past,' Mercedes said. 'It's just too dull, even for *People Magazine.*'

'The bank has been buying,' Leventhal said. 'We're hanging some pictures tomorrow. You might like to see them after dinner? I promise you there's no broken plates and no graffiti, no stick figures and no Schnabel.'

'I'd love to,' Mercedes said.

'We could,' Leventhal said, 'talk about Boca Raton.'

It was a remark surprising enough to make dinner into a mechanical affair, a mere delay before the evening's serious business. They made the proper smalltalk, and stayed until after dinner when the less privileged and the much less privileged came, and posed and checked one another, and circulated in eddies and tugs.

Chloë Leventhal said she might take Carpenter home for a drink if Leventhal and Mercedes really wanted to look at paintings. She was conspiratorial with Carpenter; she knew he was a proper, testosterone philistine.

But they went together to Security National, a tower still alive with light, until the boardroom floor which was all taste and silence. Chloë flung herself on a sofa by the boardroom door, daring the others to go ahead and look at art. 'Go ahead,' she said to Leventhal. 'Don't mind us.'

'I never mind you,' Leventhal said. 'Dearest.'

She hated him; he was off balance with her, maybe loved her; or so Carpenter thought. But however they fit together, they did seem to fit; he made no assumptions.

The boardroom door drifted shut. It was built to do that.

'You like art?' Chloë Leventhal said, accusingly to Carpenter. He shrugged.

Inside, Leventhal said to Mercedes: 'You want to see these?'

'I wanted to talk as well.'

'Talk,' Leventhal said, struggling, a little red-faced, to heft into view a large canvas that was propped against the wall. The protective wrappings came down, and there was a kind of free-floating Matisse against black lacquer. To the right, a woman's neck arced down towards a dressing table, but there was no reflection where the glass should be. There a forest began, stiff with emerald and bloodstone and brilliant colour; and birds that were trapped on the surface of a monumental vase, a domestic thing grown awesome. It was like watching how a man inhabits his mind.

'It's lovely,' Mercedes said.

Leventhal said: 'Don't get distracted. You wanted to talk about Boca Raton.'

'Yes,' Mercedes said.

'Who told you about it?'

'Nobody. I found out for myself.'

Leventhal frowned. 'I suppose we are talking about the same thing? You tell me what you mean by Boca Raton.'

'A bank within a bank,' Mercedes said. 'An arrangement whereby a client's money can be held in dozens, maybe hundreds of small accounts, and brought together by computer when it's needed. What you did for Anastasio Diaz Sacasa.'

'Did Carpenter tell you this?'

Mercedes was standing very close to him, and he could smell the musk of her.

'It struck me,' Mercedes said, 'you had some trouble once with money you didn't report. Money that just passed through. Some of it from Hong Kong, and some of it from Miami. Didn't the Feds say you were washing money for punks or drug dealers?'

'Junior officers make mistakes. They get fired.'

'But Boca Raton,' Mercedes said, 'is a machine for making mistakes just like that.'

'I don't understand,' Leventhal said. 'I assumed you wanted to use the program –' He needed to move out of the net of her smell and her look, because he was feeling both angry and intoxicated. 'And you can't possibly know.'

'I could show you,' Mercedes said. 'Give me any personal computer. Give me the one downstairs. I could show the bank regulators and the FBI and the IRS. It only takes three keywords, and I know them all.'

'They can be changed.'

'All of them? For all your clients who like privacy? Won't it worry them when they realise there's been a breach of security?'

Leventhal sat down. 'Listen,' he said. 'This is all very interesting, but what's it about?'

'You might have to take Boca Raton apart. If you do, there's money belonging to Diaz. I want that money in the Providencian Central Bank accounts.'

Leventhal shrugged. 'Just at the moment, they don't have accounts. All frozen.'

'Their assets are frozen. Their debts aren't.'

'I don't understand.'

Mercedes remembered the argument Carpenter had made. 'If you can't get paid interest,' she said, 'you'll have to make Providencia's loans non-performing. Ninety-days after that, you get to write them off.'

'For accounting purposes, we're allowed –'

'But if Diaz's money paid the interest, and paid down the debt, there would be no trouble. Nothing to write off, nothing to apologise for. You'd be in the clear.'

'First you threaten me. Now you want to save the bank by stealing.'

'Nobody knows the money is here,' Mercedes said, 'except

296

you, Ian, me and whoever knows your business in the bank. It's a simple transfer, account to account.'

Leventhal was studying the painted woman's neck. It was lovely and strong; it was also vulnerable. He sighed.

'You help me,' Mercedes said, 'and nobody has to know about Boca Raton. Nobody else.'

'You could spell out what you want. I might have tape-recorders hidden in this room. I might call the police.'

'And tell them what?' Mercedes said 'That I knew about Boca Raton? To say that, you'd have to confess to Boca Raton.'

'Then say what you want.'

'The money shifted to Providencia's loan account. The balance in some kind of bankers' draft that can be cashed when Providencia's other accounts are open again.'

'But that is millions. Tens of millions.'

'Hundreds of millions,' Mercedes said. 'I hope.'

Chloë Leventhal shifted away from Carpenter when her husband reappeared, making sure her husband saw the move. She depended on intrigue.

'The paintings,' Mercedes said. 'They're quite wonderful.'

In the elevator, they were all awkward as strangers; they had nothing left to say or do. And in the Leventhals' eyes, Carpenter fancied he saw thoughts of missed opportunities: mainly, each other.

'Give me a couple of days,' Leventhal said.

Mercedes smiled. 'Come to drinks,' she said, brightly. 'We'd love to see you.'

Chloë Leventhal performed a smile, a lifeless, political smile, and looked away.

In the car, Mercedes said: 'It worked. He wasn't too worried about the threats, but he loved the idea of paying off the Providencian loans.'

'He'll be quick, will he? I mean, there's always the chance Diaz left some envelope marked to be opened in event of his death.'

'He wouldn't trust anyone to keep it closed.'

'Actually,' Carpenter said, 'he probably left it in a safe deposit box somewhere. And they're sealed automatically when a man dies. The family couldn't touch it.'

'Then we can go,' Mercedes said.

'Go?'

'To Leon. We can't leave money in the States. We have the money from Switzerland to transfer. We can do some sums when Leventhal comes through.'

'But we don't need to go to Leon,' Carpenter said.

'I do,' Mercedes said. 'I don't want any tricks. I want to know the money reaches Providencia, and the right people.'

'You're so sure they're the right people?'

'That's the point of it,' Mercedes said.

In the apartment, he turned on the eleven o'clock TV news, out of habit.

'– guerrilla armies massing on the northern border –'

'It could be about Providencia,' Carpenter said.

'– training camps in the Florida swamps –'

A man, too heavy, swaggered across a motel forecourt in Coral Gables under a bandolier. There was elephant grass, six feet high, and when it parted, slack-shouldered men in combat gear sat exhausted at the end of a day's exercise.

'– when these pictures were shot, days ago –'

Then there was a talking head in the studio, a woman with the sly manner of the arrogant who know about the world.

'– why don't you call them freedom fighters?' she was saying.

Carpenter watched Mercedes freeze before the screen.

'– they are fighting for –'

She stood like a fighter.

'– against the Soviet threat in Central America –'

'They said my father was the Communist threat, lady,' Mercedes said. 'They know how to lie. All of them.'

'It's only the news,' Carpenter said. 'It can't be Providencia.'

She turned and for a moment he expected her to launch herself at him; but she put her arms around him gently and tugged his arms into place at her waist.

'Sometimes I think it'll be a war for always,' she said. 'The old guard, the new guard, the revolutionaries, the revolutionaries on the Right, the Americans who won't accept a change and the Leftists who won't accept a return to old times. And in the middle, the people die.'

'You're buying guns with the Diaz money.'

298

'That's what Tomás would do. Only he'd put back all the National Guard and the pimps and thieves.'

'Then it's all right,' Carpenter said. 'You chose right.'

'I was thinking about Aurelia.'

She said nothing more. Aurelia had toughened in the bush as anyone might; she had authority and experience, both denied her in decorous married life. But she also had a glaring sense of self-righteousness. She seemed to act and pose for a medal, which was a little like Diaz; and even a very little likeness was alarming.

'It's not just for Aurelia,' Carpenter said.

'Maybe she tricked us into this,' Mercedes said. She was testing the unsayable.

'It wasn't a trick. It was what I saw.'

'Then I believe what I see, too,' Mercedes said. 'I want to see the money in Leon.'

Carpenter kissed her.

'I'm not frightened,' she said. 'It's not fear.'

'I know,' he said.

When the day came, she commandeered a plane like a pirate in silks – the private 737 of a TV mogul who needed to be lifted from the Bahamas and was happy for his plane to divert to Miami. It was a beige, plush affair tricked out with flying art, an English steward, and to the rear, a Giacometti sculpture which, at take-off and landing, looking alarmingly like an assegai.

Mercedes took her seat and her glass of champagne and she looked delighted again. The weeks of fame had acted like a bodyguard; she was safe, Carpenter was safe, the money was safe. It was only a routine now, with a change of planes.

But in Miami, there were no flights to Providencia.

Carpenter asked the next counter where everyone was.

'Bust,' said the man at Bahamasair, amiably. 'They wrote so many tickets, the tickets bounced. Nobody paid.'

'Already,' Carpenter said.

'They were in trouble long ago,' the man said.

'That's something.'

He found Mercedes and told her.

'I wish we were Diacista sometimes,' he said. 'I bet we could

299

find some Soldier of Fortune to fly us in with a gunship. Take a present with us.'

'Christ,' Mercedes said. 'The diamonds. The diamonds Solomon bought for us in Zürich –'

'Stop worrying about details.'

'Seven million worth of details.'

'Then call the man.'

Mercedes did; and Solomon was impatient.

'Naturally I mailed them,' he said. 'Registered mail.'

'You put seven million dollars worth of diamonds –'

'Harry Winston once sent the Hope Diamond by mail,' Solomon said. 'To Washington, yet. It's easier to steal from a person than the US Mail.'

'But when did you send them –'

'I sent them yesterday,' Solomon said. 'You should have them today.'

Mercedes called her apartment.

The phone rang too long; she was annoyed, a mistress whose servants are delinquent. Finally, a maid answered, in tearful, squally Spanish.

'– fuego,' she could hear, and then 'bomberos.'

She asked if one of the firemen could come to the phone.

A big, Irish voice answered. 'Miss,' he said, 'you had visitors. A fire bomb.'

'Was anyone hurt?'

'The girls are quite frightened. But nobody's hurt. There was nobody in.'

'And you know who did it?'

'Lady,' the fireman said, 'I'm no cop.'

When she put down the phone, Mercedes felt relieved and shaky all at once. The Diacistas were still on the prowl, after the death of Diaz; they'd taken their revenge for the old man. To have the attack over was almost a relief. But if they'd left a day later, Mercedes and Carpenter might have been burning in the path of that bomb. The risks were very real again.

It took Carpenter an hour to find a small plane ready to fly out of Miami to Belize and then down the coast of Central America to Bluefields and across to Leon. This time, the plane lacked the luxury of the 737; it was cold, and it was slow. But Mercedes and

Carpenter sat with their files and their case of paper, their fortune ready to go home.

The plane tracked out a little over the Bahamas. They imagined Vico down on German Cay, polishing his time.

'He can't stop anything now,' Carpenter said.

'Shh,' Mercedes said. 'It's bad luck to say that.'

And they sat back to chat as though this was some ordinary flight and time needed passing. The long hours sobered them before they came down at Belize.

Then, they had nerves. A Harrier jet went screaming up the sky as they landed, on some routine mission of alarm. All round the runway there were nets and rough khaki camouflage and the soldiers in the middle of it seemed raw and white, obvious as toys in a sandpit.

The pilot had to talk to air traffic control, and his passengers went along. The controller stank of yesterday's bay rum; his wide, curled moustaches looked as though they had been turned from wood.

'You don't want to go,' he said.

'This is urgent,' Mercedes said. 'We have to get to Leon.'

'Don't,' the controller said. 'You really don't want to.' His accent was clubhouse British. 'You'll overfly the US base at Trujillo, and they're nervous. Then you overfly two hundred miles in which somewhere there are guerrillas. Then you get into Amadista territory. That's where your troubles start.' He coughed, and pulled out a packet of Capstans. 'They shoot down one of their own, it's a new martyr of the revolution. They shoot down one of the Diacista planes, it's a new hero of the revolution. Whatever they shoot, they can't lose.'

'I don't understand,' Mercedes said.

'The Diaz forces didn't all give up,' air traffic control said. 'Too scared, if you ask me. They had a lot to hide and didn't want to be called to account. So there are guns down there and they make everyone nervous.'

He lifted a chain of cigarettes to his lips with an oddly feminine impatience.

'You mean there's still a war?' She said it very blankly, as though the very thought was unbearable.

'Exactly,' air traffic control said. 'Clever girl. You go at your own risk.'

Carpenter looked at the pilot, worried that air traffic control might scare him off. But the pilot said: 'British! Scared of their own shadows.'

'As you like,' air traffic control said. 'But it would help if I knew what you're up to. The flat tops here like to know. I know it's not their show officially but it is their backyard, isn't it?' His big, soft eyes appealed to Carpenter for the support one Englishman owes another.

'My mother is in Bluefields,' Mercedes said.

'Mercy mission,' the controller wrote on a pad, mouthing the words. Then the spite in him came out, resentment at the pretty, mobile people who could fly away. 'I know you from somewhere, don't I?' He squinted at Mercedes. 'Pretty sweaty way to get publicity, isn't it? Really work at it, don't you?'

In the plane, the whine of the engines was enough to keep each passenger's doubts to himself. They were isolated, and now that night had come down they were alone under chilly stars, rushing towards Providencia and the final success of their mission. They had won, they told themselves.

'God willing,' the pilot said to Mercedes as she hung over the co-pilot's seat to talk, 'we make radio contact with Bluefields before we come into Providencian airspace. It would help.'

'Could we land at night?'

'At dawn. We can fly with this moon. The guys down there, if there are any, they don't have electronic spotting gear and their eyes don't work too well in the dark. I didn't turn on the lights.'

Mercedes was bundled in a rough blue blanket, and anchored on Carpenter's shoulder. She looked down at the coastline of Belize with its atolls, and the rivers which showed as ribs of black in a dusty grey land. She saw the black cones of mountains as they cut out a brilliant sky.

In that cold moonstruck landscape, there were no obvious fires or lights. She wondered what marked a guerrilla camp from the air: as little as possible, presumably. She wondered how to see if there were still Diacistas down there, the last feudal powers, with their gunships and M-16s.

Against that, the Amadistas had to be right.

The pilot was shouting: 'Bluefields. This is Alpha Romeo Tango. One Seven Six. Come in please.

'Come in.

'For Christ's sake, come in!'

She stirred herself. Below, morning broke out. The islands in the lagoon took shape from the blank silvered water, like a photographic negative, and houses and hills developed there. There was already a dory on the water, skimming along under stained white sails.

'Almost home,' Carpenter said, brightly.

Mercedes pulled herself up to look out of the windows properly. She had the sleepy, dazed air of a waking child.

Home.

Mornings when dawn hung on the horizon before racing up the sky. Oyster soup, fried breadfruit, hog plums, green oranges, red peppers that burned the skin. Baseball games in an old wood stadium that creaked with the intrigue of its spectators like a tree. Spider monkey on a leash.

She tried to hold those specific, benign pictures in her mind but they were quickly crowded out. She saw the body of the police Captain, bloated. She saw her father's coffin fall to the ground and splinter. The fires on the road to Leon. There could be no coming home for Mercedes Zenon.

She said, out loud: 'Home.'

Carpenter had his own memories: Aurelia coming to this place, the moment she took off her mask of make-up and became herself. But that self was not the woman he'd met again on the Diaz yacht: imperious, violent, strong. All he'd known was one possibility of Aurelia.

The plane bumped on the grass.

The hot, humid air was like a blow after the cold of the plane. Nothing moved. Raw wood shutters were still pulled tight on the little houses.

'We need gas,' the pilot said.

Mercedes said: 'I'd like to go into town.'

She tried to see things as a child sees them: to wonder at a parrot going crabwise on a wire fence, all raucous in blue and red, yellow and green. It was fastidious about each step. She saw the goats, black and white, in a jungle of flowers. The obelisk of the war memorial had been painted red, and on each side was the stencilled silhouette of Amadao, the new hero of the country.

303

She was going by instinct, like a child.

There were banners across the street, slogans on the wall: Peace, they said, over and over again.

The great banyan still shaded the park, and the three tall plinths were still in place, but the one which once honoured Diaz was now headless. The fountain at its foot was stagnant; testy, short alligators lay all alert and dyspeptic in the filthy water.

Carpenter said, 'We could have breakfast,' but she was going her own way.

The first cooking stands were lighting wood under wide, battered pots, and laying out peppers and chicken meat. The goats roamed out in search of melon rinds and old paper, defying the dogs.

She stopped before a house that was a weathered white and surrounded with green trellis. There were three doors, and a garden of hibiscus.

'Hold my hand,' Mercedes said.

A dog began to howl in a tentative way, as though half afraid to draw attention to itself.

Mercedes pushed open a wire garden gate.

An old woman came very carefully to the central door. The light seemed to shock her. Time had worn her face away although she must once have been handsome. Carpenter thought, obscenely, of the face of the Diaz matron in her casket, how history wears away everyone. But neither face allowed for any life, and this woman was still alive.

'Mama,' Mercedes said.

Her mother's eyes strained against the sun. She seemed unsure if she could see.

She said: 'Aurelia?' And then 'Mercedes?'

'Mercedes, Mama.'

The older woman turned. She seemed to be brushing something away.

'It's not safe here any more,' she said.

'Talk to me, Mama,' Mercedes said.

The fragile woman resisted her as if she were a ghost until she was very close, and then the two women held each other fiercely.

Carpenter walked away from the house. There was nothing he

could give to Mercedes, he knew that. But he wondered what
had bent and broken her mother. He remembered his own
grandmother who had been so shocked by grief when her
husband died that she fell deaf and dumb.

And Mercedes picked her way into the heart of the house. It
was worn, and dark; light was an accident through chinks and
screens.

Her mother went to a closet lined with cedar and brought
down a dress.

'You'll want this,' she said. 'You must have grown.'

Mercedes sat opposite her mother.

'I don't expect you're here for long,' her mother said.

She felt a prickle of tears. She heard such longing and such
resignation in her mother's voice.

'I could make coffee,' she said.

'No coffee this week,' her mother said.

'A soda. A fresco.'

'Nothing.'

The dark was a comfort; it seemed to invite confessions.

'I had a picture of you,' her mother said. 'From a magazine.
One of the boys brought it back from Los Angeles. He was on a
cruiseship there.'

'Did you like it?'

Her mother said: 'I didn't tell him I couldn't see it.'

Mercedes shook her head and went to sit at her mother's feet,
strong feet blackened by walking without shoes.

'I couldn't have let you stay,' her mother said.

'Don't say things.'

'The Diacistas, they used to take the family and friends. So
you had to go somewhere safe.' Her voice was flat and
commonsensical. 'And when Erasmo went, they took away my
life.'

'Mama.'

'Don't spoil your dress. I know you have a pretty dress.'

'Please come with me. I could look after you, I could'

'You don't want that,' her mother said, eyes like blank discs.
'You don't want to stir the dead.'

Mercedes stood. 'Is there anything –'

'I couldn't leave Erasmo. You understand that.'

'I could put flowers on the grave. I could make a new grave –'

'It's not good to draw attention.'

And then there was nothing at all to say. It was like sharing a room with a shell, a beloved shell which long ago lost all life and animation.

Mercedes stood on the steps of the house. The light blinded her, and a gaggle of women stood there, waiting to see her in her sharp and citified dress. For a moment, she wanted the refuge of the black velvet shadows of the house.

'I missed you,' she heard her mother saying, very quietly. 'I never stopped praying for you.'

She sensed a hunger in her mother's house, not from lack of food but lack of will, and she could not feed it.

The dog slithered under the floorboards, secure in his own small kingdom.

Carpenter had waited in the shade across the street. Mercedes joined him, and there was a trail of silver on her skin. He didn't ask if it was sweat or tears.

They walked a side road down to the water, where the tall red and white vaults of the church were beginning to shiver as someone stabbed out a rough tune on the organ.

An old lady under a black umbrella passed by, and smiled softly at Mercedes. 'Good day,' she said.

They turned back from the water, and the road had been blocked by a kid militia with ancient guns slung on frayed cord. The kids were restive.

Carpenter's first thought was to smile and patronise them, but their guns were real. He walked forward, hands to his head, and Mercedes followed.

'Commandante's office,' the oldest boy said.

They were escorted up past the sellers of scarlet hog plums before the Cinema Moderne, and past the pool hall denizens who took the air.

In the office, the pilot was sitting in a state of cold fury.

'That is my plane,' he said. 'My life. My living. If you don't arrange for it to be released –'

Carpenter said: 'What's up?'

The Commandante bustled in, a short man, young and rough, his name already prepared for a roll of heroes and martyrs.

306

'Please explain why you're here,' he said.

'Oddly enough,' Carpenter said, thinking he had a right to a little irony, 'we're here on Amadista business. We have some papers to deliver to José Mantica in Leon.'

'Mantica is in Washington,' the Commandante said, smugly.

'We need to get to Leon,' Mercedes said.

'A lot of people want to get to Leon.' The Commandante seemed sure in his abruptness, but there was a faint edginess about the man. He didn't want to be wrong.

The room smelt of oil and leather. Mercedes shifted leg over leg, and said: 'If you could just contact Leon – my sister, Aurelia Zenon.'

The Commandante stared. 'So you are the famous Mercedes,' he said. 'The one who got away.' He laughed at his own little joke.

'I am Mercedes Zenon. And I'd be grateful if you could help us.'

'I suppose I could,' the Commandante said. 'Do you have the fuel to get to Leon?'

'It'll be close,' the pilot said.

'We still have gas,' the Commandante said. 'You can go if you take some of our men with you – they're due to go back to Leon.'

'I'm very grateful,' Mercedes said.

'But you'll need travel papers. You need a permit to go from Bluefields to Leon.'

'This is my country,' Mercedes said.

'Everyone needs a permit.'

They sat in the tiny wood office, between two kids who were assiduously cleaning and oiling the barrels of their rifles, and filled in forms. The forms were taken to another room and brought back after three hours, stamped with a rough rubber stamp and signed in a florid hand.

The militia men brought them oranges, peeled down to the pith, and a bag of green gineps to suck. Mercedes said: 'I guess I expected joy.'

The militia man sitting by her, a boy of perhaps seventeen, turned and said very seriously: 'There is joy. But there is also a war. Diaz won't let us win so easily.'

'But Diaz is dead.'

'His name's alive.'

The boy pulled the wadding from the rifle.

It was almost dark when the Commandante decided they could fly. He wouldn't explain the delay, but he wished them well.

'We need friends,' he said. 'You must forgive us if we are a little clumsy still, Compañera Mercedes.'

She said: 'Thank you for your help.'

The little plane had been loaded down with a chatter of soldiers, all Spanish-speaking from the Pacific coast and notably older than the creole kids in Bluefields. Mercedes and Carpenter took unprivileged seats.

'You want me to fly this on compass?' the pilot snapped to his immediate guard.

The man shrugged. 'There will be lights at Leon,' he said.

They skimmed trees and mountains, and skirted the pudding basin hills, and they came down towards Leon at night. The scatter of lights below looked like a city's bones, lit for an anatomist.

A helicopter came up off the runway, bright like a firework, and cut in on their final approach. Four-wheelers, official looking, swarmed out of the shadows to take the soldiers away. The pilot shut down the engines, and with Mercedes and Carpenter he walked to the airport buildings.

All the airport concourse was silent. But to turn on any lights at all, every light in a section had to be lit, so that the whole immigration hall suddenly went bright, and then the whole customs area, and then the main concourse with its souvenir shops and news stands. It was like a doll's house, and behind them, each section went dark.

There had been nobody in the immigration boxes, which looked like a lost Punch and Judy show now, and in the customs hall only a half-dozen victim suitcases, battered and light blue, against a wall.

The great wood doors of the customs hall began to slide open.

Most nights, there were wide-eyed drivers past this door, straining to greet a friend or find a fare, but tonight there was no crowd. The air sung with life, but not human talk. And when the doors had opened, the airconditioned cool was broken by a wind

308

like breath – hot and much too intimate.

Outside there was one car: a long limo, on borrowed time. There was nothing else. When they climbed aboard, the driver started up immediately, and wouldn't open his glass partition to say where they were going.

Mercedes wound down the window, for the smells of the place: wood, peppers, spice, shit, coconut, peel of a dozen fruits, stoves and the fire that could clean the city. She saw the barrio roofs heaped against the sky, and trees that seemed to jostle the margins of the road. They'd left intact the concrete vainglory of the Diaz times, and hung the square white box of the Interior Ministry with inspirational banners. She looked at everything, smelt everything, trying to know it.

'At least they know we're coming,' Carpenter said, brightly.

The car came to an intersection under a slogan hung across the road, picked out in white light bulbs, burning extravagantly in the curfew. The city was alive with words. But as they passed the grey ziggurat of the InterContinental Hotel, there was no other life.

'There's another hotel in town?' the pilot asked, dubiously.

The limo swung left.

Carpenter knew these gates. He'd once seen Aurelia disappear through them, on some mission. Now the huge painted sign no longer carried the initials of the security police of Anastasio Diaz Sacasa; but there were new initials, only slightly different, for the security police of the Amadista Front for National Liberation.

Mercedes crossed herself.

The car went through the gates and came to a halt. Mercedes climbed out and stretched in the heavy night air. Carpenter saw a parade ground that was now more ragged around the edges, and the bunker still set stolidly into the volcano. Somehow, he'd hoped they would have bulldozed and dynamited it clean.

'They shouldn't use this place,' Mercedes said.

The car turned and left; they were alone.

There was nowhere to go except the bunker, and they were expected. They passed the first hall which was open and empty; the clutter of guards and bureaucrats was gone.

The lights died. It was like the airport again, except that this time the darkness was like a wall between them and the outside air. They walked towards other lights, a corridor away.

Mercedes had been nervous before, but this time she was afraid. These rooms had been fashioned to hold and preserve a dictatorship; their walls echoed with horrors. In this place, heroes and martyrs were made.

Ahead, in the private rooms, there were bright lights.

The walls had been scratched with slogans and *Frente* boasts. There was a faint smell of piss.

The light came up suddenly on Mercedes' face. She blinked, and then she used every skill she remembered: she assembled herself. She strutted forward.

There was a shriek, a cold sound beating at the corridor walls. Out of the corridor ahead came a great feathered thing, desperate for light. It came swooping low, and they ducked, then it climbed to clear them and fly on in a fury of gaudy colours.

Any man can have a parrot. They are loyal creatures, temperamental and sentimental in their way. But a man who takes a parrot into a bunker has some curious reason. The bunker must be his world.

She thought she remembered the bird.

She stood stock still in the corridor, the Diaz fortune in plastic bags and cases in her hands, and she shouted: 'George Vico, you bastard. George Vico!'

There was no sound except for the bird as it flapped to the bunker door, and Carpenter and the pilot stared at her.

But she was sure, now.

'Show yourself! George Vico!'

'For this,' Vico said, and he set a rifle on the desk. 'For the Galil 5.6. Among other things. You don't even know what it is, do you, and that's why the Amadistas needed me. Just when I needed them.'

He held up the rifle. 'Gas operation. Rotary bolt. The export version has a steel stock. Ambidextrous, if that matters to you – you can get at the mag release and the safety even if you're left handed.' He sighted them, and there was a click as though the safety catch had moved.

'Tritium night sight,' he said. 'Perfect bush weapon.' The rifle clattered back onto his desk.

Mercedes said, very coldly: 'Why did you need them?'

'There was some trouble in the islands.'

'You mean even the Bahamas threw you out?'

'They had some story about the death of Diaz. There were American cops everywhere. As a matter of commonsense, they –'

'They told you to move on. Even the islands you own.'

'You're a sweet child,' Vico said.

'And why did the Amadistas take you in? You're not such a great catch any more.'

'I am if you need guns,' Vico said. 'Guns when you don't have cash. And the Israelis make the Galil and sure as hell they're not selling it without American approval. So we set up a dummy company here, a shuffle there – the old game. And the guns arrive where people can use them.'

Vico seemed a little confused. He was in waiting for his moment of triumph and Mercedes refused to concede it.

'Your sister was very helpful,' Vico said, spitefully. 'She seemed to understand my problem.'

'I'm sure she did,' Mercedes said.

'So all that remains,' Vico said, 'is for you to hand over all the cash you collected. The cash you couldn't leave in America. I get it all.'

'Why?'

'Good question. Because I can use it and you can't, and the Amadistas can't. I can get the guns.'

'And what percentage do you keep for yourself?'

'Nobody's keeping books,' Vico said.

'You mean,' Mercedes said, like a courtroom lawyer, 'you take what you want.'

Vico shrugged, complacently.

'Then why the hell should I hand over anything?'

Vico was in a loud Haiwaiian shirt which hung over the racks of his bellies, and he looked hungry for the golf course and a Martini. Mercedes imagined his great gaudy bird, spluttering and cawing down the corridors, and now out free.

She watched the Amadista guards take up positions by the office door.

311

'You want a cigar?' Vico said, lighting one and sitting in a ring of blue haze.

Mercedes felt cripplingly tired, unable to summon back the courage that had been an instinct only minutes before. She said: 'This money is for the people. For Providencia.'

'The people,' Vico said. 'What do you know about the people? Everything you knew you've forgotten. La Rosée. The Four Seasons, Palladium and Studio 54. Where were the people then?'

'I mean it.'

'You going to stay in Providencia and build socialism, girl? Don't kid me.' He sucked elaborately on his cigar. 'You took Providencia and you pumped it for all the excitement you could get and now the game's over. Go back to New York and make a movie of it.'

But she would not defend herself. If she did, that would give Vico the standing of a judge.

'They're all embarrassed about you here,' Vico said. 'They've had doubts all along. They're not sure if they want to be associated with Parfums Mercedes Zenon, and they weren't sure what you were really doing. You were a gamble they took.'

'It paid.' Mercedes let herself go perfectly limp on the sofa, waiting for the moment when she needed anger or speed.

'It paid,' Vico said, sarcastically. 'It paid because they got to me, that's all. Nobody wants you here.'

Mercedes said, very quietly: 'That's fine. Because I have another home, another world. I even have a choice of worlds. I don't have to find the good life locked away in a bunker in a volcano in a city where I don't speak the language.'

'I survive,' Vico said. 'I do what I have to do. Like you do.'

'And you think the Amadistas want to acknowledge that you're here? Why do you think you're in this bunker and not at the Press Centre, two shows daily? Because the squeaky-clean revolution doesn't want to be linked to an old-time crook. That's why.'

'I don't get angry any more,' Vico said.

'You should do better than this,' Mercedes said. 'I'm ashamed of you. You stole whole funds, you ran whole empires, and now you live underground in a poor country.'

'You need your sleep,' Vico said. 'Kids need their sleep.'

'If you ever want to get out,' Mercedes said, 'call me.'

'You have an idea? That it?'

'My ideas haven't been so bad,' Mercedes said. 'I learned my trade listening at keyholes, but I learned it good.'

'Get some sleep,' Vico said. 'Take some time off, relax. Look at the revolution. Get some fishing. Go sun yourself in Cancun on the way back. You don't want to lose your beauty sleep.'

The pilot slapped his fists on his thighs and stood up, his whole body a shrug of annoyance. Carpenter followed, and Mercedes after him.

'You can wait for the paper,' she said.

'I can wait a while,' Vico said. 'But you know if you take it direct to the Amadistas, they'll just bring it back here. You do know that, don't you?'

Mercedes did not look back.

'I said, you know that, don't you.'

She passed the guards at the door, who seemed confused by her.

'Girl, I said –'

'I heard you,' Mercedes said, but she would not turn back.

A pale, mean light was opening up the city when they came back to the air. Shadows flickered in the façade of the hotel, along with the moves of the guards. There seemed to be L-shaped holes dug everywhere, as though for air raid shelters. The city was nervous.

In the hotel lobby the old glitter had gone; the light bulbs now were 40 watts; it was dull and cramped. At breakfast, the staff were surly, caught between the new democracy and their old, deferential habits and finding it hard.

Mercedes said: 'It would all be easier in New York.'

She went to bed immediately; she had no ambition except sleep.

Carpenter stood for a moment at the hotel door. Before him stretched an acre of rough green surrounded by shade trees. People's cabs went rattling up the hill, doors held by string, and he met the first money black market two blocks from the hotel: a lawyer who, on hearing the accent, pronounced himself Anglophile. The view of the city never changed: a spoiled mouth, over-run with creeper. He'd never loved the place.

For this, he'd risked everything. But what was this revolution, and what could it signify to him? He saw muddle and rot, just like the Diacista days; he liked acts to have consequences, and here they did not. He wondered who had the limos now, and the villas. He couldn't criticise; there was nothing else to drive, nowhere else to live. The country was bust.

If freedom was what they'd won, it was not yet useful. To be free, you must first eat.

He was almost out of sight of the hotel before soldiers stopped him. He was standing between two buildings – one a low, lazy bungalow marked POLITICAL SCHOOL: CONSERVATIVE PARTY OF PROVIDENCIA: they hadn't been popular under Diaz, and no doubt they would manage to be unpopular under the new regime. And next to their slow headquarters, there was a broken building, a house hollowed out by the earthquake and by bombs. A room had split in two, exposing its life like a museum show, and on the lower floor a family sat, staring, behind their washing.

The soldiers were polite, but firm. It would help if he returned to the hotel.

Mercedes had woken and gone down to the swimming pool, a dash of vivid blue among glossy plants. She lay there like any social lady repairing her tan.

'You look good,' he said.

She didn't move.

'I went out for a walk,' he said.

She turned away.

'We don't have to give up,' he said.

She took a glass and splashed mineral water between her breasts. 'You have to use mineral water,' she said defiantly.

He felt as though his lover was sick. She lay passive in the sun, full of anger and determined to show no feeling.

'You ought to see the town,' he said.

'I know Leon. I know Bluefields. I've brought the money, seen my mother. I even made an appointment to see my sister.'

He pulled her up and wrapped her in her robe. 'We're going for a walk.'

On the way down the hill, she said: 'It's none of your business.'

314

They turned into a suburban road which went from trees and litter to small wood houses, and sometimes shops. There was the lurid, blue-green box of a movie house, and a filling station sleepy in the high sun. A hotel taxi stopped beside them but Carpenter waved it on.

She said: 'You think there's something I can see that will change my mind? Is that it?'

'You're very tired,' Carpenter said.

'I could sleep in New York.'

A thin boy on a bicycle went careering by.

'This is the biggest thing you ever did,' Carpenter said. 'You want to leave it unfinished?'

'I don't care. Aurelia seems to think I'm a whore. Vico just laughs and asks if I want to build socialism. I don't want either of them to change their minds; I don't care what they think.'

'You don't expect miracles, not after a revolution.'

'You've been in a lot of revolutions, have you?'

They had wandered back to the main highway, where a cluster of white buildings stood together incongruously – a closed courtyard, like a convent, and a school, and beyond that the Casa di Gobierno, the official buildings.

Mercedes stopped at the convent door. It was an ordinary door in a concrete wall, but she stared. She was remembering being taken to Leon and to this convent, and then standing in a cool, green room, being offered to Vico by the nuns. Two lovely girls from Bluefields for adoption. She'd saved Aurelia from being Mercedes, and Aurelia took it for granted. She remembered the sweet, conventual smell of the frangipani: a smell of kindness and women.

She pushed the door open.

There was a crocodile of children, all bleary with tears, their faces brown and blotched. Mercedes knew, because she'd been in this corridor, that they were crying for pain or fear, not temper; a poor child can't afford the luxury of temper. She saw that the children were passing, two by two, into a white inner office.

'¿Que tienen los niños?' she asked a nun.

'Al fin, las inoculaciones,' the nun said, smiling. And she

315

explained that for years they'd wanted to inoculate all the children of the barrio, but there'd never been money or vaccine or needles. If ever there were supplies, somehow they disappeared to the army, or were never bought. Now, since the triumph of the revolution – which seemed to be a set phrase – things were better.

'*Los niños van a vivir*,' she said, matter of factly. '*Todos.*' And she swept along, comforting the children, beaming and commiserating.

'The children are going to live,' Mercedes said. 'All of them.'

Carpenter watched her. He could not enter her memories, nor know why she was on the point of tears.

In the road there was a cross batch of TV reporters quitting the Casa di Gobierno after a long wait in the high sun for a Commandante's press conference. They were turning over cases and cameras in their hands, complaining how security had shuffled the lenses and wrecked the focus.

'They haven't got anything to say,' said an ABC stringer to the street, and to Carpenter in particular. 'Just that there's Amadista activity on the borders, and they brought down an A129 Mangusta. They want to know who's giving the Diacistas helicopters.'

'Italian, the Mangusta?' Carpenter said.

'Sure. They said the guerrillas killed some nurses –'

Mercedes said: 'It's a matter of choosing sides. Neither is perfect.'

'I guess,' said the stringer. 'We'd like to do an interview –'

But Mercedes was walking on, and Carpenter ran to catch up with her.

'*Los niños van a vivir*,' Mercedes said. '*Todos.*'

'You've got a slogan. What are you going to do with it?'

'Get every penny of that money to Providencia. Cut George Vico out.'

'And then?'

She opened her eyes very wide. 'I thought I needed revenge on Chamorro and Diaz,' she said. 'But I might have forgiven them. In time. The one I can't forgive is the one who compromises everything, who spoils it all. Who takes my life and tells me it has no effect at all.'

316

Carpenter said: 'He's lying.'

'He's dead,' said Mercedes Zenon.

John Grey was on the phone very early, when Mercedes was lying between sleep and the day. Carpenter stroked her shoulder.

'It's all fine,' Grey said. 'You can take it the American authorities are very interested.'

'They believe you?'

'They want a little demonstration.'

'And you can do that?'

'Easily,' Grey said. 'All you have to do is sell it to Vico. The Americans know it could work and they know what's going to happen.'

Mercedes put down the phone. She needed help from Washington, for fear Vico's threat could go like fire through a rooming house: all through a bureaucracy with nobody knowing what to do or why. At least Americans were giving advice on which Americans Vico should threaten.

She ate dry toast for breakfast and drank thin coffee. She said: 'I'm good at the great game – good at money and people's fears. You know that?'

'I've watched you,' Carpenter said. 'I've admired you.'

'And now,' Mercedes said, 'I can play the great game for those children.'

She wiped her lips and said she'd go alone to the bunker. Carpenter regretted her going.

She found Vico red faced and impatient, a man out of focus in his underground place, as buried things lose shape and colour.

'I hope to Christ you brought the paper,' he said. 'All the paper.'

Mercedes said: 'I wanted to talk to you.'

'You had ten years to talk to me,' Vico said. 'More.'

'You got me out of Leon once,' Mercedes said. 'I'd like to get you out now. To show just how grateful I am.'

'I'm here for a while,' Vico said. 'Ain't nobody can change that. This is home, sweet home.' He flailed his arms at the walls, which still bore the Miami chic that Diaz had installed, but now grazed and pocked by bullets.

'Listen to a story,' Mercedes said. And she reminded him of

317

the vision John Grey had spun in the Bahamas: the trap in the program for FedWire, the power to encrypt all of America's money in a single move.

'I know, I know,' Vico said. 'We do it at eleven thirty, don't we? All the money is paid out but none of it has gone where it belongs. It would just be lost.'

'They wouldn't dare let it happen,' Mercedes said. 'They know there's four hundred billion at stake, not to mention whatever General Electric borrowed for the day and didn't tell the banks. It would be a nightmare.'

'I know that.'

'Then do it,' Mercedes said. 'If the Amadistas get all the Diaz money, all of it, you can have the FedWire scam. You're the only man who could ever use it.'

Vico looked sideways, parrot-like. 'You mean that as a compliment?'

'Yes,' Mercedes said. 'And because you're the only one who could do a deal. You want to get back to America, or you want to get back at America. You can do it this way.'

'You're asking me to give up my cut of almost a billion dollars,' Vico said.

'It's not much,' Mercedes said, 'compared with going home.'

He looked around the room. 'Home,' he said, and then he was sure he had showed too much feeling. 'You never gave me anything,' he said.

'How could I?' Mercedes said.

'Why should you give me back America?'

'I've gone too far, I've risked too much to see that Diaz money go to you – in fees or commissions or cuts, whatever you say. I did it for a principle.'

'Ideals,' Vico said. 'I never thought a child of mine –'

'And then we're quits,' Mercedes said. 'I get you through this, you get back to America, and then it's all over. I'm on my own.'

'What would you do if I did bring down FedWire?' Vico said, alarmingly. 'You depend on that system. You couldn't live without it.'

'I could live a hundred ways,' Mercedes said. 'I think. I'm only beginning to live.'

Outside there was the sound of a man running in the corridors.

Vico looked alert, but not concerned; there must be guards.

'How do I know this is for real?'

'See how the Americans react.'

'And how –'

'You can visit the American Ambassador. Just don't go to the embassy because they could arrest you on American soil.'

Vico cleared his throat. 'I don't think so,' he said. 'They might let the Diaz people know I'm here. And they might tell the Amadistas to extradite me. They have a billion dollars' power over the Amadistas, never forget it. That's what the poor bastards owe.'

'Then I'll go,' Mercedes said.

Vico shifted. 'I don't know what you'll say. You might just shop me.'

'I might,' Mercedes said.

The sound of running was up to the doors now, and the doors flew open.

'For Christ's sake,' Mercedes said to a flustered breathless Ian Carpenter.

'What are you doing?' Carpenter said. 'You come up here without telling me –'

'I was talking to my stepfather.'

'What about? What have you got to say to him?'

'FedWire,' Mercedes said.

'You're not giving the whole thing to him, are you? Something we can only do one time. Why my bank would pay –'

'This,' Vico said with soft satisfaction, 'is family business. You wouldn't understand.'

'I understand,' Carpenter said. 'You're such a damn fool you think this whole scam is for real. You're desperate to go home and you take it seriously.'

'But it's a serious scheme,' Vico said. 'Isn't it?'

'Serious stuff,' Carpenter said, contemptuously.

'You really don't want me to have this,' Vico said.

'I don't see why we give you –'

'It's a proposal,' Mercedes said. 'Take it or leave it.'

'You can prove it's on the level?'

'You'll see.'

Carpenter said: 'Let's get out of here. Now.'

319

He was affronted in the corridor, and she was cold to him. She turned the corner where the shade trees led to the hotel.

She jumped. She did a little turn in the air. Her lovely face was broken back to life by her smile. And Carpenter held her and waltzed her around before an astonished knot of small, serious people.

'He bought it all,' Mercedes said.

'Every penny,' Carpenter said. 'I meant everything I said and he bought every goddamn penny.'

·EIGHT·

'Home,' George Vico said. He waited for the immigration officer to notice his name.

'Yes, sir.'

'I'm expected,' Vico said.

The clerk read a thousand names a day, and saw none of them. Customs would check if anything needed checking. He looked up at Vico though, and said: 'Just a minute, sir.'

The line stopped in its shuffle, and the clerk was torn. Returning citizens might complain. It might be even worse to let George Vico into America.

'Sir,' the clerk said.

'Take your time,' Vico said.

He gloried in this brief stardom. He'd started a rumour down the line, people buzzing his name. He half heard words the clerk hissed to his plainclothes boss: like 'notorious'.

He might not be Dillinger, who pulled crime that was understood, and he was never a cracksman or a bandit; his crimes were almost abstract. But they added up to numbers which could get a man respect, and now, in this fretful line, he would have his respect.

The clerk came back, confused.

'I'm sorry,' he said. 'Sir.'

That night, he told his wife that Vico must have bought somebody very big.

And Vico, by the carousel, was sentimental as a tipsy priest. He was home, and impregnable; he would never leave again. He had the power to salvage the whole system that he might some day have liked to wreck, and the salvage was a wonderful game. The system belonged to him.

Mercedes came after him through passport control. She had dressed for glitter, in a sheath of brilliant blue; she was the proper star to be George Vico's escort. In his sentimental way, he felt his cock beginning to stir for the first time in months: love, and lust, and satisfaction.

She chose the right smile.

'You go first through Customs,' Vico said. 'Tell them I'm coming.'

In the limo, he was bright like a child, heart fluttering. He was going to Washington, a free man. He held a glass high.

'America!' he said.

She smiled, sweetly.

'They used to send the cops after me, once. Now they send the Chairman of the Federal Reserve and he's going to be polite. So fucking polite.'

Mercedes said: 'That's power.'

'Yeah,' said Vico.

She could hear the wine talking.

'You know,' Vico said, 'you don't really know anything about me, do you?'

Mercedes let the irony go past. She didn't even say that she knew far too much, from all the headlines and indictments. She let him talk.

'. . . a Jersey boy . . .'

He was under a jack in a sweatshop garage, oiled and clever. He was talking himself into Wall Street, first with things and then with ideas. He was in the mutual fund business, running rings round all the dumb others because he did what they did not dare to do. He was an operator, moving high.

'. . . bought a Boeing 727, called it Capital Flight. You get that, capital flight? We took the money out in suitcases like everyone else – the money in Uruguay, the money in Portugal, the money in Montclair. The bonds came back by mail. They were pretty, those bonds. Not worth anything, but . . .'

She felt like some dutiful daughter who must take her father to some safe hospital. He had done everything, but each time he'd run; everything he did destroyed him. His only means of survival was to cap each crime, to find something more extraordinary – from theft to drugs, from drugs to arms. It was as if he'd sold

322

his soul to the devil but sale and lease-back, and he was still paying.

'. . . they never caught up with me. They never could . . .'

They were on the boulevards, among monuments, in the heart of Washington, and the evening was crisp. It looked settled and sure.

'We have the evening to ourselves,' he said.

He hadn't even imagined the prospect of defeat, she realised, and that was reassuring.

'There's one thing,' he said. 'Grey gave me the command to bring FedWire down. But he didn't give me the command which brings the system back. He said you knew it.'

'I'll be there,' Mercedes said.

'But I don't know how to stop the process.'

'Maybe you won't want to,' Mercedes said.

Vico snorted.

She installed him in a suite at the Mayflower, which was discreetly guarded, and made sure he had the drink he needed.

'It ain't luxurious,' he said, but nothing could have satisfied him after all those years living in dreams of America.

By nine, he was hopelessly drunk. She stood by him and knew she should not underestimate him. Tomorrow, he'd bring all that fat and waste to life, and he'd have power again, the power of a whole career to instil fear.

The Justice Department had left functionaries to see that all was well.

'He's sleeping,' Mercedes told one.

'He won't be angry when he finds he's been locked in?'

'Yes,' Mercedes said, 'he'll be angry. But he expects it. You're going to tell him I'm staying somewhere else because I don't matter.'

'We cut the phones.'

'Don't do that. He might as well be happy.'

'But my instructions –'

'If you don't keep this man happy,' Mercedes said, 'there won't be an America tomorrow.'

'Yes,' said the functionary, 'ma'am.'

She took the elevator to the floor above and found Ian Carpenter lying on the bed.

'It's fine,' she said, 'so far. Vico thinks they believe him, and they do.'

'And you?'

'You're a shrewd old man, aren't you? They don't know what to make of me. I've helped bring them Vico and they never heard I knew about these things. I don't even seem to want anything. All they have to do is pardon John Grey about Greystoke –'

'They could still just arrest him. Vico, I mean.'

'They can't do that,' Mercedes said. 'They have to be sure about me, first. You see I know how to bring the system down and I know how to bring it back, so they need me. They only have an hour once Vico makes his move.'

'You have the counter command,' Carpenter said. 'They don't need Vico.'

'There's a lot they don't know. They don't know what will happen if FedWire goes down, for a start. But they're terrified.'

'So Vico could break everything and –'

'It's all a show,' Mercedes said. 'A great game. And at the end of everything, it will all be the same except that Vico will be in jail.'

Carpenter saw mischief in her, and something darker.

'You're sure everything will be the same?' he said.

The city shuffled to life. The first joggers bobbed and bounced on the Mall, and the clerks went to their offices in waves. Vico stood at his window, and saw an order he could utterly disrupt.

He watched the morning news shows. The President had woken early at Camp David, he was told; his talks with the French President were over. He was dashing back into the city. There was to be an early meeting, unannounced; staffers were unavailable and saying nothing, and phones went unanswered. Reporters simmered on the lawns and said that something was happening, unannounced, unplanned and therefore real. They read everything into a silence uncharacteristic of such an orderly, public administration.

By nine, the cameras had recorded a stiff-backed White House Chief of Staff, a Boston refugee, as his limo slid into the west basement. He was there at 7.15 as usual, but his morning meeting with senior staff had been brought forward to 7.45. That

324

fact was not meant to reach the Press, but it did.

They imagined what crisis could bring the staff together early, a dozen men scribbling on their white pads and planning the day. By nine, the tone of the TV newsmen was a touch strident: they were offended by their inability to predict.

The President came back in photogenic whirl, down from a helicopter on the White House lawns and directly to the Oval Office. He didn't smile.

Great cars came up to the White House gates, bearing the Attorney General and the Secretary of Treasury. The Vice President was seen hopping briskly across the lawns. The camera crews tried to rush him, but were held back.

At ten, the President seemed to have all the machinery in place to cope with a crisis. But nobody knew what the crisis might be. There was no obvious domestic and political issue, no reported crime; Reuters and Associated Press had nothing on terrorism, wars, nuclear tests, provocations in Eastern Europe, anything that could explain the suddenly chill atmosphere. The usual sources knew nothing, and said so, petulantly.

Vico saw the reporters shouting to the President: 'Mr President, what's happening?'

'No questions,' a sandy haired man said.

Vico was gratified by the commotion. He said to Mercedes, who stood with him: 'I never could tie a tie.'

She helped him, and she told him to use mouthwash. She prepared him for his short drive to the offices of the Federal Reserve.

'They don't know what to do,' Vico said.

'They'll know,' Mercedes said.

'I don't give a fuck,' Vico said, and although it was a lie he had the will to make himself believe it. 'They agree, I come home. They don't, they're history. I don't give a damn if the whole mess of them go up in flames.'

'Come on,' Mercedes said.

The Justice functionary opened the doors and they walked out to the elevator. Mercedes checked Vico's appearance as they went down; he was sharp as a gunfighter in some dark Western. The elevator man seemed startled by the notorious faces.

The driver had the limo door open, and Vico marched to his

seat, truculent on the half of Scotch he'd opened before Mercedes sent him to the Listerine. He was going to glory; he was sure.

'I didn't know you were coming,' Vico's guard said. 'I'm sorry Miss Zenon, but I don't have orders.'

Mercedes said: 'Take Vico. I'll catch up.'

Vico leaned across and said: 'I won't go without you, Mercedes. They might trick me.'

'It'll be fine,' Mercedes said. 'It's just security.'

The word explained everything, it seemed, and Mercedes turned to ask for a second car. It came almost immediately and she settled quickly. She would need all her wits that morning, but not yet.

The streets that passed seemed leafier than she remembered, and a little wilder. There was no Macdonalds between the Mayflower and the Federal Reserve; she was sure of that.

She tried to catch the driver's eye, but she could see the man laughing with a simple enthusiasm for going fast. He allowed her no chance to give orders, or get out.

In half an hour, the end of the world would start. They would trip Vico's temper somehow; if they didn't, they would never see the trapdoor in action, and never be able to change it. Vico would punch in the code, and money would become a perfect abstraction, like wind. If Mercedes wasn't there, then the curse would not be lifted. It was so simple, and she had wanted it this way: in the end, it would all depend on her.

But she was out in some Georgetown street, between neat trees, and the limo was coming to a halt by a triangular building. Above its door hung a curious symbol, the Rosicrucian eye of Central American states.

'You get out here,' the driver said.

'I have to be at the Federal Reserve –'

'Lady,' the driver said. 'You get out here.'

She swung herself out of the limo, long silky legs in perfect array. She stormed the entrance hall, an oval of marble. She thought how provisional it looked.

A girl on a kitchen chair said Mercedes was expected.

The double doors opened onto a long, carpeted reception room which was blank except for a superannuated sofa.

326

Mercedes took the stairs. There was an air of tenuousness about the building, occupied but not inhabited.

She came up against a soldier. He hung from the wall, eyes wide and white, rifle ready. It was only a hanging, she told herself, some woven piece of revolutionary art, but it was shocking between the chandeliers and the silk walls.

On the first floor, the glass and mirror doors to a great ballroom had been broken. Through the cracks she could see filing cabinets, cardboard boxes, metal tables and piles of papers on the floor.

'You're here,' she heard, and turned.

Aurelia was standing in a doorway.

'Come in,' Aurelia said. 'We don't have all day.'

They put George Vico to wait in a panelled room with an Adam fireplace and a view of domestic trees. It seemed a quiet, rather academic place: where a committee sits to tease and block the nation's money supply, and to fix interest rates. It could have been waiting for a seminar.

Vico had summoned himself. He was no longer a wrecked man, lost out in dreams, and he was tempering his usual bluster. He knew he had work to do.

They had to believe not just that he could do this thing, but that he had the will to do it. They must be close to that belief or they would not have let him back into the country; every minute George Vico went free was a scandal. But now he might have to deliver on his threat. One command, on any terminal connected with FedWire, and he had brought down money.

It might help that Mercedes was not yet here. They would think she, too, had access to some bank terminal, or maybe some terminal in a big corporation linked to the system. You need only one keystroke to end the world.

But it was his world. He needed the systems to beat. Without them, he had no more games. And it was his home, this place. Perhaps not this genteel atmosphere, and this cold sense of power without exhilaration, but this country.

The doors opened, and it was too late for doubt.

They had sent the Chairman of the Federal Reserve, a

crumpled man whose features were as disordered as his suit. He smoked a dollar cigar.

'Mr Vico,' the Chairman said. 'I think I'm meant to say it's a pleasure to meet you.'

'Likewise,' Vico said, and smiled.

The Chairman lowered himself into his customary chair, half a table away from Vico. He sprawled, but he looked disquietingly alert.

'The Great Crash all over again, I suppose,' he said, stabbing the air with his acrid cigar. 'Except that we know exactly when and where and how it will happen, and it's going to be quick: 1929, in the made-for-TV version, you might say.' He smiled at his own joke and pushed across a pack of cigars.

'I'll smoke my own,' Vico said.

'The President,' the Chairman said, 'insisted on giving me a box of Romeo y Juliettas. Can't see why. I like a small cigar, and often.' He beamed.

Vico felt like a man in the Chairman's club, and he was clearly not a member. The Chairman's calm was beginning to annoy him.

'We don't have a lot of time,' Vico said.

'God knows,' the Chairman said, expansively, 'I know that. But there is the usual muddle with the political gentlemen. Some of them want to free you, and some of them want to hang you and none of them wants to get caught. They seem to think it's like giving in to terror.'

'They do that all the time,' Vico said, 'when it's only a matter of lives.'

'Only,' the Chairman said, 'implies an interesting moral view. But I guess you don't want to talk morals this morning?' He rumbled to the sideboard and poured himself a glass of iced water. He flourished the carafe at Vico.

'I'm going to bring down the whole thing,' Vico said.

'I take it all very seriously,' the Chairman said. 'But I don't know what the President thinks. He doesn't like grey areas, you know, and this is very grey indeed. We don't know what happens if FedWire is wrecked for ever, do we?'

'Work it out,' Vico said. 'Run a computer simulation, or whatever you do.'

'And then, of course, they're embarrassed. They don't want to have to explain what George Vico, fugitive financier, is doing at home in Wyoming, or wherever you want to go.'

'I have never been convicted –'

'Let's be honest with each other,' the Chairman said. 'We don't try people *in absentia*, and you have been absent a long time.'

'I didn't come here for discussions.'

'We have to fill the time. We may as well be civil.'

'There won't be survivors.'

'Well now.' He puffed, and puffed. 'That's a matter of opinion. I accept there will be complete chaos for weeks, maybe months – no more money, no more credit, no more trade, for a bit. I suppose payrolls won't be paid or goods sold. And we don't know what all that would do. But I do think psychology may be against you. People need to believe in systems, or everything would make them fearful. It wouldn't be much of a life if we could take nothing for granted. So I think it quite possible,' puff, puff, 'they will simply refuse to accept that the system fell apart.' The Chairman grinned. 'They still believe in economists, after all.'

'They'll burn the banks,' Vico said. 'Feds first. Because the Feds and the banks will have to tell them that money means nothing any more. Nothing at all – not even bread, butter and rent.'

'You may be right,' the Chairman said. 'Of course, we economists are so far from everyday life –'

'I don't see what we're waiting for.'

'For a pardon,' the Chairman said, 'since that's what you want. The question is whether the President will sign one. He doesn't like to be seen as weak, you know. I really don't know what he'll do when it comes down to signing and not talking.'

Vico had his arms pressed hard on the arms of his chair.

'While we wait,' the Chairman said, 'you'll have some coffee, of course? And you can explain this very ingenious trapdoor of yours. "Trapdoor" is the word, isn't it?'

'The program accepts a command, once a quarter. If it gets no command, it runs as usual. If it gets the command, it anticipates a second command.'

'And the first command,' the Chairman said, with the air of a patient man trying to grasp complexities, 'has already been given?'

'Yes,' Vico said.

'So what happens if you simply don't give the second order?'

'The system unscrambles,' Vico said. 'At random. If I do give the order, then the system encrypts all the figures, and then in an hour it has a kind of nervous breakdown. It's not good, either way.'

'But if you give the second order –'

'You buy some time.'

'And the process can be reversed?'

'It can be reversed but only within the hour.'

The Chairman said, complacently: 'Then we have an hour.'

'Yes,' Vico said, shifting in his seat. He had expected a committee to browbeat, not this singular, bear-like man with his infuriating air of interest. And besides, there was the problem of Mercedes.

'I really wanted Mercedes Zenon to be here,' Vico said.

'I don't know if that is appropriate –'

'It's appropriate,' Vico said, coldly. 'Today, I decide what's appropriate.'

The Chairman made calls, and Vico watched him. He was a cool, clear-headed man, a theorist who thought in grand terms; his body was a testimony to lunch and carelessness. He was a little like Vico himself, except that he had chosen power over trouble, theory over crime.

'I'd have thought the Bahamas were a little dull,' the Chairman said when he sat down. 'Lovely in spring of course.'

'We have only twenty minutes.'

The phone rang, and when the Chairman had spoken he shook his head. 'Your friend Miss Zenon,' he said, 'doesn't seem to be available. Nobody knows where she is.'

The Chairman saw horror in Vico's great grey discs of eyes, but he did not know what to make of it.

'She must be at the hotel,' Vico said. 'Someone must know.'

'Does it really matter?' the Chairman asked. 'I can't imagine you being so sentimental that you need a mascot.'

Vico calmed himself. He couldn't say why Mercedes mattered.

If he did, he gave away that George Vico lacked the power to reverse what he had started. Vico could be set aside.

'It's important to me,' Vico said.

And if she couldn't be found, Vico had no options left. He would have to watch the banks of America unravel before him without the ironic glory of posing as their saviour.

'Very well,' the Chairman said.

It was like a trial, Mercedes thought, but in an open, shabby room looking out over a garden to a chicken restaurant and a video store.

Aurelia had settled herself behind an old kitchen table which served as a desk.

'What are you doing?' she asked.

Mercedes looked around. She had an absolute obligation to be close to Vico in the next hour, but she had no wish to be hurried into answering. She saw José Mantica in the corner and he looked almost apologetic.

'I said, what are you doing?'

'I don't answer to anyone,' Mercedes said.

'You have the Diaz money,' Aurelia said. 'The Frente decided that money should be channelled through George Vico, and then suddenly George Vico isn't there, and you aren't there, and George Vico is in Washington.'

'Things change.'

'That won't do,' Aurelia said. 'There are proper procedures and you disrupted them. We had control of that money –'

'George Vico had control,' Mercedes said. 'I know the man. He doesn't do things for charities.'

'Then why are you with him?' Aurelia said.

'I was his daughter for a while.'

'You haven't seen him for years. You don't love the man. You're here for a reason.'

Mercedes looked at her watch. Down the road a large dog was barking out of anxious boredom, and a siren sounded very far away. She could hear birds.

'Why are you here?' José said. 'It would be so much easier if you'd tell us –'

Mercedes said: 'I have business in town.'

331

'I'm sure you do,' Aurelia said. 'But you're not leaving here until we have an explanation.'

'I could call the cops –'

'Not to an embassy,' Aurelia said. 'This is Providencian soil, remember, and they can't cross the threshold unless we ask them in.'

'You're telling me I am a prisoner?'

'We need explanations,' Mantica said. 'There's been so much changing of sides.'

'I never changed sides,' Mercedes said. 'Maybe you changed.'

Aurelia said: 'You're working for yourself, are you? Some kind of individualistic trip. You want to be the heroine.'

'You wouldn't listen if I told you why I did all this,' Mercedes said. 'It was for justice –'

'And what do you think justice means without politics? You think you can decide the right thing to do, always, on your own?'

'I knew Diaz stole his money. I knew Providencia needed it.'

'And you think it's your gift, that you decide how Providencia shall take it?'

Mercedes said: 'I have to be back in the Federal Triangle in half an hour. Maybe we could talk politics some other time.'

'What business have you got with the US Government? You're a model, for Christ's sake. You show your face and your body for money.'

'At least I didn't sell them,' Mercedes said. 'I didn't marry the aristocrat my family arranged for me.'

'That was another Aurelia. She's dead now.'

'So is Chamorro. So is Diaz.'

'You regret their deaths?'

'I'm sorry you became an executioner. Did you do that for justice or for politics?'

'It was necessary,' Aurelia said.

'But who says it was necessary?'

'Would you rather some judge said it, and some paid executioner did it? Does it offend you that the people –'

'We've been in different worlds too long.'

'Perhaps we have. I was in Leon all those years when you were in Switzerland and Manhattan. I was learning a trade, being a wife, and none of them ever thought it might make me angry. I

332

didn't believe it either. I went to kill Chamorro and even when he was dead I hardly believed I could do it. But I was angry enough.'

'I understand that,' Mercedes said.

'I know. That far we go together. But then I went underground and I went on learning. I learned about class and money and politics. I learned how to make some sense out of the world I knew I hated.'

'But you went there because you hated. You killed Chamorro because he killed our father. And Diaz, as well. Your reasons were as personal as mine.'

'But I understood what happens next,' Aurelia said. 'You can't run a revolution for ever on passion and hate and soul. You have to make the machine work.'

'I know that.'

'We make compromises. We buy time. We do deals. We don't stay pure and idealistic. It isn't all justice.'

'And people get hurt in that process, don't they?'

'Some,' Aurelia said. 'Life's imperfect.'

'Then how would you judge between our two ways? You talk about politics and class and the people, but what finally matters is what happens to the people. Doesn't that matter more than theory or correctness?'

Aurelia said: 'That's a very naïve way –'

'If individuals give people food and medicine and schools, is that worse than the Frente giving them?'

'Who's giving?' Aurelia said. 'The question is taking. Who's taking the Diaz money and where is it going?' She leaned down to Mercedes, her manner like a policeman. 'What business do you have with the Federal Reserve?'

Mercedes stood, faced off against Aurelia, and for a moment it seemed to Mantica that the two women might physically fight, might wrestle each other down. He stood back.

'I came here to get Vico out of the way,' she said. 'So that Providencia could have all the money Diaz stole. All of it.'

Aurelia said: 'We need Vico. He's a fact of life. You need friends and some of them you have to buy.'

'But if you need Vico, who else will you need? He sold guns to Tomás Diaz. Did you know that?'

'We don't ask that our helpers are pure.'

'Then why the hell do I have to think the right things the right way?'

'I don't care how you think, Mercedes,' Aurelia said. 'You come from a different world.'

'You're patronising me.'

'I don't think you have much to say about revolution or the economy of the Third World. I look at your dress and your make-up and your shoes and I see a woman who doesn't know about revolution.'

'You could answer my confusion,' Mercedes said. 'You could show me that this is all right.'

'You're not sure why you stole the Diaz money, is that it? And now we have to justify ourselves to get back what Diaz stole – justify ourselves to you.'

'Yes,' Mercedes said.

Aurelia spat on the floor.

'Please show me,' Mercedes said. 'I wanted to believe.'

'What in? In some spotless revolution where the world was just like Park Avenue when we'd finished? It isn't like that, Mercedes. This isn't your world; it's the making of a new world.'

'I know,' Mercedes said, 'that there'll be medicine for the kids. The nuns said that. I guess you'll make schools and send teachers. There won't be the great ranchers any more, and Diaz won't take his cut. It'll be better.'

Aurelia stood at a window, looking down on the raggedy garden and its mess of vines and bushes. 'We had nothing under Diaz, not even the knowledge that we'd live. I know that.'

She turned. 'You want to be sure, don't you? Sure like you're sure if you send a cheque to the Red Cross. There is nothing sure in all this.'

'Then you're gambling for millions of people.'

'We know what to change,' Aurelia said. 'We know how to change it. There won't be private land, there'll be collective land; then the peasants can work five years ahead –'

'But they only work a year ahead. They borrow and they pay back at harvest. They'll be terrified to work in five-year plans.'

'We'll see,' Aurelia said. 'And the fishing out of Bluefields, of course.'

334

'But they go where they want, when they want. That's the joy of their life. They can set out and lose themselves for days.'

'We have to organise.'

Mercedes said nothing, and Aurelia glared at her.

'It's necessary,' she said.

Mercedes said: 'I know we needed change. That's all I know we needed.'

'It's not your country any more,' Aurelia said. 'You can't expect to make the rules and the plans. We have to do that. We'll do it better because you brought back the Diaz money, I promise you that. There'll be fuel and food and drugs and guns, and we can get on with making our own history.'

'Is that all you can promise?'

'Yes,' Aurelia said. 'You're gambling on us all.'

'Your own history.'

'You're not coming with us. You're not going to give up everything to live the revolution. You're going back to your own life. So you don't get to give the orders either, any more than the President of the United States gets to give us orders. That's why we fought.'

Mercedes said: 'It's like a child, making its own way.'

Aurelia slapped her hard across the face.

Ian Carpenter drummed a spoon on a saucer. There had been calls for Mercedes from George Vico at the Federal Reserve; but Mercedes was supposed to be with Vico at the Federal Reserve. A woman at the next table glared at his steady percussion on the china and he stopped.

If they didn't have Mercedes, they had no way to stop the cataclysm. He had to find her, or he had to find John Grey, because they alone knew which simple word could bring back FedWire from the dead.

Of the two, the easier was John Grey. He'd taken himself south to the Bahamas, with a friend who was sick. He seemed much occupied with the friend, and all too little with the game he had set in motion.

Reception at the Lyford Cay Club was distantly polite, and warned it might take some time to find a guest. Perhaps Mr Carpenter would care to leave a message? But Mr Carpenter hung on.

He looked at his watch. Twenty minutes from now, Vico had to tell the program to encrypt whatever was on FedWire and not just abandon all the day's transactions like flotsam in a flood. Twenty minutes.

John Grey sounded lazy, and serious all at once.

'Where's Mercedes?' he asked.

'She isn't here. And she isn't with Vico. She seems to have disappeared.'

'Check the embassy,' Grey said. 'They must think she's stealing the Diaz money for herself.'

'I don't know where to look,' Carpenter said. 'The point is, she can't tell Vico what word stops the program. You have to tell him.'

Grey said: 'You want me to tell you the code?'

'Yes, if you can.'

There was a silence on the line. Ian Carpenter found himself drumming again, fingers on the metal of the telephone cabinet until the sound began to irritate him.

'I can't do that,' John Grey said.

'You mean you don't trust me?'

'I mean as few people as possible should know that code and I don't know you.'

'We both know Mercedes. We both –'

'Yes,' John Grey said, tartly.

'At least call Volcker at the Federal Reserve. Call his mother, call his wife, call anyone who can get through to him. Tell him how to stop this thing.'

'Leave it to me.'

'And I'll find Mercedes,' Carpenter said, like an oath.

It was a very open prison. She could see light and sun, and there were no guns or bars. But she was effectively in prison all the same. No cops could come to rescue her, and she could send out no message. She was guarded by very young, very serious men who were a little like automata; only the spirit of the revolution animated them, and it seemed to inspire them to take orders.

'If you keep me here,' she said to Aurelia, 'there will be a catastrophe. A real catastrophe.'

Aurelia knew she was serious. But she did not know how

seriously to take her. Mercedes' values, and her sense of drama, were a mystery that she had no skills to unravel.

'Let me explain,' Mercedes began. 'There is a system called FedWire. It carries all the money that goes between banks in America, every day. There are billions and billions on that wire. In an hour, it's going to come down unless I give a password.'

Aurelia said: 'The system's not so weak,' and she turned to leave the room.

Mercedes was furious and miserable at once, but the fury won out. She said, crisply: 'I know much more about this than you do.'

Aurelia said 'How could you?'

'I know what the systems are actually like – what a rackety thing they are. I know it's faith that holds them up, faith and string. Vico taught me.'

'Capitalism might come down from its own internal contradictions,' Aurelia said. 'But not because you have some codeword.'

'Why do you have to believe your enemy is so strong?' Mercedes said. 'It's fallible, like any machine. It can be tampered with, adjusted –'

'You mean,' Aurelia said, 'you can improve it. You don't have to break it.'

'God help me,' Mercedes said, 'I mean that I have already broken it.'

'I don't have time for your fantasy,' Aurelia said. 'Revolution isn't fantasy. It's guns and sweat, and patience.'

'Listen to me,' Mercedes said.

'Due to circuit congestion . . .'

There is a simple comedy when a man makes a phone call and the call fails. He dials again, and then again, each time more briskly and less carefully. He reaches numbers almost at random. But John Grey was dialling fastidiously, and still he heard the same acid voice.

'. . . in the country which you called . . .'

Country code. City code. Number.

'. . . your call did not complete . . .'

Try the operator. The operator, at least, will try and try again.

337

'I'm sorry,' the operator said. 'Please try again later.'

'But this is an emergency. Life and death.'

'I'm sorry sir. I can't mend the lines.'

'Emergency!'

The line went dead.

John Grey put down the phone with too much force, and then tried to dial Washington one last time. He held the receiver like a man's last grip on a mountain.

'Please try later . . .'

Try the US embassy. They could telex Washington. They must have dedicated lines.

He left his friend curled on a daybed, watching two wrapped figures playing tennis out of habit, and drove furiously along the sea road into Nassau. He sprinted up to the American embassy.

He stood before the glass cage with a girl and two Marines. The girl said: 'Sir' with studied detachment, and the Marines looked blankly out.

'I want to report . . .'

'There's nobody here at present, sir.'

'How can you have an embassy with nobody present?'

'It is lunchtime, sir. We open again at one –'

He couldn't bring himself to say it. By one, the banks would be down and there would be nobody to call. The disintegration, the collapse would have started.

'Time,' said the Chairman. He had marked his seriousness by setting aside his cigar. His hand felt unoccupied.

Vico said: 'You fixed a terminal, I guess?'

He was sharp now, every nerve alert. He must not give away his own inability to fix what he was about to tear apart. He had another hour, after all.

'That terminal,' the Chairman said, 'accesses FedWire directly.'

'You have access in the boardroom?'

The Chairman shrugged, and Vico felt obliged to sit at the keyboard without threat or any show of force. He found the Chairman impressive.

He stroked the keys.

John Grey had made his trapdoor as an amusement and an

indulgence, and also as superstition, so he had used his usual joke. To identify himself to the computer, Vico typed:

'G.R.E.Y.S.T.O.K.E.'

He was acknowledged.

He gave the password: 'T.A.R.Z.A.N.'

He was acknowledged again, and now the screen was alive and ready. It asked for a bank, an account, an amount, but instead Vico typed the command which over-rode the usual business of the wire. His fingers seemed too pudgy for the keys; he typed once, wrongly, and then corrected hismelf:

'G.O.T.O.J.A.N.E.'

He was acknowledged one more time, because there were no casual ways to blunder into this trapdoor.

He typed the last instruction, John Grey's joke:

'C.H.E.E.T.A.'

Nothing happened. The Chairman felt across the polished table for his pack of cheap cigars and could not find them. He did not take his eyes off the screen.

'The problem with FedWire,' the Chairman said, 'is that it doesn't have the capacity we need. Three deals a second, that's all. That's why it takes time to register.'

Vico said: 'But if we're too late with that –'

The Chairman fidgeted with matches and the cigars. He seemed to make a decision, and set them aside. He would celebrate with a cigar when things went wrong.

The screen went blank.

The Chairman fumbled for a match with unusual graceless-ness. 'Is there any reason,' he said, 'why you shouldn't correct this thing now? Immediately?'

'You have an hour,' Vico said. 'I need to see the pardon, and I need to know all the conditions.'

'You wouldn't let this happen, would you?' For the first time the Chairman's voice betrayed his fear.

'I don't give a shit,' Vico said, but he was transfixed by the screen.

'But you gave your word –'

'What good is the word of a fugitive financier?'

But he longed for Mercedes to arrive and end this nightmare. He wanted to come home. He was old enough for the idea of rest.

He was middle-aged, he was short of breath at the third drink and his heart was suspect. He didn't know if his body had the strength to run again.

But he could not show such feelings. He had to mask all his humanity and stay steely.

'I almost think,' the Chairman said, 'you might be bluffing.'

In the main New York offices of Security National Bank a tall, thin black man was saying: 'Holy shit!' He kept saying it.

He reworked the keyboard. Transfer. Eighteen million. First National of Boston.

Pause.

The screen remained blank.

He picked up the phone and said, very quietly, 'You're not going to believe this. FedWire's down.'

'You checked the plug?'

'I checked. FedWire isn't there any more.'

'Then money isn't there,' a laconic voice said. 'Get some coffee. Try again.'

Aurelia said: 'If that's true.'

'If it's true, you're in trouble. Don't you see? You'd be making your revolution without banks or credit or money or spare parts or food or –'

'I'm not stupid,' Aurelia said.

Mercedes wanted to ask why she'd turned off her passion, subjugated it to a formal set of rules called revolution. But she kept quiet.

'Funny you should be the one to do it,' Aurelia said, 'and not me.'

Mercedes said: 'Vico's started the process now. We don't have much time, less than an hour.'

'I wonder what would happen if we just let it run,' Aurelia said. She looked across to José Mantica who was startled by the women's talk, unsure how to respond. He only nodded.

'You listen to him?' Mercedes said. 'You take orders from –'

'I respect the leaders of the revolution,' Aurelia said.

'If you compromise everything to get power and keep it,' Mercedes said, in a voice that was measured like steel, 'then for what reason should anyone let you take power?'

José Mantica said: 'We ought to talk.' He began to manoeuvre Aurelia out of the room, but she had time to say:

'I will not be grateful. Whatever happens.'

A soldier stayed with Mercedes and gave her a glass of water. He wouldn't let her not drink.

George Vico's cool had mostly been alcohol, and alcohol wears off.

'You can't tell me what's happening,' he said to the Chairman. 'I want to see the others. I want to see the President.'

'The Attorney General is coming,' the Chairman said.

'That's not good enough. I demand –'

'Please don't demand,' the Chairman said. 'I'm only the technician, the keeper of the mysteries, whatever you want to say. I don't do the politics at all.'

And on a cue, the double doors opened again to admit a retinue, neat men in pencil suits with a terrifying blandness, surrounding a man who seemed angry at the very existence of Vico.

'Paul,' the Attorney General said, and sat down abruptly. His aides clustered around.

'If it were up to me,' the Attorney General said, 'we wouldn't be here. One man can't do what Vico says he can. We all know that. But there are some folks,' he glared at the Chairman, 'who want to believe he can. So we have the pardon.'

Vico said: 'The President agreed?'

'He agreed,' the Attorney General said. 'You bring back FedWire, you go pretty damn nearly free. Though why we're so kind to some sort of goddamn financial terrorist –'

'Don't overdo it,' the Chairman said, quietly. 'The situation is really quite grave.'

'I want Mercedes Zenon here,' Vico said, flatly.

'You don't make conditions,' the Attorney General said. 'You take our conditions.'

'I'm not talking unless she's here.'

'The whole American banking system at stake,' the Attorney General said, unbelieving, 'and you're whimpering for some broad –'

341

'You don't say that,' Vico shouted. He could show his anger at a line which somehow impugned his daughter's honour. It gave him the diversion he needed.

'Get some sense of proportion,' the Attorney General said, but backing off like a blusterer who knows how a bar-room fight can start. 'She'll be here when she wants.'

'She is not a broad,' Vico insisted.

'What the hell else is she?'

'My daughter,' Vico said, melodramatically.

'Well, pardon me,' said the Attorney General. 'I never would have guessed. Days in the bush, was it?'

The Chairman sighed. 'Gentlemen –'

Vico was up on his feet, grateful for anger. 'I want her here,' he said. 'I want you to apologise. I want –'

The Attorney General picked up the papers he had laid on the table and put them in an untidy bunch into his inside pocket. 'I don't think there's any point in reading you the conditions,' he said, 'because I don't think you can stop this thing. I think you're bluffing.'

The Chairman said: 'It had crossed my mind.'

'We're wasting our time,' the Attorney General said. 'He can't deliver. He can't earn. Why the hell we don't take him here and now and find a jail for him –'

The aides looked ready, but for taking notes and not for action; they would have made a poor posse.

'I want to see the pardon papers,' Vico said. 'We can see if they're in order.'

The Attorney General harrumphed, but he sat still. 'Is there,' he said to the Chairman, 'any reason we don't just arrest this man.'

Mildly, the Chairman said: 'Only the future of capitalism, I suppose.' He had lit a second cigar while one burned in the ashtray.

And Vico tried to stare them all down. They had reason to be afraid, and he had nothing at all to lose now. Nothing. He had to work his luck until it was worked out, like some prospector.

'The papers,' he said.

In the New York office of Security National Bank, the very tall black operator said into the phone, no longer guarding his words: 'It don't look good.'

'Twenty minutes is nothing.'

'It's damn nearly four thousand transactions,' the tall man said. 'You tell me what four thousand times eighteen million – at least –'

'You don't know how much,' said the voice on the phone, which was metallic and anonymous. 'Maybe it's just us.'

'Chase is down too. So is Manny Hanny. I checked. And someone at Chase said Citibank –'

'You been hunting up rumours?'

'You,' the tall man said, 'you thought what this might mean? Sir?'

'It must be a line fault.'

'It's FedWire that's the fault,' the tall man said. 'You check with Washington.'

'You work your buttons,' said the laconic voice. 'Leave the questions to me.'

The tall, black operator could hear the prickle of fear.

There was nothing to see, nothing to hear; it was like an infection, moving silently and bringing on horror only later. Carpenter was glad that John Grey was telling the Feds all he knew, because if he had not –

There remained the question of Mercedes. She must have gone somewhere and he didn't know why. But if it was so important that she was missing her own melodrama, then it must be something to do with the Diaz money. John Grey had said check the embassy; he would go calling. He wanted to be moving while he waited to hear that everything was settled.

He took a cab up to a very settled street, where the houses were proud like castles even before they needed to be defended. The shade trees seemed to call back some rural past, and there was space and a sky that looked painted.

A dog barked out of turn.

The sound was shocking. He looked around at the stillness of the street, its white paint and Buicks and evergreens cut into shapes; he felt conspicuous as a stranger in a marriage bed. But he had no reason to back away, or hide; so he told himself.

He saw a wood-framed station-wagon prowl along and park among the other, elderly cars before the embassy. He followed the driver into the entrance hall and stood there for a moment. The girl at the desk smiled, without enthusiasm.

'Miss Zenon,' he said.

'Could I have your name?'

The driver was moving into the embassy, and Carpenter lost his politeness. He barged after the man and cleared the doors. There was a scuffle behind him as the guard, sprawled on a kitchen chair, pushed himself into life, but he was into the open reception room.

Mercedes wasn't here, not in some public room. She must be talking in some private place, for some reason that he hadn't grasped. He didn't want to be excluded any longer from her life.

He sensed some kind of danger, although he did not know what. He had never been in this building before, but he knew it had been stripped by the Diacistas and left an unlovely, pretentious shell of itself and he felt the emptiness. He reckoned he could stand on the stairs and hear any talk.

But he could not stand for long. The guard had broken through the doors and was shouting. There were armed men in the building; they would be mobilised soon.

Carpenter bolted up the stairs and found himself between the spoiled ballroom and some other, echoing salons. He could imagine a reception here, the polite talk and drinks and the buying of support; and he listened, very hard, for the sound of Mercedes' voice.

He heard Aurelia.

'She can stay a while,' Aurelia was saying. 'José can talk to her. I have other things to do.'

He crashed the door and stood before Aurelia like some movie hero who has come through the glass in pursuit of his lover. 'Ian Carpenter,' Aurelia said. 'They all come after a while, don't they?'

'Where's Mercedes?'

'She's in a meeting,' Aurelia said. 'Isn't that what you people always say?'

He listened to the little, mean phrase, and said: 'They tamed you, too, didn't they? Just like Mario and your mother and the people around Leon.'

344

'You can think what you like.'

'But they didn't spoil Mercedes,' Carpenter said, proudly.

'She spoiled herself.'

He lost patience.

'She's in the room at the end of the landing,' Aurelia said. 'You could interrupt, if you wanted.'

He pelted down the hallway and found the only door Aurelia could mean. He thought of knocking, with an odd and formal impulse, but instead he threw himself at the door.

He fell into the room, which in his own way was a declaration of impatient, incoherent love.

He looked down the barrel of a gun.

On the boardroom floor of Security National they had stopped their lunch. The life died in a dozen bottles of mineral water.

There was a conference phone with an open line to Washington, and Leventhal was shouting:

'Get FedWire back,' he was saying, 'and get it back soon. We've lost our books, we've lost our billions. Billions, I said. All that money is out there in limbo. It disappeared, *capisce*? Money disappeared.'

'Please be moderate,' said a starched voice from Washington.

'I am a very moderate man,' Leventhal said. 'I just want you to know, very moderately, that every moderate bank is moderately bust if your moderate system isn't working again inside an hour.'

'That doesn't sound very moderate to me.'

'Listen,' Leventhal said, his face pressed down to the phone as if he doubted any other way to send his message. 'You don't have to sound like the phone company to me. This is the biggest disaster in financial history and it is the one we can't repair. You understand.'

That featureless, official voice said: 'I will convey your opinion to the Secretary, when it is appropriate.'

Leventhal listened to a dead line.

'Due to congestion in the country you called –'

John Grey looked at his watch. There was almost no time left.

He had been proud, privately, of his trapdoor – an elaborate, harmless joke at the expense of all those innumerate people who commission grandiose systems without any clear idea of how they work. He had needed the trapdoor, so that he knew the system was imperfect, and precisely where the error lay. It had only been a gag to ensnare George Vico, to save the billion from Diaz, to win a pardon for John Grey and let him settle his life at last.

But the telephone said: 'Due to congestion in the country you called –'

George Vico stared at the screen. He said: 'I don't have that information.' He sounded ignominiously like every clerk and manager he had ever outfoxed.

'I don't understand,' the Chairman said.

'I don't have the information,' Vico said. 'Mercedes has the information and the man who wrote the program has the information. Mercedes never told me the words. I guess she wanted to be with me.'

The Chairman sucked in his breath.

'You were bluffing,' said the Attorney General. He had an almost mediaeval faith in confession.

'That shouldn't seem so strange,' Vico said. He found himself watching a tiny American flag on the mantelshelf, rigid in an imagined wind. He stood, defeated.

'You've got thirteen minutes,' he said. 'You find John Grey or you find Mercedes.'

The Chairman tried to remain methodical. 'Is thirteen minutes exact or an estimate?' he asked.

'I did all I know,' Vico said.

It was true. He hadn't imagined that he would cause the very worst without intending to, and that he would face confinement and forensic duels and finally a verdict. He'd let himself be judged.

The Chairman said: 'Listen. We can't reach John Grey. Can you tell us where Mercedes is?'

He saw the Attorney General had the sweetest sense that all his suspicions had been confirmed, and that he was terrified.

The soldier was very young, but very competent. Carpenter saw the gun and the innocent face and he felt menaced by a child.

346

But it takes a second to prime and aim a rifle. In that second, he could kick out and then punch, throw his weight at the kid and bring him down. The kid was wiry but insubstantial, and he went crashing down under forty years of bankers' living. Carpenter grabbed at the rifle.

'We're going,' he said to Mercedes.

'You're playing at war with them,' she said. 'That's what they want.'

'Get moving,' he said. 'And if anyone asks, you're Aurelia Zenon and you changed clothes.'

He pushed her out of the door in an elaborate charade, the rifle held to the beloved head. He was terrified that he would make some false move with an unfamiliar weapon and kill this woman. He was suspicious of the word love but he knew he felt for her in ways it would take time, and living, to understand.

He pushed her on the stairs. He had to make the whole affair look real, to make the staff think that a newly glamorous Aurelia, indulging some Commandante's whim, was now at risk. He counted on their calling the cops.

He passed under the shade of the woven soldier hanging on the wall and down the steep ceremonial stairs to the empty reception room. The women who had been drinking coffee there had melted away before the sound of the coming drama.

He came to the double doors.

The guard stood aside. He had done what he could; he had called the police. He had to let the man through for fear Aurelia would suffer. The heroine of the revolution did not yet aspire to the higher plane of martyrdom.

He tried to smile at the girl in the entrance hall. He didn't want her to be alarmed.

He came to the door and kicked it shut behind him. He dropped the rifle and released Mercedes. And the cop cars screamed into place.

He held his hands above his head, and the cops moved in.

George Vico said: 'I don't think she could make it now. There isn't time.'

The Chairman retained sense, even *in extremis*. He said. 'If we find her, she can presumably go to any major branch of any

347

major bank. Or to any corporation that can access FedWire directly. Is that right?'

His own aides had come into the room and they nodded.

'Then if we sent out one more call. An all-stations police call.'

And aide said: 'We have eight minutes. That's assuming FedWire takes instruction.'

'There are no other deals to get in the way,' the Chairman said, with persistent common sense. He looked like a fat man who had run for his life.

'I hope she remembers,' Vico said.

The cops had Carpenter covered. But he could hear the radio blaring behind them: even in the focus of their guns he knew they must listen.

'. . . all points call for Mercedes Zenon. Black female, mid twenties, five nine . . .'

'That's her,' Carpenter shouted.

The cops were in doubt for a moment, but then the faceless authority of the radio voice overcame their instinct for a siege.

'Lady,' one cop shouted. 'They need you on the radio. Can you get away from that guy?'

Mercedes ran to the nearest cop car. The police were clearly startled that she had escaped so easily; they wondered how much of a menace Carpenter could be, with his gun thrown down and his face of surrender.

She took the microphone.

'Miss Mercedes Zenon?' said the disembodied voice. 'Hold for the Chairman of the Federal Reserve.'

The windows of the embassy had filled now and there was at least one liberal journalist ready to write of the outrage committed there by the cops of DC.

Volcker said: 'Miss Zenon, it seems you know the password for ending our present troubles. You know what I mean. We can't reach John Grey and Mr Vico appears quite ignorant on the matter.'

Mercedes said: 'I don't remember.'

The Chairman said: 'We only have five minutes, Miss Zenon.'

'I'm sorry,' Mercedes said. 'So much has happened this morning – if I could get to a computer terminal, perhaps I would remember.'

'I do very much hope that you can.'

Mercedes turned to the cop and said: 'Listen to what he says.'

The Chairman told the cops to take Mercedes to the nearest computer with access to FedWire. The cops both looked and sounded blank.

'I'm sorry,' the Chairman said, and shouted for information. He gave an address, of a company in outer Georgetown whose corporate headquarters had the proper link.

Carpenter listened, and watched, and the situation that he'd assumed was under perfect control began to splinter in his eyes. 'Jesus,' he said. 'There's no time left. There's no time at all.'

'I'm going home,' the tall, black operator said.

'Your job just got easy,' said his sidekick.

'These systems have a tight MTBU,' the tall man said, tugging on his jacket. 'Maybe one hour at most. It's down that long, it's down for ever. Bye-bye money.'

He took the elevator down to the street, and he thought to take some cash for the evening. He put his card into the streetside machine and punched in his personal identification number. He knew what it would say:

'UNABLE TO PROCESS TRANSACTION AT THIS TIME.'

The queue didn't move in the banking hall, and there were angry people shouting to get in. The bank officers had begun a tactical retreat from their usual corral.

The banks don't have books any more so nobody can use the banks. Logical, he thought. But the people who'd gone from the electronic tellers to the human kind were not so patient. They had thought the machines were suffering from some new moonphase; now they knew it was something more fundamental.

He saw the security guards up against the doors and sprinted for the safety of the subway.

They were waiting for Mercedes at the corporate door, with an absurd little electric truck that still seemed faster than walking, and which buzzed over padded floors and glassed corridors to the accounting room.

'We accessed FedWire,' a brisk company official said. 'But you know, there's nothing there.'

Mercedes sat down at the terminal.

Remember. Everything depended now on her memory. But it was compromised by talking with her sister, and imagining her mother, and seeing Vico. She felt like the drowned man who reviews his life in minutes, but she did not have even the drowned man's time.

Greystoke. Tarzan. Jane. Cheeta. She could get that far. But what was the word that completed the series.

Think of John Grey. Imagine his sensibility and his mind, his frame of reference. What word unlocked the damage they had done to FedWire?

The rescuer. The hero. The one who could save them all. Greystoke. Tarzan. The one who played the hero, who was playing a game by saving the world. The player.

Of course.

She typed in: 'W.E.I.S.M.U.L.L.E.R.'

The aides did not allow themselves to think, but three men had their private thoughts in the oaky, panelled room at the Federal Reserve.

The Attorney General remembered. He had been a master of political damage control; he had never faced a true disaster. He remembered the smell of surf.

The Chairman clung, by a hair, to rational thought. He tried to imagine any economic model which could predict the results of this catastrophe.

And George Vico sat sullen. He had been betrayed successfully, for the first time in his life, and by Mercedes. He imagined the details would be clear all too soon. Hanging Vico would be the last official act before anarchy.

The three men could not take their eyes from the screen. They seemed to fix their wills there, to revive the cursor.

The little flag on the mantelshelf toppled in some draught. The Attorney General shuddered.

It was there again on the screen, the little green cursor. It danced, and the first screen of the FedWire instructions scrolled up.

It was there again.

The Attorney General said: 'Thank God!'

The Chairman was more precise. 'Be sure what you're thanking Him for,' he said. 'We don't know what damage all this has done – what happened to all the day's money. We just don't know.'

'You're fired.'

His supervisor had caught the tall, black operator at home, where he had opened a bottle of prophylactic Scotch.

'Computers scare me,' the operator said.

The maid came thoughtfully from New York, having arranged the mail, some essential changes of clothes (a Dianne Brill to celebrate the return to Megalopolis) and an invitation to use a Lear jet waiting, conveniently, at National Airport.

'The fire,' she assured Mercedes, 'was only an inconvenience.'

They waited on the plane for half an hour. Carpenter had been released from police custody on direct Federal orders, and although the men had grumbled about the papers, they surrendered to true *force majeure*. Vico, though, had simply been put away. Nobody could raise the five million dollars bail that the local judge required to grant him even temporary liberty.

'You think she'll come?' Carpenter asked Mercedes.

'We have all the Diaz money,' Mercedes said. 'She'll come.'

And in time, she did: Aurelia Zenon, fierce in the righteousness of the revolution which barely covered her sisterly embarrassment.

'Mercedes,' she said. She moved as if to shake hands, but Mercedes held her and Aurelia relaxed into the embrace. She seemed grateful.

'We have the money,' Mercedes said. 'We always meant you to have it.'

'Things could have been easier,' Aurelia said.

'You don't know what George Vico organised for us,' Mercedes said.

'Aurelia knows,' Carpenter said.

And Aurelia said: 'I think I do know.'

Carpenter shuffled through the letters and the cards and found a registered package, securely made.

'Please,' he said to Mercedes. 'Open your mail.'

Mercedes pulled at the box and tore at it until it reluctantly spilled open. Inside, there was a rubble of styrofoam and within that a chamois pouch; and when the pouch was opened, it spilled out a trickle of blue fire. Mercedes raked the diamonds on a little table.

Aurelia put out a hand to the stones and sorted and picked away the styrofoam. They had a glorious light which transcended any monetary worth, and she saw that cold light reflected in Mercedes' eyes.

'These are ours too?' Aurelia said.

One diamond fell away to the floor, where it lay inert, away from the light.

'They're yours,' Aurelia said. 'Your commission. Our thanks.'

'You thank me, after all this?'

'I thank you,' Aurelia said.

'God be with you,' Mercedes said.

She'd meant, somehow, to compromise Aurelia by bringing her onto this plane and making her share a life she had affected to despise. But she did not want to do that, not now. She wanted Aurelia to go. She wanted things to be possible again in Providencia.

'I couldn't have done it without you,' she said, most directly to Ian Carpenter, and she scooped up the diamonds, all rolling and burning, and threw them high in an arc of light. It was like a rainbow in a dream, and it lasted only a second.

She said: *'Los niños van a vivir. Todos.'*

Without the great game, he was edgy like an uncle with someone else's child, afraid he wouldn't be amusing, that she would be bored or tired. He was looking for signs of disenchantment.

'There's a party,' she said.

She needed light again. She seemed to slip easily back to her old Manhattan times: to dine, to dance, to dance and open shows and dine again.

'We could just see –'

The corner stand already had the Sunday *New York Times*. Carpenter bought a copy and the print stained his hands.

He scanned the front page. There was one story from Providencia, down the page.

'Look,' he said.

It said the Diacista guerrillas had been beaten back from the borders, once again, and there was no more bleeding. It said the worst of Providencia's debt problem had been paid. On both counts, the paper seemed a little peeved.

'*Los niños,*' Mercedes said. '*Todos.*'

They stopped first at a video club which was a poseur's temple, chrome and white with a lengthy bar and banks of bottle glass and blue-white glass and video monitors all around. The screens showed muslin, bands, strippers, galleons, neon streets, floodlights and singers.

Mercedes walked into the lights and the walls of glass shimmered around her.

One hundred of the screens flickered as one. There was a fanfare, and a scroll of pictures – gold, mansions, champagne, a Rolls-Royce and a steel mill, a fur coat and a line of black and white servants.

And on every screen, Mercedes Zenon.

'You did this?' Carpenter asked, impressed by her celebrity career and its easy transition to prime time television.

'I'm a model in the show,' she said.

A bright-eyed man stood behind them. He said: 'You were wonderful, Miss Zenon.'

'I'm the heroine,' Mercedes said.

And as they waited for coats, she turned back to the hundred coloured images of herself all round that modish room, occupying all those eyes and minds. She saw her glamour, and herself.

She smiled. And, with Carpenter, she walked away.